The Tangled Trees

Book #3 The Eden Chronicles

S.K MUNT

Edited By:
Donella Brown

Printed By:
Author S.K Munt

Dedication

To my twin Prince Charming's and godsons, Evander and Elliott

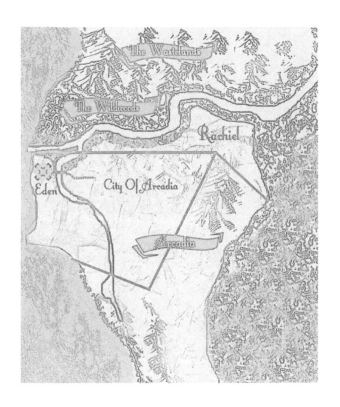

The Tangled Trees

Book#3 The Eden Chronicles

PROLOGUE

Loss of consciousness is a funny thing. Sometimes when you awaken it can feel like mere heartbeats have gone by and sometimes it can feel like eternity has passed. Either way, you always come to feeling somewhat panicked and completely robbed- shocked that your mind- your everything- was just switched off without your choosing to do it on purpose, like when you decide to fall asleep, and alarmed to think maybe you have just experienced what death might be like, and that one day your life could be taken from you that easily.

It's the truth of course- sudden death is a reality and it happens to a lot of people, but none of us like to think about that sort of thing, do we? We want to imagine dying in bed surrounded by our families and gently, sweetly, falling asleep as those who love us affirm that our life was a tremendous one, that we will be missed, and that the world will never be the same without us. It is the ultimate storybook ending.

I had lost consciousness before so I was no stranger to that feeling of panic upon waking, but my life had not been playing out like any of the favourite fairy tales for a very long time, so this time when I came to, I cared not for whatever I'd missed or how long I'd been out for, because all I wanted to do was weep for the sudden death that I'd just been denied after the worst day of my life.

And who could blame me? The last thing I remembered seeing before I had fainted was Satan asking me to help her step through the mirror so that she could enter the mortal realm and answer the prayers that I'd apparently been screaming at her for years, while my best friend/captor/borderline rapist had been soaking in the bath in my en-suite- cleaning the strong, sensual and duplicitous body that I was now legally bound to for the rest of my life due to a massive lapse in judgement on my part and a cataclysmic one on his.

My daughter? Did she call me 'My Daughter,'? My mind raced, but I rejected the recollection as though I were allergic to it. *No, my father wasn't my father, but I know that my mother was my biological one! Why did she say it, then?*

I shuddered and tried to claw away the fog blanketing my mind. What I'd seen in that mirror had either been the world's worst hallucination on record, or a sneak-peek at my new and terrifying reality and I wasn't ready to deal with either scenario because either way, I'd clearly lost my sanity in conjunction with my liberty.

'She's coming to,' a soft female voice said, and I recognised it as Cherry the healer's with a sinking heart. No way would I imagine *her* into a nightmare, or the cool cloth that she was pressing to my forehead. 'Her pulse is stabilising, but her eyes...'

My eyes! The blood! The healer's words snapped me into action and I sat up with a start and pressed my fingers to my face, knowing that if my eyes and face were still all bloody then I was in even more trouble than I had been earlier that evening. The Six Books of Creation were more widely-read now than the Bible had been in the time before, and there wasn't a person on this earth that didn't secretly fear one day crying bloody tears as Satan once had- of being hurt beyond redemption. And although I wasn't surprised to learn that my heart truly had been broken, I was dismayed to think that maybe *I* had been broken too and that the evidence was all over my face. Satan had never recovered from the anguish of losing Miguel to another woman, so if my pain was as absolute as hers, then did that mean that pain was all I'd ever know again? What of my plans to find a way to escape this so-called Paradise? What of my intentions to fake my death and start somewhere else, as some*one* else? What of my dreams of liberating Kohl too, and riding off into the sunset together?

My mind had been assuring me all night that nothing was finite- that where there was a will there would indeed be a way around the contract that I was bound to Kohén by now, but what if those bloody tears had been a sign that my will was weaker than I believed, and that I would never know happiness again?

I smeared the blood all over my face like war paint! I realised, thunderstruck. *But that was before I realised that I'd summoned Satan into Eden's walls with my misery! If anyone finds out that I did that... God if it's a slight to God to cry too much, what would he do to me for crying blood?*

'They're incredibly red,' I heard Kohén say softly, and then fingers were trailing through my hair. 'Nothing sleep won't fix, right?'

The sound of his voice scratched against my nervous system like fingernails against concrete, but he sounded so normal that he temporarily suspended my belief that the worst had just happened. My eyes and face were wet and my fingertips felt oddly cool, but as I pulled my fingers away, I was a little stunned to see that though my fingertips glistened with moisture, they were clean and blood-free, as was my vision, which immediately blurred my mind, of course.

Was it just a nightmare or a hallucination? But it felt so real!

'Sleep, and rest,' Cherry said pointedly to Kohén, while I looked around, dazed. I was on the bed, not on the floor in front of the mirror where I'd been last, and my hair was still wet from the bath. How long had I been out for, and why had I fainted in the first place? Because I'd been overcome with fear of Satan and myself as I'd believed at the time, or because I was, as Cherry had said- merely exhausted? 'Lots of both, and plenty of water too.'

'When you say rest...?'

'I mean exactly what you think I mean,' Cherry said, still holding the cool cloth to my forehead, and I was someone mollified by the sharp tone that she was taking with her prince on my behalf. She'd sounded concerned for me earlier when he'd first called her inside to heal me, but now she sounded outright disgruntled. 'This poor girl has had a taxing day, and needs the chance to recover, or a healer stronger than myself to restore her completely.'

'You'd better not be suggesting what I think you're suggesting for the *second* time this evening, Cherry,' Kohén growled, standing up and glaring at her over my body, which was thankfully covered with the thin sheet from my bed this time.

'Prince Karol is three times as strong as I am, and he has made his affection for Larkin clear today,' Cherry said stubbornly, and I winced as I felt Kohén buzz beside me- buzz, and begin to glow a warning shade of blue. 'I don't know why you think you have anything to fear from him but-'

'If I hear that you have breathed a word to Karol about Larkin's condition or anything that breeches the privacy contract that you have signed in order to work here, then I will have you dismissed immediately,' Kohén snapped, and I looked up at him, alarmed that he would speak so harshly to a Nephilim employee.

'Kohén-' I began, wondering where he got off being uppity with anyone this day.

'I am gladdened that you are so concerned by Larkin's welfare,' Kohén went on, ignoring me in a way that was out of character for him, and even more alarming to me because it made it clear how insignificant my feelings had become, 'and I can understand how strange all of this must look to you- suspicious, even- but I assure you that if my elder brother gets his hands on her due to a lapse in your judgement, it will be the last bad decision that you ever make!'

'Kohén Barachiel!' I snapped now, horrified, turning to Cherry with an apology in my eyes. 'Don't be so rude, she's just trying to help me!'

Kohén whirled to glare at me. 'Do *you* want Karol in here, Larkin? Will you welcome his healing hands on your body? Do you crave his company and assistance right now?'

I narrowed my eyes to slits, thinking of how disastrous that would be, and resenting the fact that for all of the wrong he'd done by me, Kohén was still the lesser of two evils as far as the Barachiel men were concerned. I didn't want this imprisonment but Kohén was right- I needed it, at least until after the ball, because now that Karol had released his own companions, this harem was the only place in the Eden that his brother was not permitted to step foot in. Those were my tasks: to keep away from Karol until he was safely engaged (hopefully to Ora) and forbidden to pursue me- and to keep Kohl believing that I was happy to stay with his twin, so he wouldn't cause another scene over our feelings for one another and give Kohén grounds to punish him for the rules we'd broken. 'Of course not.'

'Good,' Kohén motioned to Cherry. 'Then how about you dissuade Cherry from sticking her nose into our business in your sweet, charming way- so I don't have to talk to her the way that I just did, hmm?'

I ground my teeth together. Being tethered to this new, deceptive Kohén was a living nightmare that warranted me crying rivers of bloody tears... but there was another potential rock-bottom for me to hit sitting below this one and letting Karol and Kohl discover that I was miserable would surely get me there. I didn't want to have to lie to Kohl- for him to suffer, believing that I'd gotten over my feelings for him in a heartbeat- but if I didn't cause his suffering then Kohén would, and Kohén had enough on him to get him booted clear over the fence and to the Banished on the other side of it. And more than that, if Karol made a fuss over trying to get to me, then there was a good chance that Ora would find out about it and go running for the hills herself, and I didn't want to scare *her* off because I honestly believed that the entire world would be a better place if Karol just sucked it up and married someone as lovely and level-headed as the first-daughter of Rabia. So the only option I had was to keep everybody calm... and out of my business. Everyone except for Kohén, that was, who needed to be convinced that I loved him and him alone.

This in mind, I turned to Cherry, who looked beyond perplexed now. 'Please,' I said to her softly. 'I thought we went over this earlier? Yes I have had an emotionally-draining day, and I suppose it is clear that Kohén and I are treating one another in a way that is unusual for new lovers, and out of character for old friends, but-'

'It's not out of character,' Cherry said quickly, 'he's been treating you like…' Kohén sparked and she rolled her eyes, 'like trash instead of like an old friend for months!' she turned to glare at Kohén. 'And if you threaten my life for saying so, then you'd better prepare yourself to dismiss the entire castle's staff and the community while you're at it, because I'm not the only one that has noticed or spoken about it, Prince Kohén!' she looked back at me. 'Your being in here doesn't make sense! You were released today, Larkin! How could you be so foolish as to give up your freedom, for a man's companionship?'

I winced, as her words wounded me. I wanted to scream that I had not given up anything for a man, but that wasn't exactly the case. Regardless of which Barachiel brother I'd believed I'd been giving myself to earlier that evening, my virginity had been the only thing about me that I'd had going for me still and *I'd* sacrificed it for a few moments of passion, spite… and the foolish belief that Kohl and I had what it took to survive together outside Eden's walls once we were banished together for going behind Kohén's back. A somewhat optimistic plan to make, considering I hadn't been sober enough to know that I was plotting an escape with the wrong twin, and because we hadn't had so much as sensible shoes, a map or a canteen of water between us to escape with. *I'd* accepted Kohl's love like a lifeline, despite the fact that just ten minutes before, I'd been completely sure that I was still besotted with Kohén. *I* had nobody to blame for any of this, but myself, and if I didn't start convincing everyone that I was where I wanted to be and soon, *I'd* end up with Kohl's death on my conscience and Karol's hands on my body.

'I've worked towards many goals during my time in Eden,' I said softly, returning Cherry's probing gaze with shuttered eyes, 'but today I simply realised that none of them would hold any joy for me without my prince by my side.' I shrugged slightly. 'Kohén has promised to make all of my other dreams come true if I stay here with him, and I believe him. I concede that it was a spontaneous decision that will shock some people, but it was my decision to make, healer, so please...' I looked to Kohén and smiled sadly, taking his hand. 'Being freed did not change the fact that I am infertile, so if this is the only way that I can be with my love...then I'll cling to it. So long as I am his *only* Companion now.'

Kohén's eyes softened to a misty blue, and I silently scorned him for believing my performance. 'I'll never touch another woman again,' he promised me. 'I am as indentured to you, as you are to me, and I refuse to let people judge you for choosing to follow your heart.' He leaned over and kissed my forehead, and I closed my eyes and tried not to cry. 'That being said- are you done with your inspection, healer? You said yourself that Larkin needs to get some rest, so...'

'That she does,' Cherry said softly, giving me an odd look. 'I apologise for sticking my nose into your private affairs, your highness, but as I said, speculation is rife and as a healer it is my duty to report-'

'Report to everyone that it is possible to have an Academic's mind and a woman's heart then, seeing as they are all clearly struggling to believe it for themselves,' I said, lying on my side and rolling over to face her once more, comforting myself with the knowledge that my fraudulent cover story was a lot less embarrassing than the real story was, and a lot less dishonourable. 'And thank you again for seeing to me. I am sure I will feel better after some sleep.'

'And fluids.' Cherry stepped back from the bed and moved towards the door, her gait drooping like a wilted flower as she opened the door and closed it behind her without saying goodbye. She hadn't believed that I hadn't wanted a white knight to come to my rescue before but she did now, and though I should have been relieved for Kohl's sake, I was anything but. This was so hard already, and it was only just beginning! How was I going to convince an entire kingdom that I was happy, when I was anything but? Especially after the big fuss that Karol had made about me earlier that day in front of everyone? How would all of this affect Atticus's decision to appoint Kohl as a general of Pacifica? What were the other Given girls thinking about me now that they'd been kicked out of their comfortable rooms and told that they were now to service the public instead of the crown? Where was Kelia and what hell was she raising, and how on earth was I going to make sure that Karol didn't change his birthday wish for the sake of the other released Given to get me, when I couldn't risk going near him until he'd made an official promise to be faithful to Ora?

And most importantly, what had happened before I'd blacked out? Was Satan truly here in Eden, looking to cause trouble on my behalf? Or had I imagined it all?

The bed shifted behind me as Kohén lifted the sheet and snuggled up against my back. 'Thank you,' he whispered, kissing my shoulder and my lips tightened into a thin line at the feel of him against me. He was naked and still humid and slightly damp from the bath, and so fragrant from the bath oils that he'd used that I immediately grew dizzy from it all, like I was suffocating in his aura. I supposed that I smelled the same way, but he was a man and his pheromones were reacting differently to the cloying fragrance, and I was loathe to admit that he smelled incredible. 'You handled that well.'

'One of us had to,' I pointed out, and Kohén chuckled and ran his finger down my bicep. I had the sheet pulled up under my armpit, and now as my skin broke out in gooseflesh in response to his touch, I wished that I'd tucked all of my limbs away out of sight.

Please god, don't let him instigate… that. Not now. Not while I ache so!

'I'll admit that I lost my temper,' he said softly. 'But the idea of Karol seeing you like this…' lips touched my shoulder again, and his finger trailed back up my arm, leaving a delicious, invisible trail. 'How can I expect him to resist what I cannot? There's nothing I wouldn't do to have you, Larkin- *nothing*.'

'A fact that I am all too aware of,' I said sardonically, and Kohén moaned and buried his face into my neck, making the diamond choker around it tinkle.

'You don't understand,' he complained, pulling my hair over my shoulder so that he could kiss the top of my spine. It tickled as sweetly as his other touch had, and I pressed my lips even more tightly together to keep in a moan. Was it unfair for his touch to feel so good despite how much I hated him? Or was this the universe's way of softening my fall from grace? 'You don't understand what it is to love someone with all of your heart.'

I breathed in sharply and turned to face him. 'How dare you!' I hissed. 'I loved you with all of my heart, Kohén! And you threw it all away because you wanted another woman's body more than you wanted my devotion!'

Kohén's eyes narrowed. 'If it's rest you want, little bird, turn your face away! For I will not be held responsible for the things I do to you when you're looking at me like that and declaring your love! When you're damned near challenging me to prove my devotion!'

'You will find a million excuses to fuck me because you are an entitled brat, and which way I am facing at the time will matter none!' I poked him in the chest. 'Own your short-comings, Kohén, and learn to overcome them when it's appropriate to.'

'I have a million excuses as to why I want to fuck you, but I need only one,' Kohén sat up taller and pulled me against him so that we were face to face on our sides, and I gasped when I felt his erection slip between the gap in my thighs and send a murmur of pleasure across my sex. 'Feel that?' Kohén leaned in and kissed me hard on the mouth. '*That's* my excuse for my behaviour, and due to your own poor conduct of late, that's *your* responsibility now and yours alone. I will apologise for the multitude of mistakes that I have made that have caused you to lose faith in me, but I will never ever apologise for how much I want you. Nor will I apologise for how you got yourself into this mess by going behind my back with my brother.' His blue eyes flared like fire. 'I love you, but I hate you for loving him, and I do intend to punish you for it- when it's reasonable to do so.'

'Punish me?' I demanded. 'How? By taking me into that special room with the whips and chains?'

'I don't need to chain you up to get you to submit to me,' Kohén whispered, kissing my lower lip, then my chin, then the underside of my jaw. My thighs clenched around his cock when I felt it throb, and something inside me throbbed in response. 'But I plan on punishing you by making you cry out my name as many times as your heart cried out for his.' He kissed my neck, and slid himself in and out of the gap between my thighs, sliding his cock against my clitoris like a violinist with a bow. 'How many times was it, Larkin?' he whispered, coming back to maul my mouth with his as his erection began to pump in and out of the tight space between my thighs- bringing pleasure to one place that was demanding it while making the inner walls of my sex clench up wantonly with need. 'Five? Ten?'

'Kohén, stop!' I whispered against his mouth. 'We can't talk about this stuff, it won't do either of us any good!'

Kohén tore his mouth away and leaned back to stare into my eyes. 'Was it more than that?'

I looked down at his chest and immediately wished I hadn't, because it was sweaty and tanned and beautiful- and heaving due to his thundering heart and laboured breathing, as was mine. 'Kohén... please...'

'Oh God...' Kohén lifted my face to his and stared into my soul, his anguish evident. 'Larkin... did you ever crave me at all? Or was it him you were picturing every time we touched or kissed?'

I looked up at his face sharply. 'Don't be a fool,' I whispered. 'I had disloyal thoughts about him, but never when I was with you, and they never overshadowed how I felt about you until...'

'Until?'

My heart twisted as I realised the truth. 'Until today, in the hall.' Tears misted in my eyes. 'When I agreed to run away with him.'

Kohén inhaled sharply and pulled me closer still. 'So I was right? The most you ever loved him was today, when you believed that my words were his? That the look in *my* eyes was his?'

The tears slipped down my face. 'When I believed a lie? Yes.'

Kohén's face broke into a beautiful smile that blinded me. 'Then is it possible that you never loved him at all?'

'If that is true, then it is possible that I never loved either of you,' I pointed out, though I knew that if those bloody tears had been real, then that wasn't the case, 'only craved what I could not have.'

Kohén's eyes narrowed and he eased himself out from between my legs so that only the tip of him pressed into my clit now, making the cluster of nerves beneath my hooded bud spasm. One thrust and he would be inside me, and my wretched hands grasped his hair in fistfuls in need. 'You can have me now,' he whispered against my neck as I arched my back. 'You are wet and gasping and pulling at me so tell me, little bird... are you imagining that I am Kohl right now?' he bent his head as I writhed and kissed one of my nipples chastely, making it pebble.

'No!' I gasped, and that was the sordid truth.

'Are you wishing that I would stop?' he suckled my nipple and nudged me a little more purposefully, making me buck and gasp. I hated my body for responding to him so passionately, but I had no more control over that than I did over my destiny. I hated Kohén Barachiel with a passion too, but I wanted him still and that made me hate myself even more. And seeing as how I couldn't possibly despise myself more than I already did, what was the harm of giving into my base desires? They were the only ones I'd be free to entertain from here on out anyway, at least until I thought of a better plan than 'Duck and cover'.

Sensing my crisis of conscience, Kohén rolled me onto my back and gripped himself and circled the tip of his cock around my clit, making me shudder. 'Well? Is it rest that you want?'

'No!'

Kohén groaned and pressed himself into my labia, parting them and taunting the entrance to my sex. 'Is it *me*?'

Fuck I hated him so much, it felt like I could snap his neck off his shoulders. But I yanked his face closer to mine and kissed him while hitching one of my knees over his perfect hip. 'Yes! Yes I need you!'

'Who?'

'Kohén!' I cried, my heart thumping hard enough to combust. 'I need you inside me Kohén!'

Kohén growled and thrust into me and my eyes rolled back into my head with pleasure as my back lifted off the bed so that I was sitting up and hanging onto him for dear life, meeting the intrusion eagerly. In response, my aching body was given every inch of what it hated but wanted with equal measure and it felt so good that I honestly feared that I would combust- just burst into heat and flame as a result of our chemistry. Kohén met resistance inside me, but I cried out in delight as he grunted and speared me with more purpose, forcing his way up into my taut, cramping heat until he was almost completely sheathed within me. Our coupling was erotic and nonsensical and completely erratic, but I rode him eagerly while he thrust up to meet every twist of my hips, and I only flinched when Kohén's lips claimed mine and whispered the last thing in the world that I wanted to hear from him right then:

'I love you, Larkin! I will love you forever!'

My eyes sprung open as I sank my teeth into his muscular shoulder, but he interpreted the hostile act as one of passion and grunted, crying out the same vile words again, and earning himself a look of utter contempt for it- not from me this time, but from the woman in the mirror. I gasped to see her, clenching around him as I did, but she held a finger to her lips and winked before vanishing.

We'll see that he means that, I heard her whisper, but only inside my head. *And we'll see him suffer forever for it- together.*

And then the only sound I could hear was the blood inside my head and the jingling of the diamond rope around my throat as I began to climax around my master, who I now knew was as imprisoned by our passion as I was.

1.

I lost count of the amount of times that Kohén and I made love while buried under my downy comforter, but when I woke up in the morning- it was almost afternoon and we were both covered in bruises, claw marks and tooth imprints. My lips were swollen, my hair was so snarled and frizzy that it was broader than his shoulder span, and he looked so utterly fucked that I couldn't help but feel a surge of pride. His usually red, full lips were scarlet and swollen, his hair was mussed up and when he moved to get out of bed, he moaned and sank to his bare backside, rubbing his thighs.

If that really was Satan in here watching us right now, it's safe to say that she's a lot more pleased with me right now than the lord would ever have been...

'Jesus...' he muttered while I pulled my slip off the lamp (I could neither remember dressing in it, or taking it off). 'What have you done to me?'

I pulled the slinky nightgown over my head and then smoothed it over my thighs, whimpering when my flexing back muscles twanged unhappily. 'Nothing you deserved then... and ironically- nothing you don't deserve to suffer for now.'

I heard him chuckle and then his arm was around my waist, dragging me backwards. I yelped for it made me ache all over and made my mind spin, drawing my attention to the fact that I hadn't eaten in over a day. I did remember him bringing in a tray of strawberries and chocolate dipping sauce at some point near sunrise, but I'd been so pissed off with him for trying to make even my forced diet the sensual sort that I'd smashed it across the room. I looked now and saw them scattered across the threshold to my bathroom still, and lost my appetite.

How can he stand to cuddle me, knowing how much I hate him? I swear, I whispered that to him as many times as I whispered 'harder' to him last night, didn't I?

'I didn't mean in a bad way.' Kohén pulled my head into his lap and appraised me upside down. 'I mean... I feel *human.*' He lifted his hand and wriggled his fingers and they didn't glow or spark at all. 'I can always hide my charge well enough, except for in my eyes, but I can't even *feel* it now.' He pointed to his eyes. 'What colour are they?'

I lifted my lashes, and was slightly startled by the appearance of his dilated pupils, for the ring around them was the colour of bright ice. 'Glacier blue,' I whispered, 'like your mother's.'

'Really? I always thought I had my father's eyes- that steel blue.'

But I shook my head. 'No they're that topaz colour.' I pressed my fingers to his brow and stared closer. 'They're...' I caught myself and my breath, and turned, sliding off his lap and picking up a half-drunk glass of stale wine. I threw it back quickly, and then swallowed my feelings down with it.

Drunk... I need to be drunk all the time! Maybe if I'm inebriated, the days will begin to blur together and pass as quickly as the hours did last night...

'They're what?' he whispered from behind me.

I put the empty glass down and turned away, pressing the fingers of one hand to my temples to muffle the echo within. "Beautiful," I'd been about to say, and the word was still lodged in my throat, like I'd swallowed a sharp-edged gemstone. I couldn't throw around compliments like that! False ones meant to placate him yes, but not real endearments, for he didn't deserve them. And like my father and God, feeding this Barachiel any sort of affection was only going to strengthen him while weakening me.

Don't be as weak as the duchess! Do NOT be as weak as the duchess!

'Don't you have somewhere to be?' I asked frosting my words like the hue of his eyes. 'Some Basket-Racket match or a morning tea or another one of Karol's many festivities-'

'I've already missed the first two events for today, and the flower show downtown is well underway. You were fast asleep but father came to see me at about eight this morning to demand our attendance, and answers for what the hell had gotten into the both of us... but I told him that I was in your bed, and that I had no intention of leaving it, and so he left with the warning that we will be discussing all of this further when he returns.'

'This?' I repeated, glancing back at him.

He gestured to us then offhandedly toward the door. 'You. Me. Kohl's resulting tantrum...'

'And what are you going to tell him?' I asked coldly.

Kohén met my gaze steadily. 'That Kohl was hoping to pursue you once you were released, but was thwarted by our inevitable coming together... and that you had no feelings for him in return, outside of friendly ones of course- and are very regretful that you may have unwittingly encouraged his during your few interactions.' Though my nose tingled, I nodded. It was a reasonable explanation, all things considered, and a generous one on Kohén's part but still... poor Kohl! And when the duchess heard that I'd chosen her crowned prince over her favourite and was trying to deny ever having felt anything for him at all- poor *me*!

'And do you think he'll believe you?'

Do you think Kohl will play along? Will the duchess let us get away with it? Or will she be so insulted that she'll raise hell without pausing to contemplate why I would tell such a lie?

'I'm not going to give them any other option,' he said smoothly, but with an undercurrent of determination in his voice, 'and neither will you, all right?' I nodded again and moved to go to the bathroom, knowing that I was probably going to have to tell the duchess something about all of this to keep Kohl safe, but Kohén hooked his fingertips around mine, halting me, and said in a softer voice as he rose to his feet: 'Larkin...? What were you about to say about my eyes?'

I shook my head, accepting a kiss on the cheek before trying to pull myself free of him again, finding it harder to endure the intimate nature of our scenario, than the sexual part. Why did my traitorous flesh have to hum at his every touch? Why did I suspect that convincing everyone that I was madly in love with Kohén was going to be easier than I'd previously thought, thanks to the way that my body *reacted* to his touch? Tears pricked at my eyes and clogged my throat, making my voice crack when I responded to him: 'Nothing of import.'

There was a tense silent before he whispered. 'Yours are that periwinkle colour again- shifting like a mood ring.' He cleared his throat and I narrowed my gaze at the crystal water jug on the shelf across from me, wishing I could break it over his head. 'Your lips are swollen and a perfect pink, and you're glowing so much that I... I have fallen in love with you at second sight. At the sight of you as a woman now.'

I buried my face into my hands. 'Stop...' I pleaded.

I heard a drawer open and then Kohén huff a breath. 'I'll never stop loving you, or saying so,' he said, and his tone was decidedly cooler. 'And you can pretend to hate me all you want, but you love me too. So hide your feelings from yourself, if you're so determined to deny this absolute truth... but know that I will always find my way to you, and inside you; body, mind and soul.'

I was about to turn around and let him have it again, but I saw myself in my mirror when I moved and was startled silent by my dishevelled but radiant appearance- and especially at the sight of the necklace hanging around my throat and glittering in the shards of sun light spiking through the slats in the lattice and across the room. I waited for Satan to flicker to the mirror's surface again, but was disappointed that the only evil temptress staring back at me- was me.

'Yes, you're an angel...' Kohén said, then chuckled softly. 'But an utter hellion between the sheets and thank fuck for that-' there was a rapid knocking on my door. I spun around completely to face Kohén again, but before I could ask if he was expecting frantic company, he smiled at me. 'I sent a message for Kohl to stop by this afternoon,' Kohén said quickly, seeing the alarm on my face.

'What?' I hissed. 'Why?'

'Don't you want your chance to save him from himself? To stand up for me so that I won't be moved to stand up for myself?'

'Of course I do,' I said quickly, irritated to realise that I'd have to play-act before having a morning coffee. Hell, I needed more than a coffee to prepare myself for seeing Kohl again- I needed a month of meditation! 'But why *now*?

'The castle is all but abandoned at the moment, so if he pitches a fit or tries to make a scene as I suspect he will, we should be the only witnesses to it, which is safer for him. And if I need to calm him down, it'll be safer for me too.'

I scowled at Kohén. 'What do you mean by saying: "Calm him down?" Kohén?'

His eyes sparked with the promise of voltage and violence. 'I mean-'

'Kohén?!' Kohl sounded irate as he knocked again. 'Larkin? If he's got his hand over your mouth, I swear to Lucifer that I will…' he knocked harder, and my nerves shook like the door did in its frame. He was going to get himself electrocuted! 'What's going on in there?! Why hasn't she come out all day?! You said that she was FINE.'

Kohén and I stared at the door for a moment and then looked at each other and I realised that he'd managed to get himself a pair of gold, silk drawstring slacks. My eyes went straight to the bow that he was tying low on his hips, noticing that the skin of his abdomen was as gleaming as the fabric, and he followed them, then looked up at me with an arched eyebrow.

'I thought you'd want to settle this clown-' he jerked his thumb toward the door as hip jerked in a similar fashion to form a quickly-given, salacious smile. 'But if you're gonna look at me like *that*-'

'Don't even *joke* about it!' I hissed, and he must have seen that I was deadly serious, because some of the brightness faded from his eyes. *Easy...easy... you're supposed to be convincing him as much as you need to convince Kohl, remember?*

'You know, there's nothing wrong with enjoying sex, Larkin...' Kohén tied off the bow and then sauntered toward me, dipping his hand into his pants to adjust himself and my core burned like a coal even at that. 'And there's nothing wrong with admitting that you enjoy it with me, or that you'd gladly do it again right here on the floor. Do you think you're the only one that's been overcome by what we've done in the last twelve hours?' His eyes glowed and my heart thumped. When had he become such a... *man*? When had he begun to walk so completely with Karol's prowl, or look at me with that same constant level of heat? And when had I started wilting toward him for it, like a rose positioned too near to a fire? 'You set me on fire, woman. I feel completely turned inside out- I never knew that pleasure could *be* like that. And it's not just because you've got a body from Hell and the face of an angel and this way of twisting your hips...' his eyelashes fluttered and I gulped. With every step he took, a memory flashed before my eyes- Kohén's lips teasing my inner thighs, Kohén's tears of joy when I draped my arms around his neck and rocked back against him... Kohén's hot stomach against my back, spooning me... filling me... loving me... by the time he reached me, I was flushing all over and breathless. 'It's because you're always going to be my best friend. You have my heart, you have my history and now- you have me by the balls,' he pulled me against him and I almost swooned. 'And that means you can have me whenever you want, got it?' he kissed me gently and whispered. 'I am your slave, and I could not *be* more willing.' He smacked my ass gently and smiled even more gently. 'And I cannot wait until you admit that you feel the same.' He winked. 'And you will.'

Oh God.. oh God he's right... I am beyond redemption... I was growing wet and I was ashamed of it, I looked away, closing my eyes and struggling to breathe through the cloud of lust that had formed around us. *No you can't have him now- Kohl's on the other side of that door!*

Kohén sighed and stepped back. 'Are you sure that now is the time to deal with Kohl?' he asked coolly, while I gulped air down to force down the need to pant lustfully. Maybe what I needed was to dump the crystal jug of water over my own head, not his! 'I need you to pull yourself together Larkin and hold it together enough to convince him that he's fighting a battle in a war that he's already lost.' He lifted my chin with his thumb and stared into me hard, assessing my hue, no doubt. 'I know we've thrown a lot of ugly words and threats at one another over the past eighteen hours, but I wasn't joking when I said that I could kill him and Karol both for putting our relationship at risk. So if you want him to make if off this particular battlefield in one piece and with a bright future ahead of him still- then convince him that he'll have no part in yours, understood? And that you wouldn't want it any other way.'

'I will,' I said earnestly, my panic overshadowing my desire at last. 'I told you as much already! But we need to stop him from kicking up a fuss before he gets EVERYBODY all worked up and curious to know what's afoot, all right?

'Larkin? If he's holding you down or covering your mouth then just kick something and-'

'Shut the hell up!' Kohén bellowed, spinning away from me and moving for the door. 'I'm coming!'

Ahh! I'm not dressed, but! I'm not ready! Oh...

With a thunking heart and wild eyes, I caught sight of my robe hanging on a hook by the bathroom door and snatched it up quickly, trying to shrug into it. There was another glass of that peach elixir sitting on top of the fireplace mantel beside the water jug too- his from the evening before- and I paused in my dressing to throw it back as I had the last, making an awful noise as the flat, warm, too-sweet peachy flavour drenched my taste buds.

Oh Lord, I wish I could have seen Cherry before I had to go through this! She'd be able to calm my nerves, oh dear... she's probably never going to want to come near me again after the way that we spoke to her last night! How am I going to do this?

'Are you decent?' Kohén hissed and I nodded, putting the glass down with an unceremonious thunk, and Kohén wrenched the door open just as I was trying to catch the belt ends of the robe with my hands. 'She's fine, all right? Look.'

'Where?' his twin stumbled into the room, and I spun and retreated a few steps, knotting my belt as I swallowed down the flat, too-sweet champagne, and scanned Kohl for damage with my eyes.

'Right here,' I whispered, noting the long, angry pink scar running down his bared right bicep, and cringing to see that it extended almost from his collarbone to his elbow. What had it looked like before Karol had healed him, if it was still so red now? And what was he feeling on the inside, for his exterior to be so shadowed by his grief? There were dark shadows under his equally dark eyes, his facial complexion was pasty and beaded with sweat around his hairline, and because he was wearing a tight-fitting white tank with grey, low-slung shorts, I could see how every one of his muscles was clenched with tension and his skin rippled with gooseflesh and stained a pale blue by his surfacing power. 'Good morning, Kohl.'

Kohl halted, looking shocked, and then turned to Kohén. 'What is that around your neck? Are you insane? I'd assumed that you'd fooled her, or blackmailed her- but if you've bribed her with Pacifica's treasure, then you're even more fucked up-'

'He didn't,' I said quickly, seeing the way Kohén's eyes slitted dangerously, even though he had no right to look indignant because Kohl was right on all three counts. 'It was gifted to me by Atticus- his offer to secure my future in Pacifica.' I swallowed and reached for Kohén's hand. 'At my lover's side.'

Kohl's eyes almost bulged out of his sockets. 'Your LOVER?' he took a step between us and Kohén clenched mine almost hard enough to hurt. 'You honestly expect me to believe that you have gone from being torn between us, to plastered to his future, after seeing you run off with him while wearing MY clothes, seconds after Kohén revealed the fact that he knew about us?' he shook his head. 'No, I'm not a fool! And mother swears that-'

'The fact that you've busted in here to accuse your identical twin of rape proves otherwise, for you should know me better than that,' Kohén pulled me to his side and kissed my head, and I almost fainted with relief that he'd cut Kohl off before he could finish repeating what his mother had said, because whatever it was, it probably hadn't been meant for Kohén's ears. I stared hard into Kohl's eyes, trying to communicate what I knew I could not with a single look.

No, we're not escaping together now- but you still need to go, and quickly! I'm sorry for it all- so sorry- but SCRAM!

'... and the fact that you saw her pull me more deeply into her luscious body last night ought to convince you that *you* are the one who has made some very foolish miscalculations regarding the depth of her affection for me!'

Kohl's eyes flared and my cheeks flushed, but as humiliated as I was to remember the way Kohl's panting had steamed *his* side of the poolroom door as he'd watched Kohén and I fornicate, I could tell by the identical sets of balled-fists that I was the only one who was capable of dissolving the tension in the room, rather than escalating it. So I pressed my other hand to Kohén's chest and patted it in an affectionate way.

'Do not speak for me, please darling- the innocent always sound the most guilty when defending themselves.' I turned back to Kohl and saw that his face had puckered up in distaste at the words 'darling' and 'innocent,' and I could not blame him, for they tasted as sour in my mouth as they had probably sounded. 'You are right in presuming that I sought out Kohén's company yesterday, believing that he was you. And yes, he played along and allowed me to believe it while I confessed our wrong-doings to him.' I smiled sadly. 'But Kohl... I gave him your ring back while under the impression that he was you, and it doesn't matter that he wasn't, for the fact remains the same: I chose *Kohén* because I know that we belong together.' I saw disbelief fill Kohl's eyes so I pressed on, remembering how the excuse I'd fed Cherry the night before had evidently convinced her of my stupidity and my willingness to be enslaved too: 'And because being free will not change the fact that I will be just as infertile, and as ineligible to marry Kohén now as I was before, I decided that I'd rather live out my life as his companion that is free to love him, than as his friend that is forbidden from touching him.'

Kohl blanched. 'Just like that? No way! Larkin I know that you've always been torn between your feelings for him and your feelings for me, and I'm not surprised to learn that what Karol did yesterday forced you to ponder a change of heart... but you could have made the decision to throw away your life for him an hour, a day or a *week* later- so why would you make it in the heat of the moment like that, given how much he has hurt you? You're too smart for that!'

'There were other factors that forced me to speak quickly,' I said quietly, thinking of Kelia, 'but I admitted everything that I have ever felt within this palace's walls to him yesterday- for you *and* for him- and by the time I'd explained it all to him, I realised that I'd just finally explained it to myself- that I love him more than anything, or any*one* else on this earth.'

Kohl flinched. 'Even me?'

The words tasted like poison, but part of me suspected that it was the truth to them that repulsed me so, not the fact that I was forced to say them out loud.

'Even myself,' I admitted, and saw Kohl's face crumple, telling me that my confession had been more poisonous- and more destructive- than even I had suspected. I looked to the mirror again, hoping to see Satan once more, and praying that she'd offer some sort of wink of encouragement or smile of empathy as she had the night before, but all I saw in the looking glass was Kohl's devastated reflection- a reflection that revealed more about my character than anyone else in that room, even Kohén.

2.

The silence was unbearable, but when I saw Kohl's eyes fill with tears that would get him into even more trouble if they were seen by his parents or other citizens, I discovered a new level of unbearable. This poor boy would never know anything but suffering until he distanced himself from me, and because he seemed incapable of removing himself from a potentially lethal situation, it was clearly up to me to give him the shove he needed, even though it was killing me to act so dismissive of his feelings- and of everything that we had shared.

'I can't believe this…' Kohl was whispering brokenly to himself and the floor. His eyes moved to the choker around my neck, and narrowed. 'And what's more- I *don't* believe this. I cannot!'

Shaking, I smoothed my hand down Kohén's chest and felt his pounding heart again. 'I know that this all must be hurtful and confusing to you and I am sorry for that Kohl… you cannot know how sorry. But I stand by my choice, so please…'

'Please… *what?*' I couldn't tell if Kohl was choking on tears or rage or both, but the sound of his voice breaking speared me through my heart. 'Forget that we were in love? Let it go? Assume that this is our new destiny, and that you will be happy like this?' Kohl's dark eyes were bottomless. 'Larkin, after Kelia confronted him yesterday, he was threatening to drag you to the harem by your *hair-*'

'He had every right to be furious with us,' I agreed quickly, not wanting to hear the ugly threats again, 'and he has been generous enough to agree to look the other way over our betrayal, which I am thankful for.' I swallowed. 'But he will only do that so long as I agree to stay here in Eden with him as his only Companion, and to cut ties with you.' Kohl's eyes flashed with indignation as they turned to Kohén, but I pressed on: 'And I think we both know that that is fair- because as innocent as our affair was, we have hurt him irrevocably, Kohl, and we both need to take steps to make it right.'

Kohl blinked rapidly at me, then looked to his twin, then back to me, his cheeks gaining colour as he did until he was flushed red. 'He doesn't LOOK hurt now that he's had his fun with you! Don't you question the depth of feelings that can be wrecked by betrayal, but healed by getting his end wet? You sure did on Caldera!'

I cringed because Kohl was right, but Kohén's suddenly thunking heart felt like a countdown to an explosion. 'He loves me,' I said softly, and my voice sounded pitiful, even to me, 'and I love him. That's more than I thought to hope for when I was younger and alone all the time so-'

'You're not that girl anymore, and you didn't need a pity screw and lukewarm affection from his Royal-Entitled here, to give your life purpose and meaning!' Kohl stepped forward, and Kohén buzzed all over in warning. 'Your freedom was granted to you yesterday, Larkin! You could have chosen him down the line and found a way to make it happen, but *now*?'

'She promised to stay at my side willingly yesterday before *any* of this came to light!' Kohén snapped and I flinched, remembering that tender moment on the common after I'd been released. Yes I had promised Kohén that I wouldn't leave Arcadia any time soon without him, and I had meant it... just not under these circumstances.

'No, she didn't! She wouldn't have...' But I saw Kohl's gut buckle as his face did. He turned to me with a million questions in his eyes and a lifetime's worth of pain etched into the lines around his downturned mouth, and though I wanted to assure him that I had not gotten over him so easily to spare his feelings, that would have been stupid. He *needed* to be hurt- he needed to think me fickle and unworthy of him and then, he needed to get back on the ship to Pacifica and sail to his freedom and never look back!

'He's telling the truth, Kohl.' I inhaled and exhaled, digging deep inside me and coming up with something honest to offer him. 'I gave up my freedom when I realised that it is not worth losing Kohén over.' I shrugged as though it were no big deal. 'He has proven that he will help me make my dreams come true, and agreeing to be his will keep me out of Karol's reach indefinitely.'

Kohl's brows drew together. 'How? *Why?* How could your heart just change so swiftly?"

I leaned against my prince and smiled, feigning a sort of bliss as the other prince's eyebrows rose. 'Because I took your advice Kohl, and confessed the deal that I made with Karol to Kohén, and you were right: he forgave me, and has sworn to protect me from your eldest brother at all costs, and without giving me that dreadful golden brand that I so fear.' I looked up at Kohén and gave him a fraudulent, adoring smile, before looking back at Kohl. 'And because I cannot have children or hope to marry Kohén anyway, I will take this path, and remain at his side however I can.' Under my hand, Kohén's heart gave a deep, contented and relieved throb that was notably slower than the others. 'And I beg that yes, you let it go, and try to find a way to make your peace with it so that we can all put this behind us and start again.'

'Yes…' Kohén ran his hand down my shoulders, and the hairs on my forearm crackled with his static energy as a rumble of thunder- stirred by Kohl's emotions- rattled the windows. 'I would very much like that, and though I know you don't care for me Kohl, you can respect her wishes at least, can't you? If you love her so much? Or wish to escape this little clusterfuck unpunished?'

'Her… wishes…?' Kohl ran his hands through his hair in an agitated manner, looking from me to Kohén and back as though waiting for the other shoe to drop. '*Is* this your wish, Larkin? Is this what you'd be asking me to do if he wasn't in the room?'

It wasn't, but I'd still be asking him to leave. 'I guess we'll never know, because we have not earned the right to exchange even one more confidence in privacy,' I said honestly. I tried to communicate as much apology as I could with my eyes, but I was afraid to look at him for too long, lest he saw my fear and understood that yes, Kohén had an invisible gun, but it was trained on *Kohl's* precious head, not *my* unworthy one as he suspected. 'You just need to take me at my word, and my apology for leading you on with it- and then let things be!'

'How?' Kohl demanded. 'I don't believe a word, and your eye colour keeps shifting, telling me that you don't believe it either! He's not only closed his hand around my firefly- he's balled his fist, hasn't he? And if you have faded so much overnight then you will be a walking shell by the end of the week-'

'*Your* firefly?!' Kohén thundered, eyes sparking. 'How *dare* you?' I could not hold on to Kohén or contain my yelp of fear as he ripped himself from my side and got in Kohl's face, creating the illusion of someone who was very displeased with his own suddenly fearful reflection. 'How heroically you rise to save her from a man who actually loves her!' he snapped. 'But tell me, where was this cavalier attitude when *Karol* was the one hoping to treat her like a whore?'

Kohl blanched. 'That was her decision to make-'

'One you were going to let her follow through on, because you knew it would make her unequivocally ineligible to marry me, right? Leaving her as fair game for YOU, third-born brother of mine?' Kohén asked softly, and my stomach lurched.

Wait… what?!

'Oh, go to Hell!' Kohl snapped, but he did not meet my eyes and suspicion crawled over my skin like a million spiders. 'Some of us don't have to manipulate our way into a woman's future!'

'No, some of us stand aside and watch her fuck it up so badly that she'll require rescuing after- by someone who has nothing to lose by scooping her up!' Kohén shot back. 'And that's YOU!'

Kohl's eyes gleamed and I realised that even if Kohén's accusation was mostly unfounded, it probably wasn't completely inaccurate. Kohl had gallantly offered to live with me regardless of what status I held when he did, and yes that was sweet- but not once had he offered to intervene on my behalf when it came to Karol. Was that because he'd been afraid to, or because part of him hadn't *wanted* to, because me being released as a non-virgin would have disqualified me for Kohén's hand indefinitely?

What does any of it matter now? You can't stand here and let these two duke it out because it won't change the end result of Kohl getting himself killed or banished... will it?

Fear and adrenaline sluiced through me when I heard thunder rumble again, bringing my brain back to life after an eighteen hour hiatus. Thinking quickly, I gave Kohl one final look before I chose my next course of action, realising that he looked completely out of place in my room with his sexily bare feet and agitated posture, in comparison to Kohén and Karol had always looked at ease within the harem. He'd been denied his birthright and that wasn't fair, but he deserved better than to be groomed the way his brothers had- he *needed* sunlight and salty air and hard work, and would grow to be twice as glorious as his 'elder' brothers if granted those things and denied me.

But if he pushed Kohén too far or attacked him, and that bible was thrown onto a pile of evidence, not even the duchess would be able to dig him out of that hole. I cared for him, very deeply, and I didn't want to accept the fact that I'd never have another chance to make things work with him and I really didn't want to break his heart beyond repair- but I would, because Kohl Barachiel deserved a woman as sweet and selfless as him- not a used whore with a conflicted heart.

'Some of us are smart enough to know that the prospect of being married is off the cards for me, always has been and therefore, is a waste of breath!' I turned around suddenly, breaking the silence of their stare-down, took Kohl's ring off the top of my lowest bookcase and stepped up to him, folding it into his hand. 'I'm sorry to have caused you pain and thank you for your concern- but I am Kohén's Companion now, and your intervention is not deserved, required *or* wanted, Kohl.' His hands were clammy in mine and I stepped back, pleading with my eyes. 'Please; do not make any more accusations against Kohén's character for the sake of mine, because neither of us have the right to plead innocence or cry injustice.' I looked him hard in the eye and said: *'Everyone who makes a practice of sinning also practices lawlessness; sin is lawlessness!'* *

Kohl stared at me as Kohén pulled me back into his arms, and I saw realisation dawn on him when he realised WHAT I was quoting. His darkening eyes immediately surveyed my room, looking for the bible, but I knew that Kohén had already hidden it away, and the way he blanched when he met my eyes again communicated that he understood: we were both fucked, so best off being fucked quietly and with a degree of kindness.

'Really?' he whispered.

'Remember what you said, about the cage?' I kissed Kohén's cheek. 'He is barring the door yes- but he is still in here with me and for that I am grateful enough... but there's not room enough in here for three, Kohl, so you must let yourself out and relinquish the idea of taking me with you, for I have made my choice. I choose for you to walk free of this- not I.'

A tense silence followed this statement, and I could hear my pulse in my ears as I returned Kohl's stare, willing him to believe me, but it was not Kohl who broke the stalemate, but the sound of the door cracking open once more.

'Oh my god!' the shrill voice was akin to a firecracker going off in the heavy silence, and we whirled as one and found ourselves gaping at Kelia with matching expressions of surprise.

Oh no... !

'Kelia!' Kohén snapped, stepping back and taking me in his arms. 'Why aren't you at the flower show?!'

'Greeting that snotty Amelia-Rose bitch like the rest of the kingdom while choking on rose-stink? Not likely!' Kelia scoffed, and I was momentarily distracted by the fact that Amelia-Rose Choir and her rich, renowned step-father, Shepherd Choir, had arrived in Arcadia to haggle for Karol's favour at last. Would that affect how things were progressing between Karol and Ora? It was common knowledge that she had always had a 'thing' for the Barachiel bloodline, after all.

Oh and she'll be so excited to learn that he's dismissed his Companions- she'll probably have to be pried off the birthday boy with a crowbar! But Karol's always hated Amelia-Rose though... right? Ugh, I hope a change in tune on her part won't instigate one on his!

But Kelia's hazel eyes flared with outrage after she'd taken the three of us in, and I remembered that I had interests of my own to safeguard that were in far more peril now than Ora's were, and snapped back to attention just as she exploded:

'What's going *on* in here*?!*'

'How did you get past the guards?' I demanded, excited to think that there was a crack in Kohén's security- one I would willingly fall through if it meant getting a few minutes alone with the duchess to warn her of Kohén's hold over Kohl!

'There's no guard on the door right now,' Kohén grumbled, looking aggravated. 'I dismissed him for a few hours.'

'Oh.' My heart sank, knowing that he'd had getting away with the murder of his twin on his mind when he'd done that, and Kohl gave him a foul, knowing look.

'Are the security cameras off too, big brother?' Kohl snapped. 'Or were you just going to turn one to face the front gates while you dragged your likeness's body out the rear gates?'

Kohén's face creased, but as he turned and opened his mouth to express whatever emotion was making his fingers spark (so much for me having screwed him human!) Kelia lunged forward and stole focus once more.

'What is she wearing, Kohén?!' the irate girl demanded, locking her gaze on my neck. 'You were supposed to be punishing her, not frosting her like a cake!'

'Get out of here, Kelia,' Kohl growled, motioning toward the door. 'This is a private discussion and you have already interfered enough!'

Kelia rolled her eyes. 'Oh *I'm* the interference? You're the one who fucked her in the first place, so *you* get out!'

'I did *what*?' Kohl whipped around to gape at his twin. 'That's what you thought she was guilty of doing? That's preposterous!'

'Like Hell it's presumptuous!' Kelia got the word wrong but none of us deigned to correct her. 'I saw it written in your own hand- you recollected making love-'

'Oh!' Kohl whirled back to look at me, and he was green. 'THAT was the letter that he read?' I nodded and he turned on Kohén, his face draining of all colour as he put two and two together. 'You didn't know that she wasn't a virgin still when you did this to her, did you? *That's* why...' He gripped his face in his hands like he was going to tear off his skin and hair in exasperation, and my blood turned to dread and began pumping away like mad. I'd so hoped to keep Kohl from learning that! Not only would he be more convinced that I was lying when I said I was happy now, but he'd have to live with the knowledge that he could have had me if he'd pushed hard enough. 'You *idiot*. If that's what you suspected, why not ask me outright?'

Oh god Kohl stop trying to solve this mystery and get the HELL out of it!

'Because *you* were being so forthcoming with me?' Kohén jeered, but then sighed. 'I didn't know that asking would make a difference. Your letters said all that I thought I'd needed to hear.'

Kohl looked at me. 'Are you... are you okay? Did he-'

'She's fine,' Kohén protested, cheeks pink. 'But for the record, clearing up the misunderstanding was such a delightful experience that I'm rather glad that it was made in the first place.' He kissed my temple. 'For both of us, right darling? Now we don't have to argue over whether or not we'll be together forever- because it's been decided *for* us.'

I wanted to kill him, but I did not. The look on Kohl's face made it pretty clear that I wouldn't be able to beat him to it if the opportunity arose anyway, so all I did was nod and smile tightly, my own cheeks pinkening to know that Kohén had a point- physically I *was* better than fine. Once the initial obstacle had been taken out of the equation, having intercourse with Kohén had been, well, nothing sort of magical.

But Kohl's not going to believe that, and he's not going to give up! And my hint about that bible will only convince him further that he has cause to fight! I need.. I need... I need Martya's brain! What would she do?

'You better be joking, Kohén!' Kelia shrieked, drawing our focus back to her. 'Yesterday afternoon you were ready to rip him limb from limb to beat *her* with them, and now you're in love again? It's sickening.' She pointed toward the door. 'You've had your fun with her, your highness, and I won't tell a soul that you used someone who wasn't pure, for your sake! But get rid of her NOW or-'

'Yesterday afternoon, you led me to believe that Larkin had been unfaithful to me with my twin,' Kohén said softly, calmly and in that dignified way that made him seem years older than the rest of us. 'But that was a false allegation- one derived from a double entendre, in fact, and so Larkin was as pure as the driven snow when I-'

'Ploughed her?' I suggested dryly, turning to face the mirror and pretending to smooth my hair. My hands looked calm, but I could feel my fingers trembling.

'Yes, that.'

'Gross!' Kelia exclaimed, and rambled on- tearing my character to shreds and keeping Kohén distracted. The new full-length mirror revealed Kohl's reflection within it and behind me. Sensing my gaze immediately, his eyes drifted from the arguing pair and latched on mine and he bit his lip, asking me what he could do, and making my head swim with the want of being rescued by the handsome prince, just like in my books.

This is it! You can either signal that you need help, or ask for him to send his mother or communicate that you are scared and that he is in grave danger- or you can get him out of it by giving nothing away.

Blinking back tears before their sheen could be seen, I shrugged, moved my fingers from my hair, to the circlet of diamonds around my neck and stroked them lovingly, letting my gaze drift from his to it, as though the sparkling stones held more appeal for me than his beautiful eyes did. I allowed my lip curl in the hint of a bittersweet smile, and then met his gaze again, seeing that his brow was now furrowed in confusion. I needed to get a message to Constance for his sake, but I could not risk involving him.

'I'm fine,' I mouthed, then allowed a sweeter smile to develop, before turning and resting my head on Kohén's shoulder lovingly. 'I'm *his.*'

Kohl stared at me like he was waiting for the punch line, and I took it as a credit to my character that it was so hard for him to believe that I was actually content with my lot. But then I moved my lips against his twin's shoulder in an affectionate kiss, and I saw Kohl's muscular abdomen notably suck in beneath his shirt-like I'd socked him- and I supposed that I had.

Either way, I knew that I'd shattered everything that he'd believed that he knew about me, and it was a bruise that would never fade from my ego.

He thought I was a Companion now, too. And just like that, the rain began to fall.

3.

'I don't care what she did or did not do, she broke rules!' Kelia was still raging on. 'She had a bible in her room! She's been lying to us all and manipulating everyone and when she leaves on Sunday, it had better be with a criminal brand and a slut one!'

'She won't be leaving here on Sunday,' Kohén said quickly as I spun around, feigning offence, 'so I am not obligated to even discuss branding her until I intend to travel outside of Arcadian perimeters!' he turned to Kohl. 'And would you knock that rain shit off? You'll ruin the flower show and we're already in enough trouble with father!'

Kohl gave him the finger.

Kelia flushed purple, drawing me out of my mental ramblings. 'But she had an affair with your twin! That makes her a whore in every sense of the word and people need to KNOW it! And then they need to watch her being swept to the gutter!'

'Watch your mouth,' Kohén snapped. 'Larkin corresponded with my brother, but she *never* slept with him!'

'Lies!'

'No, it's the truth!' Kohl came back to life and stood at Kohén's side, staring Kelia down, and I blinked owlishly, stunned at the sight of them standing united once more. 'I swear, Kelia- your jealousy will be both of our undoing- not just Lark's!'

'As Larkin will be this kingdom's!' Kelia countered, her voice shrill.

'They had a crush on one another, Kelia, and they corresponded via the letters that you showed me,' Kohén said quietly, resting his hands firmly on her shoulders and looking her dead in the eye. 'I am wounded by it, but it's not a crime and if it were, it is one that you are guilty of having committed just a while ago when it was YOU corresponding with Kohl and trying to win time with him alone.' He held his hands out. 'How can you demand that I brand Larkin a criminal, without expecting me to extend the same courtesy to you?'

She narrowed her eyes at him. 'This was a little more intense than that!'

Kohl quirked up the corner of his mouth. 'Because I wasn't interested enough in what you had to offer to nibble at your rancid bait?'

Ouch!

Kelia's eyes bulged and then suddenly, she was turning around and throwing open the door. 'That's it! I won't be offended like this for a second more! And I'm certainly not sharing this place with her!'

'No you won't be!' Kohén said firmly after exchanging a heated look with his brother. 'Because Larkin will be staying, and *you* will be leaving. And if you go quietly, you will be compensated generously for-'

'I am NOT leaving, and a noble girl cannot be compensated for being treated so poorly!'

'You're not a noble anymore!' Kohl reminded her.

'Neither are you!' she spat back. She rested her hands on her hips and looked back at Kohén. 'We had a deal, Prince Barachiel and if you think you can worm your way out of it and send me off to the Corps, then you've underestimated me!' She pointed out into the foyer. 'A crime has been committed here, and I am going to report it! ALL of them!' She spun on her heel and marched out and Kohl and Kohén were hot on her heels. 'The affair! The bible they were passing around! The fact that she wasn't a virgin when you-'

'She was!' Kohén roared, and my heart lurched in my chest. 'I am sorry if you are upset but making more false allegations will not get you a golden brand, Kelia- but whipped!'

Oh no, if she talks, I'm going to be investigated anyway!

'Oh, I'm so scared!' she taunted, storming along the corridor ahead of us. 'In fact, I am so scared that I think I need to seek a Shepherd's counsel immediately and confess that I am being made an accessory to a crime, and threatened! And I think I'll find one at the garden show, and SCREAM the truth so that all of Arcadia hears it before you can silence me!' She laughed. 'Welcome to Arcadia, Shepherd Choir- have some SIN! And some unseasonable frost because the inconsequential twin has blue balls!'

I came to a halt and stared after her, aghast. Kelia was going to ruin us all, Kohl would suffer the most and the goody two-shoes Amelia-Rose would have a field day with such scandalous information! And why? Because Kelia was a demon who wanted to hold shiny things in her hand more than she wanted to shine on the inside!

Breathing heavily, I reached behind my neck and unclasped the choker, and then took off after her in a sprint. 'Kelia, wait!'

'You'd try and take down three of us just to spare yourself a few years in the Corps?' Kohén demanded, sounding incredulous as he loped after the angry redhead.

'Of course she will! She's a lazy little shit!' Kohl grunted, matching him step for step.

'Says the guy itching to get the hell out of the Corps and now can because he just HAPPENS to be born the same year as the incredible Martya? Pfft! What a load!' Kelia waved her hand over her shoulder. 'There are strings being pulled all over the place here for the chosen few, and I won't be hung from one while *that* whore grows old and fat in the lap of luxury!'

'Kelia, please!' I hugged myself so my breasts wouldn't bounce as I ran after them all. 'I'm sorry you're so upset, but so am I! Nothing in my life has gone as planned either, but making things worse for someone else won't make them better for you!' I had the necklace pooled in my fist. 'But I know that all you want is to feel safe and cared for so here-'

'Get away from me!' Kelia whirled around suddenly, causing Kohl and Kohl to hurtle past her and out into the centre of the harem, where the hot baths were gurgling under the misty glass-autumn above. 'What position are you in to be doling out advice?' she spat toward my feet but I yelped and backed up in time so that it hit the tile, not me. 'Slut! Everyone thinks you're an angel, but I know you're the spawn of Satan in some way, and so was Martya!'

'Hey!' I lunged forward and shoved her back, hard. 'Say what you like about me, for I am inclined to agree with you! But leave her out of this! Martya was a saint!'

'Martya's six foot under, not high above!' she hissed. 'And thank goodness for that! She didn't read books that were nearly big enough to hide her wretched face well enough, so good riddance!'

I saw red, as though I'd been set on fire. 'God, you are hideous. How did it take me so long to see it? I though Kohén sodomised you because he was a pervert, but clearly- he just couldn't tell the difference between your mouth and your arse hole, because the stuff that comes out of both orifices is the same!'

'He did *what?*!' (Kohl)

'You told Larkin what?!' (Kohén). 'You KNOW that we haven't technically done ANY-'

'I hate you!' With a mottled face and an indignant gasp, Kelia pulled back her hand to slap me but I swung out my own arm to block her and suddenly, I heard a loud crack.

What was THAT?

Kelia let out a blood-curdling scream and reeled back, holding her right bicep with her left hand so that I could see the way that her forearm was dangling unnaturally. 'Aahh!' her shriek bounced off the high ceiling and hit me directly in my chest. 'You broke it!'

'Oh my god...' I recoiled, pressing my hands to my lips in a prayer position. I'd barely felt the impact, but evidently I'd been right when I'd told Kohén the night before that I was perfectly capable of defending myself.

'Oh! Oh... my arm is BROKEN! Bitch! Hellion!' Kelia bowed at the waist and screamed again and I pressed my hands to my ears, certain that my eardrums would rupture.

Kohl and Kohén raced past me and flanked her like bookends. 'Oh! Make the pain stop!'

'Whoa- it *is* broken!' Kohl exclaimed, sending me an awed and slightly shocked look.

Oh no, oh no oh NO! I AM a hellion!

'Both the radius and the ulna,' Kohén confirmed grimly, leaning over to regard it up close, and I sobbed and turned away because blood was dripping from the webbing of Kelia's fingers to the floor, and I knew that if she held her arm the other way, I would see bone pressing through her perfect, noble skin. 'She needs a doctor or a healer- and soon.'

'I'm sorry!' I cried, feeling worthless. Elijah and the duchess were going to be so mad to learn that I'd done something so awful on such an important day. 'Kelia, it was an accident!'

'It was self-defence, actually,' Kohl pointed out, crouching beside her to peer at her arm. 'It's not your fault that she doesn't have the bone density to support her bad temper!

'No one will question what happened here with us as witnesses Larkin so please, calm yourself.' Kohén waved his hand at me and then bent over to address Kelia, but I wasn't comforted by either of them. I didn't care how much trouble I was going to be in, only that she was in agony because of me!

What have I done? Oh my God, I am evil!

'Kelia I know you're in a lot of pain,' Kohén said, his voice velvet as he rubbed her back. 'But you need to stop screaming and breathe.' He looked at me, and his face was red. 'And whatever she said, please know that I never penetrated her-'

'Shut up!' I pressed my hands to my ears again. 'Not a word more!'

'Fuck you! All of you!' Kelia hacked out, and I spun to see her staggering toward me but around me by the pool, giving me a wide berth. 'This is evidence of how twisted she is! I'm going to find a healer and I'm going to tell them that

I swore to tell the truth about her and so she attacked me and-'

'Kelia, NO!' Kohén moved after her, his face white and I knew that this was *bad*. One spoiled brat the palace could ignore, but one with bone jutting out of her skin? The only person that we could possibly call to help us now was Karol, and I doubted that he was even in the castle, or would help without strings attached anyway.

'Stop her!' Kohl roared, hurrying past me to block her exit.

'Kelia, here!' I tossed the necklace to her feet. 'Take it! Keep your mouth shut about Kohl, and it's yours, please?'

'Larkin what the fuck?' Kohén moved forward to collect it but Kelia snatched it up first and growled at him.

'Mine!'

'Let her have it!' I spat. 'She deserves to get something out of all of this, doesn't she?' Kelia looked up at me, and seemed thrown off by my coming to her defence. 'Yes I'll admit that she's a lying, sleazy, uppity little creep, but we all know she wouldn't have been if she'd been left with her mother!' I pointed to her, meeting Kohén's eye. 'This is your fault, and mine, and Arcadia's for allowing it to happen- *this* is what I've been trying not to become for the last twelve years!' Suddenly I knew that Satan had been in my room, not just in my imagination, and I knew that I probably wasn't the only one that had summoned her there. 'You think I want her to suffer? You think she's an extreme case right now?' I laughed harshly. 'The morning that I went to Karol, I had a serrated bread knife in my belt, do you know that? I had Martya's cure in one hand, ready to do the right thing, and a weapon waiting for the other- just in case doing the right thing got me nowhere! Maybe you don't understand being pushed to one's limits, but *I* do! How can people on their hands and knees be expected to do anything that isn't low? If it had been MY backside hoisted up for your royal pleasure I can assure you-

'I don't blame you for protecting yourself in such a way!' Kohén cried. 'But the circumstances were different! You were trying to do the right thing- she never has!' he shot her a dirty look. 'And no one pushed her to her hands and knees- she was already crawling!'

'She was taught to perfect the application of lipstick and elbow her way to the front of a pack,' I reminded him. 'And that could have been me, if not for Kohl and his books. Tell Atticus that I gave the necklace to her as I felt sorry for my best friend having to leave him with so few adornments, and she will be able to make a comfortable life for herself with it!'

Kohén blanched. 'I hear what you are saying Larkin, but in the name of what is fair and equal, I cannot allow Kelia to have something so valuable as a reward for behaving so atrociously.' We all looked to her, and saw that despite her discomfort, she was already trying to get the choker on, one-handed, and it was a sorry sight indeed. 'She is the rough- and those diamonds are priceless.'

'I will NOT have Kohl's life on my head in any way!' I pointed out, and he blinked, clearly remembering that if Kohl went down, he'd lose me too. But in the same sense, fighting too hard for Kohl could inspire him to string himself up in order to fight back for me, and I couldn't have that either so I hastily added: 'Not after I've led him on like this, only to end up more in love with you than before.' I pointed at it. 'If it was a gift, then I can buy Kohl's freedom with it and her silence, and you'll be able to quietly convince Atticus that it was a decision that will benefit Pacifica, because it dug their new lieutenant general out of a ditch.' I wet my lips. 'But if it was a collar, then snatch it back and chain me once more and I will KNOW the depth of your love, and you will feel mine in response! Or lack thereof!'

Kohén's face contracted, but he simply pressed his hand to his forehead and stepped back, shooting his brother a loaded look. 'Then I guess this is your issue now, Little Kahuna, not mine.'

'Larkin…' Kohl sounded hoarse as he stepped forward again. 'I'm moved that you would go to such lengths to secure my freedom, but you know me better than that. Maybe those diamonds are a fair trade for you and Kelia to crawl on your hands and knees to attain, but I'd sooner be imprisoned for what she intends to accuse us of, and see the worth of that spent on freeing the oppressed like us- before I allowed her to keep it just to save myself.'

I stared daggers at him, finally understanding how his piousness had managed to rub Kohén the wrong way on so many occasions in the past. I was saving his life so he could go on to save others! Not giving up one pretty thing so I could enjoy the others I'd receive with a clear conscience after!

Kohén chuckled, clearly enjoying my turn of coat, which he'd easily glimpsed, as he knew me so well. Had my eyes turned violet in indignation? 'What Kohl means- I'm sure- is that despite your heart being in the right place, those jewels are now in the worst hands.' He lifted his brow. 'You do not agitate a wasp, and then give it means to amass a larger hive.'

I cringed again, for he had a point. With eleven million dollars, Kelia would be able to fund some dark, selfish deeds indeed.

'Who are you calling names, asshole?!' Kelia squeaked, tuning in at last. 'Larkin gave these to me because she knows that she's white trash who doesn't deserve them, but *I* do!' she shook the necklace in her fist and I closed my eyes, exhausted by her and realizing that I'd never left my bratty, vain and spoiled older sister Jaiya, behind- she'd been here since Kelia had arrived- right down to the freckles.

And I'll bet that's why I loved her so… oh boy, I need to be evaluated by a psychiatrist before I get a whipping, just so they know that they're punishing the right personality!

'And I'm keeping them!' Kelia was backing away from us, holding the necklace high while blood dripped from her forgotten arm and along the tiles, and tears dripped from her nostrils. 'And I'll keep Kohl's crimes a secret if you let me leave with them-' Kohén opened his mouth to argue, but she hurried on: 'But I am STILL telling Shep who broke my arm, and I will laugh until I cry while I watch her get whipped for it!'

'No deal!' Kohl barked, stepping forward. 'I'll tell him the truth and go down willingly, just to prove what a cunning little liar you are.'

'I concur,' Kohén said, and his voice was acid. 'Tread carefully, Kelia- you are getting on my last nerve.'

'I'm not scared of you!' Kelia whirled on Kohén. 'You're only second in line, you know, so there are plenty of heads I can go over to see this situation handled the right way!' she smiled a wicked smile. 'In fact, now that I know that my instincts were right about Karol's fixation on duckling here, I might tell *him* that Larkin's a big whore and fair game for all three Barachiel brothers now, huh?' She began to hobble past us and toward the entry doors, moving incredibly slowly because she was trying to fasten the choker on herself, one-handed. 'With any luck, he'll take her down into that dungeon and make her scream good and loud on her hands and knees, once he knows that she's been had by *both* of his little brothers!'

Both twin's expressions became instantly murderous, and I saw them look into one another's hate and agree silently, that they hated someone else more.

'You nailed that wasp thing on the head, Big Kahuna,' Kohl said coldly after a moment, and my fingertips went numb to see him smile grimly as he said it. 'Good thing there's no one else in the harem right now- it's downright dangerous to have one buzzing about so.'

'That's an excellent point,' Kohén agreed, looking just as at ease, and my blood became lava again when I saw his hand twitch with a spark. 'We should probably take care of it, before she stings the wrong person.'

No, no NO! What about your souls?!

'Together?' Kohl asked, but they were both already turning and walking past me, following Kelia who was still too busy trying to fasten her necklace to hurry as she ought to be doing. 'Like... brothers?'

Kohén's eyes darkened. 'We're both allergic to this particular breed of wasp, Kohl so yes, I think it's only fair that we bid it *Aloha* together so there is no finger pointing after. But brother is not a term I'll be throwing around lightly ever again, so don't push your luck.'

'That's how I feel about the word 'Banished' right now,' Kohl said frostily, sauntering forward as though they were going to play golf and not closing in on someone they were about to murder. 'I mean, I'm already in a lot of trouble aren't I? So I'm hesitant to tempt fate further by giving you something else to blackmail me with...' He raised an eyebrow. 'But maybe, if I had a certain book in my hand, well, I might just be inclined to help you flatten a bug with it...'

Kohén didn't even blink. 'Done. I don't have it on me because I've hidden it away, but I tell you what-' he glanced at his twin as their swaggering turned into strides, and I snapped out of my stupor and hurried after them. 'Agree to a condition, and I'll see that you get that evil book back.'

'Which would be...?'

'I want you to help me keep Larkin safe,' Kohén said, and my brows pulled together in consternation, for that was not Kohl's responsibility! 'Karol will be thirty in a few days' time, and I don't think either of us want him changing his wish to free her so that he can call himself a hero again, and then take advantage of her after... right? And he can only justify doing that sort of thing, if he can sell it to others that he is saving her. So... convince him, and others, that Larkin is blissfully happy at my side and will refuse to leave me- now that you've seen it for yourself, of course- so that he gives up the ghost, and once he realises that there's no point waiting for her, and no evidence to justify liberating her, I'll bet he proposes to Ora, and leaves Larkin alone.'

'Why do you need *me* to-'

'Because he won't believe it coming from me anymore than you did, and I'm not letting him close enough to her to give her the chance to prove it for herself, because that's like waving a mouse in front of a cat. But it's common knowledge right now that you hate me, so if you vouch for her happiness to mother and father and Karol, especially grudgingly, Karol will be more inclined to accept the fact that he'll turn grey waiting for her, than if he hears it from anyone else.' Kohén's eyes darted after Kelia, flashed and then suddenly, he was walking faster. 'Do that, and stay away from her also, and when you set sail on Sunday, you will have a book in hand, and a brother waving you farewell once more.' He smirked. 'But naturally, one who will be hoping that you stay away until you're over her, too.'

'Aren't you afraid that I'll double-cross you, and either rat you out to mother who doubts that this has come to pass naturally, or team up with Karol instead, so we could share the spoils of this war?' Kohl asked blithely, and Kohén didn't miss a beat as he whirled, grabbed Kohl by the neck and slammed him into the wall hard enough to audibly knock the air out of Kohl's chest, and my own. I pressed my hand to my mouth to smother my scream, and saw that Kelia had finally looked behind her to see what that noise had been, and dropped her jaw. No surprise there, for Kohén had a blade to Kohl's forehead- the small switchblade kind, and was pressing it into his skin just beneath his hairline.

He did not just say that! I thought, staring at Kohl with the kind of horrified expression that I usually reserved for his eldest brother. *He could not have!*

'I'll wear your scalp like Miguel wore Satan's feathers if I entertain the notion that you are *that* fucking sick for even a moment, little brother,' Kohén said his voice low and eerily calm. 'So tell me- *should* I be afraid that you'd sink so low as to bat Larkin around with Karol for your own enjoyment and put you on *your* hands and knees now... or will you retract that vile suggestion?'

Kohl looked furious but fortunately for my racing heart, more intimidated than mad. 'No,' he choked out. 'I'd die before I touched her against her will, and you know it!' he glanced at me with an apology in his lightening eyes, but then looked back to Kohén, causing them to darken with anger again before adding: 'You are the one that will take a woman against her will to sate your lust.'

Kohén exhaled, and his eyes lightened from black, to navy, to azure. 'I didn't touch her against her will,' he whispered, letting Kohl go. 'I'd sign a declaration to that in my blood attesting to that- and so would she.'

Kohl looked at me questioningly, and I nodded, hating the way his eyes blackened again. I should have been relieved to see Kohén release his brother, but the truth was that Kohl's not-so-funny threat still had me eyeing the switchblade and contemplated a triple homicide. How could angelic Kohl even joke about sharing me with Karol, like two dogs with a bone?

Um… because you told him that you loved him and then slept with his brother?

'Then I'll believe you,' Kohl said grudgingly, rubbing his neck. 'Until she tells me otherwise.'

'Good,' Kohén swallowed hard and then said: 'Larkin? Now might be a good time to go back to your room.'

I'd been temporarily distracted from the point of their wheeling and dealing by the terms that they were laying out, but now that Kohén shot a glance Kelia's way, my blood turned to ice. Leave… so that they could do murder? I shook my head, unable to speak for my fear, but neither boy broke off eye-contact long enough to look at me and see it, so when Kelia sighed and took off again, as though they'd spoiled her fun by calling a draw, I panicked. She didn't suspect what was truly going on! She was too busy plotting *my* demise to sense that her own was swiftly approaching.

You can't let them do this, because that will make you a silent witness and a passive supporter of this system, just

*like your mother! Yes, they're scared for you and for Kohl
and so are you! But does that justify murder? No!*

Adrenaline chugged through my veins and I stepped
forward and reached for her. 'Kelia WAIT. You guys I-' but
she sensed the movement and turned and ripped out a snarl
before I could latch onto her.

'Get away from me!' She spat at me again. 'You're so
grotesque that your own mother didn't want your touch, so
how dare you reach for MY noble arm?'

I recoiled in horror. 'We're equals, Kelia! And I am
trying to *save* your noble ass!' *And Kohén and Kohl's souls!*
I added silently. *They are descendants of the great Miguel
Barachiel- how can they even consider ending a human's
life to protect their own interests?*

'You've already failed to save me, so now I'll take your
advice, and save myself!' Then, she smiled and she was the
grotesque one. 'Which I plan to do. I have no intention of
going ANYWHERE, before I watch Karol do to you, what I
did to your dumb soccer ball using his royal cock!'

My throat tightened like it was being crushed by an
invisible hand.

'That's it: *one*!' Kohén shouted loud enough to make
Kelia and I both jump, and she twisted back to stare at him,
puzzled but not yet alarmed.

'Two,' Kohl rumbled and above us, the sky did the
same as his eyes locked on Kohén's and shone an identical
shade of blue. I saw it then- the understanding on Kelia's
once pretty, pale face, and when she turned to me, her anger
had melted away and she was a little girl again- opening her
mouth to ask for her best friend's assistance- her golden
copper hair turning blue as the charge of two Nephilim
beings filled the room like atmosphere.

But it was too late- I was too hurt and scared and
appalled by her words to utter a sound and the room was
already blue, so instead of taking the tiny hand that shot out
to grasp me, I turned away from it so I wouldn't witness
what I didn't have a hope of preventing, practically feeling
Satan's arms slither around me just as they shouted:

'Three!'

3.

A ghastly scream ripped me apart from the inside and made me stumble forward toward my room without grace. The room lit up as though the fog were burning, and then flashed repeatedly as water sizzled, skin burned, and copper hair fried. I wanted to turn back and scream at them, but there was no point, and I knew that if I saw my friend's body simmering in a puddle of their creation because of me, I'd never stop.

Forgive me! Forgive me, forgive me... God! Satan! Anyone? Stop this!

I caught myself on the wall and sucked in a shallow, acrid breath- gagging on the scent of burnt hair and wishing that that foul breath was my last- wishing and praying that they'd both remember their anger with me and dispose of me in the same way so I wouldn't have to go on to cause even more damage to the Barachiel's once near-perfect world.

'Larkin, how have you not noticed that every wrong-doing within Eden has you as the common denominator...?'

I made it to my room by blocking my ears and closing my eyes and using my elbows to guide me back along the corridor, and fortunately, the door to my cage was still open so I fell into it, sobbing, glad now that the window was closed up, so that I wouldn't have to see Lady Liberty gazing vacantly back at me and through me.

I am wicked, and my Nephilim power came to me in a moment of fear in my youth as my mother said it would- my beauty! That has to be it, right? After all, lust for me is what makes these boys act the way they do!

I heard the rain ease off and the lock in the door click behind me then- confirming that committing murder wasn't distracting enough to force me out of Kohén's mind for even a few minutes- and that was when my tears really started to fall for real- fat, ugly, tears that were accompanied by mucous. Smothering my face into my tangled sheets in order to absorb some of the moisture and the sound, I cried harder and harder until I felt a headache coming on, wanting to feel sorry for myself but knowing that I didn't deserve to.

This is all my fault! Every sin they have committed is because of me, and if I stay here, it will just go on and on! I would slash my face to shreds, but they'd just have me healed anyway!

As the pillow grew soaked beneath my flushed face, I fantasised about cutting myself again, only instead of imagining ripping my face to ribbons, I imagined smashing the mirror and using one of the glass shards to slash my own throat instead. Yes, Kohén had threatened to kill Kohl if I did anything to hurt myself... but what if my influence on him was an enchantment that could be broken if my heart ceased beating? What if he came in upon my lifeless, bloody, chalky white corpse, saw only the useless whore I had become and came to his senses at last?

'They are the evil ones, dear girl, not you... and they are the ones that need to be stopped!' a serene voice said then, and I reared up from the bed, horrified not only by the sound of Satan's voice and the knowledge that she had been watching me again, but the sight of my pillow- which had soaked through with so much of my bloody tears that crimson pools had begun to form on its previously pristine surface. I whirled around to look into my mirror, horrified, and screamed when I saw my reflection superimposed over hers- for I looked like a living nightmare. A bride, wearing her own blood as a veil.

Satan winced. 'Must you? They won't be able to hear you well due to the sound-proofing, but *I* can!'

'Am I losing my mind?' I choked out, wiping at my tears and only succeeding in smearing them more fully over my face. 'Is it truly you, or am I hallucinating?'

'Take my hands, and find out.' Satan pressed her hands to the glass as she had the night before and when she did, my reflection vanished and hers grew opaque, like I was looking through a window, rather than into a looking glass. Behind her was a dark abyss.

'I'm not touching you!' I snapped, getting to my feet and looking wildly around the room for anything that I could use as a weapon. 'I-'

'Don't bother. We are in different realms right now, so you cannot swing a lamp at me any more than I can swing one at *you*. And even if we were in the same realm, well…' her lip curled. 'I'd anticipate anything you'd attempt to do before you could even make up your mind to do it.'

'Can you read my mind?' I asked, horrified.

'In a way.'

'In *what* way?'

'In a way that I won't be explaining to you- until your desire to kill me fades… and sadly, I can see that's not going to be happening any time soon.' Satan clucked her tongue. 'You're going to be harder to talk sense into than God was, aren't you?'

'Don't you know that for sure?' I demanded, and she laughed, wagging her finger at me.

'Nice try, but you have to get up pretty early in the morning- a couple of millennia ago, in fact- to trick me into admitting anything that I don't want to reveal to you, so don't offend me by attempting to manipulate me, please. I'd hate for us to get off on the wrong foot.'

'I'm not intimidated by you!' I cried, but my heart was pounding so hard against my ribs that I imagined it bruising like fruit until it became mush inside my chest. 'You've already told me that you can't hurt me, so what am I supposed to be afraid of? You leaving fingerprint marks on my mirror?'

The lights flickered in my room then, the electricity flowing through the power lines buzzed and suddenly my light bulb exploded with a pop so that the room went dim, lit only by the thin strip of light shining through the edges of my boarded-up windows. I ducked and sucked in a breath as hot fragments of glass from the bulb and shattered light cover rained down on me, and felt my heartbeat accelerate from pounding, to racing.

'I'm incorporeal- not impotent,' Satan pointed out as I slowly began to stand on my shaking knees, and shake the glass out of my bloody, tangled hair.

'You didn't do anything just now that Kohén cannot,' I muttered, even though my mind was begging me to stop provoking the wrathful demon. *Stop mouthing off! This isn't Karol you're hurling insults at but Satan. SATAN!*

'Yes it is, and I much prefer you continue to refer to me as Satan, because I do not care for the pet name 'wrathful demon' at all,' she interjected and I blinked at her as she continued: 'I can do many things from where I stand right now Larkin, but helping *you* isn't one of them, so if it's divine intervention you want, then you're going to have to get over yourself and let me in before Kohén comes back!'

'Let you into this room, or this *realm*?'

'Into *you,* little bird- into *you.*'

My heart did a flip and landed with a slap. 'I must be going fucking crazy, for you to think for even one second that I would agree to such a request!'

'You're crazy if you don't. In fact...' she shrugged. 'You're *dead* if you don't.'

My muscles seized up. Had that been an assumption she'd quoted, or a fact? Still... 'I'd rather be dead than Satan's vessel!'

'I'd rather be a pastry chef than the devil- but we don't all get what we want, sugar, and the only chance you have of getting anything that you've ever wanted *is* to become my vessel now, understood? I've seen the path that you are on in my dreams, and with every word you say and step you take, it is growing shorter!'

'I-I don't care,' I stuttered, even though I did, kind of. 'If my life is coming to an end, then I will spend the remainder of it making the most of what I have, not giving you the opportunity to raise Hell on earth with it!'

'Interesting choice of words... and evidence that despite your high intellect, you understand nothing... least of all, Hell.' She sighed when I shrugged. 'I'm not here to rape and pillage your soul- Larkin. I am here because *you* have called to *me*. You're the one that has summoned me here, time and time again with your pleas for help and your scarlet tears!'

'I have no choice but to cry those tears!' I protested. 'My regular ones either! I know they are sinful but-'

'And I have no choice but to respond to them!' Satan argued. But she held up her hands and sighed once more. 'I understand why the notion of sharing your body with me is a shocking and terrifying one, but if you let me in, I can convince you otherwise!'

I snorted. 'You're not the first person to tell me that letting me into their body will win my heart, you know. Karol and Kohén have used the same argument before and as you can see-' I gestured to my blood-streaked face, 'I'm not convinced.'

'And I don't blame you. But I'm not asking for a permanent change here- only the opportunity to borrow your energy until I've generated enough power to give myself human form of my own. Once I have done that, we will work side by side!'

'Why do you need *me*?' I demanded, pointing to the face she was wearing. 'I've seen you on the castle's grounds wearing that face twice now, so I know you're getting out of that realm and into this one of your own volition somehow!'

'Usually I would ask Siria or Gabby or one of the many others who care for me to assist me, but if the crowned prince of Arcadia can't get into that harem right now, then how can a Blue-Collared waitress and a Companion from another kingdom be expected to manage such a feat?'

My knees and fists locked up into taut balls. 'They're real people? The twins, I mean?'

'Dear friends of mine,' Satan conceded, 'and before you ask, yes they are dark Nephilim and no, that won't help them get in. Kohén has a guard on that door that has a power that no other Nephilim in the world has- even *me*.'

I frowned at her, perplexed but curious still. Every question she answered was rising a million more questions! 'And what power is that?'

'The ability to mute any other Nephilim's powers.'

I furrowed my brow. 'I've never heard of that before.'

'Well it's kept quiet, of course. Usually he stays by Elijah's side, guarding the kingdom's greatest asset- the king- but Elijah has agreed to post him at the harem door this week, which tells me that he suspects as I do: that *you* are now the kingdom's greatest asset, little bird, and so blood will run before that door is breeched- *divine* blood, and I will not risk my friends lives for someone who is to foolish to fight for her own. I'm sure I could get by the guard somehow, but that won't help *you* anyway Larkin, because you don't have what it takes to defend yourself, and you won't until it's too late... which is why you *need* to surrender control to me, and let me do what you cannot in order to extricate yourself from this situation!'

I narrowed my eyes at her, refusing to fall for the old apple and the snake routine. She was pretending to have my best interests at heart, but I knew that she was just trying to scare me into doing something that I would surely regret! After all, I'd read the bible- I knew what happened to those who gave into temptation, especially when that temptation was offered up by Satan!

'You had to refer to the worst fictional book ever printed to affirm the notion that temptation leads to sin?' Satan asked, looking incredulous. 'What... waking up utterly fucked in a locked room this morning didn't do that for you?' She smiled cruelly. 'Or did the pleasure you experienced in his arms take the edge off the betrayal and your intelligence?'

I glowered at her, embarrassed to know that she'd witnessed such private goings-on. 'I know that I'm an idiot for succumbing to what I believed was Kohl's plan yesterday, but I'd have to be utterly brain-dead to believe that *you'd* steer me and my body along a more rational course if given the chance! I've read the six books of creation- I know how you work, and I know what happens to those that follow you!'

Satan arched her borrowed eyebrow at me. '*Do* you now?'

'Of course! The Bible may have been a work of fiction, but the six books of creation weren't!'

'I never said that they were,' Satan conceded. 'But there is only so much information that can be fit into six books, Larkin, so if you want the full story, then you're going to have to let me into your world!'

'So you can destroy it?' I asked, tears flowing down my face again. 'And take my soul along with you?'

'So I can salvage what is left of your soul before it is too late!' She threw up her hands. 'Why is it that zealots can always quote what they regard to be scripture and yet miss the main points entirely? I didn't destroy the world- *God* did! I *saved* it, remember?'

'*After* you set off nuclear weapons!'

She bubbled her lips and waved her hands. 'I caused two cesspools to be obliterated at the prayers of others! And even if millions hadn't wanted the same thing, I had my reasons for doing so, and the world would have already been a better place if God had left the remodelling to me!'

'How?' my voice cracked. 'What's in it for you, if you remodel the world? And why do you care enough about my measly little soul to concern yourself with salvaging it?'

'Plenty, and I will explain it all-'

'Because I'm a dark Nephilim too, and you want to be able to use my powers for your own purposes, the way you use Siria, and Gabby now?' I asked, voice pitching as the hysteria began to return to me. 'The way God feared that you wanted to use Miguel?'

Satan's eyes flashed. 'You speak of things you do not understand, and though I long to set the story straight and wipe the bloody tears from your eyes, I cannot trust you enough to know my motives, my truths or even to see my true face until you trust me enough to let me inside you!'

'I cannot trust the devil!'

'Then I cannot help you!'

'So leave!' I pointed into the mirror and into the swirling, misty blackness behind her. 'I committed a sin when I asked for your help, and I see how wrong that was now! I'm sorry that I've wasted your time but rest assured-it will not happen again!'

Satan smirked. 'You say that now-'

'And I will say it forevermore!' I stepped closer to her, reaching for the water jug on the shelf beside the mirror as I did. 'You don't have to believe me, but I swear on my soul that I will cut out my own tongue before I call for you again, and plunge a blade into my heart before I pledge it to *you*!'

Satan did not flinch. 'That's precisely what I'm afraid of, Larkin, and exactly what I've come here to prevent. You think that ending your life will end everyone's suffering with it, but it will be the beginning of the end for everyone that you still care for- and no-one more than Kohl. In fact, there is very little that you can do from hereon out that will keep Kohl-'

'Kohén really will kill his brother if I take my own life?' My palm was sweaty around the water jug's handle, my heart palpitating in my throat. 'You've *seen* that?'

'Haven't you? If you want to know your fate as it currently stands in its entirety then you have to-'

'I don't,' I said coldly, and that was the truth because I'd felt manacles closing in around my wrists and ankles since Satan had spoken sweet Kohl's name. 'You've told me all I have to know, so-'

'I haven't even begun to tell you all you need to know!' Satan raged, and I went stumbling back from the mirror as heatless flames sprung into vibrant life behind her, casting flickering shadows on my walls that were incandescent despite their darkness. 'And I won't stop trying to tell you how important your life is-'

'Help!' I screamed, turning and smashing on the harem's door. 'Kohén! Kohl! Anybody? Satan is-' and just like that, the words were cut off, as a cold, hard fist clenched my larynx and squeezed tightly. Gasping and choking as though she physically had me against the door and was strangling the breath out of me, I whirled around to face Satan and understood that I wasn't going crazy, not at all. I was going to Hell!

'It is a sin to discuss me with others- both in their rule book *and* my own!' Satan exclaimed, and just as suddenly as the pressure had come upon my throat it vanished, and I fell to the floor in a heap, gasping and gaping at her with wide eyes, stunned by how quickly she'd transformed my pristine bedroom into a nightmarish place of fire, smoke, shadows and fear.

'You took my voice?' I tried to ask but of course, I failed. Still, she read the words in my mind and responded to them with a cruel sneer.

'And I will hold it as captive as Kohén is holding you, until the compulsion to mention seeing me- ever- has gone!' Satan confirmed, and then snarled at me again. 'That goes for writing it down too- not a course of action I'd recommend you undertake if you value your fingertips, eyesight, or functioning brain cells at all!'

Now I *was* scared. Could she do that? Crush my fingers with her incorporeal hands? Crush my mind with her balled fist? Suddenly I remembered the first time I'd met Siria- how I'd screamed for Satan's help inside my head at that ball, only to have the chandelier come crashing to the floor, practically on top of everyone that I'd been angry with at the time- and it was like someone had hit me in the stomach.

'Yes, that was me,' Satan said smugly, as I turned and began to kick the door, rattling it in its snug frame. 'My power is limited until I can walk the earth once more, but it never vanishes completely. So long as you call for me, I will hear you, and so long as there is a looking glass, I will be able to-'

I pelted the crystal jug at the mirror, and it shattered into several massive shards, extinguishing the flames and her face, but leaving the room dim and filled with dread still.

Weeping brokenly, I dropped the glass to the floor, picked up the largest part of the heavy water jug that was still intact- the solid handle- and then crawled into the bathroom, staying low and out of sight of the mirror above the counter- feeling my heart lodge itself in my throat when I heard Satan sigh above me and whisper:

'You've made your bed here as his whore with your actions, and I cannot stop you from lying in it, if that is what you have made up your mind to do in order to work off your guilty conscience.' Satan said sadly. 'But if I cannot appeal to your conscience, then I *will* appeal to your delightful curiosity.' Something big and thick smacked to the tiled- floor in front of my eyes, causing me to startle. 'You're not the first girl to fall victim to the Barachiel's legacy, and unless you help me- you won't be the last. Read between the lines of that, then we'll see if you have the capacity to understand as much as your preliminary test suggested that you do.'

I saw instantly that it was a book that she had dumped at my feet, but only as I rose and flung the thick glass projectile into the mirror. I couldn't see much in there, but there was a satisfying crack followed by a rain of glass hitting the marble countertop and as soon as the glass stopped falling, I realised that I could breathe and see again. The light remained muted, but the blood had cleared from my eyes and I knew without looking that my tears had begun to run clear again. The scent of blood had gone, along with the pungent aroma of smoke, and the general sensation of being watched.

Satan was gone, but when I opened my mouth and tried to pray to God out loud, I was dismayed to realise that she'd cut me off from contact with everybody else as effectively as I'd just broken communications between us, and her disappearance hadn't altered the fact that I was mute now.

Now what? I thought, sniffling as I sat up again, realising that blood was trickling out of my knees and palms from where Satan's surge of electricity had blown out the light bulb above *and* the glass globe that had encased it. There was a sudden pounding on the door then, and I flinched- what if Kohén saw all of this mess and assumed that I'd staged a personal rebellion against him, and took it out on Kohl?

'Larkin?' the voice was only just audible through the thick door, but because it was a voice that was on the other side of that door still, I knew that it had to be Kohl because Kohén would have let himself in. 'Larkin, what's going on in there? Are you hurt?'

I got to my feet and shoved the book into my bathroom cabinet and then I got up, wiped the tears from my face with the back of my hand, checked it to make sure that the moisture was clear, not clotted, and sighed in relief when I saw that it was. There was nothing that I could do about the glass or my wounds, so I limped out into my chamber again just as the door burst open then and Kohén barraged through, looking wild-eyed and frantic. He stumbled to a halt when he saw me, and Kohl smacked into him hard from behind as he attempted to follow.

'Larkin? What's the meaning of this?' Kohén demanded, but when I opened my mouth to answer, only a sob came out. He turned to push Kohl off him, then indicated into the hallway. 'Go finish arranging things, and I'll join you in a moment!'

'But Lark-'

'Isn't your concern anymore, remember?' Kohén demanded, and Kohl's expression tightened. He looked to me, seeking support that I could not grant him, but before I could demonstrate that I had no voice to speak with, glass snapped beneath Kohén's bare foot and he looked down at it and hissed as blood trickled from the sole of his foot and towards my white carpet. 'Good grief! This place is...' he shoved Kohl out. 'Go on! I'll handle this!'

'Well do it quickly!' Kohl spat as he melted out of my room and back into the hallway. 'We haven't a second to waste!'

'Like I don't know that?' Kohén sneered, and I was dismayed to realise that they were back to bickering again, proving that their ceasefire was temporary at best, and volatile at worst. Realising that my actions would impact how long their truce lasted, I rushed forward, ripped the clean but damp pillow case off my bed and knelt at Kohén's foot, catching the blood before it could stain my rug and indicating that he should sit down so that I could see to it- playing the devoted lover rather than the rebellious prisoner. He initially stiffened at my touch, but then sat down on the bed in front of me, lifting his foot off the ground so that I could inspect it for glass. To my surprise, he was trembling almost as much as I was.

Oh my God, how am I going to handle this? And shit! I forgot to ask Satan if my mother truly gave birth to me or if-

Do you believe that Sapphire Whittaker would have raised you, had you not come from her own womb? Please...

I gasped gently, but Kohl mistook it for concern and assured me that it didn't hurt as much as it looked like it did. So Satan couldn't just hear my thoughts when I addressed her- but when I thought of her in *any* way. Geez, the Sheps warned us off using her name, but I had a feeling that they didn't know just *how* disastrous using it could be!

And that's the way I like it.

'Thank you,' Kohén said softly, and his voice sounded strained. 'I think. Larkin... what happened to your room? Did *you* do this?' I sniffled, experienced a light bulb moment of my own- and then pointed up at the shattered and dark ceiling fixture, then to the mirror's frame. He looked up at it and then sighed. 'Oh. *I* did this?' I nodded, hoping that my streaming tears would explain away my lack of speech, then pointed into the dark bathroom. '*Both* lights?' I nodded again, and he cursed under his breath. 'Damn. And here I was hoping that I'd controlled the surge enough to contain it to the one part of the harem. I suppose I'm going to have to check all of the other rooms now too, aren't I?' I nodded, too relieved that he'd bought my feeble excuse to do anything else.

'Shit. Must have been a much larger surge than I thought, for the light to have shattered hard enough to break the mirror too! Oh! And you're hurt as well! Baby…' Kohén leaned forward and took my forearm, inspecting the tiny little cuts. 'Oh well, we need to cover up my injury so no one knows I was here when this happened, but yours are too small to warrant medical attention and fit a story about you being locked in your room all morning, right?'

I nodded again, got up, reached into the lower drawer on my bedside table and pulled out a pair of my sports socks. They were large enough to be stretched around his foot so I did the injured one first, then the other while Kohén watched.

I'm doing this to save Kohl, and for no other reason! I said to myself firmly, though even that silent thought sounded like a lie to me. I could plead martyrdom for Kohl until I was blue in the face, but nothing would change the fact that I was helping both boys cover up a murder- a murder than I was now an accessory to.

'Clever duck,' Kohén said, 'I mean; swan.' He sighed sadly. 'A power surge it is- one resulting in superficial injuries to you, and fatal ones for...' He took my hand and lifted it, kissing my palm and staring at the blood on my arm with clouded eyes. 'You should go and have a shower, hon. Resonah and Rosina will return soon enough, and when they do, they'll find…' he swallowed hard and lifted those eyes to me, their colour darkening to navy and finding clarity at last. 'You know *nothing,* okay? You saw nothing- and heard nothing. You were sleeping when there was a power surge, and were unable to get out and cry for help, all right? Kohl and I will handle the rest.'

I bit my lip hard enough to draw blood, but nodded. Not just for Kohén- but for Kohl.

'Thank you. I…' his voice trailed off and he sighed, sitting back down on the bed and pulling me into his arms so that he could kiss my shoulder. 'God, Larkin...' his voice was thick with the threat of tears. 'What have I *done*?'

I didn't want to witness his pain or fear- I had too much of my own to deal with as it was, and the anguish in his voice and eyes was making it hard for me to breathe, because it was that lost little five-year old boy I was seeing again now- my best friend, not my captor.

But he is! He is my captor now and I, his captive! Satan would normally encourage suicide to steal my soul by default, so she must have been telling the truth when she said that my death would bring about Kohl's, as Kohén has threatened! So I have to find a way to live with this man somehow!

'I love you, but I have to go in order to deal with this,' Kohén whispered into my hair, and my skin crawled when I felt him slip the choker back around my neck, collaring me once more with the precious stones that he must have had to pry from Kelia's dead fingers. 'Kohl and I need an alibi after all so...' I shivered violently when I heard the tiny lath click and felt the ice-cold stones settle around my tender throat. 'Please don't be mad at me for this, my love. Everything I do, I do for you. You know that, right Lark?'

That was the last thing I needed to hear right then, so I wrenched myself out of his arms and stomped towards my bathroom door, slamming it shut behind me- and locking him out, grateful for the fact that the mirror was gone because I didn't have to see my wretched face or the diamonds around my neck again.

4.

Kelia's body was discovered by Elijah's Companions two hours after her death, and though I'd heard the screams, my door was still locked so I could not get out of my room. I banged on the door, but it was five minutes before a red-faced and wet-eyed Cherry opened it and begged me to stay in my room, for something awful had happened, but she didn't want to expose me to it until Prince Kohén had attended the scene first.

When he did come, sweaty and with a racket in his hand, Kohén pretended to break the news to me and then led me out to see Kelia's body- which they had tossed into the pool in order to stage her accident. I burst into tears without having to stage anything, because she was bloated and awful-looking by then, and knew from the way Cherry moved to comfort me but she didn't suspect that I'd had anything to do with it. And why should she? I'd been locked inside my own cell the whole time.

They knew that Kohl had been invited in to pay us a visit that morning, and that could have put him in a compromising position, but Kohén and Kohl had left the harem only minutes after Kelia's death (once they'd made the necessary arrangements and had checked on me) and had walked out together after, heading straight for the Basket-Racket courts and arguing (loudly) about me and about how Kohl had to get over his (pointless) and completely unfounded crush. According to my healer, they'd started shoving one another and throwing punches, working out their issues as men do, and then had played a heated, fiercely competitive match in front of half a dozen witnesses that were now their alibis. I didn't know how much of that interaction had been staged and how much had been for real (though I was sure that Kohl was humiliated to have Kohén write off his feelings as a one-sided crush in front of so many people!) but all that mattered was that the castle staff had seen them together away from the harem long before the older Companions had sounded the alarm.

Kohén had won the match though, and I suspected that that part had not been staged or easily done. In fact, I suspected that quite a few of the rackets were in need of re-stringing by now! And poor Kohl was probably in need of a stiff drink and a psychologist. How was that sweet, honourable boy going to survive this week?

Murder wasn't a common occurrence in Arcadia let alone Eden, and because Kelia was notorious for being a dimwit, and had been found with her stereo in the pool with her, there had been no further investigation into her death beyond a Shepherd's grimace. It was ruled rather swiftly that Kelia had dropped the appliance in the water while soaking her feet (a small, spilled bottle of nail polish had been on the ground beside the pool, giving her an agenda and one that she was known to repeat often) and that the electric shock that she'd suffered had been enough to blow out all of the power sockets in that wing that had been switched on at the time, including my bedroom lights, but only mine, as every other room in the harem had been un-occupied at the time. Not only had the current liquefied her insides within seconds, but it had broken her arm (God forgive me) and to my horror- her neck- as she'd fallen into the shallow section of the unforgiving marble pool.

I listened to this ruling with genuine tears rolling down my face, and genuine disbelief swelling up inside me, allowing Cherry to feather her warm pink light over my tiny cuts- erasing Satan's touch on me, but not her influence. I tried to ignore Resonah and Rosina's eyes on me from across the spring, but I felt their curiosity and their suspicion, and realised that I was suddenly looking forward to going back to my locked cell.

And Karol thought I was paranoid to believe that someone had masterminded Martya's death? Ha! Their ability to make an entire human being literally disappear is staggering! Why fear letting a dark Nephilim like Satan into Eden's walls, when light ones like Kohén and Kohl are capable of being this destructive?

I hated them for killing her- both of them- but only because they'd done it for me. I was glad that Kohl would be safe. I was glad that they'd gotten away with it, because neither boy had a murderer's soul, I was glad that Kelia had not had the opportunity to throw my carcass at Karol's royal boots, and I was glad that she'd been taken from a world that had caused her so much grief...

But I would never know peace again now that two Given girls had died in the name of protecting me either for my benefit, or from myself, so when Resonah came over and offered me a small pill that she said that she sometimes used to help her sleep at night, I took it gladly, and then washed it down with a bottle of champagne the moment I was back in the privacy of my cell.

*

Kohén returned to me after dinner on Wednesday evening, waking me from a deep slumber that I'd fallen into before sunset by lighting the candles he'd brought with him on my nightstand (electricians hadn't yet come to fix my lights), and trembled as he held me tightly against him, apologising over and over again for the part he had played in Kelia's eroded mental state and her death.

He drank port as he spoke, more than I'd ever seen him drink before, and as he grew more and more lucid, his nervous chatter morphed into a confession of sorts, and I knew that he'd been bottling up everything he felt inside him that day, and was only just now getting the chance to pour his emotions out- drowning me in them. It agitated me to think that he expected comforting from the last person on earth that he had a right to lean upon, but then again, I was relieved to know that he hadn't committed the heinous crime lightly.

Kohén admitted that he'd disliked Kelia intensely for quite some time, had never understood my connection with her and had only used her to get back at me because he'd known that she was the only girl in the Harem that would readily lie about having sexual relations with him. She had been a smokescreen, keeping me fooled into believing that he was over me (and as he hoped- jealous) and the other girls from questioning why he wasn't coming to them anymore.

He swore black and blue that although he'd tried to take her the way she'd said, the fact that he hadn't been able to get hard had handicapped him even before my interruption had that night in Caldera. He'd gotten no satisfaction from the orgy at all, but he admitted that Kelia had orgasmed from the way his body had brushed up against hers when he'd attempted to enter her that awful night, and because she'd never experienced that sort of euphoria before- not even with herself- she had sought him and his odd little electric hum out since, begging for him to try again, or even just to lie on top of her. He swore to God that he had not, and though she had pouted and whined, Kelia had been contented enough with their intrigues and the trinkets he'd gifted her to keep that fact to herself. Not only to keep their lack of relations to herself- but to twist the story around and broadcast it loudly whenever the rest of us were in earshot to make me jealous.

She'd told me otherwise of course, and though it might sound foolish- I believed Kohén. There is a way that people act around one another when they have been truly intimate, and I hadn't seen any evidence of a connection between them- emotional *or* physical. Whenever they'd been together, he'd had a habit of leaning away from her, the way people do when conversing with someone with bad breath, and not once had I seen his eyes follow her across a room with the slightest bit of interest. Besides, if he couldn't get hard for Emmerly or Lette, who were both sensual *and* engaging, how should I believe that he had been drawn in by Kelia's irritating nature?

Naturally there was still a chance that he was deceiving me, but I was trying to numb myself to my new lot in life so it wouldn't hurt so bad, so forcing myself to believe in the good in Kohén was just one of those things that I was going to have to get into the habit of doing. That, and drinking.

Naïve, stupid, drunk and appreciative of pretty things- that was what a Companion had to be in order to endure it, and I had to endure this for Kohl.

Kohén babbled on about Kelia, his inner turmoil and his fear of losing me for hours, but didn't seem to notice that I wasn't responding to him verbally until close to midnight. I waited tensely for him to look at my throat and find some imagined evidence of Satan's hold on me, but instead of assailing me with questions, he assailed me with more apologies instead.

'I can't bear you being this angry with me!' he cried, rolling on top of me and taking my face in his hands, forcing me to stare into his wet and red eyes. 'Larkin I love you, and I'm sorry for all the hurt I've caused you... but you shouldn't have fallen for him! You were mine! You were my everything and instead of being happy about that, you went behind my back with my brothers! You should have come to me about Lindy- I would have helped you! You should have told me that you were attracted to Kohl, so I could have fought for your interest more than I believed I needed to!' I nodded mutely and stared into his eyes, apologising for those things as much as I could without saying a word, but that wasn't enough for him and he let out a moan of frustration before slanting his mouth across mine. I tasted his tears on my lips and felt his fingers tangle in my hair as he murmured his love and sorrow and regrets to me over and over again, punctuating each with a kiss. I still had nothing to say and was terrified that he'd realise that my silence was magically-induced, not a sign of anger, and so I kissed him back, distracting him as best as I could, and melting when he practically whooped with delight and claimed my mouth more savagely than he ever had before, even the previous night.

It didn't take long for me to become as distracted by our kisses as he. I was angry and scared and depressed, but my soul and body and mind were all too weak against his sultry Nephilim advances, so it was only moments before I was gasping beneath him- tilting my hips so that his erection would hum against my groin, while he clawed my nightgown out of the way and massaged my breasts with his warm, glowing hands. He tasted like summer fruits and kissed me like he needed my breath in his lungs in order to survive, and though I don't think either of us ever stopped weeping through the experience, it didn't take long for my thighs to part around his hips, or his hands to slice my nightgown down the middle.

I deserve this! I told myself as Kohén reared up over me and tore his own shirt over his head, trying to ignore how nervous I was growing beneath him. The last time I had done this, I had been too drunk and too shocked to understand what was happening- of how intimate this was. *This is my penance for all of the sins that I have committed against him!*

I'd tried telling myself that a few times that day, but it had been hard to believe when I'd wanted to kill him for weeping over Kelia, and it was even harder to believe once he was naked from the waist up, firm, golden and glowing, but for different reasons. *This* was a punishment? *This* was torture? I knew nothing of either, not in that moment, and my sex tightened and throbbed in silent agreement. He was perfect, physically at least, I was out of my mind with lust, and when he reached forward to caress the place where my nerves knotted between my parted thighs, I practically bucked in pleasure.

'How could you have ever doubted this connection?' Kohén asked, his voice low and rough and hardening as I balled my fists in the sheets and fought against the pleasure threatening to annihilate me. I shook my head and he bit his lip, sliding a finger under the edge of my panties and pulling the fabric out of the way so that he could stare at me. 'You didn't?' he asked, gently pressing the tip of his finger into the slick, heated slit between my labia, and I shuddered, shaking my head again. 'It was always me you wanted more?'

I turned my face away and sobbed soundlessly, hating him for trying to turn the screws like this on me in such a moment, but hating him more for delaying my pleasure. No, no Kohl had never gotten me heated to the point where I'd lost my mind and all sense of self-preservation, but then again, Kohl had never made me despise him like this either! To be a lover- a soul mate- there had to be both elements present, didn't there? Someone that you could get lost in, but only because you trusted them to protect you in the interim? Kohén filled one side of the criteria and Kohl filled the other, and never would either boy get the chance to prove that they could be both to me again.

'Larkin…?' Kohén's voice was breathless and low as he pressed his finger into me and tenderly coaxed me open. I tore at the sheets, but could say nothing, and so he retracted and rubbed my clit with the pad of his thumb again. 'Larkin… answer me. Tell me that I'm the only man that can do this to you.'

I didn't know that for sure and never would and I was furious with him for that, and yet the truth was that he was the only man that could do this to me because I was his fucking captive and hadn't the free will to find out otherwise. Using the method acting approach to pad my self-esteem, and reminding myself again silently that I deserved this, I nodded the half-truth.

'Say it,' Kohén whispered, easing a second slick finger into me now and moaning as my sex clenched around him expectantly. God, I was going to black out again! 'Show me how much you want me.'

I couldn't say a bloody word, but I could show him and so I sat up, reached forward, tugging on the golden drawstring cord of his pyjamas, watching with delight as they fell away from his perfect hips and revealed his thick, hard and glorious cock, which I fisted greedily. Kohén gasped and thrust into my fist, lips parted, eyelashes fluttering, but before he could give his dog the 'speak' command again I bent at the waist and took the bulbous head of his erection into my mouth, sucking on it ardently.

'Oh God…' Kohén had already been on his knees but now he leaned back and caught himself on the mattress, staring down at me with a rapturous expression. I couldn't stand seeing the adoration in his eyes so I closed mine and worked him over ravenously, keeping one hand curled around the base of him where I knew my mouth wouldn't reach, while I clasped his shoulder with the other, holding onto him.

This feels right! I realised. *This feels honest! This isn't making love, this is earning my keep, and that's the way it should be between a third-born slave and her master!*

'Oh *God…*' Kohén moaned again, but he fell silent as I twirled my tongue around his foreskin, and soon enough the only sound in the room was his heavy breathing and the slurping and smacking of my oral assault against his hard-on, which suited me just fine. I wanted to slip my fingers between my thighs and touch myself so I could rub away that hollow, desperate feeling that he'd created inside me, but that would blur the lines between business and pleasure, and if I was going to tolerate this sort of activity night in and night out, I knew that I had to start thinking of everything that I did for him as work, until my feelings for him vanished completely. When the compulsion to pleasure myself overwhelmed me too much for me to resist, I would wait until I was alone and think of Kohl until I climaxed.

Yes! Yes I need to stop kissing him when we have intercourse, and offer up this sort of thing every time I can, until the intimacy between us evaporates!

But…

'Lark…' Kohén panted, tapping on my shoulder a beat later. 'Lark stop, I'm going to…'

I wanted him to, and so I began to bob with more eagerness, but he groaned and tried to physically pull me off. 'Larkin, no. Larkin no… I'm not going to let you… *ugh…*' He was saying one thing, but I could feel his cock humming between my lips that communicated another and so I suckled on him more deeply and sweetly, swirling my tongue around him in my impatience to see this done.

I deserve this! I deserve this! He does not, but I deserve this! I am third-born! I am nothing!

'Larkin you have to stop...' Kohén moaned. 'I wanted to make love to you, not be serviced by you...' he lifted my chin up, but I did not release him. 'I won't make you swallow my seed like some slave!'

If I could have laughed out loud, I would have, but because I couldn't, I grinned at him and then slid my mouth over him again and moaned when I felt him twitch and thicken against my tongue.

If I'm not a slave then let me out of the slave quarters! Until you do, servicing you is the only reason why I'll crawl into bed with you!

'No! The pleasure will always go both ways between us, always! Do you hear me?!' Kohén grunted and just as I knew he was about to explode, he tore me off him, sheared the rest of my nightgown off my body and then threw me backwards against the pillows. 'I won't have anything coming between us Larkin, is that understood?' I bounced on the springy mattress and tried to sit up, but he grasped my panties and slid them down my legs and off my feet until I was completely naked beneath him- naked save for the diamond choker, of course. 'Not my brother, not my crown, not your contract- and certainly not a single stitch of clothing.' He opened my thighs and crawled between them, crawling out of his pyjamas as he did so, so by the time he'd arranged himself on top of me, both of us were completely naked and pressed together. '*Is* that understood?'

I could only swallow and nod (while silently screaming in my head that I'd prove him wrong in time) and he smiled.

'Good, then keep your eyes on mine while I make love to you, so that I know you're here with me, or know that I will kiss, tickle and tease this beautiful body of yours until you do.' His arm came under my neck then, nestling my head in the crook of his elbow, and as his lips fluttered down to land on mine in a sweet, soft kiss, his fingers trailed from my collarbone, over my breasts and down between us. I undulated under the feather-light touch, my body lifting to meet the barely-there caresses, so that by the time his fingertips were trailing over my pubic mound, my hips were lifting to meet them and my lips were parting so that our tongues could tangle. Only instead of using his fingers on me when he finally brushed against my vulva, he took the opportunity to guide his cock inside me instead, opening me up slowly and purposefully, his rock-hard rod feeling like silk as it slid into me. I was still sore from the night before, and yet I threw back my head and gasped as the impalement caused my nervous system to collapse.

'Yes!' Kohén's firm ass clenched beneath my traitorous hand as he rocked into me slowly and then withdrew, paused, caught my eyes with a pointed look of his own and then rocked into me again. His pupils dilated on every thrust in, his firm ass flexed, and with every retreat, his lips found mine, keeping us connected- holding me captive with his beautiful eyes. 'Mine...' he breathed, and feathered his tongue against mine so sweetly that I would have groaned had I the voice for it. 'Mine... *mine*...' his breathing was erratic now, as was my own, and I felt his heart thud against my breast as he opened me to his erotic assault and then began to hum with the beginnings of his climax. And the moment he began to do that, I began to clench and spasm around him, holding onto him with all of the strength that I had left while his seed unspooled inside me and my tears trickled out of my eyes.

Then, with his final thrust, he pressed his lips against mine and whispered what I knew to be true, at least when it came to the subject of our chemistry: *'Ours.'*

5.

Kohén continued to assume that I was giving him the silent treatment because I was angry with him over Kelia and my imprisonment until we fell asleep that evening, and that was okay with me for the time being, because I knew that he was still feeling guilty enough to admit that he'd warranted being frozen out, and satisfied enough by our love-making to make his peace with it at least for now.

But my intentions to pass my silence off as intentional were obliterated when he asked me what I wanted for breakfast on Thursday morning. Still half-asleep and devoid of an appetite, I moved my mouth to answer in the negative, before I remembered that I was mute, and the fact that I was obviously trying to speak but failing made Kohén realise that there was nothing intentional about it. He grew concerned and went off to fetch my poor healer again while I panicked, wishing that I had an encyclopaedia of incurable diseases that I could peruse while I waited for help to come, so that maybe I could find some symptoms to fake in order to support a theoretical illness- perhaps something rare.

Preferably, something sexually transmittable.

But I didn't have any medical journals lying around, so I walked into the privacy of my bathroom, opening my mind for just long enough to inform Satan: *If concealing your hold over me is your prerogative, then forcing me to bite my tongue is wrong way to go about it! You think I'm curious by nature? Ha! Just you wait and see how deep a hole Kohén will dig, if it means getting to the bottom of some truth about me!*

To my horror, Satan's response was quick and striking:

If doing what is right is your intention, stop burying your head in the sand! Try as you like, but you are not cut out for this life, and the sooner you stop playing along with this Companion farce to make amends for your wrong-doings, the better off all will be for it!

I gasped to hear her voice so clearly in my head and immediately regretted instigation dialogue with her again, but I couldn't do anything about it now so I walked back into the main room just as Kohén's voice filled it.

'...come to think of it, I don't think she's said a word since...' he looked at me, his expression perplexed, and I almost snorted to see that he'd come back with a vacuum cleaner in his hand- one of the few electrical appliances that was used daily in Eden. 'Actually, I don't know if I've heard her say a word since I... since I showed her Kelia's body yesterday afternoon. Gosh, could it be grief affecting her so?'

'Possibly. So you're saying that you haven't heard her speak a word since after noon yesterday?'

'Yes, I guess that's right...' Kohén was examining me strangely, and I knew he was trying to remember if I'd spoken since he and Kohl had agreed to kill Kelia. I had, but he hadn't heard it and that suited me just fine. Let them think I was in shock if it spared me a thorough medical investigation!

Cherry gave him a sharp look. 'And that didn't strike you as being cause for alarm until now? Your highness... perhaps you need to brush up on your conversational skills. I confess that I didn't realise that Larkin wasn't speaking yesterday either... but I was only with her for a few minutes. But you.... well... I'm fairly sure that if I were engaged in a one-sided conversation, I'd notice that something was amiss well before the second hour was up, let alone the eigh*teenth*.'

I snorted gently and Kohén flushed. 'I knew that she wasn't talking to me,' he defended himself, looking sullen. 'I just assumed that she was giving me the silent treatment intentionally for-'

'For...?'

'For keeping her in here... for her protection.'

'Well yes, I suppose that is grounds for the silent treatment. Question is- will you do anything about that now that you understand how upset she is?'

'Not if it puts her in danger.'

'Because *this* situation is a healthy one, of course.' Rolling her eyes as Kohén scowled at her, Cherry motioned for me to get onto the bed. I complied and she listened to my heart, felt my pulse, pressed her hand against my forehead and stared into my eyes, and then, with a grim expression on her face, pronounced that I was in shock and told Kohén that nothing would heal that but time and a lot of comfort- and still more fluids. Her voice was more gentle now, but the contempt in her eyes had not lessened, and I suspected that she suspected foul play, both towards myself and Kelia now.

Shock? I thought, relief coursing through me. *That sounds better than demonic possession! I can work with that!*

After agreeing to let me rest, Kohén saw Cherry out the door. But he'd only just returned and turned on the vacuum cleaner (we'd both been wearing slippers or shoes on my glass-covered floors since the day before) when a knock on the door sounded again. Irritation contorted his handsome face, and he did not open the door again until he'd asked who was there. Cherry answered that it was her again, and so he turned off the vacuum cleaner and opened it a crack.

'What is it?' he demanded. 'I cannot have people coming and going and expect to keep Larkin secure. Why do you think I'm performing the maid duties myself?'

'I'm sorry, your highness, but your mother is at the harem door asking to come in, and because the guard you've stationed there has refused to let her in without your consent, she has asked me to appeal to you to give it.'

'No!' Kohén had paled already. 'No, and I've already told her that! There are people in Eden who wish to steal Larkin away, so I cannot permit a single soul to enter here without due cause!'

'I know. And I understand that it is not appropriate for her to come into the harem while Resonah and Rosina still dwell within- but couldn't you allow Larkin out so that they may talk in privacy somewhere *else*? A bit of maternal affection and fresh air will do her a world of good, you know.'

I knew it was pointless to hope that Kohén would break his rules for me, I gave him a pleading look anyway.

Oh please, please let me go! I cannot talk to her, but I could at least nod and shake my head and communicate the fact that Kohl is in danger here somehow, right?

Kohén scratched his morning stubble (something I'd not been aware that he even got until we'd become roommates) and studied me, but eventually shook his head while I deflated. 'I'm sorry Cherry but no- my mother hordes her maternal affection for my twin, and has none left to spare anyone else, so I don't see Larkin benefitting from girl time with her right now.'

I pinched at my bottom lip with my fingertips, wondering if Kohl had upheld his end of the deal that he'd made with Kohén to placate their mother. Was she coming to throttle me for breaking my promise to be with her favoured son? Or was coming to sneak me out? I desperately wanted to know the answer to *that*, at least!

But Cherry frowned. 'Well, with all respect your highness, I have worked here for eighteen years, and not once in that time has the duchess cared enough about anybody in the harem to deign asking for entry so that she might visit with them-'

'Which indicates to me that she seeking an audience with Larkin to scold her, not comfort her!' Kohén slid onto the bed next to me and folded me into his arms. 'Ask my mother to leave please, and assure her that I am more than capable of giving Larkin all that she needs- which is precisely why she *chose* to stay in Eden with me in the first place. And tell her that she and Kohl have already talked this out with no hard feelings left on either part, so her concern for Larkin and her favourite son is unfounded anyway!'

Cherry looked at me, obviously perplexed again and clearly aware that I would like nothing more than a few minutes alone with Constance Barachiel, (and obviously still convinced that I'd not volunteered myself for this particular job) but I was still too floored by the idea of her having worked there for eighteen years to give her anything in return but a slackened jaw. She looked twenty-one, tops! Had she been working since she was three? Or was she deceptively older than she looked, like Karol, who seemed to be permanently stalled at twenty-one, and Elijah, who didn't look a day over thirty-five even though by my calculations, he was ancient?

They get graceful ageing and awe-inspiring powers and what do I get? Beauty that gets me screwed and a green thumb! Terrific!

'But... the Artisan concert is being held on the common in central Arcadia today, isn't it? I was of the impression that you yourself were performing. I hear that Amelia-Rose Choir is looking forward to your recital very much... seeing as how you weren't there to greet her when she and her father arrived yesterday afternoon.'

'Well, she will have to be disappointed because I am needed more here than I am on the stage.' Kohén scooped me up in his arms and wriggled me back to the top of my bed, pulling back the covers and sliding me under them, and I willingly went because I was exhausted from his nocturnal ravishments and weakened with hunger to the point of trembling. 'Please inform my mother of that too, and assure her that I will touch base with her later today, all right?'

'Yes, your highness,' Cherry said softly, and left us alone, and though the lock hadn't clicked shut behind her, Kohén's arms were binding enough.

'Boy, she's getting nosy...' Kohén muttered after Cherry had left, and I raised my eyebrows at him. Who *wouldn't* be fascinated by the sight of the castle's long-standing agitator- me- acting like a malleable lump of moulding clay all of a sudden? He took in my expression and exhaled softly, looking abashed.

'I'm sorry, you're right, why wouldn't she with all of the odd things that have been happening?'

I turned my face away from him, staring blankly toward the boarded up window. 'Odd things'? Could such a simple term be applied to the loss of someone's liberty? The murder of a dull-witted virgin? The destruction of a fraternal bond? A tear burned in the corner of my eye and scorched a trail down my cheek and onto my eardrum. Yes, the fact that I hadn't seen sunlight in days now was odd indeed. The fact that I was now used to feeling my best friend's body warmth against my naked skin, and that I was beginning to crave it and nothing more- that was odd. The fact that I'd been feeling too listless to eat or even read for two whole days- yes that was *very* odd.

They were more than odd events though; they were symptoms. They were evidence of the fact that I was dying from the inside out, and it hurt me that he didn't realise it. If he had ever loved me at all, shouldn't he be able to see that I was falling apart?

But that's the thing, isn't it, Little Bird? Satan's voice taunted me. *He never has loved you, not really not if he can stand to see you suffer like this- and you know it. The only reason why you're not riling against him is because you don't love yourself enough to fight back, not anymore. And I don't see why! Virginity has always been highly overrated in my humble opinion...*

I moaned softly, rubbing at my brow as I chastised myself for letting her back in. She was as bad as Kohén! Obsessed with you one moment, holding a grudge the next!

You're onto something there, little bird. You think Kohén went to astonishing lengths to get his hands on you? Just you wait and see what I will do!

My stomach tightened in anger. *You're already raping my mind and holding my voice against my will! And like Kohén, you wonder why you always came in second-best to your greatest rival? Ugh- I'd choose God and Kohl over you two assholes any day!*

You little-

God! Help me God! Save me God! Satan's after me God! God, God, god, god GOD!

'Headache?' Kohén asked, and I nodded slowly, moaning softly again as Kohén began to rub the wings of my shoulder blades gently, melting some of the tension I'd had stored in there almost immediately. I had a lot more going on inside my head than pain, but Satan had evidently been shoved out of my mind as I'd prayed to our creator, so I made a mental note to do that until God himself showed up and offered to absolve me and then fly me the hell out of there.

I wonder if there's anything else I can do, to keep her at bay? Crosses? Holy water? Garlic? Surely there's some truth to the old wives' tales about banishing demons, right?

'Then I'll finish the floors later, so the noise won't agitate you, okay?' I nodded, though I had been rather amused at the second son of Arcadia acting like a domestic on behalf of his slave. Sighing Kohén massaged his way up the back of my neck and to the base of my skull. 'I know you're probably going stir-crazy in here Larkin...' he said softly, and I nodded again. 'But I know from talking to my father yesterday that my mother blames us both for Kohl's misery, and I won't have you abused for making the only choice that you were allowed to make as my Companion.'

The notion that he was doing me a good turn by locking me in the slave quarters and fucking me around the clock should have made me laugh, but I heard the fact that he believed what he was saying in his voice and that made me want to cry instead, so I nodded mutely, realising that Kohén wasn't really trying to comfort me- he was trying to come to terms with his own behaviour, which was something that *I* should have been doing too.

'Believe me, if I had it my way, we'd be out every day- drinking, dancing, celebrating... but I really can't risk sending you out there until the future is a little more certain, and I know you understand why right? Just a few more days, though, and then Kohl will go back to Pacifica, most of the nobility will bugger off to where they belong, my former companions will leave and Karol...' Kohén kissed the back of my head. 'He will propose to Ora, I am sure of it. And once he's spoken for, you will be given your freedom to walk the castle halls again.'

I sighed again, but nodded in acquiescence. I didn't want to walk the castle halls- I wanted to bolt through them, climb the fences standing between myself and the tidal falls and then dive right off the side- a swan dive!

'Good.' Kohén sat up. 'I'll clean your room and stay with you for a while today, but unfortunately I will have to leave for a few hours at some point. My father wants to talk to me about the protesters, and I would feel a lot better if I could see Kohl and Karol in the flesh and gauge how they are handling this business on their ends, you know?'

I rolled over in his arms and frowned at him.

Protesters? What protesters?

Kohén frowned back. 'If you don't want me to go-'

I shook my head firmly and wheeled my finger, indicating that he should rewind. He frowned and then said: 'Oh, the protesters. I haven't mentioned them?' I shook my head. Kohén shrugged. 'A bunch of miscreants have been loitering around the perimeter fence for days now. Banished individuals, Godless folk, pirates... I suppose they caught wind of the fact that a lot of people have come to Arcadia this week, and have sensed the opportunity to make a nuisance of themselves. Most are just asking for food, water and blankets, and we've given what we have of course, but a few are begging to be allowed in, and others are demanding it or more supplies. It's not a big problem, but it is causing us strife. A lot of the other leaders are watching closely to see how we handle it here in Eden, and there's a fine line between us being thought generous and compassionate, selfish and hard-hearted, or weak.'

I nodded. I could imagine Elbert Yael calling Elijah stingy for not helping them enough just to cause trouble, while secretly thanking God that the ruffians weren't banging on *his* door.

Kohén cocked his head at me. 'I'm sure you have a million questions, suggestions and recriminations- about everything- so if you care to write them down later, I'll happily answer all that you need me to once I return. But rest first, all right? I miss your voice and your smile, so if you need to spend the day in bed as Cherry suggested, feel free to do that and I swear I won't try to molest you in it, okay?' I made a face at him, but he chuckled. 'Hey, it's going to be hard for me to keep my hands off you too, but I want the old Larkin back more than I want to ravage this silent one! Last night was amazing as always, but I miss you crying out my name...' he ruffled my hair over my face. 'Even if you do tend to follow it up with a cuss word.'

I was glad that I could not respond, for I was certain that he would not appreciate my answer: I was never going to be okay or 'normal' again. My hopes were gone, my happiness was gone and now, I'd lost my voice as well and Kohén was beginning to believe his own lies. I mean, only three days had passed since he'd broken my heart a second time- so how long until I faded to transparency, like my father, thanks to Kohén's blind faith that this was the garden I was destined to grow old in, when it was obvious that I was more like the ivy on the windows- suffocating the castle, and leaving everyone in shadow?

*

The rest of Thursday morning passed slowly and rather pleasantly despite my duress, and I was very entertained for about an hour when Kohén took it upon himself to straighten up my room, proving what a fussy thing he was by cleaning for so long that he exhausted the solar-charged power pack on the vacuum. He stripped my bed and vacuumed the mattress, inside my closet and even our slippers, poking his tongue out at me when I snorted, and then re-starting the machine by giving it a tiny blue zap so that he could finish doing the skirting boards with the brush head.

'Shut up, dust is gross, and spiders crawl over people when they're sleeping,' he said as he strained to suck up a tiny spider's wed from the corner behind my door. 'I yelled at our maid for not getting all the Spiderwebs and cobwebs when I was like, nine, you know. Mother said I was rude for talking to the help like that and punished me by making me do it for myself for a week, and I enjoyed it so much that

I've been doing it since.' He chuckled at himself. 'In fact, I asked for my very own vacuum cleaner on my tenth birthday, and I still have it now. Not that I need to charge it in the sun, like the others.'

I lifted my eyebrows, surprised to learn that. All these years I'd imagined Kohén putting up his royal feet while a maid vacuumed around the spoiled prince, so to learn that the opposite was true was disconcerting. I hated the fact that though I'd grown up in his house, I'd never seen him in the part of it that he actually called home. He ate breakfast in there, and read, and studied and chatted with his family- and I'd never seen *any* of that because I wasn't deemed worthy of it!

Kohén chuckled again. 'And you know what? After she saw what a good job I did in my own room, she ended up swapping maids so the other rooms upstairs would look as good as mine did.' He made a face. 'Not Karol's, though. He's a slob, and he doesn't like people in there so I doubt it's been cleaned properly in years.'

I made a face back at him. I'd seen Karol's sloppy bedroom once, and didn't particularly want to see it again.

After he'd finished cleaning, Kohén took out all of the trash and dirty clothes and lines and returned with clean sheets to make up my bed with, a bottle of champagne with more strawberries and a tray of tiny finger sandwiches, motioning for me to go to my vanity to eat while he re-made my bed. But I couldn't- the nibble I had of the strawberry tasted bitter, and the chicken on the sandwiches smelled funny to me, so when Kohén went into the shower, I slid most of it into the trash can that he'd just emptied and opened the wine instead, taking it and The Count Of Monte Cristo onto the rug in front of the fire that he'd started for us, after remarking that it was getting colder and colder outside and that later he'd bring a thicker blanket in for me. I'd only shrugged- I'd been feeling sweaty in that room since the moment I'd awoken in there on Wednesday night and suspected that claustrophobia was going to guarantee that I'd feel toasty warm right through the rest of the fall and winter. Possibly even for every day of my life from thereon out. Why would I need a blanket, when I was going to have a Nephilim wrapped around me until I lost my looks?

I tried reading but the words blurred together, so I lay down and stared at the book on my side and pretended to be absorbed by it, while Kohén produced a lovely golden guitar, propped himself up on my window-seat and began to play softly, providing me with background music. Once I realised that he was too focused on singing and strumming to pay much attention to what I was doing, I gave up on reading and watched the flames dance only inches away from my numb skin in the lit hearth instead, amazed that Kohén had passed up the opportunity to show off his incredible voice in favour of housekeeping and performing a private concert for a hostile audience of one. I wanted to appreciate him for trying so hard to please me, but thinking about the fact that Kohén wasn't in the spotlight where he ought to be reminded me of how the world had also been deprived of Kelia's beautiful voice because of me, so I sipped from my third glass of marshmallow champagne for the day and willed myself to get drunk. I'd always enjoyed the taste of alcohol but now I enjoyed how it softened my most violent thoughts around the edges, so I drank it without tasting it at all, and marvelled over how I was losing sensation in my body too, along with my senses. Experimentally, I extended my fingertips towards the coals where the flames were flaring the most brightly, frowning when I did not feel them overheat and wondering how close I'd have to roll to that fire in order to absorb any warmth from it.

Why can't I feel the flames? Shouldn't a fire be hot?

This went on for hours: me roasting without burning, and he serenading me with that voice of his, which was as rich as hundred year-old scotch, but as silken as the downy fur mat beneath my body. Sometimes Kohén played popular tunes and hummed along with them, but sometimes he played things that he'd clearly written himself, and not a single lyric of his original songs escaped my drunken notice, because they were obviously about me. There was one about my 'ensorcel' eyes- that was unfinished, one asking why the deck of cards didn't have a princess of hearts, one about a mermaid, one about a being who stole his soul with every kiss... songs that spoke of a girl who was so much more than a third-born whore to him, and that made me ache and wish that I'd taken him at his word on Tuesday afternoon, and had run instead of lingering to plead my case or take the fall that I still hadn't hit the bottom of. How differently could this have all gone, if Kohl had leapt to our defence by making it clear that he had not taken my virginity, instead of drawing his sword? How completely could I have loved this boy with his velveteen voice and eagerly given heart, if he had not slept with so many girls to spare my purity, only to rob me of it and my freedom in the end anyway?

How happy would I have been if I'd agreed to his terms at his ball last year, instead of assuming that mine were the only workable ones?

It was an unwelcome thought, but one that I couldn't drown out, even with the alcohol. I'd had a destiny, like every other third-born, and I'd done nothing but fight against it, only to end up in the nightmare I'd feared and under the worst case scenario- when if I'd just surrendered years ago, he would have released the other girls as virgins, and we could have had something more than this.

No, I didn't think that I could live like this, but I am living it now, and it's not so bad... is it? We have chemistry, and something more than that, only it's gotten lost under our deceit. But if I'd asked him to take me... it could have been wonderful...

As flattering as it was that Kohén had written so many songs about me, I was vexed by the way they referenced me constantly as some sort of mythical enchantress; a mermaid, a siren, what sounded like a succubi, a witch... how were those lyrics fair? He was the one who had lain the trap that *I* had been snared by! *He* was the flawlessly beautiful one that had dazzled me for ten years before my looks had kicked in! He was the one who I ought to have stabbed in his sleep, and yet when I awoke in his arms, I was overcome by the need for him to be inside me! *He* was the one with the power, so why was *I* the siren? I was moved to the point of tears a few times, but they did not actually spill over my lower lashes until he began to sing an old Hawaiian song that I'd heard many times in Pacifica. In fact, it had been the song that had been playing when I'd stumbled onto Kohén's orgy: 'Somewhere over the Rainbow.'

Kelia sounded beautiful when she sang that... she should have aspired to be an artisan, not a noble... oh God! Why am I just LYING here, accepting this fate? I should be rebelling! I should be fighting back! I'm an academic or a farmer, not a whore!

Really? That glass of wine you just finished while wearing a negligee in the middle of the day suggests otherwise...

Drunk and clearly in a maudlin frame of mind, I rolled over and clawed at the throw pillow under my head, weeping soundlessly into it, and Kohén must have seen my shoulders shaking with each wracking sob because he immediately stopped playing and came over to hold me. I tried to wrestle away from him, and wished that I'd had the voice to tell him that I needed to cry- I needed to feel all of this and if he didn't allow me to, I would never be able to expunge my agony from my system.

But I could not say the words and he would not let me go, and so I let the embrace happen and allowed my hurt and anger to bubble back up to the surface again and evaporate my tears. Those he could wipe away, but my growing anger and resentment he could not, and it was only a matter of time before I decided that a world without either Barachiel twin was better than living in one where Kohl was alive and well, but where Kohén was my keeper.

That's what I thought anyway, but as far as my actions went, I simply continued to lie there and allowed Kohén's fingers to stroke my skin with his exquisite touch until I fell asleep and began to dream dreams that were as dominated by thoughts of him as my existence was in front of a heatless fire.

6.

I woke up at about four on Thursday afternoon in the worst mood that I'd been in yet. My head felt achy and my eyes blurry from the champagne and too much sleep, my mouth felt dry as did the rest of me from dehydration, I was so hungry that my stomach was actually cramping up painfully and to top it all off, remnants of a nightmare were clinging to me.

In the dream I'd been in a garden on a freezing cold night, trying desperately to pull weeds away from the plants that Martya and I had planted together. It had been too dark to actually see the weeds so I'd had to feel for them, and each one had been not only slimy and hard to grasp, but full of spikes and barbs that had stabbed into my skin, making my hands slip constantly, and then burn with what had felt like a million paper cuts. And as though that had not been awful enough, I'd quickly begun to realise that every time I pulled one weed out, a new one had regenerated somewhere else nearby, making the task entirely pointless anyway.

But I was Larkin, the stubborn one, so I'd weeded on until the soil had been soaked with my blood and tears and probably would never have stopped- until I'd realised that it wasn't weeds giving me so much trouble, but the very pumpkin vine of Martya's that I'd been trying to *save*. It had mutated, turning against me and the garden that it had grown within, and when I'd seen this, I'd screamed in fury and the entire garden had exploded into a cloud of ash that had transformed again, becoming a swarm of glowing locusts that buzzed around me, thicker than a fog- choking me.

Fortunately, my imagined scream had been loud enough to snap me out of the nightmare, but when I'd awoken needing comfort- even Kohén's- and had discovered that I was alone because he'd slipped out to go on living his life, my terror and confusion had become fury. I'd stomped around the room, silently raging at him, Karol, and pretty much anyone that had ever wronged me in my life- so lost in my anger that I had mouthed to the polar bear rug under me to go fuck itself when I tripped over the corner of it that I had kicked up.

I was pretty sure that I was losing my mind, and although I knew that it was the stupidest thing that I could conceive of doing, I reached for the rest of the peach wine that was still chilling in the ice bucket next to my bed, and then after a long swig from its neck, had stalked into the bathroom with the bottle still in hand, fishing out the book that I'd been trying to ignore for two days. Yes it was foolish to read it, but I was bored and my brain was dying from a lack of mental stimulation and too much physical indulgence, and reading something that was apparently going to arouse my curiosity- and possibly even answer some of the questions that I was too afraid to ask Satan directly- was a temptation I was not strong enough to turn away from, not anymore.

If I'm going to Hell anyway, I want to know what it's like, what she's about and what company I can expect to keep when I'm down there! I thought defiantly, opening the ancient cover and watching a fine mist of dust swirl up from within. I held my breath as I turned that dangerous first page, wondering if the questions about my father and mother were finally about to be answered, sort of excited to think that doing as I was could potentially set into motion a chain of events that would see me ejected from Eden and into the afterlife more rapidly. It was a scary thought, for sure, but scarier still was the possibility that the rest of my life would carry on as it was- of me drinking myself stupid enough to fool Kohén into believing that my glassy-eyed gaze was an adoring one. Days, weeks, months I could endure it for... but for the rest of my existence? No, I was fairly sure I'd sooner die and take Kohl with me!

The book was titled: *'As it is In Heaven: A History Of Eden's Founders,'* with the words 'First Edition' printed beneath the title, and I exhaled a stream of air through my nose, disappointed after reading it. This wasn't contraband! I'd been handed this book as part of my studies years ago!

To be certain, I walked over to my bookshelf, scoured the titles with my puffy eyes and then plucked out my own copy, looking from one to another and thinking that although they didn't look much alike, they were titled the same. The first edition that I'd been gifted was larger, thicker, smellier and older-looking, but the author was the same: Cadence Verity, a renowned Arcadian Academic/historian. She'd been interested in the Kingdom's history growing up as an academic, and had spent a great deal of time researching the royal family during her apprenticeship, penning this text before her twenty-first birthday. She'd done such a wonderful job that she'd been transferred to the nobility upon completion of it, and had caught the King's interest. His son Aidan had been about to turn thirty, so the king had pushed for the two to be joined, telling Aidan that he would give him the crown immediately if he chose a woman that was not only beautiful, noble and intelligent- but interested enough in the kingdom's history to devote her life to it. Aidan had taken him up on the suggestion and had made Cadence his spouse and soon after, his duchess, and the book had been published and made accessible to the public after their first child had been born as the king's gift to her.

But according to ancient gossip, Aidan had been a neglectful spouse during his reign because he'd been far too preoccupied with raising a kingdom in Tariel to have time for anyone else, even his children, who'd been raised predominantly by his duchess with little to no assistance from him. Like Elijah, he'd preferred to spend whatever free time he did have inside the harem with women he'd grown up with who had demanded nothing from him but his pleasure, so rumour had it that the king and duchess had probably only gone to bed together twice in all of those years- both times in order to procreate, and never for any other reason. The entire kingdom had felt sorry for her, and yet when the time had come for him to seriously consider marrying Cadence or releasing her, he'd opted to spend a few weeks getting to know her at last, and had shocked everyone by falling madly in love with her!

Tariel had been an established kingdom by then thanks to all of his hard work, and their sons were turning thirty and twenty-one, so Aidan had abdicated to his eldest child, Raoul and then had released the women in his harem in order to spend the rest of his life as a devoted spouse rather than a king and eventually, a husband. Naturally this delay in their decision to take vows meant that Cadence would never get to be the queen (not in a way that was officially recognised seeing as how her husband's reign was already over), but they had been happy together anyway, and the kingdom had been as in love with their story as I had first been to hear it. After so many years of playing it safe, a Barachiel King was finally going to commit to a woman in a way that could not be undone! How pleased God would be! How lucky she was!

But sadly, their happiness was destined to be short-lived. To celebrate their love and mutual success, the couple had decided to take a honeymoon of sorts, and had sailed down to St Miguel, intending to tour this side of Calliel- especially Tariel- before marrying and before their sons could start giving them grandchildren. But unfortunately, their ship had been wrecked by a storm between St Miguel and Tariel and they'd both perished as a result- along with their entire crew.

Well- it was presumed that a storm had wrecked the ship, but there were people that believed that pirates might have had something to do with it because back then, we'd had a few foreign vessels attempt to dock on our coastline and the waters were considered dangerous for most. But we'd never know the whole truth, because the coastline that the ship's debris had washed up had been wild, so no witnesses had been present to see exactly what had happened that day- only settlers close enough in St Miguel to report the fact that the entire region had been inundated by a terrible storm a few days before, one that had could have been powerful enough to wreck an Arcadian ship, because it had damaged buildings and ships in St Miguel as well.

Either way it had been a tragedy that had made it clear that seafaring was as dangerous then as it had been six hundred years before, which was why their youngest son Cole, then Duke of St Miguel, had started campaigning for a highway to be built between Arcadia and Tariel soon after. His brother the king, Raoul, had been a bit of a weak ruler (the only one to die young and without children or a spouse due to a few troubling incidents in his childhood) but Cole's son Lloyd had inherited the throne when Cole had passed it over (he hadn't wanted to leave St Miguel after having called it home for so long), and Lloyd had gotten the highway completed during his reign, earning the continent's respect.

Apparently, Calliel had felt very disjointed before Lloyd's reign, but the building of that highway had made the entire continent feel safer and more united afterwards, and because Elijah's own successful reign had followed it, bringing many more advances to our civilisation, the previous sixty years had been touted as being a true golden era. People had been sad about Cadence's passing and the king's too, but they'd rejoiced when her book had finally been printed shortly after her death, so even though she hadn't broken through the Barachiel glass ceiling as far as love, marriage and monarchies went, she'd certainly made enough progress to inspire every little girl in Calliel into believing that maybe someday, people might find cause to celebrate *her* life too for being more than just a spouse or a wife- but as a success.

It was an interesting story, but I didn't understand why Satan had decided to give me a book penned by Cadence Verity to read now, especially seeing as how I'd not only read it, but had been forced to study it before. Still, being reminded of that woman's success certainly hit a nerve (I should have been in the academic caste aspiring to nobility, Martya too!) and I was just about to toss it across the room when I opened the cover and realised that the book I was holding had not been printed using a press as my own copy had been-but written by hand!

Oh wow! I thought, sitting up and flipping pages. *Is this a first edition, or a first* draft?

To my delight, every single page had been filled in using cursive handwriting rather than typed print, and I'd only turned a few before I realised that the paper it had been written on was the handmade sort too- the kind that we hadn't used since we'd built factories to recycle paper with.

It is a draft- a mock-up of what was eventually printed! What a neat little treasure! How foolish is Kohén to frost me with diamonds, when it is the scent of old paper that thrills me so?

The book's scent was indeed strong and old, but it wasn't pungent, like most of the books that Kohl had excavated for me had been, proving that it had been stored somewhere dark and dry in order to preserve it, not buried away by accident. It was a history text, but one of our history and not the time before and so it had been mass-produced, not locked up in a museum somewhere. The fact that this was an original copy was thrilling to me, (I hadn't lied when I'd told Elijah that I was drawn to rare things, not just rare things of monetary value) but I frowned as I turned page after page of painstakingly-illustrated family trees, knowing that this book had to be well over one hundred years old and irreplaceable... so how much trouble was I going to get in if it was found in my room? Was that Satan's only intent- to agitate my situation?

I should have been thinking of a way to hide it until I could entreat someone to smuggle it back into the Collection room or the library for me, but curiosity had me now and it wasn't letting go. Satan had told me to read between the lines of this to prove my intellect, but what was it she wanted me to notice aside from what I already had? I did not know, but I hadn't come this far to go on not knowing, and so I started reading.

The book wasn't nearly as interesting as an autobiography on Cadence's life would have been, but it was full of information, and information was something else that I usually prized so I stuck with it. It was divided into sections, each titled with the surname of one of the twelve originals, followed by a series of family trees tracing their lineage. This was where I quickly noticed another difference- the second edition that I had contained information that had been updated to include the most recent twins' births, whereas this one ended just over one hundred years ago, to when this project of Cadence's would have been considered up to date. The first entry, of course, was Prince Elijah The First. The last was Prince Aidan, who was our current King Elijah's great grandfather.

So old... I mused, reading the names at the top of each page. *Kohl would love to see this!* I felt a pang in my heart then and remembered that there were a lot of things that Kohl would have loved to do, but a lot of things he'd never get to do- book-sniffing with me included. Groaning soundlessly, I paused and took another long sip of champagne to sedate my nerves with. *Please, let Atticus keep his promise to make a general out of Kohl! Let him find a way to shine without my help or Kohén's, but on his own merits!*

I turned page after page as I sipped my life away, my eyes blurring over the squiggly lines connected Barachiel to duchess, to Barachiel, struggling to find anything to focus on while under the influence of fermented peaches and nursing a sore head from drinking even more the day before... but try as I might, nothing snagged my interest because frankly, the book wasn't that interesting. I knew quite a bit about the first three Arcadian Kings (Miguel, Elijah and Elijah's son, Michael) and a lot about the kings that had come after Aidan because *that* was the branch of family tree that I had grown up in the shadows of, but I knew very little about the sixteen kings that had reigned between both points because as far as I knew, they'd all led rather dull, predictable lives. Sure they had done their part to keep Arcadia growing and moving forward, but none of them had left much of a legacy or done anything to render them notorious, not the way that Aidan, Lloyd and Elijah had. After all, God had left the Barachiel's in charge of keeping the human race happy, equal and safe- not thrilled, excited and rebellious, so unlike the history texts of the world before, there were no monsters between the pages *or* between the lines as far as I could tell. And thanks to how careful the Barachiel men had been about promising women they loved anything that they could not surely deliver (no more bloody tears!) there were no epic love stories or tragic back stories to these couplings either, at least not until you got to recent history and started looking hard into the duchess's current predicament, or my own. I was sure there were more interesting stories when it came to analysing the prior kings, princes and their Companions, but those illicit stories would rarely have made it out of the harem, let alone into an important text.

Hmm, maybe that's what I should do! Research the whores before me and give it to Kohén for publication! I probably won't get a royal title out of it, but I might get banished... I giggled at the idea of producing such an 'important' history and presenting it to Elijah, and bubbles of champagne went up my nose. *I could name it: 'He giveth Liberty, and then he taketh away!'*

After I'd recovered from my drunken giggle fit, I read on until my eyelids growing heavy and the lines on the page had begun to dance in front of my eyes. The pages concerning the other twelve originals were more interesting than the ones about the monarchs, and I lingered on the page about Rosa Fernandez, Miguel's step-daughter longer than I did on any other, realizing suddenly that I knew next to nothing about her, which was strange because we knew a lot about the others-even the ones that *hadn't* been named in the six books of creation. Had she been overshadowed by her infant brother's 'angelic' conception and existence? That hardly seemed fair! Typical from a sexist standpoint, but not fair!

Cadence's book showed that Rosa had married one of the other original twelve, a young man named Jasper- a fact I'd already known-but her family tree had been smushed in next to Miguel and Gabriella's, and only extended to include a branch for her daughter before it hit the bottom of the page. I turned the page over, remembering that Adeline had mentioned being related to Rosa and interested to see if her and Martya's great-grandparents had made it into this book at some point, but to my surprise, the family tree on the next page was Amalie Sanchez's, not a continuation of Rosa's.

I flipped back, re-reading the last name on Rosa's tree- Luciana- and scratched my head, wondering if Luciana had died, therefore voiding any further history. But then I remembered that Jasper had been the teenage son of Carol, another widowed survivor and Korbin, the doctor that Miguel had saved during Armageddon (both two survivors of the original twelve) and so, there was a chance that Jasper and Rosa's family tree had been embellished upon on *their* page instead, which made sense. But more quick page-turning proved that although Carol and Corbin's tree showed their union, the child they'd had (Jasper's half-brother) and all of the descendants that followed them- there was nothing else there to show what had become of Jasper and Rosa's descendants after they'd had Luciana- merely a spike after Jasper and Rosa's marriage that indicated to go back to the original Barachiel Tree on the first page, which I already knew was a dead-end as far as Rosa's genealogy went. Why?

We didn't learn much about Rosa's life during our education either... I mused, squinting as I stared at the bathroom door and into my memories. I knew that Rosa had taken an interest in gold-mining so she and her husband Jasper had been given land to excavate in Nitika, but that was all I did know, and it made no sense. Why would this book go into detail about every generation of the original twelve up until one hundred years ago, but fail to elaborate on what had become of Miguel's step-daughter's line? How could the history of Gabriella's firstborn child be dismissed as inconsequential? The girl had met *God*, for Heaven's sake! Didn't that warrant an autobiography or two? A painting? A public holiday?

Intrigued now, I pulled out my notebook and tentatively marked Rosa's name onto the page, followed by Jasper's- and then waited nervously for Satan to smite me for putting lead to paper. But nothing happened (obviously she was only going to 'get' me if I tried writing stuff down about her) and so I quickly jotted down the twelve names that had a section in the book, until I had listed all twelve of the originals, and then traced their lines to their castes, trying to make sure that I knew where everyone was and that no pages were missing.

Miguel and Gabriella had been the first nobles, Amalie Sanchez the first athlete, Cole the war veteran had had the Corps named in his honour (many, many years after his passing) Carol the widowed architect had married Korbin the doctor, and along with Maryah the scientist and Cohen the engineer, had had the academic caste founded after them... Raoul the homosexual had had no children but had had the Artisan caste created in his name... leaving Aura the nurse and Trojan the labourer to head up the first Blue-Collar caste. Those people had married or joined with either one another or other survivors that had made their way to Arcadia after hearing God speak and their genealogy had been charted for centuries... and their names had be recycled time and time again to honour them (I'd always known that Karol had been named after Carol the female survivor, but I hadn't known that Kohén had once been spelled Cohen) but even after going through every individual family tree, I realised that I could not find a link between Luciana, Rosa's last named descendant and anyone else of note because there wasn't one. So had Luciana perished? Had she been forgotten? Or had she simply lived out her life without having any children of her own?

No that can't be! Both Martya and Adeline have mentioned being related to her, so unless they're like, six hundred years old and both secretly named Luciana, then they have to have ancestor's somewhere, yeah? Ancestors that ought to be recorded here?

The first option was possible, but I knew that a family linked to Miguel Barachiel's (even if only by marriage) would have been encouraged- if not forced- to procreate for the good of mankind. After all, repopulating the earth had been Miguel Barachiel's highest priority in the beginning, and it had stayed that way until about one hundred years ago, when Tariel's limited natural resources had been strained by their initial settlement. They'd adopted the one-child only rule once they'd realised that repopulation could equal famine in their environment (gold they had, but arable land they had not), and Arcadia had adopted the practice soon after when hundreds had fled Tariel, hoping to be taken under Arcadia's wing. So, after centuries of trying to plump up the population, we'd suddenly had exactly as many as we could sustain and swift action had been taken against it expanding much further- and that was yet another shadow that I'd grown up beneath during this supposed golden era.

In fact, now that I thought about it, I realised that a lot of things had changed around that same time or just before then, but I had no idea exactly how or when, because it hadn't been documented. But somewhere during those sixteen uneventful reigns, the Arcadian kings had decided that they could not take on the responsibility of ruling or marrying for love until they were thirty and had created first the Given caste and then the Corps caste and finally, the Companion one.

Companions had been a 'thing' before the population cap, of course (it really was the world's oldest trade) but it had been a strictly voluntary position that I knew had been started when two farmers had offered up their infertile daughters to the crown, so that the first crowned prince Elijah could 'take care of them' back in the very beginning- trading sexual favours and companionship for food, shelter and safety on the grounds that their fathers could not provide for them, or marry off girls that could not have babies to anyone else.

Miguel had never married Gabriella, but he had been in love with her and faithful until the day he died, of course, and that we all knew for a fact. But it had been difficult for his son Elijah to find a girl that he could be as devoted to, because there simply hadn't been many to choose from back then, given how many had died or had been taken up to Heaven or down to Hell during the apocalypse. Terrified of growing old alone, and suffering due to his powerful Nephilim urges, Elijah had taken on the responsibility of the two (for all intents and purposes) 'smitten' young women in exchange for the right to be intimate with them, so long as they understood that he could not make a commitment to them that would impede his chances of procreating with a fertile woman one day, and risk breaking anyone's heart as Miguel had Satan's. They'd agreed not to fall in love with him, and Elijah had been so satisfied with their company and the arrangement that he had not ended up joining with a fertile woman until he'd been in his mid-thirties... one that had allowed him to go on acting intimately with his whores, so long as it was understood that as soon as their child had been raised by them both, she would be free to return to the man that *she* loved, who had also been infertile due to radiation poisoning, which had been common back then.

Elijah's temporary spouse, Arytha, had sadly died from pneumonia when her son had still been a child so she'd never gotten the chance to return to her old flame, but the bottom line was that the Barachiel line had found a way around God's strict rules that had seen everyone's needs getting met without tears being shed, children being abandoned, or feelings being hurt.

Naturally, the people that hadn't been directly involved had been suspicious of the odd arrangements in the beginning, but the truth was that the woman that Elijah had 'used' had been well provided for and content with their lot, as Elijah's child's mother had been, so where was the harm in it all? Besides, it would have been pretty dangerous to suggest that being prostituted was beneath anyone, as Elijah's mother Gabriella had been a sex worker once too- so if that had not prevented an archangel from falling in love with her, or hampered her ability to be the female ruler of the new world, then who was anyone to suggest that the life of a prostitute was a wasted one?

I don't think the Barachiel's had actually intended to keep that arrangement going for centuries, but breeding had continued to be difficult but also a priority for all in Arcadia for a very long time, while falling in love had remained a high-risk activity that was not to be undertaken lightly or easy to find, so I guess it had made sense to fashion our country's laws around the Barachiel's example of having it all originally: around the concept that love, procreation and lust were three very different things that ought to be kept separate, especially if it meant safeguarding their souls, while keeping re-population under control.

Yes I could easily understand how it had all come to pass, of course, but at some point, the women offered to the crown had stopped being the penniless, infertile, voluntary and easily pleased variety, and had started becoming the reluctant sort, and *that* was what drove me insane. I did not know when it had been decided that all women given to the crown must be virginal, accomplished, indentured, attractively presented, sit with their hands to form a bowl and trained to heel and 'fixed' as far as fertility went despite having no fertility issues to begin with- but I suspected that it had something to do with the ushering-in of the third-born rule, and that it probably wasn't a story that I was going to like very much, which was probably why I had never looked very deeply into it. It, or the reason why after all of these years, the royal family had yet to give us a female heir. There were just some questions that I didn't want answers to, not if I wanted to sleep at night while under the same roof as a Barachiel, let alone in the same bed!

And THERE you have it! The disembodied voice slithered through my brain like a snake, causing me to jump and knock my champagne onto the floor. *Find the Barachiel daughters, and you will find an answer to every question you've ever had regarding this family, little bird, and your place in it! And why not? It's not like you're sleeping at night anyway, is it?*

I screamed, but no sound came out.

7.

I cringed to see the puddle spreading over my freshly-cleaned tiles before looking around for Satan accusingly, searching for her with a stuttering heart, but of course, she wasn't in there with me- not in the physical sense anyway.

Thanks for that! I told her silently and angrily. And then I thought about what she had said and snarled at her as I got off the bed and began mopping up the wine mess with the towel that had been wrapped around my head earlier. *And what Barachiel daughters are you talking about? There are no Barachiel daughters! They've only birthed sons since the beginning of our time!*

That's true. But there is a difference between being birthed and being conceived, isn't there? And just like that, the book fell off my bed and opened at my feet with a splat. *I told you to read between the lines, so if you can't manage that sober, perhaps you should stop drinking, hmm? You ever heard of a smart drunk? Because Hell is filled with people who thought they could be both!*

A prickly heat travelled up the back of my neck and I lifted the book, straining to read the elaborate, old-fashioned cursive on the swollen, brittle paper. At first glance the family tree looked like a slightly more amateurish version of the printed one, but when I peered down at the page, I saw that there was more writing on this one than on the others. Not as far as the kings went, or the duchesses- but the siblings lines were more clustered than the others starting from AA36, when Elijah had had his first child, Michael, and written beside Michael's name was something I'd never seen before, not in the second edition that I'd read, and certainly not on any family tree I'd ever lain eyes upon before!

Michael Elijah Barachiel. *Gabriella-Rose Barachiel (Dec).*

My heart was pounding hard enough to make my blood throb in my ears, and the further down the family tree I looked, the harder my head throbbed.

Dec... as in deceased? Michael had a twin sister that didn't survive? Oh my God!

I knew that multiple births were a thing in the Barachiel DNA, but what I hadn't realised that not one set of multiples had ever been born successfully together until Kohl and Kohén had come along. There had been other sets of twin boys born, and we all knew that, but now I saw that they'd all originally been triplets, and I was flabbergasted to realise that it had been kept a secret from us all!

Cadence knew, though! She worked this out during her research somehow, recorded it- and then omitted it for some reason! Was she silenced by force, or did she trade this secret for the chance to marry a monarch? I shook, and the book trembled in my hands. *Why? Why would she want to keep this secret? Why would anyone want to silence her? And what the hell is going to happen to me if someone works out that I know...?*

That's one question you should avoid having answered, believe me! Satan offered unhelpfully and I pursed my lips, thinking hard. What *did* I know, exactly? That the Barachiel's had some sort of reproduction defect that prevented their spouses from having girl babies...if that was all it was, then I had no problem. But if it wasn't...

Despite my brain screaming at me to beat myself in the head with the book until I was rendered unconscious, I read on with a racing heart, inhaling the information the way I ought to have been inhaling food and water. The stillborn issue hadn't arisen with every generation of Barachiels, for there were plenty of times when there had been just the one successful birth, or one or two brothers birthed by the same mother with a few years and no tragedies lapsing between... but sadly, at least every second or third King had suffered multiple births that had ended with one child perishing, evidently as a stillborn and *always* a girl. Sometimes it was two boys born with one girl not making it, sometimes it was one boy born and one girl deceased... but there was a pattern emerging in Cadence's penmanship that suggested that breeding with a Barachiel could see both father and mother nursing a stillborn female infant after, and that was incredibly sad. The most shocking revelation concerned Michael's twin (our third king could have been a queen and no one had ever mentioned it?) and the most awful incident involved a set of twin girls that had been born before King Aidan, to a woman that was *not* his mother. The twin girls he'd fathered first had both perished, and their mother had evidently been replaced by the next duchess of Arcadia, who had gone on to give the king a healthy son, which made me feel sick to my stomach. I opened the second edition copy of the text to the same age and compared, feeling heartsick for the poor, forgotten duchess when I realised that she'd been written out of Arcadian history all together in the published text.

Oh my goodness! How could such a thing happen time and time again without it becoming common knowledge that the Barachiel genes have issues, just like any other? Has this been hidden from the public because they were saddened or embarrassed by it… or for more sinister reasons?

I went cold then, remembering what Constance had told me- about how Elijah had immediately suggested switching the babies, Kohl and Kohén, to make it appear that the first-born twin had been the healthy one instead of the other way around. Had these infant daughters of his ancestors been born dead… or had they been *discarded* to prevent the inferior sex from ruling one day? I was going to vomit, and quickly- all I was waiting for was to hear Satan confirm my worst fears to trigger it… but her voice didn't come to me, and so I swallowed down the bile and looked back to the book, shaking my head.

No, no the Barachiel's couldn't be that evil, could they? They're not as pure of heart as they've led us to believe, but killing their female heirs to keep the crown on a male head? That's ghastly! That's demonic! And what reason could they possibly have to do such a thing? The people in this kingdom WANT to see a female heir- one would be celebrated! The Barachiel's would never fob off the opportunity to win so many people over, would they?

I looked back to the first page, to where Michael's birth (and the death of his twin) was recorded, and then noticed that his name fell adjacent to Lucinda's, only where his legacy went on, hers ended. There was nothing much interesting there, but I was just about to turn the page again when I realised that above it, and above Rosa's entry, another name had been written and then crossed out with a series of violent slashes. I wondered if maybe Cadence had just made a mistake when she'd started printing the tree that she'd corrected, but when I flipped the page over, I saw the indentations that her pen had originally left in the paper- and that the name had once been connected to Rosa's via a strike-line that had been used to represent a sibling connection in the rest of the other family trees. That indicated that Rosa had had an older sister but not one that had been connected to Miguel or Gabriella in any way, and my jaw dropped. The name was printed backwards and barely legible, but as I squinted at the little bumpy loops, I realised that it was a name written there: A-T-E-I-L-U-J

Julieta? Rosa Fernandez had an older sister named Julieta?

O-G-N-I-B! the voice whispered in my head, and after an embarrassingly long pause for consideration (I really wasn't a smart drunk) I sucked in a breath.

Who was her father?! I asked Satan, and then blinked, realizing that I already knew. Not the name, of course, because Gabriella's life had never been investigated, pre-Armageddon, but if it was Rosa's sister, then I already knew that the man that had sired both girls had to have been a rapist, and if he'd been a *serial* rapist, then there was every chance that he had been a dark Nephilim... and if he'd been a dark Nephilim, then *that* meant that there was a chance that his two daughters could have been as well...

You don't know that this Julieta was conceived with rape! I told myself firmly, once my initial hysteria had subsided. *The circumstances of Rosa's conception could have been completely different to hers! And if Julieta's mother had gone to bed with this man willingly, then there's no reason to*

assume that he was a serial rapist let alone a dark Nephilim, is there? Normal men do fucked up things all the time- look at Kohén!

But Satan snorted and just like that, my hysteria came crashing back over me. If Rosa Barachiel had been a dark Nephilim, then instead of the world starting over fresh here in Eden, full of light and purity as we'd been led to believe, it had been tainted from the very beginning. Not just here in Arcadia, but wherever this sister had lived out her life too. How much influence had Rosa had over her step-brother? Had her line been poisoning the Barachiel one from the beginning? Was Adeline dark? Martya? No! But had Rosa encouraged her half-brother to do what was right and good, or had she played the devil's advocate from the very beginning, damning mankind the second time around out of loyalty to Satan?

I heard Satan snort derisively again. *Because all dark Nephilim are evil, and all white-plumed Nephilim pure and good? Was it one of* my *descendants that locked you in here little bird? Or one of the saintly Miguel's?*

You asked me to read between the lines, and that is what I have done! I told her, growing angry. *You show me evidence that suggests that something was 'wrong' with Rosa's family tree, and then evidence to suggest that the Barachiel line was corrupt almost from the very beginning, and then mock me when I draw parallels between the two branches? If I did not decipher this correctly, then it is your fault for giving me such vague hints!*

Satan sighed. *I am trying to show you that things are not as they appear, and all you are doing is taking things at their most basic face value!*

I've been reading between the lines for seventeen years, and it has gotten me nowhere! I hollered back at her silently, standing up and flinging my comforter off my bed so that the book fell to the ground. *Do you think I WANT to be here, you stupid bitch? Do you think that it felt good to have my heart smashed time and time again by these Barachiel bastards? Do you think I wanted to fall in love with a man who I knew could very likely be my undoing?*

I don't know... sometimes I think that yes, maybe you do want to be here, you sensual little ingénue...

NO! Tears were rolling down my face, as it had finally dawned on me that not even Satan had the power to pluck me from this world- the way I'd sort of hoped she'd had- no one did! I couldn't turn to the boy I loved for help, because he was the one enforcing all of the pain, I couldn't turn to the three women I trusted the most: Ora, Constance and Cherry with my secrets, because not only were they more fond of Karol than they were of me, but because there was nothing they could do that wouldn't make it worse... and I couldn't get help from anyone else because there was no one else- just me and my stupid, fried, drunken brain. My situation had seemed like a complicated one for days, one there might be no escaping from, but now I knew it for sure- I was hopeless and it was all my own fault.

I wanted to raise cotton, and play soccer with my best friend, and exchange books with his brother, but no matter how hard I strove to make those dreams come true, something else has always come between them and me. I have not made the best decisions, but I have not had many options have, I? And I don't have them now!

You only think that but once you get out of here-

Satan if I leave this place, Kohl will DIE- you've said it yourself- and he doesn't deserve that fate. And Kohén will be the one to kill him- and he doesn't deserve that fate either! No, I don't want to sit here and rot until Kohén loses interest in me, but that is what I must do to keep Kohl and Lindy free and alive... so if you truly want to help me, then use whatever power you have and smash my brain to pulp so that I don't have to torture myself over all I have done wrong anymore! And if you cannot do that then please, just leave me alone! Don't draw my attention to how corrupt this palace is- let me believe in Kohén's love! Let me believe that there is something good inside Karol and Elijah. LET ME BE NAIVE BECAUSE IT HURTS TOO MUCH TO BE OTHERWISE!

I cannot stand idly by and watch you destroy yourself over these boys-

WHY? They are Nephilim- I am NOTHING!

I think we both know that you're a lot more than nothing! Honestly the last woman that caused this much scandal and chaos on earth was me!

I shuddered at the comparison, and I had a feeling that she wasn't exaggerating as much as I wanted to believe. I flushed hotly, feeling ill. *Then WHO am I? WHAT am I?*

You're a pain in the ass! And a card player, which means you ought to know that I'm not showing you anything until I know that you're a safe bet, and all you've ever proven is that you're too honest and kind to keep secrets that matter from anyone! Besides... I can only see where you've come from, and who you might come to be- your future isn't set in stone, stretching out with certainty with a final destination in sight the way a highway is, but subjective to exterior forces, as a ship voyaging across an open sea. Many factors could see you blown off course, sunken or capsized, Larkin- wind, rain, lightning, storm surges... but the only thing I do know for sure is that right now, I'm the safest harbour available to you, so if you refuse to follow my instructions, than it's very likely that you'll be smashed across the rocks soon enough. And what's worse is- they're submerged rocks- the sort you cannot yet see yet because you are too busy looking for the thunderbolt to strike from above, like every other god-fearing idiot since the dawn of time! But you will see all soon, and as soon as you do, it will be too late for you to do anything but abandon ship!

I rubbed my forehead. *Well that was fucking poetic. Did you have a word count minimum there, or did you eat the soul of a bard before you popped in here for desert?*

Don't be a wanker.

A what?

Stop mouthing off to me- and think for yourself instead of demanding answers! You have a responsibility to uphold here Larkin-

I'm not responsible for anyone, not even for my own actions! I pointed out, bewildered by this conversation, which was becoming more and more like a riddle with every second that it dragged on. *I've tried sleuthing as you suggested but according to you, I interpreted every clue incorrectly, so if you want me to read something other than what I have, then spell it out for me, because I am too drunk, tired and defeated to take this shit anymore!* My rage was silent, but I kicked the book across the room in anger and it made a satisfying 'thwack' sound.

It is not I that has to grow and change here, Larkin- it is you! If I have to spell the truths in your life out for you because you cannot- or will not- work it out for yourself, then there is no way that I can help you get to the bottom of what is truly going on here, or help you get out of it! Oh believe me I would if I could, but I am a fallen angel, not a puppet-master! Your destiny is your own, as is your free will, but the path you are on is going to lead you to death here, and I am powerless to stop it unless-

'Then *GO TO HELL* and *LEAVE ME TO DIE HERE ALONE!*' I screamed, and my voice filled the room with as much brittleness, volume and violence as a stack of plates being shattered. My throat burned and instantly felt hoarse and my ears rang, but as soon as I'd shouted out the command for Satan to leave, I felt her presence dissipate from the air completely, with no trace lingering after her.

I stood there, gasping and feeling the oxygen tickle my vocal folds and inflate my lungs, and realised that whatever I'd just done had not only booted her out of this realm, but out of my mind- releasing me from her hold. I was shaking from head to toe and my head was pounding from the paranoia that she and her book had instilled in me, but I was alone in my mind, alone in my fear, alone in my cage, alone in my anger… and alone with my conflicted, but still functioning soul.

'She's gone…' I whispered, knees weakening beneath me as I sat back down onto the side of the bed and cupped my heavy head in my hands. I'd overcome the temptation to give myself to Satan, even if that could mean saving my life, but instead of feeling stronger for it, I felt only more exhausted than I had before. 'And I am still here, with…' I looked over at the book, and felt tears fill my eyes, as though I had a tear for every question that I'd asked since I'd learned to speak that had gone unanswered. I wanted to sob them out so that I could rid myself of them while indulging in self-pity yet again, but instead I rolled over on my bed and plucked a bottle of peach wine out of the ice bucket that Kohén had left for me before he'd gone along with a fruit platter, cracked it open and downed a third of it in one greedy, defeated gulp, letting the few tears that had spilled over to drain back into my hair so that I would not have to taste them again.

Once I'd fortified myself with alcohol again, I bent down and began to re-stack the books on the shelves, hiding the one that Satan had gifted me in clear view of the others, because I knew that Kohén wasn't nearly observant enough to see what was in front of his nose. If he had been, I would not be here now, would I? He would have seen the adoration in my eyes for Kohl in Pacifica, and would have raked me across the coals then. People had always said that the safest place to hide a book was in a bookshelf- and I supposed by the same logic, the safest place to hide a whore, was in a harem.

When I turned my back to that bookshelf, I imagined myself turning my back on everything and everyone, God and Satan, Right and Wrong, Heaven and Hell alike… and it was liberating. Something was wrong in Eden and I couldn't deny it… but it wasn't *my* problem, it never had been, and if I'd gotten into this mess by trying to take responsibility for all that the Barachiel's had done wrong, then I guessed that the best way to disentangle myself from it all was to stop caring; period.

Yes there had been a decline in the purity of the Barachiel souls over the last couple of hundred years and the fact that a Barachiel man hadn't had feathers of his own since King Elijah The First was a testament to that fact. Apparently they'd also somehow managed to procreate twenty-one generations of princes without a princess ever being born alive despite the fact that they'd been conceived, which reeked of foul play, and yes, there was possibly something very wrong with a supportive branch of the family tree... but although some people might have found all I had just learned to be cause for alarm, as far as I was concerned (and as far as I cared to be concerned) the darkening of Barachiel souls probably had less to do with demonic possession... and more to do with evolution, just as Martya had predicted.

They were weakening- becoming more human than divine, and so long as that evolution continued to level out the balance of presumed piety and power between the Nephilim race and the human one, well, I didn't see any reason as to why I should fight against it anymore, especially not while so many eyes were watching the kingdom of Arcadia... watching, and waiting for one of them to put a step wrong so that the power could be taken from their entitled hands by force, and handed to someone that had earned it, as it had been in Rabia.

True, I was a prisoner here, and Kohén couldn't sugar coat that for me, but that meant that he was going to struggle- and obviously was already struggling- to sugar coat it for *others* too. Perhaps Cadence Verity's truths had been swept under the rug, but my life was already more public than hers as a Companion to a prince rather than as a bride, so when I did not show up at that ball, there would be questions. And if Karol changed his mind about marrying Ora or changed his birthday wish because he wasn't ready to part with his dream of having *me* then there *would* be consequences- and I didn't fear being held accountable for them this time, because I had nothing left to lose now.

The Barachiel men, on the other hand, had everything to lose, and they were gambling it all away on the utterly male, and utterly human belief that they had the right to take whatever they desired- even the forbidden fruit.

But they were wrong, and if all I had to do to make that clear was drink wine that I enjoyed, go to bed with someone that I was insatiably attracted to, and accept diamond ropes that were worth more than the treasury of most countries in the world and stop worrying about what was to become of us all, then I would do it.

I'd be a Companion, if it meant there was a chance that I'd be the last one.

8.

The afternoon passed slowly in a blur of champagne and Kohén's comings and goings after I'd banished Satan from my head, and though I'd regained the ability to speak, I decided to keep that fact to myself for a little while, mostly because I knew that my silence was still weighing on whatever was left of Kohén's guilty conscience and I rather enjoyed that. Besides, my mouth had been getting me into trouble for years anyway, so I knew it would be easier to lie to him and pretend that I was happier with our arrangement than I truly was when I didn't have to actually *vocalise* the falsehood.

Though Kohén returned to check on me as often as he could that day, he kept his word, and began to make a habit of popping in on his brother's birthday celebrations to keep up the façade that all was well between the Barachiel brothers, despite the fact that those of us in the know understood that they had never been worse. Family strife aside and insatiability when it came to me aside, the kingdom was full of people that he had to impress while he had the chance, like Shepherd Choir (who'd been a wealthy count before he'd retired to spread God's love) and the new Baron of Janiel, Alton Breech (a shipping magnate who'd only just recently been titled and was contemplating investing in Pacifica's future). It was unfortunate timing for the royal family, and it sucked for me to be left alone in there for hours at a time, but Kohén pointed out that if he wanted to work the wonders that he intended to on Caldera and Isthmus in the future- for both of our sakes- then he would need people like them supporting him financially once he'd been crowned. And schmoozing them before his coronation was an integral part of that plan- one that he'd let fallen to the wayside for too many days already while he'd been making *me* his singular priority, irritating his father and giving his mother an abundance of chances to introduce Kohl to the people that she should have been gushing about Kohén to.

So though it was clear that it physically pained him to leave my side (once his eyes had glistened with actual tears) as soon as it become apparent that I had been rendered mute, guilt-ridden, cooperative, subdued and decidedly pickled with peach wine, Kohén began to leave me with more regularity.

The first event that he attended was a basket racket match between Ora and Amelia-Rose earlier that afternoon while I'd been hanging out with Satan (Amelia-Rose had won, to my dismay) and the next was a sunset sail along the coast that evening- one that was cut short by an hour to the unseasonably cold weather. The third was a Shepherd service that had followed the cruise, in the throne room in Shep Choir's honour, where he'd apparently regaled the people of Arcadia (the service was open to everyone in the kingdom except for me) about what he and his daughter had been up to since he'd visited Eden last. And as he'd talked, the castle staff had handed out warmed cinnamon milk to the assemblage in an attempt to ward off the late-Autumn draft sweeping through the cavernous halls.

My room was sound-proofed, so I hadn't been able to hear any of what was going on, but there must have been hundreds of them in there, collectively shivering until the room filled with body heat and laughter- because I could actually *feel* the buoyant energy swelling within the castle and filtering under the millimetre-high-gap beneath my door, where it clashed against my fragmented aura. It made me want to cry, but there was nothing that I could do but sit there and wait for it all to be over so I could stop feeling like I was missing out on something, so I picked at my eleventh uneaten meal of the week listlessly while the hours ticked by. I'd promised both myself and Kohén that I would eat something, but like with my temporary loss of voice, I knew that there was no point trying to force my body to do something that it simply was not ready to do yet. Besides, I liked my wine diet- it was keeping me pleasantly numb to things that I knew I wasn't ready to cope with sober. Like the sight of all of the love bites on my neck, or the fact that Kohén had managed to bird nest the underside of my hair so much that I was probably going to have to shave it all off soon enough. Sober, that would have pissed me off, but drunk- it was all kind of funny. I didn't know exactly how many Companion rules I'd broken that week, especially when it came to the personal grooming ones, but I knew that if Maryah could see me now, she'd be cooking up some way to punish me even though it was Kohén to blame for it all.

The alcohol was definitely a crutch that I was leaning heavily upon, but when Kohén returned after the Shepherd service, looking peaceful and bemused and, well- *hugged*- I'd sobered up quickly, and had made a horrible face at him, seriously considering flinging my now-cold mashed potatoes at his head... while they were still on the *plate*. He knew that I'd always loved the Shepherd services, and I'd been interested in Shep Choir's career since I'd read that he was the one who had restored order as resident Shep after the Bastien Birch scandal, many years ago, and was eager to see if he was as gifted when it came to easing people's restless spirits as I'd heard that he was... but I'd missed my only chance to hear him talk, and why? Because I was the castle's secret shame! It was humiliating.

Like a drowning person glimpsing the surface, the urge to rebel- to stick my ruffled feathers in Kohén's face and cuss him out or break things rose to the surface of my very being along with Kohén's cheerful smile- as it had earlier that day. But I knew that my violent mood swings and scattered emotional surges were the result of alcohol and lethargy and cabin fever and were more likely to inspire Satan to champion my freedom again then they would inspire Kohén, so I refrained from acting out and listened to Kohén's recap of the evening's events while pulling a brush through my hair.

Remember, you need to start numbing yourself to all that aggrieves you here, and just start being thankful for what isn't so bad! Okay yeah you're a prisoner, but it's not like you're chained up in a filthy cold cellar and being raped by guards or anything, is it? You're a white collar captive at best- a palace pet at worst. Hell, you even had to gag and starve yourself because the people around here would polish your fingernails while feeding you peeled grapes before they'd let you go hungry!

'Father hopes that Shep Choir will be able to do something to disperse the outlaws at the fence,' Kohén said softly, gently tracing patterns on the bared skin of my left shoulder blade while I combed my hair over the other, and I grimaced to think of all of those cold, hungry and scared people out there- then grimaced again to be reminded of how lucky I was to be here despite all of the laws that I'd broken. The temperature in the harem was maintained using heaters that were hooked up to the solar energy source, but I knew from Kohén that the temperature outside had been dropping for days and would soon reach zero and even I with my embarrassed, constantly-flushed face would shiver at zero. 'But there are already too many do-gooders interfering, and if I know Shep, he won't go and see them until he's certain that no one's watching him, you know? He hates all of that attention.' Kohén's finger slipped under the edge of my toga as it outlined a heart, and because I wasn't in the mood to let it feel good, I began to tear the brush through my hair more vigorously, shaking it off.

'Kohl's one of the do-gooders, of course...' Kohén sighed as he lent back against my bed head, looking dejected and fiddling with the cuffs of his shirt now that I'd made it clear that I wasn't in the mood to be touched. 'Kohl and Amelia-Rose... they're quite the pair now. Practically inseparable.'

What? Kohl and Amelia-Rose? No! Why?

I dropped the brush and twisted to gape at him, and Kohén smiled a smile that told me that he knew he had me. 'Oh... haven't I mentioned that either?' I shook my head, frowning at him, and Kohén shrugged, trying to look nonchalant. 'I don't know how he can tolerate her harping on, or she his sulking- but yeah, Kohl and Amelia-Rose have been as thick as thieves for past few days. I guess they haven't gotten their way on other matters lately, so they've taken up the Banished cause instead... waxing on and on about the value of human kindness and charity and all of that and making themselves ringleaders... it's so *weird*. I get that it's easy to bond with people when you have a cause in mind... but Amelia-Rose Choir *isn't* people. I don't think a lot of Kohl right now, but even *I* know he can do better than her.'

I turned away from him again, fiddling with my hair to hide the fact that I wanted to wring them together and pace. I was jealous that Kohl was spending so much time with a girl that wasn't me, but on the other side of that coin, I was irritated with myself for being jealous of a girl I didn't like the sound of- on behalf of a boy that I had no right to get jealous over. *She-who-would-not-be-named* was sure to be laughing at the emotional swamp that I was currently trying to navigate a path through!

'They're really out of control too,' Kohén went on, watching my fingers weaving my hair with interest. 'I mean, Kohl's always tried to be the champion of the underdogs, but Karol apparently had to talk him out of going out there to shake hands with these people today, and that's just crazy because the Banished guys that seem to be the ringleaders have already threatened to kidnap someone of import if their demands aren't met.' My mouth popped open and Kohén nodded. 'Mother practically had a stroke when she heard about *that*, but although Kohl's never put much stock in mother's opinion, he's disrespecting our father now too. Can you believe that he practically ordered father to open the gates and let the huddled masses in before they freeze to death? And Amelia-Rose actually tried to open the gate herself! And the only reason why they backed off was because Shep Choir stepped in and reminded his daughter that he hadn't raised to her to act so irresponsibly or disrespectfully, and promised to pack up their things and leave Arcadia tonight if she continued to make a nuisance of herself. It's crazy! All of this fuss over a bunch of heathens.'

I pursed my lips, irritated with Kohén for the mocking tone of voice he'd used when he'd said: *Huddled masses...* like people freezing in the northern winter were nothing but a big joke to him! And Heathens- that was one of his mother's surly words- since when had Kohén started emoting her? I wanted to break my silence just to point out that Kohl would never say anything so cruel *or* use the word Heathens, but I knew that doing so would only make Kohén resent him more, and the last thing I needed to do was provoke Kohén further on the subject of his brother.

Kohén tickled beneath the clasp of my necklace. 'Anyway, they've settled down a bit since Shep went off at them, but I know they're secretly proud of the fuss they've made and the attention they've brought to the plight of the poor nomads. A lot of people are being charmed by the sight of two noble kids ladling soup into cups to those on the other side of the fence- but anyone smart enough to know it's all an act is getting incredibly irritated by it- father and Atticus included. And what does Kohl think he's going to accomplish anyway? Atticus is going to make him a General and Kohl's apparently over the moon about that, but a General's primary responsibility is to keep the outlaws under control- not to get them all worked up and not to coddle them when they misbehave! I tell you... if Kohl doesn't pull it together soon, he's going to be sailing right back into the Corps on Sunday as an underling, not a bloody leader.' He shook his head. 'Actually, I honestly don't know why Atticus hasn't rescinded his offer already. I get that the whole rain thing will help with the farming industry but when it comes to Kohl's temper, when it rains it *pours*. I guess mother's much better at promoting her son when I'm not around than I thought, for Atticus to be going out on such an unstable limb for him.'

I turned my face away, pretending to be inspecting my loose when really, I just needed to hide what I knew would be my pink cheeks. I knew why Atticus hadn't retracted his offer to Kohl yet- because of *me*. Yes, he'd obviously locked me in via the necklace now that Kohén and I were a package deal, so there really was no chance that I'd get to run off to Yael... but he obviously feared that I'd do as I threatened and spend my time in Pacifica sunbathing instead of helping him build an empire, so he was keeping his promise to keep Kohl on a pedestal in the hopes that it would foster good feelings between us. It did... but I sort of wished that Kohl would get his act together. I wanted him earning the respect of men like Atticus, not their frustration! Like Kohl, I had a soft spot for the underdogs of the world, and I'd be quick to hand anyone cold and hungry hot soup... but I'd certainly think twice- perhaps fifteen times- before I contemplated letting *any* of them inside the castle's walls... and I would never ever embarrass myself or my father the monarch by ordering him to do so in front of other people! The discarded third-born children and adulterous women that were stuck on the other side of that fence pulled on my heartstrings of course, but Arcadia didn't throw people out without just cause, so the 'huddled masses' that Kohl was trying to accommodate were likely full of murderers, rapists and thieves, *not* martyrs. And any one of them could pull Kohl into the electrified portions of that fence in a heartbeat if they thought they could get something out of doing so, even if it *was* just his coat.

Actually Arcadia doesn't throw out third-born children either- they take them in like they took me in. So if there are any innocents on the other side of that fence, then it's because they made a poor decision, or because whoever is responsible for them made several of them. They need help, certainly... but should they be allowed to re-join society because it's cold out? Not necessarily. Kohl should be doing more thinking, and less demanding! And he shouldn't be doing anything within an inch of this Amelia-Rose person! She who wants Companions herded up and put into the Corps like criminals!

'It's definitely suspicious, and it's not like Atticus to tolerate a loose cannon swinging about. I swear, if I hadn't noticed the chemistry between him and Jovi, I'd assume that mother was fucking him to buy Kohl a military career.'

I flinched before darting my eyes at Kohén and he snorted. 'What? You didn't know?' I nodded and then pointed to him and he waved a hand at me. 'I conduct electricity, remember? Which means that I pick up on charges between others- and Jovi and Atticus are downright uncomfortable to be around sometimes.' I laughed gently and soundlessly and he perked up a little, resting his elbows on his knees before leaning over to gently turn my face to the side, eyeing my hair. Only then did I realise that I'd started fishtail-braiding it. 'Nice. I've always wondered how that's done. Anyway... for better or for worse, Amelia-Rose and Kohl have barricaded themselves away in the kitchen to cook huge batches of soup for like, three hours a day- but only when there are no official events on, of course.' Kohén shifted, sitting so that his legs were open on either side of mine and then took my hair from my hands and to my surprise, began to twist the strands together while wearing a thoughtful, focused expression. 'They're eager to help the homeless, but not so eager that they'd pass up on a single wine tasting or miss the opportunity to have their portraits painted in the common during the markets, you know? It's all so... choreographed.' I nodded, making a face because that was exactly how it sounded to me too and trying to ignore how good he smelled. 'But hey... whatever keeps her out of my hair and him out of father's good graces...' Kohén kissed my shoulder, tugged on my braid and whispered. 'You're not jealous, are you? Of the fact that Kohl is going out of his way to spend time with another girl?'

I swallowed hard. I was of course, but I shook my head no, and then backed it with an eye-roll to make it a bit more convincing.

'Good,' Kohén went back to braiding my hair, 'because I have a feeling that that's what he wants- for me to report back his antics to you until your skin is as green as his was when he saw us together, which is ridiculous because Amelia-Rose isn't in your league- not even with all of her money and life experience.'

I had a feeling that there was a lot more to Kohl's new friendship with Amelia-Rose than a strategic move to make me jealous or as a means to make a martyr of himself, because he was far too kind a person to use anyone for personal gain... but I didn't know what he was trying to accomplish by forming an alliance with her and I didn't want to know, so I merely shrugged, and Kohén chuckled. I twisted to raise an eyebrow at him, silently demanding to know what was so funny, and he reached up to cup my cheek while gazing adoringly into my eyes.

'Your voice- or lack thereof... why do I get a feeling that it must be as convenient for you during this time in our lives, as it is *in*convenient for me?' He brushed my hair over my ear as I blushed furiously. 'Oh, don't think I'm not aware of how relieved you must be to have a genuine excuse to remain silent on several hundred subjects right now, my sweet little swan. I mean, I know it must be torture for you to have to keep all of the nasty things you'd like to say to me to yourself while you're so angry with me as well... but we both know that Kohl's chances of getting back to Pacifica without me beating him to a bloody pulp increase with every day that passes by, without you having the ability to point out how superior you think he is, compared to me, don't we?' I snorted twice gently out of my nose in a subtle laugh that I almost couldn't curtail, but Kohén chuckled, grabbed me by the back of the hair and pulled my face up against his so that he could growl gently and bite on my lower lip. 'Cheeky girl... if you weren't so unwell I'd prove just how superior I am to him right now, by bending you over this bedhead, and fucking you so hard and fast that I'd pound every thought of him out of your head forever.' I gasped as the mental imagery assailed me and made my sex cramp up in anticipation of such violent passion- the kind that would dull my thoughts much more quickly than the wine would- but Kohén sighed and disentangled himself, leaning over me to pull a sack off the floor, which he deposited on my lap. 'But I promised Cherry that I would not so here... I offer a consolation prize. Though it may not prove me to be superior to Kohl in your eyes, it may prove me to be as thoughtful.'

Practically panting and overwhelmed with disappointment now that he'd heated me to my very core but was making no move to put the fire out, I poked open the sack automatically, raising my eyebrows when I saw a stack of books within. He'd brought me books? I looked up at him and was debating whether or not to speak at last just so that I could tell him that I'd much prefer the first thing he'd suggested, but Kohén smiled.

'I told some of your friends that I was going to go to the library to try and find something that you hadn't read already to help you pass time while you convalesce, and when I suggested it, your friends offered to supply you of a collection of the ones they'd brought with them,' Kohén said, tapping on the bag. 'There's a Pacifican History book in there from Atticus, a few romances from Ora, one about meditation from Lette, and an adventure book from my uncle, Ewan.' He smiled crookedly. 'Karol and mother said they'd see if they had anything for you too, but I told them that I'd be checking them very carefully for private correspondence hidden within, and strangely enough, they opted not to trouble themselves by lending you books after all. Funny, isn't it?'

I gave him a withering look, reached into my bedside table and produced a notepad and pencil. He watched with interest while I wrote down: *'Do you honestly still suspect that I'd take up an offer to correspond with anyone behind your back, given how much is on the line?'* Kohén sighed before I'd finished writing and said:

'No actually I don't- but I wouldn't put it past *them*. Mother's getting angrier and angrier with every day that passes without me bringing you out of the harem, and Karol practically isn't talking to me- which suits me just fine. As far as I'm concerned, both of my brothers can go fuck themselves for trying to come between us anyway. Mother too.'

I frowned, and then wrote: *'Is there nothing that can be done to ease tensions between you all? It can't look good for the entire royal family to be giving each other the cold shoulder at a time like this.'* Of course I was hoping that their family dramas were bringing heat upon them and the Given caste, but he didn't have to know that!

Kohén snorted. 'Short of turning back time? No. But our strife isn't as obvious as you'd think. After all, mother's devotion to her other two sons is as rock solid as it always has been, Kohl and I are being incredibly civil towards one another in public despite how we feel about each other in private, and now that I am getting back out there and joining in on the celebrations again, father is pleased with me for handling all of these crises in a circumspect manner. He's even happy with Karol's birthday wish now that he's seen how it has won the public over without putting him out too much.'

I'll bet he is! I thought snidely, knowing how freaked Elijah had been at the prospect of having to buy my allegiance to Arcadia after one of his sons had released me, because his other son had failed to seduce me. Kohén hadn't just kept me duty-bound to Arcadia, but he'd done it without spending a cent, and had managed to make it look like I'd sacrificed my freedom for love of a Barachiel. How romantic!

'And how does he feel about Kohl?' I wrote. *'Aside from the issue with the Banished, I mean?'*

Kohén shrugged. 'He's pretty much forgiven him for developing a crush on you and for the scene he made when we burst his bubble on Tuesday night... but only because he believes that it was a passing fancy, and because he knows that Kohl has not been groomed to keep his composure in the face of drama, as I have. He, mother and Karol do not know that you cared for Kohl back, or that he encouraged you to betray me with him, and so long as they go on believing that, all of this will eventually blow over.' He lifted my chin and looked into my eyes, and I hoped he couldn't see my panic in them. No, Karol didn't know that I'd had feelings for Kohl, and neither did Elijah- but *Constance* did, and that was precisely what was allowing her to maintain her anger. 'But that is only if you and Kohl hold your tongues about all of the other stuff that went on, and agree to leave whatever feelings and hopes you had for one another in the past, understood? Kelia was the only person that had enough inside knowledge on these sordid matters to pose a serious threat to us from the outside, and we need to keep it that way. One confession from you, Kohl or myself to anyone that doesn't have as much to lose as we do could get us all disinherited, banished or killed- depending on the intensity of the confession. Admitting that you wrote Kohl could get you in hot water, and I suppose *that* we could write off as a harmless crush... but admitting the truth to Kelia's demise?' He shuddered. 'We'd all be done for- even you for having witnessed it, because not speaking the truth about what happened makes you as much of a criminal according to Arcadian laws as if you'd killed her yourself.'

I cringed. Perhaps there was a part of me that sort of hoped that all of our secrets would be revealed, because not having to keep them anymore would be a relief and could unlock a door that might see me thrown out of Eden and out of Kohén's reach and Kohl's accountability for it. But no, I wouldn't go down for Kelia's murder, and I didn't even want Kohén to be held responsible for it. That knowledge made something inside me wither. When had been rendered a Companion gone from being to my worst-case scenario, to my best-case one?

Um... when you met Satan, maybe, and realised that Hell wasn't just a hypothetical state of mind or being- but a physical location that she's eager to suck you into?

'Exactly,' Kohén said. 'Everything else I could deal with, but not that, which is why I'm not giving mother a hard time about parading Kohl around like a prized trophy, or teasing him too much for martyring himself at Amelia-Rose's side. It's a struggle to keep my temper and the sparks that can come with it in check, but that kid needs something else to look forward to or live for- something that has nothing to do with you, because so long as there's a chance that he will be overcome enough by sadness to confess everything to someone else, there's a chance that all of us could end up on the other side of that fence, you know?'

I nodded, because I did. *'Yes,'* I wrote quickly, squinting and struggling to make my handwriting legible given how drunk I was. *'I'd wipe the last five years from his mind, if I could, if only to bring him peace and end his suffering.'*

'I could,' Kohén gave me a crooked smile. 'Say the word, and I'll put him into a coma or in the very least- hurt him enough to give him short-term memory loss.' I gave Kohén a foul look and he chuckled. 'Yeah okay, okay… I'll behave. Besides- we only have to wait two more days until the party ends and he goes home now. I know it'll take a lot to get over you, but the distance and time will help, I'm sure of it. Karol wouldn't shut up about letting you out of there all of yesterday, but he's been plastered to Ora a lot, so there's only so much he can say on the matter without making his crush obvious too, you know? It would be so much easier if Kohl actually developed feelings for that Choir bitch, but who *could*?'

I snorted and wrote: *'Too bad that Kohl doesn't have a harem of his own, hmm? Certainly kept your mind off me for a while there.'*

It was Kohén's turn to scowl. 'It did nothing of the sort and you damn well know it, Larkin! How many times do I have to remind you of that fact? I've had sex and experienced release with someone that wasn't you ONCE, my love- ONCE! Which is exactly how many times you would have been unfaithful to me, had it truly been Kohl in that corridor on Tuesday, rather than I!'

My stomach flipped but I scribbled furiously: *'Actually no, I'd still be a virgin because Kohl wouldn't have taken advantage of me like that- and you know it.'*

Kohén read the words and then looked at me, raising an eyebrow. 'Do you actually believe that?'

I realised that no, I didn't, the moment I saw Kohén's eyes fill with scepticism. Not just because Kohén understood male insatiability better than I did- but because Kohl had already confessed to me that he probably wouldn't have made it past my sixteenth birthday without taking me either, so I truly did know better.

But before I could write an apology, Kohén waved my hand away from the page. 'Don't bother, Larkin. I don't want you to rush to his defence, even if I do get a bit of a kick out of knowing how wrong you have us both. I'll let you go on believing that he is as pious as you both believe, and allow you to treat me like the only monster within Eden's walls because-' I yanked him back to me by the collar of his white shirt and smushed my mouth against his, silencing him while desperately trying to soothe him. He pulled back and attempted to wrestle my hands off his collar. 'Don't,' he said gruffly, though his eyes were already darkening with lust. 'I've told you that I need more from you than this, and until you believe me…' he pushed me gently back down on the bed and adjusted himself. 'Read, Larkin. Read, heal… and believe what you will. Time is all that will prove to you that you have overestimated him and underestimated me, but luckily for us both- we have a lot of that now.' He straightened his collar and smoothed his hair. 'Now if you'll excuse me, I think I'm going to sleep in my own room tonight. I trust myself to keep my hands off you while I am awake, but not in my slumber.' he flickered his eyes over my notebook again and scowled. 'Although right now, I kind of want to wring your neck more than I want to do anything else.'

He was leaving me? I froze with my hand at my mouth, and although Kohén shot a longing look my way, he turned his shoulder and opened my door. 'Good night, little bird. Sleep peacefully in your cage unmolested, and I shall see you in the morning, hopefully in better spirits for not having been forced to tolerate your captor's presence all night long.'

'Please don't go!' I whispered hoarsely, but not quickly enough. The door clicked shut between us, and though I knew that Kohén had left me only to resist temptation and to make a point, the fact of the matter was that I'd never felt more like a whore than I had in that moment, to be left in my harem room alone with my thoughtlessness, ingratitude- and the stack full of books that I'd not thanked him for.

9.

I slept restlessly and with a heavy heart on Thursday night, regretting pretty much every minute of my life except for the ones I'd spent playing soccer with Kohén as a child, but the alcohol in my bloodstream was strong enough to render me unconscious somewhere around two a.m., and when I woke up in the morning, I was amazed to see that although Kohén had kept his word to stay out of my bed, he'd let himself back into my chamber, and was sleeping curled up on my bearskin rug in front of the fire like a faithful dog. That sight made me smile, not just as I reflected on the jokes that Kohl, Emmerly and I had made on the night of the formal banquet regarding Kohén's faithfulness to me (in matters of the heart, at least), but because there was an innocent beauty to his peaceful features now that was so much more beguiling due to the fact that he was sound asleep and for once, not trying to intentionally win me over. The curve of his cheekbone, the strong line of his jaw, his full, flushed lips, his thick black lashes- all of it detailing his coppery skin... he truly was divine, half an Indian Brave and half a Roman God, and my lips ached to brush against the smooth, sweet skin behind his ear against his hairline where he always smelled so good.

I'd fallen asleep without touching the sack of books, and now I crawled off the bed and over to Kohén, taking the notepad with me, knowing that I had to make him forget the fight we'd had the night before and convince him of my loyalty to him over Kohl before he reverted to being violently paranoid again. He stirred when I straddled his hips and rolled him gently onto his back, smiling in his sleep and whispering my name, but his eyes did not open until I kissed him gently behind his ear and then bent to inhale his freshly-washed and still neatly barbered black hair.

'Lark?' Kohén asked, blinking slowly as he awoke, and I felt something else stir- something that was pressed into my pelvic bone. 'What's going on? Why are we...?' He looked around and then made a face. 'Right, I forgot. I snuck in here when I couldn't sleep, didn't I?' I shrugged. I didn't know when he'd come in, but I was glad that he had because it made me feel less like a discarded sex worker, so I softened that shrug with a smile. Kohén wrinkled up his nose. 'How embarrassing. Guess it's pretty clear which is the girl in this relationship, hey?'

I smiled, but then thought it over and wrote on my notepad: 'Is it?'

'Yeah well, I'm the emotional one, and you're the one that keeps trying to push me away because she has more important things to do than be in love.'

'That shouldn't be the defining line between being a woman or a man, should it? The fact that you're a die-hard romantic is the one thing that you have left going for us, as far as I am concerned. Without that trait, I would have tied you to a tree and thrown a jar of wasps at you last year!' I showed him the page and he rolled his eyes.

'Gee, thanks. I feel so much better about sleeping on your floor like the bitch that I am now.' He looked around, asking with a wry expression; 'Where are your slippers? Shall I fetch them using my teeth?'

I smirked, then wrote: 'I'll bet I can make you feel better.'

Kohén raised an eyebrow. 'What are the stakes? Because it would take me a hell of a lot to make me feel better about anything right now.'

I wrote: 'If I win... I want to see your bedroom.'

Kohén's eyebrows shot up. 'What? Why?'

It was a point that had been bugging me for years, and as I'd been trying to sleep the night before, I'd realised that it was bugging me even more now that we'd been intimate. I had to stay in Eden- I had no choice- and *that* meant that I'd have to put up with being intimate with Kohén for God knew how long? It was going to be a miserable experience on many levels, but for some reason, I knew I'd feel better about one of those levels, if at least *one* door was unlocked between us, however briefly.

So I wrote: *'In books, best friends hang out in each other's bedrooms. Though you've been in mine plenty, all we've done in here is, well... things that have ruined our friendship. If you want to salvage any of it, then I'm gonna need to be let into your life the way you've forced yourself into mine, and seeing your bedroom will make me feel better. Then, next time you stomp off and leave me here so that you can sulk in there, at least I will be able to imagine what you're doing, and where you are.'* I flipped the page around and Kohén read it, eyebrows shooting up.

'That's a big ask, Larkin. For starters, it's not safe for you to leave this room and secondly, you're not technically allowed into our wing.' I glared at him and he cringed, holding up his hands. 'Okay, okay... we have a deal. I don't know when I'll be able to get you in there, but if you can cheer me up now, I'll do it.'

I smiled, put the book on the end of my bed and then slowly began to lift my nightgown over my head. I heard Kohén's breathing hitch as I bared my breasts to his gaze, but after I tossed it off, he sighed and said: 'That's it? They're the most beautiful breasts that God has ever created Larkin... but it's my ego that's aching right now, not *that*.' He frowned and shifted beneath me, and I felt him stiffening a little more. 'Okay that's gonna be aching in about thirty seconds, but you're only compounding my troubles, not alleviating them!' I reached for the notebook on my bed and wrote on the page before holding back to him:

'I was trying to demonstrate which of us is the girl, and which of us is the man.' I wriggled on his hips, and his eyes rolled back into his head. *'Don't the sight of my breasts remind you of who is who?'*

Kohén grunted and bucked beneath me. 'Point taken, but still... it doesn't help me shake the feeling that if I hadn't acted quickly, you would have done this willingly for Kohl someday- not for me just because you feel as though you don't have a choice in the matter.' He pouted, and it was disarming.

I bit my lip, thought it over and then leaned down, touching lips against his in a kiss that was soft at first, but quickly grew tentative and breathless. And as I kissed him I caught his hand and pressed it not onto my breast but my heart so that he could feel how it was pounding, before steering it down into my panties, so he could feel how they were soaking.

'Oh sweet Jesus…' Kohén breathed, straining up off the floor to kiss me back. He pulled on my braid and leaned back to look into my eyes. 'You *want* me?'

I leaned over and scribbled on the paper while he caressed my lower back, and held it up so he could see me printing: *'I've made my peace with the fact that Kohl and I will never go to bed together already, believe it or not. Perhaps that is spurned by concern for him, I don't know… but I do know that I've gone only one day without making love to you, and I'm certain that I won't last another. If you wanted to punish me for hurting you- it has been done. Please Kohén… forgive me? And take me because I cannot beg for it without a voice!'*

Kohén's eyes sparked, turning neon blue as he wrenched me off the floor and pulled me to my feet before making a beeline for my closet. I had no idea what he was doing, but when he returned from my closet he had a toga in his hands- and a very prominent erection in his silk night slacks. 'Put this on- now!' he hissed, glancing at the clock on the wall. 'We have minutes to make this happen, possibly less before…'

Before…? I gave him a confused look, but he huffed and looped the open end of the toga over my head before yanking it down, holding out the single side strap so that I could get my hand in.

'Before the castle wakes up, and catches us!' he said, and I felt my breath rush out of me. We were leaving the harem?

'Only if you act fast!' Kohén said, and that was all it took to get my heart pounding, my mind racing- and my feet moving.

*

Leaving the harem stressed me out more than I cared to acknowledge, and the sight of the burly and shocked-looking guard that was standing by the exterior door startled me (I'd never seen anyone so big!) but there was no time to stop and gape, because Kohén's fear of what might become of me if I left the harem had become my own. What if I ran into Constance, or Karol? What if she caused a scene? What if one of the guests called out to me, drawing everyone's attention to the fact that the prized, grief-stricken whore was finally out and about? They'd have questions for me and I wouldn't know how to answer them, even if I *did* decide to speak.

'I haven't the time to explain,' Kohén said quickly as we passed the guard. 'But no one aside from father, Resonah and Rosina are permitted in while we are gone, and no one is to know that we have left Larkin's room, all right?' The guard nodded and shot me a quizzical look, but Kohén was already pulling me away and leading me up the stairs to our right, which I already knew led up to his family's wing because I had sneaked up there once before on the day after my sixteenth birthday.

Remembering how scared I'd been when I'd gone to make that deal with Karol that morning- and how much of the suffering I'd experienced since as a result of that deal since- made me feel sick, but the castle was still dark enough to suggest that it wasn't yet five a.m., and so I knew that there was a good chance that no one was going to see us at all, which made it easier to breathe. I was still full of anxiety as Kohén turned his winged ring in the locked door, but to my relief, the interior hall of the royal wing was as dark and silent as the exterior hall had been. I pretended to look around me with wide, awed eyes as though I'd never seen any of this before, but when Kohén quickly beckoned me into the very first door on the left after using his ring to unlock it again, my feigned awe became genuine awe, because I was in Kohén Barachiel's bedroom at long last- and it was nothing like how I'd expected it to be.

'I apologise for the mess...' Kohén whispered, taking my hand as he led me into the centre of his room. 'I did not expect a visitor- least of all- one as important as you, so it's still in the state I left it in when I came back to your room this morning.'

I snorted, for the mess he'd referenced was non-existent. I remembered that Karol's study had been in disarray that time I'd visited him, with books and luggage and papers tossed about, but Kohén's room was spacious and uncluttered, and the colour palette that he'd chosen to decorate it in made the room seem more vibrant than the rest of the castle did. Several things in there caught my eye immediately, but it was the stained glass window above his bed that snared my attention. It was the exact width and length of the massive bed beneath it, and four thick brown posts extended from all four corners of the bed to meet the corners of the window, making the mural above a canopy of sorts even though there weren't any drapes to complete the look. It was stunning, and I envied Kohén for growing up with a bed that would allow him to experience every one of the sky's moods like that without having to go outside.

I want a bed like that one day! I thought, soul lifting in response to the beauty. *But no glass! Just the open sky above me!*

The dull morning light glowed gently through that window from above, casting green prisms over his navy-blue comforter and the floor, which was carpeted in that same navy blue. His featured colour should have given the room a dark, shadowy and melancholy vibe, and yet he had a crisp white fur rug in the centre of it all, and white linen sheets and cushion covers peeking out from beneath all of that blue, which set it off crisply. He'd used a second contrasting colour- a bright sea-glass green- here and there in the trims and curtains and a few knick-knacks, and because his massive bed, roll top desk and chaise lounge were all crafted from a dark, heavy timber, I couldn't help but conjure up images of an old ship ploughing through a bright ocean.

It was lovely- too elegant to be thought of as a boy's room, but too bright and cheerful to belong to a grown man, and I thought it captured him perfectly. And as I'd always assumed, being allowed in there made me feel less like an accessory to his life, and more of a part of it. I supposed that was why Companions were never allowed in to their master's chambers- for it gave us a false sense of belonging that could prove to be problematic for their future brides.

But Kohén *wanted* me to feel as though I were the focal point of his life and not a hand-maiden, and although I'd been rebelling against that for so many years now for fear that it would raise my hopes for a future with him to a level that it would never be able to live up to, I'd decided in the middle of the night to let that intimacy back in, if he'd still allow it. What was the harm? My hopes had already been dashed- might as well allow myself to go on believing that he was mine and mine alone for as long as I could if that inspired him to go on treating me like a princess rather than a slave. It wasn't him I'd do it for, but *me.*

Sooner or later our bubble would be burst and he'd be forced to take a bride and I'd either be released as a common prostitute or kept on as his side-piece, and that was going to hurt me if I allowed myself to feel like a lover now. But if I treated him like a lover too- adored him, doted on him and made his body bend to my will then hopefully, it would hurt *him* more. Hell, maybe, it'd hurt him enough to put an end to the Given caste forever, to spare his own future son the same anguish.

Tell yourself that... the thought sneaked into my head unbidden. *You know, if it helps you sleep at night when you don't have another one of those pills.*

Kohén released my hand to go turn on a lamp by his bed, which had an emerald and royal blue stained glass shade over it that was a replica of an old-time globe, and when it began to glow, I saw that though all of his walls had been painted that same dark blue with white trim, the one across from his desk and behind his bed had been painted with a mural of white-watered waves, similar to those depicted in the old-time Japanese art. Stunned by its beauty and the intricate detail, and free to do as I pleased as Kohén hurried to straighten up his comforter and pillows, I moved to the wall and touched my fingertips to it, certain that I could feel those waves rolling beneath my hand.

'I had ocean envy growing up,' Kohén said softly, and then came up beside me, pointing to his surfboard in the corner. 'Strange isn't it? Almost like the wrong twin was born second. Were it not for your presence here, I think I could have been okay with Kohl's lot in life, you know?'

Tears stung my eyes- he had no idea how right he was, or how close he'd come to being the prince sent to Pacifica, and he could never know. To distract myself from that painful secret, I moved to look more closely at the few books lined up on the top shelf of his open desk, but that was when I noticed the picture frames on the opposite wall. Curious to see which moments of his life he'd chosen to keep on display, I moved towards them- and promptly froze when I saw that the first one was a picture of *us*.

Oh my gosh! How does he have this?

Kohén and I couldn't have been more than six in the picture, but we were sitting on a two-person swing, our shoulders pressing together- our heads thrown back with laughter, and it was so beautiful that the tears in my eyes began to form little pools that I could barely see through. I wasn't pretty in that photo- I looked pale and scrawny, like a plucked chicken, and yet Kohén had wanted to look at it every day anyway. How curious!

'Um… yeah…' Kohén cleared his throat. 'Once again, I didn't know you'd be coming up here so… I'm embarrassed.' He snorted softly as I moved from the first photo to the second- one that had been captured of he and I hiding under the pristine white skirt of a table at a ball-laughing again as we spied on the adults from our little hidey-hole. We were older then, possibly ten, and because I'd been forbidden from going in, Kohén had had to sneak me in so that we could eat some of Constance's birthday cake. We thought we'd been so clever, but evidently at least one adult had seen us- the photographer- and had captured the moment perfectly in black and white with shades of grey.

There were more photos than that- photos that spanned across the width of the wall, artfully arranged in matching dark timber frames around the fireplace that documented our friendship from the beginning, right up until our trip to Pacifica. The most recent one was of us posed on either side of his surfboard, and it was the only posed photograph in the whole lot. In it we looked carefree and happy and I had to admit, pretty damn good together, but resting on the ground beneath that photo was a whole stack of frames that had been turned around to face the wall, and they caught my attention immediately- especially when I realised that there were empty picture hooks jutting out from the walls between the photos of Kohén and I. Were these pictures of him and the other Companions? Had he taken them down since he'd released them? My heart sank. I knelt to peer at one, but only caught a glimpse of two identical, gappy Barachiel smiles before Kohén pulled me back up to my feet.

'Don't turn those over, please?' he asked, sounding choked up. 'I can't bear to look at them Larkin- that's why they're there. I... I took them down after...'

After you took my virginity, fearing that Kohl had gotten there first? Oh God! Oh... poor Kohl... he's been written out of the story of Kohén's childhood, just as that duchess was written out of Cadence Verity's book! I felt a lump form in my throat, but when I turned to look at Kohén, the anguish in his eyes was so clear that my empathy swished his way instead.

'He knew, you know?' he stared forlornly at the stack of discarded photographs. 'He knew that I loved you more than anyone else did- he *knew* that my life would become meaningless if I lost you… and yet he tried to take you anyway. I…' he screwed up his face and looked away. 'I haven't given up on our bond because I don't love him anymore- I've done it because… because by taking you- he proved that *he'd* stopped loving *me*.' Kohén lifted his knuckle to his eyes and wiped at a tear. 'I know you think I'm heartless for denying him forgiveness and threatening his life… But Lark, when I read his letters, promising you things that I could not, and asking for the only thing I've ever wanted in the world- *your love*- he sank a knife not only into my back, but into my heart from behind.' He waved his hand at the pictures. 'He killed me. My own twin *killed* me. And now I cannot look at him without remembering that.'

I pressed my hand to Kohén's arm, trying to get him to turn to look at me so that I could shake my head and communicate the fact that Kohl had been more loyal to him than he realised, but Kohén shook his head and twisted away, making a hacking cough sound that he'd obviously intended to be a laugh at he wiped at more tears.

'I read the first letter, Larkin! After he left here that first time… one day he knew you for, Lark- one fucking *day*! That was all it took for him to strike! So don't tell me what *I* don't see-' he grabbed my arm roughly and walked me closer to the wall, forcing me to stare at the photos. 'Look at what he blinded *you* to!'

I looked at the photos through rivers of tears. The most moving one was of us sitting in 'our' tree when we'd been thirteen- just after I'd learned about the role that I was to play in his life, deep in conversation about something, and the most beautiful one was of us racing after a soccer ball. I'd begun to blossom by then, even though I'd only been about fourteen, and although I hadn't seen it then- I could see it now in the way my long fair hair gleamed in the sun. And judging by the look on Kohén's face in the picture, he'd seen it too. I was the one that had been blinded to the depth of his affection for me, just as he'd said. I didn't think it was

Kohl's fault, but I couldn't help but feel like it hadn't been Kohén's either.

'I love you, and I always have,' Kohén whispered, wrapping his arms around my waist and resting his chin on my shoulder. 'I didn't want you to be my Companion, Larkin, but he left me no choice, so I will take it, if that's the only way I get to have you!' I felt his hot tears on my shoulders. 'I know that's selfish, and I will burn in Hell for all eternity for it and gladly if it means that I get to hold you like this for the rest of my life first. I do not belong to my country or my parents, my twin *or* my God, little swan- I belong to *you*. How can you look upon that wall, and think that you are the one trapped when it is I that has been on my knees since the first moment we met- begging for you to love me?'

Tears were streaming down my face, and the pressure in my throat was insane. I was grateful that I had to go on pretending to be speechless, because I knew that only that excuse was standing between me and him- and me admitting that I loved him too in that moment. Because I did. Heaven help me- I loved him more than I could barely stand. I loved him more than I hated him.

I loved him more than I loved myself. I just wasn't sure if that meant anything, seeing as how much I currently loathed myself.

I sniffled, and Kohén's face lifted. 'I'm sorry,' he whispered. 'I know you hate it when I make such promises to you, and in light of how many I've broken of late, it's foolish for me to believe that you'd take me at my word now. But I have a bad habit of speaking my heart when it comes to you, don't I? And having you in here... Larkin this is where you belong, and I will do everything in my power to see your head rest upon my pillow as my wife one day, and if you don't believe that-'

I whirled in his arms and pressed my mouth against his. I didn't believe it, but I desperately wanted to.

10.

Kohén moaned softly and wrapped his arms around me, kissing me back with salty, lush lips. I moved my hands to unlace Kohén's slacks, knowing that coming together in here would be not only cathartic but amazing, but Kohén shook his head gently, batted my hand away and then placed it back on his shoulder.

'No...' he whispered huskily, scooping me up in his arms and carrying me back towards his bed. 'There's something else I'd much rather do in here- something I've dreamed of for as long as I can remember...' he kissed me again and then began to sink onto the bed, twisting as he did until I was lying on the mattress on my back, with him leaning down to kiss me from above. My eyes fluttered open, curious to see where he was going with this (and a little scared to think of what nasty things he'd imagined doing to me with so much time to plan ahead) but Kohén just kept on kissing me, slowly and sweetly, sighing into my mouth and moaning when I kissed him back. His kisses were lovely, and I loved the way my scalp tickled when he tugged the fastener out of my hair and began to work free the braid we'd woven together the night before... but soon enough my hair was out and we were still just kissing while my body was throbbing all over for need of his intrusion, so I started to worry that he'd forgotten that we didn't have long up here, and moved to unlace his slacks again. Kohén was hard against my hip and I moaned in need, but he chuckled, fished my hand out of his waistband before I could stroke his silken skin and laced his fingers between mine- pinning my hand back to the bed and squeezing it gently.

'Stop trying to undress me,' he scolded me gently. 'Can't you see that *this* is my ultimate fantasy? Kissing you! And I won't have you ruin it with your wanton ways!' My eyes and mouth popped open with shock but he chuckled again and nuzzled my nose with his. 'Seriously... I was forced to... well, to do that thing in a bit of a rush the first time, and every time I look at you, I get so excited that I end up rushing again.' He twisted his lips gently against mine but then leaned down to chastely kiss my chin, then my collarbone. 'But when I imagined making love to you, I imagined it happening after months and months of doing other stuff first, you know? Kissing you... courting you... taking you up to my bedroom so that we could hold hands and flirt and inch closer and...' he moaned and kissed me again, rolling over on top of me a little more so that he could take my other hand, and my heart skipped a beat, tripping some kind of wire and loosing what felt like a million butterflies into the pit of my tummy. 'Can we do that?' he whispered, breaking contact with our lips just long enough to ask: 'Can we start over, Larkin? Your hair... you look almost as exactly as you did that night of the ball, when things truly began to go off course with us, and I'd like a second chance to get them on course again. I mean, I still feel like a virgin every time you touch me so... can't we pretend that we are, and build up to... to doing that other stuff?' He fanned my hair out using his fingers. 'Not as a master and slave... but as two best friends who know they're meant to be together?'

My lips parted in surprise. *Can you?* I thought, incredulous, and he smiled angelically- an illusion made all the more authentic-looking due to the gentle morning light filtering through the stained glass above him. *Can you actually have me, without having me?*

'Of course I could,' Kohén answered my silent question, robbing me of my breath as I realised just how many times he'd already done that- read my mind perfectly. 'If you would like that too, I... you *know* I'd give you anything you asked for!' he cupped my face and began kissing it all over, and the butterflies in my tummy flapped their wings. I moaned and re-directed his lips to mine and then suddenly we were kissing deeply and breathlessly. My hands reached up and caressed Kohén's smooth, muscular biceps, and he slipped one arm beneath my head to cradle my neck while his other reached around and pulled my face more forcefully up to his. It only took a moment or two for my heart to stop pounding with joy and start pounding with lust, and I felt Kohén grind his erection against my thigh quite a few times to take the edge off for himself as well, and yet every time I moved to caress him again- to let him know that I was perfectly happy to do everything that came naturally to us now that he'd gone and gotten me hooked on it- Kohén would growl and press my hand somewhere else- against his face, his chest, his own... and soon enough I was certain that the pressure building up inside me would explode.

When it got to the point that I simply couldn't take the wanting any more, I rolled swiftly, getting myself on top of him and rocking myself against him. He opened his mouth to say no but I leaned down and kissed him hard, catching both of his hands and pinning them to his soft comforter- assuming the role as master whether he liked it or not. I rolled my hips a few times as he gasped and grunted and then suddenly he hissed a warning and forcefully tore his hands from mine. I gulped and pulled back just as a barely- visible wave of spark-encrusted energy rolled across the open room behind him, and for a moment, it felt like the entire room had trembled.

'Shit!' he whispered, sitting up and glancing around him as a book toppled off the top of his desk and fell to the floor, along with a small free-standing mirror. 'Was that loud? What's with my power lately? It's like I keep shorting out or something!' he looked back to me as he moved to sit up saying: 'Larkin we're probably going to have to play this game in your room-' but I pounced him again, mesmerised by the way that his lower abdominals had crunched together and bulged when he'd lifted his shoulders off the bed. So beautiful! He was just so damned beautiful! And the light glowing down on him through the sky window above wasn't exactly hurting the whole 'angelic' thing that the Barachiel men had going on!

Kohén moaned and wrapped his arms around me, sitting up as he returned my heated kisses until I was straddling him with my hair falling around us like a crinkled veil, and though I knew he was determined to get me out of there, and although I knew I would eventually comply given how likely it was that the rest of his family would wake up soon, I milked the moment for all it was worth, soaking in the scent of him, which was what I loved the most about being in his room. Kohén always smelled incredible, but usually, his natural scent was diluted by environmental factors and lately- one of those factors had been the white rose oil of the harem, which I despised. But this was Kohén's environment and his scent was potent and everywhere and it was the most incredible aphrodisiac I'd ever encountered, so though I was happy that Kohén had finally brought me here, I was already feeling sorry for myself and how miserable I was going to feel once I'd been returned to the harem again. I waited for my sub-conscious to pipe up and point out that it was all going to be my own damn fault for letting the charade I was supposed to be playing for Kohén's benefit get this far, and that this was all going to end up hurting me more in the long run... but I'd evidently killed my inner voice with wine and sex the way I had killed Satan's with God's name, because she didn't say a word, allowing me to do the one thing that I never got to do- live in the moment without a single regard for the consequences. That was a dangerous way to live for someone who had everything on the line like I did, and no sooner had I thought how lovely it would truly be to take everything good at face value and turn a blind eye to everything bad, then a 'consequence' came barging through the door.

'Darling we're being attacked!' I heard someone cry. 'Amelia-Rose and her father have come to warn us that-' I looked up just in time to see the duchess duck under Elijah's arm and enter the room (the king's angel ring was still pressed into Kohén's door lock) and though she'd been making a beeline to the bed to 'rescue' her sleeping son, she came to a sudden halt halfway between his bed and his desk when she saw me. In fact she stopped so suddenly that she almost lost her balance and fell over, which was exactly what King Elijah looked like he was about to do when his gaze shifted to where I was- on *top* of his son. That would have been mortifying enough as it was, but when I saw two strangers gathered in the hall behind them- an older man and a very young, very beautiful girl- my mortification found a new rock bottom to slam into. The man turned his face, embarrassed- but the girl gawked at us blatantly.

'Oh My God!' Constance cried, exactly as her spouse bellowed: 'What is the meaning of this?!' and Kohén practically shot me across the room when he sat up swiftly. He caught my rump with his hip to prevent me from flying off of his lap, but there wasn't much he could do to keep me in his arms because Constance had regained her equilibrium, darted across the room and was now dragging me off the bed and her son using my bicep. Her nails were long and sharp and they cut into me and Kohén's expression immediately transitioned from 'OOPS' to indignant, but before he could lunge after me, his father appeared behind him, grabbed him by his arm and threw Kohén backwards so quickly that Kohén didn't have the chance to defend himself- especially seeing as how his eyes had been on his mother and full of concern for me instead of looking out for his own interests. As I landed awkwardly on my backside, my prince hit the wall hard enough to cause the clock that he had hung on it to shake free and crash to the ground on top of him, and I gasped, horrified when he flopped face first to the floor- his back so red from the impact that it looked like second-degree sunsting. The strangers in the doorway gasped as well, and though Constance stepped in front of me to prevent me from going to Kohén's assistance, she also cried out for her husband to calm down.

'Calm down?!' Elijah repeated, grabbing Kohén by the hair and hoisting him violently off the floor. 'Why? These disrespectful little bastards have humiliated me for the last time this week!'

'And you believe that throwing them about will garner your respect?' the duchess asked, incredulous. 'Because it's not enough that they're drawn to whores like you are- now you must teach them how to solve their problems with violence too? You reap what you sew, Elijah- and you have sown some wild oats with your seed so do not attack them for being uncultivated! That error is *yours*!'

My jaw dropped as Elijah gave her an ugly look over his shoulder. 'You are right, so allow me to harvest them before they grow beyond my control- a chore I will see to now, by putting my foot down- on their matching, ever-smirking faces!' Elijah dropped Kohén again and lifted his knee, and when I saw that he was about to stomp Kohén's head, a garbled scream began to gargle out of my throat. I lunged forward off my knees but only made it to the edge of the bed by the time Constance grabbed me again- just as Shepherd Choir raced forward and pulled Kohén out of Elijah's reach.

'I understand that you have reached a breaking point after a chaotic week, your highness-' Shepherd Choir was a tiny, white-haired man, but when he pulled the still-dazed Kohén behind him, he made himself look ten feet tall to me, '-but I think we both know that Kohén here should not be held accountable for all of your troubles. It is advice and guidance that the young prince is clearly in need of- *not* the physical manifestation of anger that has built up inside you.' He turned around and pushed Kohén gently towards Amelia-Rose. 'See that he gets out into the hall with his brothers, darling, and then all of you retreat to the ballroom as we've been instructed. The duchess, king, the young lady and I will follow quickly.'

'Yes daddy,' Amelia-Rose said in a voice that was so mellifluous that it actually made me flinch. She turned and placed her hands on Kohén's shoulder, attempting to steer him away while giving me a loaded look that I hadn't a chance of deciphering, but Kohén stepped out from underneath her arm and walked back in, shaking his head as his eyes fixed on me.

'I'm not taking a step without her and-'

'YOU WILL DO AS YOU ARE TOLD!' Elijah thundered and I cringed as Shep went white and stepped back, giving up. 'I'm not playing here, boy! Allowing a Companion into our private quarters has a punishment of fifty lashings for each of you, and if you do not move quickly to save your own back, then I will administer all one hundred of them to *her,* understood?'

Kohén's eyes widened as he stopped stalking towards me and turned on his father. 'Those punishments are never actually enforced, and you know it!'

They weren't? That was news to me!

'Because no one is ever stupid enough to break the rules!' Elijah retorted, and I cringed. Yep, trust me to be the first Companion to get hit over the head with the rule book!

'Must we discuss this now while there are people bombing the castle?' Amelia-Rose demanded, fiddling with the pearl buttons of her white, high-necked, tight-fitting blouse. 'We need to protect those that matter, not fritter away time on those that don't!'

'They're bombing the castle using the kerosene that you and Kohl so generously snuck out to them without my permission to keep them warm, and don't think I won't be having a serious chat with you two later about that, either!' Elijah snapped at her, and Amelia-Rose cringed and cowered a little as he pointed out the door. I looked to the Shepherd for a reaction, but his face was too composed for me to know if he took offence to the king reprimanding his child. 'But you're right, I don't have the time to parent or punish anyone right now so I'll say this only once more: You have five seconds to get out of this wing and downstairs, Kohén Barachiel, because that will give me about twenty seconds to sneak her out after you and back into the safety of her wing before anyone else notices that we have a displaced Companion! And if you waste one more second of that time then I won't bother returning her to the harem, but to the cells! Five, four-'

'But she can't be exposed to other people!' Kohén spluttered. 'There are too many people out there who would abduct her! Especially if the opportunity presents itself during chaos!'

'Three-'

'I'll see her returned to the harem unharmed!' Constance cried, waving her arm. 'Just go, Kohén, or you'll only cause her more grief!'

'Two-'

'I'm GOING!' Kohén exclaimed, and then stormed from the room after sending me an anguished look that wasn't without a trace of warning- warning me not to do anything to antagonise his parents further, or betray his trust. I heard him pounding a path down towards the foyer as Constance sighed in relief behind me (she still had the back of my toga and was holding me in place) and Elijah threw up his hands, whirling on us.

'*One!*' he began to step around the bed towards me, face still red and furious, distorting his own good looks gruesomely. 'Right- *you*! Will a day ever pass in this castle during which I don't develop a headache as a result of your actions?'

I furrowed my brow and pulled back from him, swallowing hard as I swallowed down all of the nasty things that I wanted to say to him, because Constance had expressed it all rather eloquently herself a few minutes beforehand with the whole seed-sowing thing anyway. I didn't want one hundred lashings- but I didn't want one-hundred and fifty lashings even more, so I figured that the only smart thing that I could do in that moment was to do what I'd done all week- bite my tongue.

'I've heard that she cannot speak for she is already in shock and mourning the loss of a close friend...' the shepherd said, looking to me and cocking his head. 'Is that true?'

I swallowed again and nodded, wiping away the tears that had started to trickle from my eyes when I'd seen Kohén hit that wall. I felt awful for lying to Shepherd Choir and pretending that I was still mute, but I had thrown myself on the sword too many times before in the past in the interest of doing what was right and had nothing to show for it but multiple stab wounds to the heart.

'Well then, that means that she cannot speak for herself or for Kohén, so it would not be fair to speak *at* her either, especially not when you know that she's also suffering from an awful week.' He glanced at Elijah. 'Nor would it be honourable to whip a girl as punishment for a crime that she is incapable of committing.'

Elijah turned to him. 'What do you mean by that? She's in a wing that she's forbidden from entering, and you see it with your own eyes!'

'Ahh yes, but I also saw you unlock this door with a specific key made to fit a specific lock to get in here, and I would assume that she does not have a copy of that key in her own possession, correct? It had to have been in Kohén's?' Elijah nodded and the shepherd shrugged. 'So she could not possibly have made her own way into the monarch's wing- she had to have been invited, and as Kohén's Companion, she is not allowed to turn down any invitation from him, is she? So punishing her for breaking the boundary laws, would be akin to punishing her for following the ones that demand her submission... and that doesn't sound very kind *or* fair to me...' Shepherd's pale green eyes landed on me and they were full of empathy that made my eyes water, and triumph that made my heart sing. What a kind, wise man he was... and how little he must think of me! 'Does it to *you*, your highness? Because I'm beginning to wonder if it's this girl's actions that require correcting- or the guidelines that she must adhere to.'

Elijah's draw dropped in response to the syllogism that the shepherd had just flattened him with and I wanted to applaud. But...

'It's not the guidelines that need correcting, it's the fact that she's here at all that needs to be addressed!' Amelia-Rose said, shooting me a look that was less-difficult to figure out due to the disgust in her brumous eyes. 'Kohén shouldn't be punished for fornicating with a woman in his chamber- he should be prohibited from having access to ill-fitting women, *period*!'

Ill-fitting? I thought, glaring daggers at her and making no move to hide it. *The only thing ill-fitting here is your hideous blouse! Your cup may runneth over lady, but the neckline of your shirt certainly doesn't!*

Elijah sighed a long, low sigh. 'I suppose you have a point,' he grumbled. 'But something has to be done to prevent this from happening again, and I don't have time to - '

'No, you must go and check on the rest of your people, I agree. So let's postpone dealing with this matter until later on, all right? I'll speak to Kohén myself and stress the importance of leading by example- even when it comes to following the most insignificant rules- and we'll see Larkin back to her harem on the way, so long as you're certain that it's safe.'

'The Harem is a fortress,' Elijah said quickly, shooting me another look that communicated that if Kohén hadn't already forbidden me from leaving it, he'd be doing it himself. 'But we cannot simply stroll downstairs with her on our arm. People will see her and wonder how she came to be-'

'I'll give you the chance to leave, hold her here, and then escort her to the harem door myself once you, Amelia-Rose and Shep are out of sight, Elijah,' the duchess said quickly, and he gave her a sceptical look. 'Not only will it give me the opportunity to make it clear that she will never allow herself to be coerced into this part of the castle again...' she gave me a dirty look that let me know that I was in for it, '...but it will give the majority of those fleeing the rear lawn the chance to pass first, covering Kohén's dastardly tracks.' She motioned impatiently for Elijah and the others to leave, and although I saw Amelia-Rose swipe her mane of burgundy ringlets over her shoulder and sneer at me, she blessedly turned her back to me quickly after.

'But it's not proper-'

'There is enough speculation running rife about Larkin's hold over the Barachiel men right now as it is- do you think it better that she is seen leaving our chamber on *your* arm, darling... or a woman's?' Constance did not wait for him to answer that before she smacked her hands together. 'Out, now! For the love of God, people are setting off explosives on our lawn, and you think we have another second to waste debating Larkin's reputation? Go check on my sons- all THREE of them, please.'

Elijah made a frustrated sound but began to leave, steering Shepherd Choir out with him and muttering apologies. 'I don't know what you must think of me and my family right now, Shep, but I assure you- the behaviour you've all witnessed this week is completely out of character for all of them...'

'Not for her though, right?' I heard Amelia-Rose sniff as her voice faded away. 'You see, this is exactly why the Given caste offends me! I've heard that Larkin is intelligent and personable and charming from the men in your family, and yet every crisis you have seems to swirl out from her like the eye of a storm...'

My face flushed hotly- so hotly it was like I'd fallen into a fire, and I moved to go after Amelia-Rose, wanting to point out that all I'd heard from the Barachiel men on the subject of *her* was a lot of teeth-grinding... but then Constance moved in front of me and slammed the door, barring my exit, and my blood turned to ice when I saw that her eyes had turned the same shade.

'I have a million things I want to say to you, and a million questions that I want you to answer, Larkin, but before I start, let me preface it by making one thing crystal clear to you!' And then she pulled back her hand and struck me so hard that I went reeling into the post at the end of the bed.

11.

I sobbed as the side of my head hit the bed post hard, not only because it hurt, but because it was Constance that had struck me. It seemed so cruel to me that she and I had evolved from being enemies to allies to actually affectionate with one another- only to end back up as enemies again... and it proved to be the straw that broke me. I sank to my knees, cupped the throbbing side of my head and wept silently, distraught to understand that lying to myself in order to make my existence here tolerable was only going to work if I stayed isolated. I could get myself drunk and even fool myself into believing that Kohén was enough for me now... but every time I looked into someone else's eyes, like Constance's or Elijah's... I'd be reminded of all of the awful things I'd done, and how adding all of those awful deeds together made me an awful *person*.

You were an idiot for trying to think otherwise! Perhaps Kohén and you can find redemption in one another's arms for the pain you've caused each other, but that only makes what you've done to Kohl worse!

Ahhh there was that pesky sub-conscious of mine again! Of course she'd choose now to resurface... to state the obvious only once it was too late to avoid a collision course with it!

Don't tell Constance a thing! Especially not about the murder! She'd never tell anybody about that, especially once she understands what happened and how it all came to pass... but once she knows, it will break her heart and she will not be able to look at either son without them instantly realising that she knows! And once that thread is pulled at, everything will unravel into a pile of blame, water and electricity!

'I... I just don't even know where to begin!' the duchess exclaimed, and I could tell by the sound of her footfalls that she was pacing madly. 'You tell me that you love Kohl and that you'll do anything to escape here before Kohén locks you in, and then an escape is handed to you and what do you do? Lock your*self* in! At first I feared that my son had taken you against your will, and I was trying to find out exactly what had happened from Kohl so I could get to the truth of the matter and maybe find some sort of loophole that I could sneak you out through... but to walk in on you in the middle of...' her voice sputtered out again, but only momentarily. 'Well what *did* happen? Was I right about you all along? Damn you if I was! I will encourage Elijah to whip you, and *hard*!'

I looked up at her, just in time to see her swing on me, her pretty, pale blue nightgown swishing behind her. Her eyes were a matching shade of ice blue, and she was wringing her hands. 'Well?' she demanded. 'I know you cannot speak, but from what I saw a few minutes ago while you were on top of my son, you have use of all of your body parts, so nod or shake your head, child! Did you deceive me? Did you fall in love with Kohén again? Or have you been in need of my help but simply powerless to ask for it?'

I thought quickly about all three questions, and then shook my head- a no to all three. I wanted her help, yes- but she wasn't in a position to help, only to agitate matters further.

The duchess moaned in exasperation. 'What? How is that even possible?

I sniffled and wiped away my tears. 'I cannot tell you how that is possible- only assure you that it is and beg you to leave it at that, for everyone's sake!'

Her eyes bugged further. 'I thought you'd lost your voice! Have you been lying about that, or has *he*?'

I shook my head again, taking her hand when she offered it and allowing her to help me off the ground- but turning my face away from her fingers when she winced and tried to touch the spot where she'd hit me, and where I'd hit the bed after. She retracted her fingers and stepped back, looking hurt, but I had a feeling that she was a lot more upset with herself in that moment than she was with me, so I combed my fluffy hair over my face and hugged myself.

'My voice returned to me late yesterday afternoon, but I have kept that fact to myself, for not having to speak has been a godsend to me these past few days,' I said softly, wincing a little when I reflected on what I'd just said. Losing my voice hadn't been a gift from God, but a punishment from Satan, and if I didn't mind my tongue, I'd end up on the receiving end of another! Bearing that in mind, I quickly crossed to Kohén's desk and turned his small free-standing mirror over without first looking into it, knowing that so long as there was one in the room, Satan would be able to spy on me. 'But please, don't tell Kohén all right? If he believes that I was unable to converse with you, his paranoia regarding what I may have said to you after will be less, as both of our interrogations will be. In fact, you cannot confide to anyone that we have spoken, not Kohl, not Elijah and certainly NOT Karol, okay? All you will do is get me in even more trouble, and I need you to understand that I will never speak another word to you if I hear that you have quoted me to anyone!'

The duchess paled and grabbed me, as the anger within her eyes burned away, leaving only fear behind. 'Why?' her voice broke. 'What did Kohén do to you? What does he have *over* you? I know that he's learned of Kohl's affection for you… but has he learned of your intent to run away with Kohl too?' her face crumpled. 'Oh Larkin, did my sweet boy rape-'

'Please, stop!' I grabbed her arms back and shook her gently. 'I cannot say anything about it, duchess- not a word! I know you think you want the truth but trust me, you *don't*, all right? All I can tell you is that Kohén, Kohl and I have made a plethora of mistakes that we are trying to keep between us, because if those mistakes ever become public knowledge they will not only ruin the three of us beyond repair, but your entire family and none of us want that- not even me.'

'Ruin my entire family?' The duchess looked stricken. 'How? Tell me, so that I might do something to help!'

'You can't help!' I repeated, growing frustrated. 'I know you don't want to believe that but it's the truth! I am sorry that I have broken Kohl's heart, but he is not the only one suffering that affliction right now, and a broken heart is going to be the least of everyone's problems if you keep agitating matters!'

'How am I agitating anything?' Constance demanded. 'I know *nothing* except for the fact that there is something to know!'

'And that's how we need it to stay, so you need to stop pushing your way into our confidences or trying to get to the bottom of things!' I exclaimed, frustrated tears coming to my eyes. I'd wanted this opportunity to speak to Constance for days so that I could urge her to keep Kohl safe- but the only way to keep Kohl safe was to get him onto that boat with that Bible... and *that* wouldn't happen if Kohl or I screwed Kohén over first, either by willingly confessing all of our secrets to Constance, or by allowing her to draw them from us because she'd most definitely take matters into her own hands and that would be cataclysmic for all of us, for she simply didn't know how to control her temper, or know how to protect one twin without causing harm to the other. 'Look, Kohl, Kohén and I are all currently tangled up in a complex web that we created with secret-keeping, lies and broken promises and it's borderline unbearable... but because the three of us are all aware of the fact that we're equally to blame for how bad things have gotten, we've all agreed to do what it takes to get ourselves out of the predicament we're in, *together*. And the most important thing we need to do is keep all that has transpired between us between *us*, all right? So do not pester Kohl to spill his secrets, or look at Kohén like he is to blame for everything, or dig for information to sate your curiosity, because all you will do is cause the foundations of our tentative unity to crumble beneath us and incite chaos!' I reached forward and grasped her hands. 'Just be patient, and everything will work out okay for them, all right? Not brilliantly... but bearable.'

'What about for you?' the duchess demanded huskily, eyes glassing over. 'How are you ever going to be okay, now that you're stuck here?'

I blew out a long, low breath. 'I've made it three days without killing myself so far, haven't I? I'm sure I'll be fine. In fact, I think there's a chapter in the guidelines somewhere about Companion PTSD and how to orgasm your way out of it...' I joked, but my smile pulled in discomfort and her eyes overflowed. 'Sorry, that was an impolite thing to say.'

'Fuck politeness. Lark...' she pushed my hair over my shoulders. 'You're not okay, are you? How can you ask me to stand by and watch you sink like this? There must be something I can do to help! Anything?'

'There is.' I gulped and grabbed her wrists again, pulling them down to squeeze her hands so she'd feel my desperation, even if she was too beside herself to hear it right now. 'Firstly, you can encourage Karol to propose to Ora by exercising every ounce of influence that you have over him, all right? And it wouldn't hurt for you to mention the fact that you saw Kohén and I acting passionately on his bed this morning either- because the more people that believe that I am here willingly, the better off we will all be. Secondly... you can convince Kohl to make his career a priority in the hopes that it might distract him from his broken heart and thirdly... you need to start treating Kohén better or in the very least- stop giving him the stink eye and assuming that this is all of his doing, because it is not! Your rage hurts him Constance and when he hurts, Kohl and I feel it!'

Constance blinked rapidly. 'I agree that the fact that people suspect- as I did- that you were seduced against your will is causing us a lot of trouble right now and it's important to snuff out that fire if Kohén truly did not light it alone...and you are not the first person to point out that I am favouring Kohl over Kohén's with no obvious grounds to justify doing so... and of course I will do whatever it takes to get Kohl's mind off his broken heart right now...' she squinted, 'but what has pushing Karol into marrying Ora got to do with anything?'

'More than you can imagine, and more than I am at liberty to explain,' I said quickly, relieved that she'd more or less agreed to my terms. 'The short answer is that it will help keep Kohén's jealousy at bay, but the long answer is, like everything else, too volatile to expand upon now, all right? Just... just do whatever is in your power to keep him away from my wing of the castle, and you will help us more than I can express.'

'But *why*?' Constance demanded, and my short-lived relief began to dissipate. 'Honestly Larkin, your answers invite more questions than they do provide answers! It's frustrating!'

I wrinkled my nose, thinking that I'd accused Satan of something similar the day before, and not enjoying the idea that she and I were alike- in any way. 'I... I already told you, I can't say anything else, all right?' And then, I had a flash of inspiration, and clicked my fingers. 'But I will, I promise. Do exactly as I've asked, and on Sunday, if Karol is engaged to Ora and Kohl sailing safely back to Pacifica- I will explain *everything*.'

Constance narrowed her eyes sceptically. '*Everything*?'

'The moment Kohén gives us the space to speak privately, I will divulge all,' I said and I meant it. Kohén really would relax once Kohl was gone, and given the time and the right setting, I knew I'd be able to find a way to tell the duchess what had happened without that instigating more trouble. That time just wasn't now- everyone was too edgy and paranoid, and her favouritism regarding Kohl was her Achilles and Kohén's alike. 'I swear it,' I added quickly, crossing my heart, 'but only if *you* swear not to do a single thing more to agitate the situation further before then, all right? Be a mother to them, Constance- *all* of them, equally and know that although I am a prisoner here, it is only because I chose to be, and so long as Kohén keeps his promise not to brand me, there will always be a chance that one day, I might walk free with enough gold to make my dreams come true…' my voice caught because I knew that I was lying and that Kohén was never going to let me go, but so long as Constance saw hope in my eyes, she'd feel it in her soul, I knew it. What mother doesn't want to believe the best in their children? 'But only when I have earned it, and after I have made amends for the evil things that have been done in my shadow.'

Constance hugged me hard. 'You're not evil, Larkin, you're trapped by it!'

'All the more reason to encourage Karol to marry Ora,' I said softly, wiping at my tears as I pulled back. 'She will put an end to this hateful system, I know it, and perhaps my release will follow her coronation.'

'That is what I pray for, and between us… I believe that is exactly what is about to transpire.' Constance pulled back and beamed at me through her tears. 'Karol has been spending hours with her every day and ignoring every other-' a scream sounded from somewhere that sounded further away than it was and Constance and I both looked at one another before she went flying towards the unlocked door, pushing it open and poking her head into the corridor.

'Oh my goodness, the raid! I completely forgot about it all!' Constance stepped out into the hallway. 'Now I don't know if we would be safer off staying here, or doing as Elijah instructed…'

Constance did not know which option was safer, but I sure did and so I eased past her and out into the foyer. 'I have to get back to that harem before everyone comes out of the ballroom, sees me and makes the scandal surrounding me worse!' I whispered as I crept forward. I looked around for a weapon but saw only art and so I hurried faster, beckoning for Constance to follow me. 'How many are there on the grounds?'

'I have no idea,' the duchess whispered, catching up with me just as I got out onto the landing. 'Amelia-Rose and

Shepherd Choir just pounded on our door seconds before I came to wake the boys and found you-'

'Kissing,' I whispered, ducking down so that I could sweep my gaze across what I could see of the hall beneath us, which wasn't much. 'That was all we were doing.'

'And all I want to know about,' Constance grumbled. 'Anyway, they said that about four had been seen running across the grounds after having scaled the fence.'

'How did they scale the fence?' I squeaked.

'They bombed the electric exterior fence, giving them the chance to put out the current and then practically smashed a section of it flat as they all scrambled over at once- and then they began to lift one another up over the solid brick part of Eden's fence once they'd inundated the walkway between, getting at least four of them over.' She sighed heavily. 'And now that they've done that, I suppose it's only a matter of time before they try it again. I wager that Elijah will have the exterior fence topped with razor wire now, and every section of Eden's fence that has been left open to give the townspeople a view of our grounds bricked in by the end of the week!'

'Four people doesn't seem like many...' I mused, thinking that I could probably take out that many. I'd bested six in a gauntlet of sorts on order to earn my PCE score... then again, that had been one at a time in controlled circumstances, not six on one in the midst of chaos.

'Well they were screaming that they would sever the necks of every noble person or Nephilim that they met, so four people with the strength to get themselves over a ten foot fence with vertical bars *and* the gall to threaten decapitation seem like plenty to me. Can you imagine the damage done if even *one* succeeds? besides, who knows how many have made their way over behind them since Shep informed us of the initial breech?'

A murder in Eden? That did sound shocking, even though I knew that it wasn't the first that had been committed there that week. 'Mmm...well, let's see that they don't succeed with *you*, okay?' I said, creeping forward more and motioning for her to stay back while I scoped out the immediate vicinity. The entrance to the harem lay beneath the shadow of the stairs and under the entrance of the monarch's wing on the upper level, so in order to see my door, I would have to get out onto the staircase and look down, behind me and slightly to the left. I assumed that my guard would still be standing there, but what if he wasn't? How was I going to get in?

You don't... my sub-conscious whispered in my ear. *You run now, while there's a chance that your disappearance could be mistaken as a kidnapping!*

The idea was so tempting that I swear my mouth watered, but when I leaned over the railing, I saw Miguel Barachiel's marble stand- without a head on it, because the head itself had been jammed into the door of the harem, keeping it ajar. Beside it, the security guard was staring up at me and waving his arms madly.

'Now Miss Whittaker!' he whispered. 'This is your only chance!' He pointed across the room. 'One's just gone that way! Hurry!'

I followed his gesturing hand with my eyes just in time to see someone filthy looking vanish behind the wall that cut off my view of the throne room and grand foyer beside us. I nodded, turned back to Constance and waved my hand and she took it so together, we ran down the stairs. I was halfway down when the security guard gasped and exclaimed: 'Duchess!' he dropped into a low bow. 'I did not see you there!' he looked to me and something strange crossed his face- was it an apologetic expression? And then he stepped aside from the door and waved me his way. 'Come miss- Prince Kohén asked me to leave the door open for you and close it after, and I suppose I will see the duchess across to the ballroom once that is done!'

'Don't be ridiculous, T'are!' Constance picked up the hems of her long silk pants and ran faster, overtaking me as her dressing gown flapped behind her- and I thought how strange it was that I had not known my keeper's name until now. I remembered seeing him around the castle over the years, but King Elijah's guards had always been silent and stoic- never doing anything that would draw attention to themselves, and I suppose T'are had become like one of the many pillars in the hall to me by now- part of Eden's structure that you were distracted from noticing due to all of the more ornamental parts surrounding it. He had an impressive frame though, and his eyes were a rare shade that were warm despite their pale blue hue, and I hoped that Constance hadn't heard him address me as 'Miss Whittaker' because that was a big no-no; I'd surrendered my surname when I'd surrendered my uterus, and was Larkin of Eden now- not of the Whittaker family. 'It is too chaotic to try and cross the grand hall now!' the duchess went on. 'I will hide in the harem with Larkin until the crisis has been averted!

'No!' T'are's eyes bugged. 'I cannot-' another scream sounded- this one much closer, and suddenly Cherry came flying around the corner, holding onto the hands of a man that had both fists wrapped around her pale pink ponytail, and was attempting to drag her backwards with it. Knowing that I owed her more than one, I forgot about the notion of hiding inside the castle- and went about protecting it instead.

12.

T'are launched into action as I did, except he didn't scream like a girl the way that I did, and he didn't bother to pause to search for a weapon because he had the kind of body mass that made him one by default- a luxury that I did not share. There still weren't any obvious weapons lying around, but the torches that kept parts of the castle illuminated at night were still alight, and because one was set into the curve of the stone wall to my right, I plucked it out of its sconce automatically and then jumped down the last three steps bellowing to Cherry to look out and arriving on the marble floor just as she lurched past the bottom step.

Please let them have trained me well for something other than the tasks I've been performing for Kohén's benefit lately! I thought as I fell into the fray. The man wrestling Cherry was very tall but very skinny, and the pink-haired Nephilim was incredibly petite, so it was easy for me to duck between the two bodies and press the flaming torch into the man's stomach while I forced her away from me with the way I bent forward. My body went into a kind of shock then, but I liked it. It already felt like it had been far too long since I had last used my muscles for anything other than Kohén's pleasure!

But my physical euphoria was short-lived, because the man grunted and jerked down on Cherry then, stabbing one of his elbows down and into my cheekbone hard enough to make my eyes water in reflex. I gasped and almost dropped the torch, but locked my knees and shoved the flame forward instead, holding my ground as he attempted to hold his. All Nephilim were precious and in need of protection, but none as much as the healers were in my opinion!

'Miss Whittaker, be careful!' I heard T'are exclaim as the Duchess cried: 'Mind your lovely hair with that torch!' but I'd already committed to this course of action so I had to see it through while T'are focused on wrestling Cherry out of the man's grasp. The Banished man's shirt had been filthy and torn, worn underneath an open jacket that was much too small for him, and both articles of clothing caught alight at once, making him cry out sharply. He looked down at me briefly as he cursed me out, and I grew dizzy from the way his clothing and breath reeked, but fortunately the shock of being on fire dominated his focus, causing him to relinquish his grip on Cherry's hair as he smacked at the flames that were licking their way up his front.

'Damn yah gal!' the man garbled in a thick accent that I did not recognise before he pulled his fist back to slug me. 'Why, I ought-' I slammed the torch up into the underside of his beard and he made a strangled sound that was drowned out by the whump of his whiskers catching on fire and making an acrid stink.

'Oh!' I cried, surprising myself when the urge to apologise overcame me. I hadn't been trying to kill him, but he must have been covered in kerosene already, because he became a human torch in a matter of seconds.

Oh boy, I'm glad Kohl isn't here to see me setting fire to the people he's trying to champion! I thought as I came to a halt at the edge of the shadows, knowing that it would be best if I didn't draw attention my way by making myself visible from the back of the foyer that the outlaws were all evidently passing through. *Though his powers would come in handy right now to put this fire out...*

I heard the duchess scream as the burning man gave up on trying to slap his flames out and charged me instead, but I glanced back at her in time to see Cherry stumble to her feet, snag the duchess's sleeve and drag her back behind the cover of the stairwell, while T'are leapt forward and knocked the burning man to the ground by tackling the frayed cuffs of his dirty pants.

'Put him out!' I cried, 'the king will want him alive!' They both went down hard but T'are rolled clear of him and then reached over to roll the man over- again and again until the flames clinging to him began to wither away, making me slump in relief. I wouldn't have a murder on my conscience this day, thanks to T'are's quick-thinking. But we were still in the middle of quite the imbroglio, so I twisted back and jerked my head towards Cherry.

'Get the duchess into the ballroom Cherry!' I cried, thrusting the torch out to indicate towards the corner, making faint shadows flicker and dance around me. 'Now! They're after Nephilim and nobility, and that makes you two more in danger from them than any of us are!'

'What if someone crosses our path?' Cherry asked, inching forward with the duchess. 'I don't know if I am strong enough to defend her- I've already had to heal one person with a bad laceration on my way down from my room! If the duchess gets hurt-'

'I'll see you as far across as I can then!' I cried, flipping my hair back over my shoulder and then holding my torch out to the side. 'But move quickly! I am supposed to be locked up in the harem, not frolicking about in the halls!'

'Miss Whittaker you cannot do that!' T'are bellowed, and I shot him a look.

'It is only Larkin, not Miss Whittaker, and I got an incredible score on my PCE!' I snapped. 'I'll bet I can do it more quickly than even you could, muscles! And if you think you'll get in trouble for letting me out of my labyrinth, imagine what hot water you'll land in if the duchess gets slain because you wouldn't allow a whore to defend her!' I turned back to Cherry. 'Go- NOW!'

'Oh! What happened to your face?' Cherry darted forward and touched her warm fingers to my cheek. 'And when did you get your voice back?'

My stomach flipped as I touched my eye. 'I didn't know I had a voice until I screamed out to you,' I lied, averting my eyes. 'And the man elbowed me in the face when I was fighting him off- I'll be fine.'

Cherry's eyebrows drew together. 'Elbowed you- with an open hand that has caused you to develop welts in the shape of fingers... and a cut where a piece of sharp jewellery has pierced your skin?'

'What?' It took me a moment to remember how I had gotten such an injury, but I stupidly looked at Constance as she sucked in a breath- and then all three of us looked down at her hand- and the large canary-yellow stone that had been encrusted into her ring. 'Oh... I...'

'Walked into a door?' Cherry drawled, releasing the duchess and cupping my face, slanting it to the light. 'Not surprising- how can one avoid walking into doors when they are all locked around you?'

'Oh God... Larkin...' the duchess pressed her fingers together as though she were saying a prayer and then touched them to her lips. 'I didn't realise I'd slapped you so hard! Oh, darling I'm-'

'*Darling?*' Cherry demanded, and I was taken aback by how venomous she was allowing her tone to be in front of her boss. 'You hit her one moment and call her darling the next? How alike the members of this family have become! And to think of how I once cursed your husband for doing the same to you!'

Tears sprang into Constance's eyes. 'He didn't hit me, well, not-'

'I'm sorry, after your spouse electrocuted you during your pregnancy!' Cherry spat. 'There! Did *that* sound better? It didn't taste any better! And it didn't make my task of healing you any easier, did it?'

My jaw dropped. 'Whoa! *You* were her healer? When she was pregnant, I mean? You look younger than she is by half!'

'Because as a healer, I have the ability to reverse the damage inflicted upon my seventy year old features by time- but not the power to erase the damage that has been done to me in here-' she pressed her finger to her temple, '-in my mind, by all that I have seen! Yes, I was the one that came to her aid after her spouse hurt her!' Cherry stepped back from us and held up her hand. 'But not anymore!' She turned to the duchess. 'I should have walked then when I saw Nephilim doing such wicked things to someone he'd promised to marry, but like a fool, I stayed- believing that the incident was an isolated one! But seventeen years have passed and not only has he not honoured his promise to marry you and give us a queen at last, but I see that violence is spreading through this family like an infection, and I won't help cover it up anymore- so I *quit*! Get across the damned room yourself! And Larkin...' Cherry turned back to me as the duchess sobbed, her pale pink eyes flashing as she lifted up the chain she was holding, showing me the charm on it- a large, three-dimensional set of wings with steel feathers- a skeleton key to the doors! 'If you truly want out of this place as badly as I believe you do, then you should follow me! This ring won't get us anywhere beyond the harem door *inside* the castle- but it can get us both out the front gate if we move quickly!'

I gasped and shrank back. 'Are you crazy?' I squeaked, although I glanced longingly towards the front doors and out to the courtyard, which I hadn't stepped foot in for days and had always loved so. 'I can't do that!'

'*Why*, Larkin? Because you want to stay here so badly?' Cherry demanded, advancing on me, and I was shocked to see that although T'are was holding the man he'd captured down with one foot, he was watching our exchange silently and intently, but without making a move to break it up as he certainly should have. 'Tell me! Tell us *all* why you can't leave!' she pushed me gently. 'ADMIT THAT YOU ARE A PRISONER HERE! Admit that Kohén raped you! He raped you in the name of love, just like Elijah beat Constance for it, and the only reason why you aren't screaming it as I am, is because he has something on you that will end your life if you attempt to live it without him!'

I almost fell over, and Constance actually swooned back against the door. 'Don't scream out such things!' I said quickly, looking around anxiously, seeing that the people that had been racing about and screaming before had started to slow down and look our way. 'They're not true, and if anyone overhears-'

'Lies!' Cherry shouted. 'You are too strong to have succumbed to temptation! You-'

'That *is* her!' someone else cried out then, and my heart sank- not just to know that someone had overheard our exchange, but because Cherry's claim that I was too strong to falter in the face of temptation was utterly untrue, and I was devastated to realise that someone could think so highly- of someone as low as I had proved to be. 'It's Liberty! And she's been beaten!'

Liberty...? I swivelled to my left and was stunned to see three people come to a halt at the corner of the wall and gape at me- me and the torch that I was holding away from my body. *Liberty?* I thought again, rather dumbly, then looked down at the torch in my hand and snorted gently. *Oh that's cute...*

'Raped... and then beaten by the duchess!' someone else cried, and my knees went weak as my body flushed with radiant heat that made me gasp. These people were as dirty and dishevelled as the others that I had already seen had been, but they did not have weapons in their hands or ferocity in their eyes- all they did was stare at me the way the Arcadians had initially gaped at my statue: shocked to find themselves in the vicinity of it. 'Grab her!' a young woman began to scurry forward. 'Let's get her out of here before-'

'You leave her alone!' Constance raced in front of me, yanking the torch out of my hands, splattering kerosene everywhere and thrusting it at the people closing in on me while I stood there, thunderstruck to see that my fingertips had caught alight so quickly- my fingertips and the hem of my dress. I moaned, balled my fist and then snuffed out the flames with them, thinking that Constance wasn't nearly as graceful with something that was on fire as she was with her salad fork. Oh well, at least I hadn't been ablaze long enough for it to hurt- either that or I was in shock. 'Get out of my palace, now!'

A hand grabbed my forearm. 'Don't cower behind the crown, Lark!' Cherry whispered, tugging me her way. 'Run from it! I know a place where we could go- a place where you'd never have to fear them finding you, once we take care of that tracking device! A place where you belong!'

'Tracking device?' I repeated dumbly, wrestling my arm from hers and backing away from her. I didn't want to get too close to the people that clearly wanted to abduct me, so I headed further away from the corner, looking from side to side, wondering who would make a grab for me first: T'are... or the strangers? 'What tracking device? What *place*? You have read so much into everything I have said, and yet I cannot decipher a word coming out of your mouth!'

'Come with me now and I will explain it all and-'

'Larkin!' a male voice cried, and I looked up in time to see Karol racing across the massive foyer, wearing only a sleeveless, fitted shirt and the track pants that all of the royals wore when working out. He was sweaty and wild eyed and his long hair was all tangled, and it occurred to me that I'd never seen anyone look so handsome- or so terrifying as he flew across that room. In complete reflex I screamed and sealed my fate by turning on my heel and not running but *sprinting* towards the harem door with my heart in my throat.

'Close it behind me!' I shrieked to T'are as I leapt over the prone, singed man on the floor. 'Close it behind me and then get Constance out of here!'

He can't get me now! If he does, while everything is so chaotic, who knows how long I'd have to fend him off for before Kohén manages to intervene?

I heard several voices call out my name or just cry out in frustration but I was so determined to get away from Karol that I made excellent time getting across that corridor, and once I'd slid inside my own prison again, I twisted, ducked and then gave Miguel Barachiel's head a mighty shove, sending it rolling across the corridor behind me- praying that Karol would trip over it and smash his perfect face. The door clicked shut and then the lock inside it clunked a second later, and because this door wasn't as thick and sound-proofed as my own was, I was able to hear what was being yelled on the other side: Karol was demanding that T'are catch the door before it could close and deadbolt, Constance was screaming for someone to apprehend Cherry, and the others simply screaming. I pushed up off the floor and flew back to my room, sobbing after I'd rattled it only to discover that it was still locked. Imagining Karol busting down the harem door behind me, I raced on, trying handles and calling out to Resonah and Rosina to let me in, but they were either elsewhere or still fast asleep because no one came to my aid.

Crying openly now, shaking to think of how close that call had been and hearing the words 'tracking device' replaying over and over inside my head, I staggered past the first wing of rooms, through the foggy pool area where Kelia had met her end and towards the very rear of the harem, knowing that it was pointless to go over to the rooms that we used for grooming purposes because the beauticians didn't come in to work until eight most mornings and it wasn't yet six.

Just find somewhere dark and quiet to hide until Kohén comes for you! I thought, but I was crying and breathing too loudly to have a hope of hiding any time soon, and I only made it another ten steps and around the left-hand side of the corridor before I realised that I'd come to a dead end that I hadn't known had been there until now.

Shit! I thought, pulling up when I found myself face to face with a shut door where I'd believed that the corridor had been. *What now? The map of the castle indicates that this is a passageway, not a full stop! Good thing I'm not running from a fire- I'd be dead already!*

The harem was shaped like a horseshoe, with two corridors on the left and right side that had doors on either side, so that the exterior rooms had their backs to the outside of the castle, and the central ones backed up against one another- twenty private cells in total according to Maryah and the map- seventeen of which were currently un-occupied. The outer rooms like mine had windows but the interior ones had skylights.

There was a break in the very centre of the harem not far from my room and that was where the spring was, and directly across from that was the group of rooms that we had come to know as 'the labs' where we went for personal upkeep, although its official name was the spa. There was a small room for physical therapy, a larger room for hair and skin treatments (six girls could be seen to in there at once) another tiny room for medical purposes (dubbed 'The Gyno' by Lette, who was constantly itchy down there and didn't know why) a room where our seamstress worked when we were in need of her, and a small lounge and bathroom are that backed onto the harem staff's private office.

The spa took up the same space as four of the harem rooms that it backed up against did, and the springs combined with our private dining room/kitchenette took up the same amount of space across from it, with four more rooms behind *it*, so because that middle section was flanked by a corridor on either side the entire wing had a symmetrical feel to it that I'd always seen replicated on the map.

But I'd never had cause to venture down to the back of the harem before- in fact I'd never thought much about the four rooms behind the dining room because they'd always been empty, but I'd always assumed that the corridor had snaked around them in a curve, as demonstrated in the castle's blueprints, so I was rather surprised to discover myself facing a door instead of continuing around in a U-shape like it was supposed to.

Curious as always despite my current anxiety, I examined the door, wondering if Resonah and Rosina's rooms were all the way down here, which would explain why I barely ever saw them getting around. Elfin, Lette, Emmerly, Kelia and I had been scattered around the entire wing, proving how embarrassed Kohén had been about having so many of us, but I wouldn't have put it past Elijah to lump his whores together like Karol had, (the royals didn't have to work for sex so why walk too far for it either?) so I raised my fist and knocked thinking that if I wanted tips on how to survive here, then I was probably best off seeking advice from those that had survived here the longest.

But my knock on the door went unanswered and echoed through the darkened corridor, giving me the creeps. If Karol burst through the main door looking for me, then the only way I'd be safe from him was if I got behind a door that his key wouldn't be able to access.

'Hello?' I tried, voice squeaking when I heard banging on the main door. 'Resonah? Rosina? Are you in here?'

But I was met with more silence, and when I heard the main door swing open with a thump, fear got the better of me and I twisted the door handle frantically, trying to rattle it loudly- and sucked in a breath when it opened to reveal only the silence, darkness and stillness that was lying beyond it.

Oh my God! I swallowed hard, not wanting to step into that ominous, windowless space, but doing so anyway when I heard haggard breathing and heavy footfalls coming from the first corridor where my room was. *There's no windows in here at all! Ugh! No wonder it's empty!*

I moved stealthily, taking care to nudge the door shut behind me and then fumbled, desperately hoping to find a lock- but there was no such thing on my side, just the little slits where a ringed wing was supposed to slot in, and when I tried the door handle again, I was dismayed to realise that it could not be opened from this side now, even though no one had turned a key to lock it from the other. More deadbolts! More claustrophobia!

Stuffing my fist into my mouth to smother my horror and sweating dread from every pore, I backed away from the door, becoming acutely aware of how stale the air was in here- and how much it reminded me of the stink of old leather. I banged into something that was hard and cold but it did not make a sound to betray my presence, so I turned and felt my way around the room hoping to find somewhere that I might be able to hide in case Karol glanced in there.

Why are there no windows? I thought, beginning to panic as I bumped into unrecognisable object after unrecognisable object. *God, I can't breathe!* Becoming clumsier and less cautious in my distress, I lumbered towards where I thought the interior wall must be and whimpered gratefully when I put my hands directly onto a bench that was covered in things that I did know by feel- a book, a bottle of something and finally, a lamp. Whimpering again I felt around the copper base of the lamp that was identical to touch as the one in my room and pressed the little switch on the stem to turn it on. A warm, red light immediately illuminated the darkness, but the colour was strange and unsettling and did nothing to make me feel better. Panting, baking in my own skin, sweating profusely and wet-faced, I looked up- and directly into the eyes of Satan.

'Bad move, Lark,' she whispered, shaking a long, polished finger at me, and I didn't know what stunned me more- how beautiful she was this time, or how terrifying she looked because her anger with me was evident. Her nails had been painted with a pearl lacquer though and that struck me as odd: shouldn't such a woman have fiery red talons sharpened to points and a skin-tight gown to match? 'Boy when you make a wrong-turn, you do it thoroughly, don't you?' Her nostrils flared as she exhaled. 'I wanted to ask if you've made good use of your time since we spoke last but I can already see the love softening your eyes, mouth and soul towards him once again. You're slipping, aren't you Larkin? You're slipping *fast.*'

I gulped and gaped for I could do nothing else. This wasn't Satan in Gabby's face or even Siria's- this was the Satan depicted in murals, only more so- more authentic than any painting could have ever hoped to be. Black coils of hair spiralled all the way down to the back of her knees, hanging like a cape of snakes behind her, and her eyes were so large and dark that I could see most of my upper body and face within them without having to strain in order to do it. They were glistening black pools, and they were full of anger and disappointment. Her lips were so perfectly sculpted that they came to thin points in the corners of her mouth, but instead of being a ruby red they were a deep plum colour, contrasting brightly with her white teeth.

She was beautiful and fierce-looking and because she was being reflected back to me not from just one mirror but in a panel of nine that stretched all the way along the wall, there was no escaping her or my thoughts, which were begging me to analyse everything that I'd just seen and heard. What had Cherry meant about my having a tracking device? Had she truly just quit her job in the castle after decades of service because of me? And if so, where was she going now?

'Oh Jesus...' Satan put her hands on the waist of her sage-green gown (another surprise, I'd imagine her wearing black or red) hips and tilted her head to the side. 'Are you finally using your brain again... or are you just so far under the Barachiel thrall now that we have to communicate in blinks? Once for yes and twice for no- Larkin. Is any part of you still alive in there?'

I blinked rapidly at her, then shook off my haze. 'You can't see for yourself... because my thoughts didn't concern you, right? You didn't want me to know... but that's how I can keep you out of my mind isn't it? By not thinking about you at all?' I clicked my fingers. 'And that's why it's me you're torturing instead of those you claim to hate... yes? Because Constance, Karol, Kohén... they don't think about you, do they- not *ever*.' I smirked triumphantly as Satan's eyes slitted. 'Constance told me that once- that she'd never prayed to you and *never* thought of you... I didn't believe that was possible, but I do now! Despite everything she's been through, her love for God knows no bounds, therefore, your ability to grasp her and manipulate her the way you wish to manipulate me knows nothing but *boundaries*, and *that's* why you leave her in peace! Because you have no other choice!'

The room burst into flames or at least appeared to and I shrieked as Satan laughed. 'Think you can use that information against me, little Larkin? Think again! True, I cannot access the thoughts of those who do not invite me in, but once the door is opened, a simple kick is all I need to keep it open, and so long as you breathe, you will invite me in!'

I staggered back a few inches but immediately crashed into something else and whirled, eyebrows lifting in mystification when I saw an oversized bench in the centre of the room- the same bench I must have bumped into beforehand, because it extended almost all the way to the door. I whirled to regard it, but there wasn't much to see for it was nothing more than a long, solid timber table that had been covered in supple-looking black leather. However there was another bench behind it, closer to the other side of the room and it was peculiar-looking indeed. Once again it was a solid timber structure, but it had more than the one leather clad surface, and it was apparent that they had been attached to hinges so that parts of the structure could be moved around. But why?

'The prey kneels on the lower pads with her ankles bound to the legs...' the woman behind me said as her flames dissipated, and I could hear the cruel lilt in her voice as she finished her explanation: 'Then she bends over the other with her torso flat to it so that she can be mounted or whipped from behind by her predator... perhaps both simultaneously, depending on how naughty or arousing or responsive or out of control the girl has been...' Satan chuckled a low, velvety chuckle as my mouth went dry. 'So it's a good thing you're none of those things, right Larkin? Because if you were, it would be safe to assume that you just ran into the very place that every Barachiel man has dreamed of cornering you within for over a year...' She sighed as my heart spasmed. 'You really are borderline suicidal still, aren't you?'

I felt like I was going to be sick and when Satan laughed, I knew that she *was* sick- sick and wrong... and very, very right: I'd unintentionally cornered myself in the dungeon room, and at any moment, someone was going to find me in here and I'd be almost completely at their mercy when they did.

But only *almost* completely. With a racing heart and mind, I scanned the room, located the wall full of whips and chains and rushed over to it, selecting the nastiest looking one before I turned back to face Satan.

'Borderline suicidal,' I said softly, running the length of leather through my fingers, shuddering to think of who had been struck by them last. 'But I'm not quite there yet!'

Which was more than I could say for whatever man tried to take me in there.

13.

'That's the fighting spirit I've been waiting to see re-emerge,' the pretty elongated corners of Satan's lips tugged to the right in a smile. 'But what I've just explained to you is not as horrible as it sounds...I don't imagine that *you'd* enjoy it much, but with the right lover, submitting to unbridled passion can be rather exciting.'

My face flamed hotly, and I wrapped my arms around myself to hold my insides together while still clutching the handle of the whip tightly in my hand. I couldn't believe that I'd looked myself in the one place that I'd prayed I'd never have to see!

'Kohén wouldn't bring me in here to submit to anything,' I hissed, hugging myself even more tightly. 'So thanks for the tip, but I'll never have to find out how I feel about this nasty stuff because he won't ask me to explore it with him. I'm imprisoned here because he's *too* romantic, not because he is a deviant!'

'He'll never have to bring you in here, because you brought yourself here! And although I could shake you for being so foolish, I must admit, if anything's going to push you over the edge of insanity and back into reason, then seeing all of this ought to do it!' Satan pressed her hands up to the glass again. 'Take me into you Larkin, and though I know my word isn't worth much to you, I can swear to God that you'd be better off accepting me into you here, than anyone else!'

'No,' I stepped around the bench, putting it between us, wondering why I couldn't see myself reflected in the glass beside her. 'No I don't fear this room, not more than I fear you. Kohén would never-'

'Elijah has already threatened you with one hundred lashes today- where do you *think* that will transpire? And despite what you believe about your vanilla beau, young Kohén will lead you in here by the hand within the next forty-eight hours if you don't let me help you escape NOW!'

'What?' I gasped, looking around at the odd instruments, which looked like they'd been crafter solely for the torture of making a woman scream. My Kohén, in this place? Never!

She's just trying to scare you! Don't fall for it!

'I am trying to scare you to *save* you!' Satan smacked her hands against the glass. 'I've told you over the past few days that you're doomed if you stay here, but you ignored me and now you have mere seconds to turn this around, and the only way you can do that is by taking my hand!'

I glared at her. 'Well I won't be doing that, so why don't you go haunt Amelia-Rose instead, hmm? Because I'm fairly certain she's evil- and almost one hundred percent certain that she'd take your hand.'

'This isn't about who is good or who is evil- we are all both!' The devil shook her head. 'And even if I wanted to explain what's gone wrong, I haven't the time, not since you blocked me from coming into your room. *Now* is your last chance to escape this place with your soul intact and with my complete assistance, so take that chance and take my hand or you will be wiped from the pages of Eden's history as I was the first time-'

The lock rattled and the door was flung open, and I screamed and stumbled back into the bench behind me when I saw a man stride in. 'Lark? Baby?' A light flicked on- a bright white light that muted the red and all at once I felt a million percent better about a lot of things and a million percent worse about others. Kohén saw me in one beat and was crossing the room in the next, demanding:

'Larkin! What on earth are you doing in this awful place?' he looked around with an expression of disgust curling his lip while I gasped for air, relieved that it was him and not Karol. 'And how did you get in? It was supposed to have been locked!'

'It wasn't, and I didn't know where I was going when I opened the door!' I whimpered, dropping the whip and extending my hands to him when he did the same to me. 'I feared that Karol was chasing me through the halls, and I

174

couldn't get into my room so I ran and tried every door until one opened-' I sobbed when he wrapped his arms around me, burying my face in his shoulder so I wouldn't have to see Satan for a second longer. She'd always given me the creeps, but the things she'd been screaming at me just moments before had been utterly terrifying. She'd made it sound like I was as good as dead already!

She'd been convincing, too. That thing about the forty-eight hours that would bring me back to this room under duress... she had sounded so sure of herself! So sure that for one awful moment, I'd actually considered just doing it- just taking her hand on the off-chance that her predictions had been right. Hadn't I seen enough evil things going down in that room to convince me that she very likely could be right? What was the point of striving to be good and pure like Constance if in the end, she was miserable enough to slap people like me anyway? And what good would it do me to have God on my side if men like Karol who had the same unwavering faith were still capable of doing vile things, like bringing a woman here? The Barachiels had kept Satan out of their thoughts and hearts yes- but that had not kept them from doing evil things with their actions!

Now you're getting it! Satan whispered and I shivered, burrowing into Kohén like I could wear his love and faith like a second skin. *Now, ask Kohén about the Barachiel stillborns while I'm able to listen to his answer- I'd very much like to know how much he knows, and how much eludes him!*

I squeezed my eyes shut, mentally squeezing her out of my brain. Her threats had certainly spooked me and my past experience had certainly proven that Barachiel men would bring women here if provoked... but she had to be lying about Kohén bringing me to this room- HAD to be, because even if he'd plotted such a course of action, she wouldn't have known about it. She *couldn't* have known about it, because she couldn't get into Kohén's mind; a fact she'd already given away.

It had been a lie- a very clever lie meant to dupe me into handing my body over to her and now that I had Kohén in my arms again, I took a moment to thank god for delivering him to me quickly before Satan had had the chance to turn me against my intention to do what was right, and before Karol had found the opportunity to search for me first.

'I want to get out of this room!' I whispered piteously, trying to tune Satan out when I heard her doing what sounded a lot like flipping furniture over in my mind in a fit of anger. 'Kohén please... I want to get out of this room!'

'Of course, of course- I never wanted you to see this place either, which was why I was so stunned to find you here!' Kohén squeezed me more tightly, and I felt him trembling in my arms as he pulled back to look me over. 'Darling, you're so skittish! After what I'd just heard about your behaviour out there, I had expected to come in here and find you breathing fire, not trembling in a corner.'

'What did you hear?' I asked, alarmed.

Kohén smiled. 'That you fought with the skill of a trained soldier and did your part to defend the castle... that you saw Cherry getting attacked and screamed, finding your voice at last. That she saw that my mother had struck you, quit her job, denounced us all and begged you to run away with her...' he moved in closer and cupped my chin, tilting my face up to his. 'That you *stayed*. Not only that you stayed but that you bolted back in here when you had the perfect opportunity to flee out the front door.' He kissed my wobbling lower lip gently. 'I'm so proud of you, sweetheart- proud and relieved.' My fluffy hair was plastered to my cheeks but he raked his fingers through it and pulled it away before cupping my face. 'You love me. You won't admit it yet, but I know it's true. And so long as you love me... anything is possible.'

He kissed me softly then and though I allowed it to happen for a moment or two, I could not shake my ill-feelings towards the room we were in and so, I broke the kiss off. 'Where's Karol?' I asked quickly, bending to pick up the whip again, which Kohén took from me with a lip curled in disgust. 'Kohén he saw me- he chased me-'

'He saw mother as soon as he got near to where you'd been standing, and changed tactics the moment he realised that you were safe again, and that she and T'are were practically surrounded.' Kohén said quickly, wrapping his arm around my waist and angling me towards the door as he tossed the whip onto the table. 'So don't worry, he's got far too much to deal with to justify coming in to check up on you, and because mother won't stop singing your praises, you won't have to worry about father paying us a visit to see through those whippings that he was threatening earlier either.'

'Really?' I asked weakly, and Kohén nodded, kissing the side of my head.

'Really. You raced to her defence today, darling, even after she'd apparently struck you, so I don't think you could have garnered better publicity if you'd tried-or a better good deed to perform to balance out the rule we broke together earlier.' He paused directly beneath the chandelier, scanning the side of my face as he tilted it towards the light. 'Speaking of which- remind me to trip her over in public at some point in repayment for that slap! What on earth brought that on? Not that I'm surprised but...'

My stomach rolled as I tried to dream up a quick lie. 'Nothing really- it was the first thing she did after your father left. I suppose she was mostly embarrassed over us having been caught in such a compromising position in front of such pious witnesses. And I couldn't respond to any of her questions so I guess she just lost it...' I touched the side of my face and winced when I felt the tender spot where her diamond had cut into me. 'To be fair she apologised almost immediately after, and I know she didn't mean to hit me as hard as she did. Most of the damage was caused when I rebounded onto the bedpost, not by her hand.'

'Don't make excuses for her Larkin,' Kohén said coldly, leaning in to kiss my throbbing head better. 'The duchess hasn't the right to lay a hand on a Companion, no matter what the circumstances are. You are my property and mine to manage- not hers.' I raised an eyebrow at him, nonplussed by all he'd just said and he made a face and blushed scarlet. 'I mean... you *know* what I mean. I don't think of you as my property- I just meant that if she has a jurisdiction here, disciplining you certainly doesn't fall under it...'

'Hmm...' was all I responded with, letting him know that he was on wafer-thin ice without actually saying it. I'd gladly stir Kohén in any room of the castle- but not this one! 'Anyway... I wish Cherry hadn't made such a fuss over it but she saw my eye and flipped out completely- in front of everyone! Your mother didn't have the presence of mind to explain herself or point out that I'd broken a serious rule, and even if she had- Cherry didn't give us a second to react before she flew off the handle and started accusing your mother of turning out just like your father...' I was rambling and I knew it, and because I knew I'd be able to plea hysterical babbling later, I decided to take the opportunity to clear up one of Satan's other inferences while we were on a related subject anyway. '...among other things. Hey- why is it that women are unable to birth live daughters with Barachiel men again?' I was trying so hard to sound relaxed and only mildly curious, and yet every muscle in my body grew rigid with tension as I watched his expression change. 'I'm sure it's been explained before but-

'What?!' Kohén demanded, eyes widening. 'Did Cherry say that? That's ludicrous!'

I gave him a chatoyant look. 'Ludicrous is a strong word. Has it escaped your notice that there's never been a Barachiel daughter? Because it certainly hasn't escaped *mine*.'

Kohén frowned at me. 'Well, I know that we've never had one before, but that doesn't necessarily mean that we can*not*, does it?'

'But the high mortality rate with the females stillborn into this family suggests otherwise,' I pointed out, and the V between Kohén's brows deepened. 'It might have seemed sort of normal to the former kings but come on... we're twenty-one generations in now. Doesn't it trouble you to know that there's never been a prin*cess* of Arcadia? Especially when so many males have been born via multiple pregnancies that were fatal to the female infants?'

'*What* mortality rate? What *still*borns?' Kohén looked anxious. 'Larkin... what exactly did Cherry say? I'm getting very confused. It almost sounds like you're saying that a bunch of female infants have been born to the men in my family... but that they all *died*? If you are, you should know that it's an awful accusation to make- awful and utterly fictional.'

I scanned Kohén's eyes for signs that he was withholding information, but they were as clear as ever-pinched only by his sudden distress. I sighed and waved my hand, realising that I'd been foolish to not only allow Satan to make me paranoid about more than I already had to feel paranoid about- but to raise such a scandalous subject while I was in a room that had been built in order to discipline people. There could very likely be a secret graveyard of Barachiel stillborns somewhere... but I was fairly certain that Kohén was innocent of any knowledge of it, and that was all that mattered for now.'

'Oh,' I said quickly, scratching my head and looking away. 'Oh... I guess you're right... maybe I am confused...' I closed my eyes and pretended to shake it all off. 'Come to think of it, I don't know if Cherry said anything on that subject at all. I had strange dreams last night- perhaps I have confused something that was said to me in one of them with something that was actually said by Cherry when she was scolding your mother...?'

Or perhaps Satan forged those entries in that book to waste my time! Argh!

Some of the light came back into Kohén's eyes. 'Ahh... yes well if you had nightmares about the subject than I'm not surprised to think that you'd confuse reality with fantasy, especially in light of Cherry's ranting.' He pulled me in and kissed me again. 'But as far as I know, there is nothing to stop us Barachiel men from having a daughter, and the only reason why we haven't, I've been told, has something to do with how stunted breeding was for us all back in the beginning.' He pushed my hair out of my eyes further. 'The men before me didn't have many options to choose from and everyone had been poisoned in some way during Armageddon. Satan reversed the damage done to the earth, but not its inhabitants, and we are still trying to evolve out of that.' He shrugged. 'Most families have a similar issue to ours. Some are too fertile, some are infertile, some cannot seem to make a baby without a massive nose or southern colouring, some cannot carry a specific gender, some simply have dominant male ones and in Amelia-Rose's case, I suspect one of her ancestors bred with a dog at some point, which explains why she is the way she is today.' He paused to grin winsomely me as I giggled. 'I love that sound!' he kissed me quickly. 'Everything's recessive though… sooner or later this particular defect will be weeded out too… it's just a matter of a Barachiel man finding the right woman to impregnate, I think, and we might be close now, you know?'

'How so?' I asked, prodding him to start moving towards the door again. God, how many years was it going to take for me to wipe Satan's access from my mind so I'd be able to be in a room with mirrors again and not quake in fear?

'I don't know what Karol's intentions are as far as Ora is concerned exactly, but he's made it very clear over the past few days that he will not settle for a joined union or an arranged one- he's in this for love and nothing short of it!' I raised an eyebrow and he chuckled. 'Well, that's what he says, anyway, but I don't care how genuine his sentiments on the subject are so long as he weds *some*one and soon.'

I frowned at him. 'Why would Karol marrying for love affect his chances of having a girl?'

'Because he's cast a wider net in his search for his perfect bride than any prince before him has had the luxury of doing, of course,' Kohén said simply. 'I think something like ninety-eight percent of Barachiel unions have been arranged in the past, and those matches have been made only with women from the noble Caste, which is pretty limiting, wouldn't you say? They make up twelve percent of our population, and the women within it only account for four percent, so it's no wonder that none of us have found a woman to marry out of love, is it?'

'But Ora's noble,' I pointed out.

'Yes, but she's a noble from another continent entirely, and that has to be a game changer.' Kohén shrugged again. 'And even if it's not, I think it's a great sign of what's to come. Things are changing in the world, Larkin- I think most of the customs we embrace today will be obsolete in twenty or thirty years, as will our fertility issues.'

My heart began to race again. 'Like... the Given custom?'

Kohén paused on the threshold and pulled me into his arms, kissing the tip of my nose. 'Especially that one. Once we have had a third-born queen...'

I sighed and turned my face away. 'Please, don't start that up again... I was rather enjoying your company, for once.'

'Hey, you're under my jurisdiction, remember? And seeing as how I'm not taking the opportunity to put you over my knee in here, I think it's only fair that I put my foot down on this matter: I'm marrying *you,* Larkin of Eden. I don't know how or when or how it will be received... but I'm going to make it happen, and you are no longer permitted to scoff when I raise the subject, all right? Not if you don't want to end up with my handprint on your delicious bottom.'

I wrangled my way out of his hold. 'Don't joke about that,' I said sourly, 'it's not funny. This room ought to be burned to the ground.'

Kohén sighed. 'Oh come on… it's not so bad. Most of the people that have ever been brought here agreed to come here, and apparently enjoyed all that transpired.'

I looked at him sharply. 'And how do you know this?'

Kohén reddened. 'I… I've discussed it with Karol before, all right? And a few of the guys on Pacifica once when we were drinking and the conversation turned to sex. It's not my thing- I love feeling your hands on me and hearing you cry out my name and would never limit your ability to do either… but some men simply enjoy dominating women, and some women enjoy being dominated.'

'Is your father very into it?' I asked, feeling chilled inside.

'Not anymore. He says it was a fleeting phase of his- one that he outgrew long before he procreated.' Kohén paused. 'I think he liked using the crop and from what I've heart, Resonah was the one that liked taking it, more so than Rosina.'

'Stop!' I covered my ears, thoroughly disgusted. 'The mental images will haunt me worse than the stillborn thing will!'

Kohén chuckled as he took my hands off my head. 'Well like I said, it was a long time ago. Karol's the only one that uses it now, and his tastes are apparently pretty specific…'

I shuddered. 'Let me guess- that awful mouth gag thing paired with a whip?'

'No. He once told me that he really enjoys, uh, the same thing that I do…' Kohén jogged his eyebrows and drew a line from my belly-button down to my pubic bone. 'Explorations... of this part of a woman…'

I batted his hand away. 'Stop that! And don't let me hear you say that you two have anything sexually deviated in common or I shall chase after Cherry after all!'

But Kohén pulled my hair. 'Not in the same *way*. I like to taste you and only you, but he's sort of fascinated by how female anatomy works in general, which explains while he looks at every woman he meets like she's a meal-'

'Ew!' I whimpered.

'It's definitely a fixation of his,' Kohén agreed, glancing across the room now too. 'He likes to use his fingers, his mouth and, um, other things to bring a woman to a climax- repeatedly. And when I say repeatedly I don't mean once or twice, you know? I remember he vanished with Adeline for a day and a half once and when they re-emerged, she was wearing twenty or thirty pieces of gold more than she'd had before and was grinning like…' he chuckled and looked away. 'He's addicted to the power trip and likes teasing… well he used the word deprivation a lot, so I guess he brings them to the edge and backs off so that it's like torture after a while, understand? Gives him a kick or something.'

'If that's all he's into then why does he need this room to do it in?' I asked, still convinced that it had been used for darker purposes than the ones he'd outlined for me.

'Those rack things apparently have things to attach bindings to, and he says that once they're bound spread-eagled, or bent over that other thing, then they've got no way of controlling their reactions to him and-'

'Enough!' My face was so hot I thought my features were going to melt off. I didn't want to know such private things about Karol, and I certainly didn't want to have reacted physically the way I had to Kohén's explanation, because I'd imagined being the one underneath Karol's mouth and the idea hadn't horrified me the way it should have. 'Seriously- don't you have a crisis to deal with out there- far away from in here? You know… before I vomit on the floor?'

Kohén's expression immediately sobered. 'Dammit Larkin, you're right! I completely forgot about all of that because I was so relieved to see you, but I need to get you back to your room and then get out there to help clean up that Banished mess.' He lead me out the door, flicked off the lights and then closed it behind me with a click that harmonised with my relieved exhalation. 'They didn't do anywhere near the amount of damage that they could have done if there had been more people up and about at that hour, but there are eight or nine people hurt, we have a healer on the lamb when we need her the most and a whole bunch of nobles to calm down before they get it in their head that Arcadia's become the Callielian ghetto and hightail it out of here.'

'Would that be so bad?' I asked.

'Hey the sooner the festivities end the better as far as I'm concerned, but my father will be intolerable for months if this ball doesn't happen after how much money he's parted with in order to make it the biggest party in Eden's history...' Kohén took my hand and squeezed it tightly. 'Anyway the bottom line is that I'm going to be rather busy today and I may not get the chance to visit you for hours. I'd love to have you out and about now that you've got that lovely voice back, but thanks to the way Karol shot after you...'

'I'm an indoor kitty again today,' I finished for him, squeezing his hand back. 'It's all right Kohén, I understand. Besides, we don't have long to go now, right?'

'Less than forty-eight hours,' Kohén said cheerfully, pausing by my door to unlock it and then grandly swinging it open in front of me. I froze to hear the words- the devil's words- be repeated in his angelic voice, but Kohén gave me a small pat on the backside, prodding me over the threshold, and when I turned back to hold the door open, panic overwhelming me suddenly, Kohén smiled gently and opened the door all the way- and then stepped away from it, leaving it open, 'and then you're free to come and go as you please- provided that Ora has been successful in domesticating our arrogant crowned-prince, of course.'

'What if she doesn't?'

Kohén sighed. 'Then I guess I will have to have a talk with him, won't I? Man to man- or sword to sword, if need be.' He made a face. 'Then again, I'm not sure that I'll be able to best him when it comes to combat yet, so I'll probably step in as Arcadia's first princess and go running to Shep for help. He can't do anything to physically prevent Karol from pursuing you of course, but Karol wants every shepherd in Arcadia to think the world of him, and will quake at the idea of me telling one *this* sort of truth about him.'

I worried my lower lip with my fingertip. 'I don't know, Kohén... the idea of spilling Lindy's secret to someone else-'

'Do you want a brand or not, Larkin?' Kohén asked me quickly, and my eyes popped open.

'No! I told you, if you burn me, it'll be the last time you touch me- while I'm alive, anyway.' I hugged myself. 'And I meant it, Kohén. People that love other people cannot press smouldering iron to their flesh, mark them forever as a whore and expect to use the word 'love' again after.'

Kohén sighed. 'Well that's the only thing I can do to guarantee that Karol will not chance touching you outside of marriage, so if you truly hate the idea of getting one as you say you do, then you're going to have to consider some other courses of action.'

'I'll consider it, okay?' I said quickly, looking around at the open door with renewed unease. 'But if you're still this wary of what Karol might do as far as I'm concerned, then is this wise? Your elder brother can still get into the harem, can't he?'

'The guard will still be there so officially, no, but there is a chance so... so I ask you to decide for yourself.' His eyes darkened, but remained gentle. 'Larkin if you fear Karol coming after you, or if you do not feel up for my company, then you may close the door and lock it from the inside whenever the urge to do so overwhelms you from now on.' He lifted my hand and kissed it sweetly. 'But after the kisses I received this morning, and the butterflies that are still fluttering about in my belly now, I no longer fear what will happen if you are not locked in, and trust that you will not lock me out. Not of this room, and not from your heart.'

I swallowed hard, feeling the butterflies fluttering in the pit of my stomach again. 'Because you believe that you have finally found a way to control me?' I asked, only half teasing him.

'No,' Kohén's eyes were eternal. 'Because I have always been under your control, and I think maybe you've finally realised that it is not you that will be ruined by our love, but *I*.' Kohén wrapped his hand around the nape of my neck and pressed a kiss against my forehead. 'Please, don't ruin me, my love,' he whispered, and then he turned and strode away, raking his hands through his hair so that the light above caught his silver ring and caused it to wink at me.

I watched him go for a long moment, cupping my lower abdomen as though comforting the butterflies still dwelling within, not only those caused by Kohén's tenderness towards me, but the fearful ones that Satan and Karol had manifested in there. I didn't want to take Satan's advice, but her warnings about what might happen to me in the next forty-eight hours were still lingering thanks to Kohén's words, and when I remembered the look on Karol's face when he'd come rushing after me...I couldn't take it. For better or for worse, I pulled the door closed and sank back against it with relief when I heard the deadbolt slunk into place within.

I locked myself in the gilded cage, and then I pulled up my knees so that I could hug them and cried and cried for the suicide that the swan had just assisted with, on behalf of the duckling she'd once been, and would never be again.

14.

Kohén was so pre-occupied on Friday that I didn't see him again until noon, when he delivered me my lunch, kissed me quickly on the forehead, remarked that I didn't look so good and that perhaps I should take a shower and then took off again, telling me that he was too busy to explain all that had happened since he'd seen me last, but that he would be back as soon as he could.

I didn't have a mirror in my room now and wouldn't have reached for one if I had, but I touched my swollen face tentatively and then looked down at myself and realised that I probably was a fright. After he'd left me I'd done nothing but cry and sleep, my toga was a bit grimy looking after all of the sweating and running around that I'd done earlier that morning, my hair had gone from being fluffy to lank and there was an indent in my leg from where I'd fallen asleep on top of the power cord to my lamp.

Wow, I better be careful! If Kohén starts to think that I'm gonna be like one of those wives that lets themselves go after marriage, I could be in real trouble! Well, maybe not me, but Kohl will...

Vowing to start taking care of myself now that I'd had four days to adjust to my new, sequestered life, I took my dinner tray over to the vanity that I'd turned into a desk and sat down to eat, but the moment I removed the silver cover from the meals, the scent wafting off the chicken breast was so overpowering that I practically gagged. Within a heartbeat, I'd slammed the silver cover back down over the steaming delicacies beneath like a musician with a symbol, signalling the end of a song.

Oh my gosh, when was the last time I was able to keep something down? I thought, rising from the desk and going over to the bed again, lying down on my back as the room spun around me. *Three full days? Four? Did I eat anything on Tuesday, or was I so excited for the parade that I skipped breakfast too?*

I whimpered softly to realise that I'd shrunk my appetite to the point of being non-existent and that if I didn't turn it around soon I was likely to get very unwell... but I honestly couldn't handle the idea of lifting that cover off the food again so I closed my eyes, rested my forearm over them to block out the glare rebounding off my white walls and breathed out slowly, telling myself that I'd ask Kohén to bring me something a little less overpowering next time... maybe even some of that soup that Kohl had been cooking up for the Banished. Not that I supposed that he was going to be doing that again, not after that morning's incident...

Oh dear... how much trouble is he going to be in for that? I wondered, laying my other forearm over my eyes and groaning when I remembered the way that Elijah had looked at Amelia-Rose in Kohén's bedroom earlier. He'd been fit to be tied! So if he could express that much anger towards a noble girl that he'd apparently been trying to impress for years, then how was he going to handle the son he'd *never* tried to impress? Would Kohl get a whipping?

My stomach cramped up at the idea and I turned onto my side, drawing my knees up to my chest in reflex to the pain I felt when I imagined what poor Kohl was probably going through right then. It was dangerous to think about him though, and as I balled up around the empty feeling inside me, I realised that I'd been avoiding letting Kohl into my thoughts all week intentionally, which had been selfish and unkind on my part, but a survival instinct that I'd latched onto when I'd realised that I would not be able to latch onto *him* instead.

At first I had filtered Kohl from my thoughts for fear that it would push me over the edge of my hysteria and cause me to do or say something foolish on his behalf towards Kohén (as I had the night before, when I'd drawn unfavourable comparisons between the twins) and then I'd been so furious with Kohl for tainting his soul by committing murder that I'd been unable to think of him without pain and anger boiling over inside me. Then I had allowed myself to think of him, only to chastise him silently over his dalliance with Amelia-Rose but now... now I was thinking that if Constance didn't heed my advice and help him through this awful time, then there was a chance that he was going to end up leading a miserable life regardless of what any of us did to help him, and I couldn't bear that. I was suffering enough as it was on his behalf and I was okay with that because I still believed that I deserved it, but then again, I'd done all I had to keep him alive and well and by rebelling against all the comforts offered to him, he was throwing it back in my face! He didn't have me, no, but he had his freedom, but he was using it to piss everyone off by the sounds of it, and that was just a waste. How was he ever going to win the nation's respect if he debuted back in court by first flying into a fit of rage and despair over his brother's girl, then by giving a bunch of dangerous convicts the chance to run rampant through Eden? I was sure Constance could find a way to smooth over most of the bad publicity that her sons were capable of drumming up but honestly... what had he been thinking when he'd handed dangerous people kerosene instead of coals? Surely he must have realised that... that...

My breath caught and I sat up so fast that my room spun again as the question hit me hard in the gut: What if Kohl had handed the convicts kerosene because he'd understood exactly how much damage that might be able to cause with a little firepower?

No! I thought. *No he wouldn't have!* But my heart thudded in my chest- because I knew that if Kohl had done something like that, then there was only one reason why he would have done it and that one reason was *me*. Had he intended to help me escape all along? Was this his purpose now? Or had he merely hoped that the banished would have found a way to cause mayhem that might inadvertently lead to my getting the opportunity to run?

The opportunity that I turned down...

That realisation made my eyes burn. I thought that Kohén and I had both made it clear that there was no way that I was getting out of this harem now, but what if Kohl hadn't believed that I'd genuinely surrendered my life in order to save his, and that escaping was a non-issue for me now? What if he kept trying to pull the kind of stunts that he thought might give me the opportunity to run, opportunities that I had no choice but to rebuff for his well-being? Kohén had threatened to kill him- had threatened to *scalp* him even, but what if Kohl thought they'd been impassioned threats made in the heat of a moment that would never amount to anything? *I* knew that Kohén hadn't made such threats idly- he'd never said a word in his life that he didn't mean... but if Kohl didn't then what would it matter if Constance and I were both working our asses off to keep him safe? The third-born prince would be a ticking time bomb no matter what we did, and the detonator was balled in his angry fist and well out of my reach.

I sat up again, feeling all panicky once more. Had I said enough to convince Constance to do what needed to be done to keep him in hand? Had she believed that I wasn't exaggerating how much trouble we were all in? Had the altercation with Cherry changed anything? What if right now, Constance was out there running her mouth- telling Kohén that I'd confessed all to try and trick him into admitting something that I hadn't? Weak and tired as I was I could barely think straight and sensed a full-blown panic attack coming on, so I got up and headed for the shower, tearing off my toga on the way and leaving it in a heap on the floor. Once I was in there I washed my hair twice, brushed my teeth three times and even let the water run cold over me for a few seconds to try and combat the anxious heat that was broiling me in my own sweat from the inside, but when that didn't work, I got out and dressed clumsily, leaving my hair out to drip down my back. I didn't know where this sense of unease was coming from, but I felt like I was being engulfed by a million worries from the inside out, and I was powerless to keep them at bay or the panicked sweat from prickling through me.

'Calm down...' I whispered to myself as I paced my floor, fanning myself with a book on Companion Protocol. 'Just breathe Larkin, breathe...'

But that didn't work either. For days I'd been pushing all of my worries into a little box inside me and locking it with a key after so they wouldn't get the chance to eat at me, but something had changed that morning and now I felt as though that box had exploded and I didn't have enough brain cells to sort all of my troubles out into categories, let alone the calm state of being required to soothe them. I worried about the tracker that Cherry had mentioned, and I wondered if Satan had really been lying when she'd suggested that I'd kill myself within forty-eight hours. Dying still didn't scare me the way it would have if I'd been emotionally balanced (which I clearly, was not), but worrying about what would happen to drive me to give up on my life (and Kohl's with it) was enough to make me chew my fingers at the knuckles.

Will Karol grab me, take me into that dungeon room and rape me? Will Kohén? Possibly, but why? What would I do to inspire such cruelty? I'm playing along well, aren't I? And Karol's not that dark, is he? Oh God... I don't know, I don't know! Please God, let this be a trick of Satan's! I don't want to die feeling like this!

Still so hot that I was feverish, I paced on, thinking about every single thing that could be going wrong while I was trapped in there, unaware of it and incapable of seeing it coming. I worried that Amelia-Rose had told Kohl what she had seen in Kohén's room that morning, and practically screamed in horror when I imagined her telling him that I was obviously very happy to be Kohén's whore. Then I worried about the way I'd enjoyed those kisses because I knew that my surrender did suggest that I was somewhat content to be Kohén's whore, and that made me yank at my hair and moan. *Was* I content? Could I live like this? How could I have been so infatuated with Kohl a week before, but so indifferent to him now? Well, not exactly indifferent...

but I'd found a way to shut down any feeling of longing that I'd had for him, and that made me wonder if I'd ever cared deeply for him at all, as I'd believed. *Had* I used him? Had he been a stand-in for the real prince all along? I closed my eyes and remembered Pacifica- remembered riding along on the back of Kohl's horse, and a wave of lust and longing practically smacked me to the ground. I grabbed the end of my bed, bent over, cupped my stomach and gasped for air- trying to breathe through pain that was so intense that I was sure someone was tearing my heart in two.

What are you doing to yourself, you idiot? My own inner voice cried. *Forcing yourself to feel pain for Kohl just to make sure that you're a good person? Fuck Kohl! Yes you cared for him and yes you hurt him but there's nothing you can do for him now that you haven't already! You need to save yourself, or he's dead anyway!*

'Oh, what's happening to me?' I whimpered, sinking down onto the furry rug on my knees and bowing my head to the floor while another wave of grief slapped me. Was this Satan's doing? It had to have been! What else could have possibly triggered such an emotional collapse given how I'd had a rather triumphant morning- according to Kohén? 'Breathe Lark...' I raised my head and as I did, I saw the source of my despair or rather- the reason why I was feeling worse now than I had in days. Next to my dinner plate was an innocuous silver bucket it and inside it was the one thing that I had managed to keep down for days- and the one thing I *hadn't* used to fortify myself with that morning: alcohol.

I'm sober! Oh my God! I feel like hell for the first time in days because it's the first time in days that I haven't had at least three glasses to numb myself with by now!

Gasping, I lunged to my feet and crossed the space between myself and the chilled bottle of wine in one leap before plucking it out and frantically unscrewing the bottle cap. It was wonderfully cold and I when I lifted my mouth to the bottle I tilted it and began to slug it down, hard and fast, not stopping until it was half-empty. I lowered it, wiped my mouth and panted for breath again while I tried not to choke, and after a moment I realised that already my fever was abating.

Oh that's just wonderful! Solve your problems by becoming an alcoholic, won't you? Grand plan. Tried and tested, that one.

Fuck you brain! I snapped to myself, taking the time to reach for a glass now that I'd taken the edge off the next wave of anguish. My hands were shaking and clammy but I managed to fill the entire thing to the top without wasting a precious drop, and within a matter of minutes I was reaching for the third and last glass while sitting down at my desk, chuckling as the world began to blur around the edges for me, and a feeling of serenity began to chew away at the panic.

'Much better...' I whispered, taking in a long, smooth breath and enjoying the feeling of fullness inside my tummy again before I raised it to the empty room and whispered: 'Now... who had what issue with what again?' I snorted at my own stupid joke, and it was at that moment that my bedroom door handle clicked and began to rattle. I looked over it as the door eased open and Kohén poked his head through, and because I'd already been sort of grinning at my own idiocy, the sight of Kohén's face made my grin spread further.

'Your highness!' I took a sip from my glass and then beckoned for him to come in. 'I was hoping you'd stop by soon. I'm gonna need something else to eat, I think. And maybe another bottle of wine...?'

'I already brought you some wine and strawberries for supper,' Kohén said softly, closing the door behind him and moving towards my bed without looking at me, and I frowned because the fact that his gait had drooped a lot in the past hour had not escaped my notice.

'Uh oh...' I said, standing up and swaying a little as I watched him lean over to put my new tray and ice bucket onto my bedside table. 'Who's invaded now? Pirates? Pygmy's?' I giggled. 'Salt and pepper bears?'

'No one's invaded,' Kohén said, but he sighed to my boarded-up window and shook his head. 'I have some pretty awful news though… and you're not going to like it.'

That sobered me up a little, and I was already imagining being frog-marched down to the dungeon room. 'What is it?' I asked, trying to sound calm and innocent of anything that I might be accused of. And because he still wasn't looking at me, I picked up and emptied my glass of wine. 'Is it bad?'

'Yeah. I…' he sighed again and turned to regard me while I was draining the rest of my wine glass, and I saw that his eyes were downcast and navy. 'I have to go to the ball, Larkin.'

I snorted bubbles out of my nose and then coughed, and a look of surprise crossed Kohén's face as he crossed to me, taking the glass from my hand and patting my back. 'Hey, are you all right?'

But I was chuckling. '*That's* your crisis?' I wiped the wine out from between my upper lip and nostrils and rolled my eyes. 'Fuck me, you're gonna cry like a bitch if you ever stub your toe or are forced to endure an actual unpleasant event, aren't you?'

Kohén's eyes slitted with annoyance. 'Larkin! What a thing to say!'

'Well excuse me, but what am I supposed to do? Get you a hanky to wipe your eyes with? It's a *party*, Kohén, not a hanging. And how is the fact that you have to go news to you? I assumed all along that you'd be there. Everyone in the city is invited, remember?'

Kohén waved his hand at me and walked away. 'Yeah well despite what you assumed, I'd made up my mind not to go the second we…' his cheeks turned red. 'When I realised that you couldn't…with Karol and all…'

'That I couldn't possibly go without risking the fact that Karol might find a way to separate me from you and everyone else?' I asked softly, and he nodded and I shrugged. 'Oh well, I'm all right with not going, Kohén, and I certainly don't begrudge *you* going, if that's what you're worried about.' And I meant it. I was sad to be missing *a* lovely ball, but not even slightly upset to sit out this *particular* one. Stand around toasting Karol all night? Ugh.

Though it would have been nice to see Ora again... and my friends before they leave Eden forever...

'But *I'm* not all right with it,' Kohén said, looking at me mournfully over his shoulder. 'Lark when have I ever been all right with you missing a special occasion?'

I raised an eyebrow. 'Three times a day for the last three days?'

He looked wounded. 'So you *do* resent missing out on that stuff?'

'No, well... not under the circumstances,' I said, thinking about it. 'I really wanted to hear Shep talk last night and I'm sad to have missed out on that, but I wasn't much of a social butterfly before this happened, so I wouldn't have wanted to be out in front of everyone this week anyway so... no. No I don't resent you for it.' I shrugged. 'I wish things could have been different, but you know me- I'd prefer to hold a book over a dance partner any day.'

Kohén's expression tightened. 'Before *this* happened? And what is *this*?' he twisted and took a step towards me. 'Us?'

I needed more to drink, and quickly. 'Can we not talk about it right now?' I asked quietly, crossing the room and taking my wine out of the fresh ice bucket. 'I'm sorry that you're upset about having to go to a party that you don't want to attend, but I won't let you pick a fight with me over the fact that I'm not upset too- that's not fair.'

'That's...' I heard Kohén make a frustrated sound. 'Larkin I am devastated that I can't take you to this ball, all right? *Devastated.* But I was okay with it, because I had a plan of my own. I was thinking that I'd play music in here, lower the lights, take the boards off the windows so we could watch the fireworks together and-' I snorted and cupped my hand over my mouth, but a laugh overflowed from me anyway. 'What?' Kohén sounded irate, but I could not look at him. 'Why are you laughing now?'

He'd take the boards off the windows so we could enjoy a fireworks spectacle? It sounded so pitiful that I laughed because I would have cried otherwise. I turned to him, grinning. 'Well, so long as you promise to punch a few more air-holes into the boards for me by summer so I can smell the ocean breezes, I'll make my peace with missing out on watching fireworks from my cell tomorrow night, all right?' I unscrewed the wine bottle and made to walk past him, bumping his hip teasingly with mine as I did. 'Have fun, but don't drink too much because the last thing I want to hear on Sunday is that you got pickled and started a fight with the birthday boy-'

'It's not funny!' Kohén grabbed my arm and yanked me back, forcing me to stare into his eyes. 'Larkin, don't you get it? You're the only Companion that I have left now! So if I don't take you, I am obligated to escort someone *else,* remember?' He released me and snatched the bottle of wine from my hand. 'I was afraid that you'd get jealous to learn that fact, but I'm just the guy you need around to punch air-holes into the boards for you from time to time right? So why would you care what I do?'

I felt my hot flush return. 'Escort?' I repeated. 'You have to go to this thing with another girl? Since *when*?'

Kohén raised his brow. 'Were you asleep in class when they taught you that? Yes Larkin, I'm seventeen now so I have to take another girl. It would be considered a slight if I didn't now that I'm old enough to start courting, and as father oh so calmly pointed out before- I am one more slight off an international incident!' He took a sip from the bottle. 'He told me I was bringing you now that you've gotten your voice back, and when I told him that no way was I going, let alone bringing *you,* he threatened to demote me beneath Kohl unless I asked someone else!' He shook his head looking heavenward. 'Apparently there are dozens of girls waiting for me to ask them!'

I pressed my hand to my chest, feeling my heart spin in sickening circles as I imagined Kohén on someone else's arm- laughing with her, dancing with her, filing her wine glass as he was currently filling mine, pulling out her chair... he'd have to tell her she looked lovely, and he'd have to kiss her hand and present her with a corsage. The entire city would watch them twirl around the dance floor, and where would *I* be? Here- staring drunkenly at my boarded-up windows. Jealousy made the alcohol surge to my head and I was glad that I was not still holding onto the wine glass, because I surely would have snapped the stem in my anger.

'Who?' I asked quickly, and Kohén's face turned scarlet. My heart sank. 'Amelia-Rose, right?'

Kohén handed me my wine glass. 'Yes,' he said quietly. 'She told my father that she'd keep quiet about the rule I broke this morning, if only I proved my character first by escorting a lady to the ball, as a gentleman *ought* to. Father agreed for me on the spot and then told me after, and I've been instructed to act excited and delighted about it until the last song is played tomorrow night, or he'll promote Kohl over me- because at least Kohl has proved that he's ambitious enough to put his country before a...' Kohén pressed his lips together and looked away while the word 'whore' rattled around in my brain. 'Kohl asked Amelia-Rose first, apparently, and though father doesn't like her, he says he was relieved to see at least one of his twins stepping up to win over those that would invest in Pacifica's future- and Shepherd Choir is one of those people...'

I felt like I was going to be ill- right there on the rug in front of him. 'Wait... Kohl asked her *first*?'

Kohén glared at me. 'Oh so she's capable of getting jealous, just not over-'

I splashed my wine right into his face.

15.

'I'm not jealous of her going with Kohl, you bastard! I feel sick at the idea of *you* dancing with her, and couldn't have cared less if she'd gone with Kohl!'

Kohén was spitting and wiping at his eyes, but when I said that, he had the audacity to shoot me a relieved look. 'Oh Lark I-'

'But I'm angry that you would step in front of him again like that *while* stomping on my heart again! That poor kid! How is he supposed to move on with his life if you insist on taking every single thing that he wants before he can grab it for himself?'

Kohén looked ridiculously good wet but I tried very hard not to let that have an effect on me. 'He doesn't want her!' he snapped. 'He's using her, Larkin, and she's using the both of us depending on how she wants to look at the time- like a martyr, or a noble! I can't help the fact that Kohl has nothing to lose by disobeying father, whereas as I have everything to lose, can I?'

'I honestly don't know!' I returned, snatching the wine bottle from his hand and re-filling my own glass. 'But I know that despite the fact that we've all made mistakes here, Kohl and I seem to be the only ones paying for it, and why? Because *you* were born first!' I wanted to spit out the truth at him, just to see him suffer the loss of something that truly mattered for once, but I couldn't do that to Constance or Kohl so I grit my teeth against the truth and said: 'You keep swearing to me that you won't forsake what we have by joining with anyone else, but how am I to believe that you'll bend the rules for our love from now until the day we die, if you haven't the power to get out of one fucking party date, three fucking DAYS into our supposed romance?'

'Lark-'

'No! No don't give me an excuse! You should be plotting how to fake a stomach flu to get out of going on a date with her if you haven't got the balls to take a whipping for it instead-'

'I have a lot more on the line if I don't take her than a whipping!' Kohén burst out.

'How fucking lovely that must be- to have so much to lose!' I bit back as my tears overflowed as I stepped closer to him. 'Do you know what I have left to lose, Kohén? You. *Only* you. My existence is built around you now…so do you have any idea how it feels, to know that the person you love more than you love yourself can't even make it three *days* after taking your virginity and your life before he must dance with another?' I shook my head, and my tears rolled free. 'No, you can't, and you wouldn't want to. The Barachiel men don't know how to deal with the guilt of breaking a woman's heart, do they? So they turn their back on it- and wonder why they have no wings left to shield their wrong-doings from the rest of the world anymore!'

Kohén went white. 'Larkin- I, I didn't think-'

'Yeah you did,' I sniffled and turned away from him. 'You knew I'd hate it, which was why you dreaded telling me. But I can't help but wonder… did you spend more time on your way down here worrying about how it would make *me* feel? Or more time worrying about how it was going to affect *you*?' I walked to my bed and sat down on it, keeping my back to him. 'Go to the party, Kohén and earn that crown- because from now on, I'm going to start asking for a piece of jewellery every time I take you into my arms, like a whore is supposed to because I'm starting to see how large a nest egg I'm going to need- and how *quickly*! And given your insatiable sexual appetite- you're going to go broke before you find a joined spouse that will give you babies in compensation for her time!'

'Larkin-'

'Get out!' I screamed at him, turning around and swiping my meal tray onto the floor, scattering strawberries everywhere. 'Get out! Get out! Get out! Start working on how to get kisses for free, because I won't be playing your pretend games anymore that you've proven once again how utterly fucking worthless your promises are!'

Kohén was grey now, grey and backing towards the door with tears streaming down his face. 'Sweetheart, please, calm down I'll-'

'GET OUT!' I picked up the ice bucket and flung it after him and Kohén cried out and ducked as it missed his head by half an inch. Ice exploded everywhere. 'Kohl has probably just been served lunch, so if you act quickly, there's a chance you could swipe it from him before he gets a bite!'

I heard Kohén gasp but I was sick of being ignored-sick of the way he was staring at me like *I* was the hurtful one. I got to my feet and raced towards the door, stuffing him out of it and slamming it between us hard enough to make the wall shake. I felt him turn the lock but I grasped it, holding it still and knowing that I was probably sealing my own fate within that dungeon room but I did not care, Kohén had broken so many promises to me, and I knew that if I did not get him out of my sight, I was likely to do a lot more than throw a plate at his head- I was very capable of killing him!

I'm sorry Kohl! I thought to myself, weeping like I would never stop. *I'm so sorry! God, if I die tomorrow night, let me get the chance to tell him that first, all right? I'm trying to help him, but everything I do is just causing him more pain, one way or the other!*

Kohén begged and pleaded loud enough for me to hear it for about five minutes, but I held firm to the door and wept silently against it until I felt the resistance dissipate. Only then did I slump to the floor and sob, grateful for the ice that was there for me to press my feverish brow against, because I was certain that if not kept contained, the sheer heat of my fury was going to cause me to burst into flames and take the entire castle down around me.

*

There was a thin band of light in the shape of a rectangle that glowed around my bedroom window that I used to monitor time with, and when I came to on my wet bedroom floor that afternoon, I was shocked to see that it had turned a deep pink- indicating that the sun was setting already because once again, I'd slept hours of my life away without having consciously decided to do it.

Did I truly garden once? I wondered, sitting up and groaning as my muscles ached from having done nothing at all. The door handle was rattling again, but I made no move to get out of the way- I didn't have the strength to. *Did I read, and write, and paint and sing and kick around a soccer ball? When? In this life? Surely not!*

'Larkin?' the door opened slowly, and Kohén's voice sounded strange to me- disembodied because he hadn't just walked in like he normally had. 'Larkin... are you...?'

'Armed?' I asked crossly as I felt the door bump into my rump. God I felt weak. 'No, I'm all out of fruit to hurl, so if you're here to drag me off to the dungeon, you don't have to anticipate me putting up much of a fight...'

'Funny,' Kohén said, and then I felt his eyes on me. 'Oh... Jesus, have you been down there this whole time?'

I twisted around awkwardly to glower at him. 'Of course not. I went to a horse racing carnival, then did some laps in the pool, and then-'

'Stop it!' Kohén knelt behind me and I felt his breath puff against the crook of my neck. 'Just stop it! I can't bear to see you like this!'

'Then I shall endeavour to make better use of my time between fuckings from now on. Where is my guidelines book? I'm sure I'm supposed to be doing something when I'm not busy washing your seed off me...'

'Larkin!' Kohén sounded astonished. 'Don't do that! Don't act like I only come to you for sex! We haven't made love in days!'

'Whoops, I've been a bad little whore,' I turned in his arms and slung my arms around his neck. 'Have you come to rectify that? I can't promise that I'll remain conscious throughout the act, but from what I recall, that didn't stop you the first-'

'Please!' Kohén grasped my wrists, and shook me gently. 'No more, okay? I'm sorry that I hurt you, my love, so sorry! But I came to tell you that I did as you asked, okay? I'm not taking Amelia-Rose to the ball anymore- *Kohl* is.'

I'd had several more derogatory things to say at him lined up in my head like a firing line, but at Kohén's words, someone waved a white flag and I lowered the canons. 'What?' I asked, astonished. 'How?'

Kohén looked utterly wrecked- pale and red-eyed and tense, but he smiled gently and shrugged. 'I stood up to father, like I ought to have done in the beginning, and I got my way.' He bit his lip. 'It was difficult and required some planning, which is why I've been gone for so long, but I thought long and hard about all you said and realised that the reasons why I ought to have said no were nothing to be ashamed of- so I said them all: not only to him, but in front of Amelia-Rose *and* her father.'

I blinked quickly. 'What did you say?' *And if you're not here to whip me, then how far off is your father?*

Kohén guided me over to the bed, sitting me down and clasping my hands, lifting my wrist to kiss it. 'I asked Shepherd Choir for spiritual guidance for matters that concerned the relationship between myself and my twin and naturally, he was all ears. I confessed that I often felt guilty for receiving perks that Kohl cannot share in, and asked him how I ought to handle it.'

'And what did he say?'

Kohén smiled. 'He said that no one could fault me for having to accept certain entitlements, but that I should strive to keep the ground between us level and fair whenever I could- that if I had the luxury to pass on some of my good fortune or to involve him in my many ventures, than I should do just that and eagerly.' Kohén paused, kissing my other wrist. 'So I asked him about matters of the heart. I said what should I do if Kohl and I were both attracted to the same girl? I explained that a week ago, he wouldn't have even been able to consider falling for someone, but now that

he was free and almost as eligible as I, was it fair for me to fight as hard for her as he would? Or ought I be compassionate, and step aside?' He smirked. 'Shepherd Choir
 stared at me and then finally admitted that it would be good for my soul to be generous and step aside, but that it would also depend on who the girl was most interested in too. So...' Kohén wet his lips before smiling at me. 'I turned to Amelia-Rose and said that although I would be a lucky man indeed to escort her to the ball as father had suggested, the amount of time that she'd passed with Kohl that week before father asked me to take her made me feel like I was taking something from him that I had not earned and that finally- I was *not* more entitled to.'

'No!' I hissed, stunned.

'Yep! She went red, of course, and tried to insist that it was fine and that Kohl understood... but I said that even if I hadn't wanted to sacrifice this particular honour, speculation about me and my commitment to my dear friend and lover-' he reached in and kissed my lip quickly '-*you*, was rife, and that I wouldn't feel comfortable subjecting her to the gossips at the ball, for it would surely ruin her evening.' He wriggled his eyebrows at me. 'I thought father was going to have a stroke, but I finished by saying that you truly had had an awful week, and that because you've just lost your own dear friend Kelia, I just wouldn't feel like I was being kind and good by taking advantage of my harem and the most eligible, pious girl in the world at the same time. And just to seal the deal- I confessed to Shepherd Choir that father and I had not known that Kohl had already asked her and that she'd agreed to go with him- and that it wouldn't do for her to be perceived as trading up in Barachiel princes when really, we were both just trying to placate father by agreeing to his arrangement.' He lifted my hands to his lips again, both this time, and his eyes were sparkling with triumph, probably because he could see how awed I was by his little anecdote. 'After I said that, there was nothing she could say, was there? Not without looking exactly like a social climber! Shepherd Choir turned to her and asked if that was true- if she'd agreed to go with Kohl first, and she hummed and hawed about how they'd had loose arrangements- and that was it for Shep! He thanked me for doing the right thing, then told father that I was the very personification of a nobleman, and at such a tender age! How proud he must be of me!'

'No!' I repeated, thrilled.

'*Yes*.' Kohén nodded proudly. 'He immediately ordered Amelia-Rose off to accept Kohl's invitation to the ball, and asked her to apologise for any confusion and then admit that she truly had had her heart set on going with him...and she had no choice but to do just that! And do you know what's funny? I expected my father to wring my neck the moment he got me alone, but do you know what he did? Patted me on the back and said that *that* was the boy he'd raised!'

My mouth popped open. 'He swallowed all of that?'

Kohén scoffed. 'Don't be daft- he didn't buy a single word. But he's proud of the way that I manipulated the situation to my advantage, and of how I managed to get myself off Amelia-Rose's hook without giving her the grounds to act offended. I didn't reject her- I *deflected* her, and I was apparently very convincing in my moral distress.' He squeezed my hands between his, leaned his forehead against mine and whispered: 'And he said that I couldn't very well take anyone to the ball now that Shepherd Choir had whole-heartedly agreed that it would be hurtful to poor Larkin... who had acted so bravely earlier that day!'

I couldn't believe it. 'So you don't have to go?'

He winced. 'No, I still have to go... but I'm going as the master of ceremonies now.'

I frowned. 'Isn't your uncle Ewan doing that?'

'He was, but he was one of the ones that got injured this morning... didn't you hear? Him and our Serein. Someone crushed her fingers when she tried to use her power to make them slip on the marble floors when they first breeched the castle.'

I shook my head, horrified at the thought of the pretty Blue-haired Serein that I seldom got to see and sweet Ewan being injured. 'No! Oh my God, are they okay?'

Kohén sucked a breath in through his teeth. 'Yes and no. Elasta- the Serein- has been healed by my brother, but Ewan got hit in the head pretty hard with a club that one of those Banished bastards hit him with when he rushed out into the fray instead of going into the ballroom like he was supposed to... Karol healed up the laceration, but he's still suffering concussion. In fact, he's lucky that he wasn't killed.' Kohén patted my hands. 'He'll recover, don't worry, but someone suggested that he step down tomorrow night, and so when mother learned that I was without a date again- this late in the game that most of the eligible girls have already been spoken for- she said that I ought to do it, father agreed and now I get to go alone because the master of ceremonies is expected to do just that.' He made a face. 'I mean, it's not exactly an ideal arrangement, because I'm going to have to tell little Karol anecdotes all night, which is a nauseating idea, and I'm probably going to be too busy to be able to come and check on you even once... but on the upside, I have a valid excuse for shadowing him all night, so if he gets it in his head to head into the north wing, I'll be right on his heels. And, the moment his birthday wish is granted- guess what *I'll* be doing?'

The butterflies were back. 'Returning to me?'

Kohén's eyes were smouldering now. '*Racing* back to you,' he corrected me. 'Hopefully to report that the other Given from your year are free, and that Karol is engaged to be married.'

Tears of joy pricked my eyes. 'I can't believe you did this for me. I mean, I can't believe that you almost went with another girl more but... but that was a big risk you took today, Kohén. You could have lost your crown!'

'For the girl that said that she loved me, finally?' Kohén grasped my face in my hands and kissed the tip of my nose. 'There's *nothing* I wouldn't do.'

I blinked, startled. 'What? When did I say that?'

Kohén smirked. 'I didn't think you noticed... but when you were yelling at me earlier, you said that I had no idea what it was like- when the person you loved more than you loved yourself couldn't make it three days after taking your virginity...' he swallowed hard as my eyes spilled over. 'I know you didn't mean to say it, Lark- but you did, and I love the fact that it wasn't intentional. I love the fact that when you scrape all of the drama off from on top of us, all that is left is two people that love one another more than they love themselves... and possibly even more than they already know.' He rubbed his thumb around my cheekbone- the uninjured one. 'And you can deny it all you want- but those lilac eyes... they tell me otherwise. And the things they tell me speak louder than anything you could ever scream at me!'

I was weeping again now and it was giving me a headache, but Kohén wasn't going to dance with anybody else, not this week, at least, and I could have exploded from happiness. 'I do...' I whispered. 'I love you more than even *I* know.'

'Oh God... oh god... do you know how long I've waited to hear you say that?' Kohén whispered, kissing my nose again, and then my cheek. 'Say it again!'

'I love you, Kohén!' I wept as he moaned into the curve of my neck. 'I can't stand it, but I love you!'

'I love you too! Not just for who you are, but what you bring out in me! I know you believe that your influence on me is the harmful sort but Larkin- I was a man today, and I was a man because *you* demanded it!' Kohén pulled back, eyes searching mine. 'How could I take a crown if it meant losing your respect? I am only ever going to end up being a king, because I will have earned the love of a natural-born queen! Without you...' he swallowed hard and pulled my hair over my shoulders. 'Can we kiss now, sweetheart? I promise that is all we have to do until I have earned the right to make love to you!'

I smiled at him through my tears, clutching at his shirt and pulling him closer. 'That's another promise that you'll certainly break,' I whispered, gently kissing his soft lower lip, 'and that's all right, because I will die if you keep it!'

Kohén's eyes became black- indicating that he was lost to himself, and the butterflies in my tummy burst free of their cage as I prayed our love would someday. And despite the fact that we'd just exchanged the sort of tender, delicate and heartfelt words that called to mind images of making love slowly under a star-filled sky, the heat between us was too intense to be handled slowly and sweetly and so we crashed into one another instead- hands tearing frantically at zips and buttons until they were caressing the hot, humming skin beneath, lips reaching for everything that our hands had not yet managed to caress. Feeling sweaty and feverish and frantic, I managed to slip and shoulder my way onto Kohén's lap and Kohén growled into the curve of my neck as he wrapped my hair around his arm and yanked me backwards, forcing me to arch my back while his hand roughly jerked my toga down off my shoulder, shredding it until I felt the chilled air kiss my sensitive flesh.

I want this! Heaven help me but I want this!

'*Oh*!' I breathed, closing my eyes when I felt the blood rush to my head just as Kohén palmed both of my breasts and kneaded them with his strong, smooth fingers. He groaned and hummed when my nipples tightened, and I panted, jerking about as he massaged me deeply and sweetly while grinding his hips into mine, freeing himself quickly with one hand and then tugging at my panties. 'I love you! Kohén Barachiel I love...'

I was so out of my mind with lust that I didn't notice that anything was wrong until Kohén jerked me back up, mashing my breasts to his chest so that he could reach behind me and tug off my belt. 'I'm going to make you scream that out, Lark!' Kohén swore, lifting me again and guiding himself inside me while the world throbbed before my vision- first red and then black. 'And I'm going to cum so hard when you do that you're going to be flooded with hot seed, do you hear me? I'm going to explode inside you, flip you over, take you by the hair and then fuck you from behind until your juices flow as freely!'

'Oh...!' I moaned when I felt the delicious impalement timed perfectly with his filthy promises. 'Yes!'

'Fuck!' I felt him thrust up into me, and then bend me backwards at the waist so that he was now driving down and into me while holding only onto my hips. It felt incredible and I was astonished by his strength, but when I tried to brace myself on the floor with my arms so that I wouldn't slip off of him, my arms collapsed. Rather than let me slide away, Kohén followed me down onto the ground and ducked so that his shoulders came up underneath my thighs. The penetration was borderline brutal that way and yet I knew he was holding back by quite a few inches yet- inches I desperately wanted to learn to take for him-so I pushed my feet down over his shoulders and forced him further into me.

'Oh *fuck*!' Kohén tried to pull back, considerate lover that he was but I was out of my mind with want and out of my mind in general (what was that buzzing sound that was growing louder?) so I squeezed him harder against me until our bellies were pressed together and he buried to his very hilt and he cried out, thickening inside me. It hurt at first but then the sharp pain became a dull throbbing and then a hot, sweet, slick ascension towards a climax, but when my sex began to flutter around him, I felt it echoed in my mind-flashes of dark and light that got darker and darker with every gasp of my breath.

The shift was barely perceptible but it happened fast: one moment I had been upside down and growing dizzy for it, and the next I was the right way up but feeling even more disorientated than I had before. Like someone had flipped a switch, Kohén's features became a streak of watercolours across my vision, and the dirty things he was saying were drowned out by a loud ringing sound.

'Larkin, I'm going to... are you with me...? Larkin...?'

'What?' I asked loudly, turning my face away from his because we were too close and too hot for me to be able to draw a breath. 'Kohén... *what?* OH!' the fluttering became spasms, in my core and in my heart and head but I didn't care. 'Oh... yes...'

And then I was coming undone, while falling through an abyss of watercolours.

PART II

15.

The water colours had vanished and now I was dying and descending into a tunnel of flames so large and thickly flaring that I could not tell where one crimson tongue ended and another began- and I was in *agony* for it.

As I probably deserved to be.

I knew that I'd been falling for quite some time and yet I hadn't come close to reaching the end of my descent because I wasn't hurtling through the flames as I had through the watercolours, but drifting down at an unbearably slow rate, like the first leaf of fall that has been ripped off the top of the tallest tree, that is then forced to hit every branch on its way down to the forest floor. I was meeting my end, yes- falling into Hell as Satan had predicted I would- but I was dying too slowly for death to yet be imminent and *that* was what was torturing me. I wanted to scream to let some of my anguish out, but if I opened my mouth, I knew I'd only inhale more of that unbearable heat, and the flames licking at my blistered and charred skin were painful enough as it was so I suffered with my lips pursed tight and thrashed out against the agony without making a sound.

Breathe in! My sub-conscious urged me. *It will hurt, but it will kill you faster if you do! Breathe in the flames now that you are completely surrounded by them, and end it already!*

But I could not bring myself to open my mouth. I didn't know how long I'd been falling through this fire for- minutes or years? But I was sick of being tormented by the process of dying when it was a swift death that I craved, so because I lacked the courage to inhale the fire, I curled into a ball, trying to weight myself so that I would drop like a stone through the heat, rather than flutter like a feather. Then I slowly began to release the last of my breath, using the very same trick that I'd used in the past when I'd wanted to sink quickly to the bottom of Eden's pool or Pacifica's waves.

For a moment that seemed to work: everything turned darker more swiftly, and even the flames began to turn a dismal shade of burgundy and grew louder and angrier-sounding... but when I closed my eyes and tried to will myself to exhale the last of my final breath so that I'd have no choice to suck in fire and carbon-monoxide after (surely it would hurt less and for a shorter period of time now?) something cold touched my head, and it was as though an icy wind had sluiced through me. My eyes flew open against the brightest, most painful white light I'd ever seen, and my skin hissed where that icy draft touched it, making me shiver uncontrollably.

No!

I threw out my arms and legs like a startled infant as a violently cold shudder rocked me- a chill unlike anything I'd ever experienced before that rushed into my lungs, inflating them- and then suddenly I was being pulled back towards that light and away from the promised darkness. I let out a shrill screech of protest that I could barely hear over the roaring of those flames and tried to duck-dive back into that river of lava before I lost all of the progress that I'd made, but that cold thing had gotten enough of a grasp on me to make the flames flicker and shrivel, and in a matter of seconds, the roaring began to lessen too, allowing me to make out voices for the first time in what felt like an eternity.

'God! It's like she's fighting something off!' someone cried- a voice that I recognised but could not place. They were touching me too- holding me down- but their touch was as scalding as the flames of Hell had been and I fought savagely against them. 'Look at her!'

I'm fighting you off! I wanted to scream, wincing when I realised that I could hear someone sobbing steadily. *Let me fall! Let me go AND LET ME BURN!* But when I opened my mouth to holler that, more oxygen entered my lungs, making the light brighter and the places where I'd been scalded sting more violently.

'I know...' the coldness was all over me now- like someone was rubbing handfuls of snow onto my blistered skin. It brought physical relief but more mental anguish with it. Could they not see that I didn't want to be saved? That I wouldn't want to live in a scorched, blackened body? 'It's quite astounding. Her temperature is so high and her heart rate much too accelerated- she should barely be able to lift a finger against us now, but look how she thrashes!' That cold thing swept up both of my lower legs and I cried out when it stung like I'd been rolled into a nest of wasps, but that unbearable heat clutched my hand (was it another hand?) and I heard a voice I knew all too well sob out a plea:

'Keep fighting baby, please? Come back to me... I can't bear this!' More sobbing, and then the hand released mine and pressed against my chest. 'Oh God... oh God it's lighter now than it was before! Are you sure you're bringing her temperature down?'

'Kohén-'

'I'm doing all I can!' that unfamiliar voice snapped. 'But my power is limited here- I can only keep the damaging fever at bay, not reverse the damage it's already caused!' More sobbing (a woman, I could tell that now) and then the other voice went on in a more controlled voice: 'Look, if you want to give her the best chance to live, then she needs a healer-'

'A doctor is on the way!'

'A doctor cannot do for her what your brother can, and you know it!' wailed the crying woman- was it Constance? Surely not!

'Yes! I don't know why you're refusing to let the crowned prince come in and save the girl that apparently means the world to you, but whatever it is, you need to get over it! And if you cannot, then you need to prepare yourself to say goodbye to her, or shut up and back off, for I can lose my cool and burn too, your highness! And she will surely lose her life if I do!'

I gasped. Fetch Karol? Bring Karol into heal me? No! No anything but that! I screamed, bucking against those holding me down. *Let me burn! Don't bring him in here, don't do it!*

'She's burning up again!' the strange voice cried, as I writhed against her hold on me, trying to force my way out of my own body if that was the only chance I had to escape Karol now. 'My God, her temperature just spiked another two degrees! Prince Kohén...!'

And then I was free-falling through the flames again, and the relief was so great that this time, I made my peace with floating through it, knowing that there were things that could cause me a lot more pain than flames would- and Karol Barachiel's hands were one of them.

I'd do anything to escape the promise I'd made to him. The promise I'd made that had broken Kohén and I.

Anything.

Even burn in Hell.

*

The room was so bright that I felt it like a weight against my eyelids, but my curiosity to see what was responsible for such an evanescent glow after centuries of tormented nightmares forced me to open my eyes and then immediately wince when I found myself looking at the ceiling of a room that was familiar, but not overly so. The littlest room in the harem- the one referred to by Elfin as the 'Gyno'. I had no idea why I was there, but considering as how the last clear memory I had was of kissing Kohén, I knew it was a very bad sign that I'd been moved without being aware of it.

Oh sweet Jesus... what the fuck happened this time? Fire- I remember fire! Did my room catch alight? No, no I was in Hell, wasn't I?

'Lark?' Kohén whispered, and his smile was brighter than the sun as he leaned in and pressed his forehead to mine. 'Oh God... you're awake!' I felt his sweet, minty breath join with mine as he lowered his lips to mine in the gentlest kiss I'd ever known- gentler even than when Kohl had pressed a frangipani bloom to my mouth in Pacifica. 'Praise God, in all of his glory!'

I blinked rapidly. I'd never heard Kohén sound so... devout, and it was rather unsettling. 'Have you been hanging out with Amelia-Rose while I was burning in Hell?' I asked, in a voice that burned my throat. 'Or are you becoming a shepherd now?'

Kohén snorted gently and leaned his forehead against mine once more. 'Burning in Hell? Is *that* what that was?'

'It wasn't?' I tried to sit up, but my movements were restricted by a line that was connected to the back of my hand. A needle had been jabbed into my skin, and the sight of it made my heart flip in fright. 'Oh... my!' I lifted my other hand, trying to tug the cruel-looking device out. 'What is that thing? What are you doing to me?'

'It's a cannula,' Kohén said, catching my hand and pinning it back down to my side. 'It's connected to a bag of fluids that are being fed into your bloodstream to rehydrate you.'

Rehydrate me? So I *had* burned? I touched my face, but it felt smooth if not a little cool. 'I've never seen anything like it before.'

'I'd expect that you wouldn't- I only saw one for the first time myself yesterday morning when we had to treat a young woman that was burned by one of those kerosene bombs. They still use them in the hospitals in the villages sometimes, but we haven't needed a doctor in Eden for years because we've had the luxury of having two healers around- so it was good that mother knew where to find one and how to use it, because I wouldn't have had a clue.'

I stared at him, astonished. 'Wait... your mother was here? Here in the *harem*?'

'*Was*. Nobody knows it though, and I made her leave as soon as you were through the worst of it so she could sneak out unseen...' Kohén nodded to the cannula again. 'I'm sorry if it's unpleasant, my love, but you've almost died a few times in the past sixteen hours and this drip has helped keep you stable since your last severe episode around three in the-'

'SIXTEEN HOURS?' I sat up and the room spun, so I groaned and closed my eyes, sinking back against the pillows that had been propped up beneath me. 'What are you talking about?'

'It's after noon on Saturday- you've been out of it since around ten last night.' I heard that Kohén's voice was rough too. 'I've never been so scared...' he leaned down and kissed my free hand and when I opened my eyes, saw him regarding me with eyes that were fractured with tiny red blood lines. 'Don't ever do that again, all right? Whatever that was...'

'I don't understand,' I said, and then cupped my throat and made a face when I realised how dry my throat was. Reading my mind, Kohén reached for a pewter chalice on the hairdressing stand beside me and motioned me to lean forward and drink from it. I closed my eyes when I tasted the water, and my stomach rolled. 'Oh...' I made a face and pulled back after only having taken a sip to wet my mouth. 'That's weird.'

Kohén frowned at me. 'What? It's just water.'

'Yes but it's the first I've had in...' I looked down at the cannula in my hand and frowned as it all hit me. 'Ohh...'

'Wait, you're saying that's the first water you've had in a while?' another voice asked, and I looked up in shock to see a woman with messy, titian hair making her way across the room towards me. I knew her- though I'd only ever met her once. She was one of the beauticians, but the last time I'd seen her, she'd look impeccable. Now, she looked as haggard as I felt and as Kohén looked. 'How long is a while, exactly?'

I looked at Kohén, and he nodded to the woman. 'That's Dulcie. She's a Nephilim by birth, a beautician by trade and a bitch by-'

'A healer?' I asked, looking back at her and finding that unlikely. The woman was glaring at me like she wished be ill-will, not a rapid recovery!

'No, though it would have been handy to have one here, wouldn't it?' she asked of Kohén, and he sighed and patted my hand before rolling up the cuffs of the cream shirt that I knew he'd been wearing the night before.

'Don't mind her- she hasn't had any sleep, and most of that attitude is directed towards me, all right? No, Dulcie's not a Healer- she has the ability to manipulate temperature, and conduct it through her hands. When you passed out last night, I realised straight away that you were too hot to touch and that your heart rate was too high and light, and because I knew we didn't have a healer anymore-'

'Well, we had *one*-' Dulcie broke in rudely.

'Because I knew that we didn't have *Cherry* anymore,' Kohén re-tried, giving the woman a dirty look, 'I called upon Dulcie to see to you while we waited for an actual doctor to be fetched from the village. I knew that if she could lower your temperature by pressing her icy hand to your forehead, it would draw your fever down- and I was sort of right.'

'I did what I was asked to do...' Dulcie said quietly, still regarding me with a vexed expression. 'But that was all I could do, and you were in such a state of distress that nothing could be done to slow your heart rate or calm you down.'

'Ice wouldn't have worked?'

'We tried,' Kohén said, shaking his head as though amused by it all now, 'but it melted within seconds of being pressed against you.'

I couldn't believe it. I'd melted ice with my fever? That was insane! But from what I recollected... it also sounded about right. 'I fought you off, didn't I?' I asked Dulcie quietly and when she nodded, I turned to Kohén and cringed. 'I remember. When you held me down it felt like burning-hot brands being shackled onto me.' I turned to

Dulcie. 'Not *your* hands though- if that was your hands I remember feeling- then yes, they had a cooling effect on me. I can't say that it was welcome at the time because I just wanted to melt into a puddle of nothingness to escape the pain... but if I'm alive, I dare say it's a credit to you.'

Dulcie looked somewhat mollified by that. 'Well... well that's something, I suppose.' She made a face at Kohén. 'I was beginning to fear that I was going to be punished for failing to save you.'

'Don't be ridiculous, Dulcie. I knew how bad she was and how hard you tried. If you'd failed... well, then it would have been me failing her, not you. And your cynicism regarding my feelings towards Larkin and my treatment of my staff is unfounded- when did the Barachiel name become a monstrous one to you all? Have we not been kind employers? Have you ever seen a woman mistreated in this harem at my hands? Karol is the one that has brought them in with rope burns, not I, and even then the girls seem awfully pleased with their markings!'

I made a distasteful expression, but Dulcie lowered her eyes. 'I apologise, your highness. I shall take pains to curb my tongue on such matters from hereon out.'

I looked from Dulcie to Kohén, confused. 'What are you saying? About the Barachiel name, I mean?'

Kohén sighed. 'It's not what I'm saying about the Barachiel name that is the problem- it is what ill-informed people are saying,' He closed his eyes and shook his head. 'Anyway I'm too tired to think about that right now and it's the last thing I want to discuss.' He kissed my hand again. 'I just want to drink this moment in- of you being alive.'

I bit my lip. 'It was really that bad?'

'It was horrible,' Dulcie confessed, sitting wearily down on the end of my bed and staring vacantly across at the wall. 'One moment all was well and the next thing you know, Kohén was racing out of the harem with you in his arms and screaming for help.'

My eyebrows shot up- he'd taken me out of the harem while I'd been unconscious and he panicked? Well, that explained some of the blemishing of the family name...

'We were kissing and... and other stuff-' Dulcie scowled as Kohén flushed beet-red, '-and you just fainted,' Kohén pouted gently. 'I didn't see it coming, just-'

'*Me* cumming?' I joked, and some of the light returned to his eyes while Dulcie made a prudish face.

'Well, yes that was rather, uh, riveting... for both of us,' he was getting redder and redder but standing a little taller and I knew that he'd probably been accused of being the only one having any fun because he darted a triumphant look at Dulcie, 'and then you checked out completely before you'd, um... finished, I thought.' He wiped his hair out of his sweaty brow and grew more sombre-looking. 'It was scary and no matter what I did to revive you, you wouldn't wake up. I felt your forehead and realised that your temperature was far too high-'

'Forty-four degrees isn't a high temperature, your highness- it's Hyperpyrexia,' Dulcie interrupted again, and I gasped.

'Forty-four? That's... that's a fatal temperature for a human, isn't it?'

'Usually. So you can imagine my astonishment when it climbed to forty-*seven*,' Dulcie said, her bright auburn eyebrows hoisted, and I pressed my hand to my chest.

'What? What caused that?!' I pushed at Kohén. 'Get away from me! If what I have is contagious-'

'It's not,' Kohén said quickly. 'We don't know what it is that you had, because someone with a body temperature that high ought to have been vomiting and certainly shouldn't be up and talking, but it's not viral or bacterial. How could it be? You've been isolated all week!' He shrugged. 'We suspect dehydration triggered your first episode, and that gave you a sort-of panic attack that you were too delusional to be talked down from and it all just cumulated-'

'I haven't had water in a few days now,' I admitted, sinking back against the pillows and biting my lip. 'I realise that now- only wine.'

They both snapped up their heads to gape at me. '*No* water?' Kohén cocked his head. 'Do you mean at *all*?'

I nodded, cringing. 'I think it occurred to me yesterday that I hadn't had anything real to eat or drink since Monday night and-'

'WHAT?' Kohén lifted off the stool beside my bed and regarded me with horror. 'How is that even possible?'

I cowered, making myself look as small as I felt. 'It just... happened that way, okay? I had that dinner with you all on Monday night and then on Tuesday, I was so busy curling my hair that I skipped breakfast. I remember nibblies being passed around at the parade but I was too excited to be hungry, and then when the feast was almost cooked out on the lawn... I sought you out and...' I sighed, shaking my head. 'It just happened, and I haven't had an appetite since so-'

'But that was practically five days ago!' Kohén bellowed, and I really cringed back into the pillows then, for he looked furious. 'And I've brought you meals three times a day- *with* snacks!'

'I couldn't stomach it, so I ended up just pushing the food around,' I admitted quietly. 'Sometimes I'd get hungry enough to think that I could eat something, but then we'd fight, or I'd upset myself...' I thought of the altercations I'd had with Satan and flinched, remembering why I hadn't had any water- I'd hurtled my crystal jug at that mirror that first morning and hadn't had it sitting there empty to remind either Kohén or I to fill it since, 'and I always ended up turning to the wine for comfort after, or falling asleep and...'

'So you didn't eat anything?' Kohén looked dumbfounded. 'Not even *once*?'

I shook my head. 'I realised how long it had been since I'd eaten yesterday afternoon and I vowed to start taking care of myself again. But when I tried to sit down and eat the food you'd brought me for dinner…' I made a face, 'the smell almost made me vomit. I was going to ask you to bring me some soup so I could start with something small, but then we started kissing and-'

'This is unbelievable!' Dulcie whirled on Kohén. 'You wonder *why* the entire kingdom is speculating about your little arrangement here? *Why* the last healer quit on this girl's behalf? Well it's no wonder, is it? Larkin has been almost solely your responsibility since Tuesday and you've been completely negligent!' She threw up her hands. 'How am I supposed to explain to anyone that Larkin isn't being mistreated- when passed out mid-coitus because she hadn't been able to stomach food since she was locked in there with you?'

'And she's off again…' Kohén said, deflating as he indicated to Dulcie. 'So much for curbing that tongue…'

'I have the right to say whatever I believe is right!' she insisted. 'And I *believe* that you were negligent!'

I snorted. 'Well I don't. He can be accused of being over-attentive, certainly, but not-'

'Not when it counted!' Dulcie glowered at Kohén while I bit my lip, reflecting on what Cherry had said about him not realising that I wasn't talking either. Was it possible that he'd been negligent? Or was my health and well-being my responsibility? 'If she wasn't eating, you should have noticed! People can't survive on affection alone!'

'If she wasn't eating, I should have noticed because she should have started dropping weight like crazy, right?' Kohén demanded, looking offended and guilt-stricken at once, which was a Barachiel trait that he had down to an art.

'Not straight away, and not if you had a healer seeing her on an almost daily basis, as I've heard you had!' Dulcie pointed out, jabbing a finger my way. 'Healers soothe every ailment, Kohén, but they heal by touch- it works better on the outside than it does on the inside unless they're concentrating on something specific. Cherry has kept her hair from turning dull and her skin from looking wan and the blood vessels in her eyes from bursting- but that can't put food in the belly, or water in the system. And Larkin wouldn't have known that she was starving or unwell if she was drunk all week long, as she obviously was! Anything she was showing symptoms for could have been written off as stress, inebriation or dare I say: overuse!'

'She was not overused- Cherry told me to give her a break and I have, okay? Before this incident, all we'd done since Wednesday night *is* kiss!' But Kohén looked at me then and lowered his voice when he asked: 'Is the alcohol thing true, Lark? I knew you were enjoying the wine- but have you truly been heavily under the influence of it this whole time?'

'Most of it,' I admitted, and his face collapsed so I sat up. 'Kohén I'm sorry, okay?'

'Don't apologise to him!' Dulcie spat. 'He almost fucked you until you died! This is a red flag, Larkin of Eden, and the only case like this that we've ever had! There's besotted- and there's homicidal!'

'Dulcie Garvant!' Kohén thundered.

'What? You almost got her killed didn't you? Go on, deny it!'

'No, *I* almost got me killed!' I bit back, growing impatient with her. Right or wrong, didn't she know that piling guilt and accusations on top of a Barachiel was just asking for more trouble? I knew she had no way of knowing that she was getting the wrong prince into strife with her harsh words, but she was and I had to put an end to it before Kohén decided that I'd faked everything that I'd claimed to feel for him for the sole purpose of saving Kohl's ass. Yes that had been the case at first, but it wasn't now... was it? I turned to my grief-stricken lover and reached for his hand. 'This was a hard week to get through so I turned to the bottle, and doing that led to me sleeping or drinking every time you left- when yes, I probably should have been eating. But Cherry had commanded me to rest and so I figured that that was all I was doing, all right?'

'Because you were wasted,' Kohén said, furrowing his brow. 'Every moment we spent this week... you had to be drunk to get through them, didn't you?'

I recoiled, hurt. 'No! Not... not *every* moment... just some of the earlier ones and...' I darted a look at Dulcie, hinting that she should leave, but she crossed her arms and stood her ground and I groaned inwardly. It was so hard to communicate what I needed to clarify with Kohén without putting my foot in something else with her or bringing everyone's attention to the fact that Satan had caused me the most distress that week! 'I guess it just became a habit, all right? The drink calmed me down and made me feel full.' I reached for him again, but he pulled back, and I felt wounded. 'Not *every* moment, Kohén,' I repeated softly. 'Not yesterday morning either, in your room...I was sober then.'

Kohén's eyelashes fluttered at that. 'Really?'

I nodded, stretching that little bit further and getting his hand at last, hooking his fingertips with mine. 'I love you,' I said, and his eyes immediately brightened. 'I was drunk when I said it last night, but I mean it now.' I turned to Dulcie. 'And if anyone asks you what is going on behind the closed doors of the harem, you can tell them *that*, all right?'

Dulcie's mouth was hanging open as she looked from Kohén to me, then back again and I was the sole recipient of her astonished gaze. 'Did you cheat on your PCE exam? I thought you were a genius- but you're certainly not acting like one!'

It was like taking a blow to the stomach, but Kohén reacted like he was the one that had been hit, not her. 'Do not speak to Larkin that way!'

'Or *what*, Prince Barachiel?' Dulcie demanded, curling her lower lip. 'Will you have me whipped? Brand me as a truth-teller and have me cast over the fence?' She shook her head. 'It is not a crime to express one's opinion, and if we are truly equals as God said we ought to be, I need not fear suffering recriminations for being candid with someone just because they happen to be a monarch, right? And if I do suffer recriminations for it all…' she took a step towards him, eyes slitting, 'then you'll just be proving that everyone screaming for her release is right to scream for it, won't you? Because you *will* be a tyrant!'

'Tyrant?' Kohén exploded.

'Screaming for my release?' I demanded, forcing him to sit down. '*Who* is screaming for my release?'

'Everybody, Larkin!' Dulcie cried, and I reeled with shock, turning to Kohén who winced, but nodded miserably. 'Everybody!'

'Even people that I thought new me well enough to understand that I could never have done the things I'm being accused of doing…' Kohén admitted in a choked voice. 'The girls I released from the harem- the girls Karol released…' he sighed. 'Even Ora… that *idiot*. She's now leading the movement to get you released from here!'

No, that couldn't be true! But when I looked at Kohén's despairing expression I knew that it was.

And I knew why Kohén looked worse than I felt- I'd almost died the night before, but as soon as he left this harem, his father was going to kill him for murdering the family name.

16.

'What do you mean by saying that people are enraged?' I stammered, asking Kohén and Dulcie both but staring at Kohén. 'What are you talking about?'

'Thanks to Karol's public announcement last week, everybody in Arcadia knows that you were supposed to walk free- and didn't,' Kohén said. 'And I was doing my best to convince them that you'd stayed on willingly. But no one's buying that now, not since the Banished caught wind of some of the things that have happened here- because they heard Karol's speech from the fences too, remember?' He sighed. 'You were the poster child for all that was good about the third-born cast, but now you've become the cautionary tale for it... and I the example of all that's apparently evil and wrong about the monarchy.'

'What?' I gasped.

'It's not just the people on the other side of that fence or your friends that believe it!' Dulcie chimed in. 'I know of about twenty members of the nobility that have grown anxious regarding your well-being, and twice that in the other castes!'

I cupped my mouth with my hands. 'Why?'

'Because gossip is contagious!' Kohén thundered. 'Because of how Kohl acted that first night, when he ran off and got himself and a horse ripped open in his grief!!' Kohén's eyes were black. '*And* because Kelia died! And because you lost your voice! Because I have not allowed you out! Because when you were seen out- you were sporting a black eye thanks to mother!' Kohén threw out his hands. 'All of it! *You* know how all of that came to pass, but you also understand why I can't supply everyone that wants to know what's going on here with a detailed explanation for it all, so in the absence of one, people are losing their goddamn minds! And when they discover that you've been starved to death under my watch now... Argh!' Kohén swiped a box of combs off the salon table behind him, and Dulcie and I both flinched when they clattered to the floor. He wheeled on me, pressing his glowing blue hands to his chest. 'I'm an evil villain now! Do you have any idea how that makes me feel? I didn't ask for this shit, and you know it! I *wanted* you to be released, but no one believes it now! I loved you and wanted to make you my wife and they- they've ruined *everything*!' he pointed towards the door and a burst of blue-hot electricity surged across the room, causing Dulcie to jump and the door to char where he'd hit it.

They: he'd been pointing in Karol and Kohl's general direction. Tears of fear filled my eyes and I tried to sit up. 'Kohén-'

'Are you insisting that there is a reasonable explanation for all of this that would clear your name, Prince Kohén?' Dulcie demanded, but she looked at me. There wasn't, not by half, but there were plenty of reasons to explain why he wasn't exactly a villain either, so I nodded miserably and Dulcie blinked in shock. 'Well... that's...' she scratched her head. 'Well...'

'It's how it is,' I said quietly. 'And it is unfair that Kohén is copping the fallout for it all.'

'I'm so tired...' Kohén sagged against the wall and rubbed at his eyes, clearly beleaguered by his life even though sparks were still shooting all over the place from his fingertips. 'We might have gotten through it all unscathed- especially after how you leapt to mother's defence and ran from the chance to escape yesterday... but I swear, Amelia-Rose is spreading all of her own theories all over the place now that I've turned down her request to attend the ball with her- whispering lies into the wrong ears... and it's escalating the tension because people believe that butter wouldn't melt in her mouth! Then you scared me so much that I lost sight of the bigger picture and brought you out in a panic, and needless to say- having you seen wearing a sheet while your eyes were rolling back into your head didn't exactly do me any favours, you know? And if word gets out that I didn't let Karol in to treat you-'

'Well you should have let him!' Dulcie insisted.

'I'm glad he did not!' I threw in, feeling desperate.

'Why?' Dulcie demanded. 'Why why WHY?''

'It is not your concern!' Kohén thundered. 'But you saw what happened when you mentioned it!' Kohén turned to me. 'Larkin I was going to bring him in, I swear it- all that mattered to me was keeping you alive and I knew that he would have been a fool to try and do anything stupid while you were so close to death! But then it was like you knew that I was about to agree, and you went into cardiac arrest!'

My heart skipped a beat. 'Oh my God! Yes- I do remember that!' I nodded, sitting up and swinging my legs off the bed. 'I heard someone demand it and the idea of it sent me into a panic and… and the next thing I know, I was waking up here…' I frowned at Kohén, confused. 'How did you…?'

Kohén pointed at me. 'Look under your sheet and see for yourself.'

I looked down, lifting the sheet away from my chest- and gasped to see the perfect handprint burned into my breastplate and breast- exactly where my heart was. 'You electrocuted me?'

'Mother made me- she said it was a way to get the heart started again- she'd seen father do it to me when I was stung by wasps.' Kohén moved over to me, cupping my face and forcing me to look up. 'I was so terrified that I'd kill you faster, but it worked so I guess your heart really had stopped already. And the moment your heart rate started to stabilise, mother had us plunge you into an ice cold bath. That brought your temperature down for long enough for Dulcie to recover her strength and we've been in here all night since, keeping you cool while running fluids through your system.'

I looked down at my chest again, not sure if I was grateful that he'd saved my life- or unhappy about it. 'And I didn't have any other issues after the heart failure?'

'No,' Kohén kissed my forehead, then folded me into his arms. 'I guess you just needed to be shocked out of whatever state you were in, and now that we know you haven't eaten or drunk anything besides peach wine in days, I understand while the intravenous fluids have helped... and why you were weak enough to manifest such anxiety to begin with.'

'She should be fine, once we get the healer from Rachiel in here to fix what we cannot with our treatments- the exterior stuff,' Dulcie said sombrely, bending to pick up the scattered curlers and watching Kohén's hands warily while addressing me. 'And once you've eaten again...I don't see any reason why you won't feel back to normal in a few hours. Like Kohén said it wasn't an illness so much as a *spell*.'

'But the damage done to my reputation...' Kohén sighed and stepped back, running his hands through his hair and staring at a spot above my head. 'I just don't know if there's a Nephilim in the world that can heal that any time soon, and if that's the case, then I'll just have to live with that.'

'Live with what?' I asked, not understanding.

Kohén smiled weakly, and it was a broken smile if I'd ever seen one. 'My people hating me. My people hating me and likely demanding that my twin brother be handed my crown...until I can prove them wrong about me.'

I frowned. 'People wouldn't demand that, would they? And the king wouldn't agree to it. We were scared of him taking your crown over the ball stuff last night but when you really think about it, he'd only punish himself by doing that. I mean, he knows that so long as you have me in the bag, you have *this*...' I touched the diamonds at my throat. 'But if you lose the crown, you lose the harem *and* me and Pacifica's wealth with it, right?'

'I don't know what to think,' Kohén yawned, covering his mouth as he sank onto the mattress at my hip. 'The love of his people is worth more than diamonds, you know. Like God, the king is only powerful as his subjects allow him to be...' he lay back across my hips and stared at the ceiling foggily, 'and Atticus can still buy you with them if you are released from my evil clutches, can't he?'

I frowned. 'You don't seem as frightened as I feel right now. Then again, you're not the one that's likely going to end up in a blue caste brothel to be bid on or with Kohl's well-being on your-'

'Don't be like that,' Kohén chided me as he looked sideways at me sharply, reminding me that I couldn't speak freely concerning Kohl's fate in front of a witness, 'I do not seem frightened because I do not believe it will come to that. Hold on...' He sat up and said: 'Dulcie, Larkin and I have something to discuss in private. Now that you've seen that she's on my side here, could you please go tell my mother- and anyone else hanging off that bloody door- that Larkin is up, talking, *not* screaming for her freedom and fully intending on going to that godforsaken ball tonight to shut them the hell up?'

'What?' I gasped, but Kohén waved at me to indicate to hold on, while I practically panted with fear and excitement. I did not want to go to that ball- but now that I knew that Ora was getting angry with the family and that the other Companions were making things worse now that I'd settled Constance down, well, I was probably going to need another drip soon.

'Of course, your highness,' Dulcie said softly, bowing gently before crossing to the door- all respect and submission again. I didn't know if that was because she believed that he was innocent of the crimes he'd been accused of committing, or because he'd scared her with his temper, but I didn't care- I needed to talk to Kohén alone. 'Anything else I should say?'

'Yeah- tell them that you heard her declare her love and that we're all snuggly-wuggly, okay? In fact, tell them that I'm going to have a nap beside her because I haven't the strength or desire to leave her side right now.'

'Yes, your highness,' Dulcie said, but closed the door with a clack that was louder than it needed to have been.

'She thinks we're both nuts, you do know that, right?' I asked him after she'd left.

'Actually she thinks I'm a kidnapping rapist that would have let you die before allowing my brother to come to your rescue- and she thinks *you're* a brainwashed ninny,' Kohén joked as he sat back down on the bed before laying down so that his head was on the pillow next to mine.

'Seems legitimate about now...' I remarked as I wriggled over, making space for him.

'None of that. Now, as for the other stuff...' Kohén glanced over me as though checking to make sure the door was shut, and then nodded in satisfaction to see that it was before lying back down again and taking my good hand, squeezing it. 'I'm master of ceremonies now- or was, they may have changed their minds about that- but regardless of who does all of the announcing tonight, I've already seen what Karol has planned for the evening, and so I know that after the fireworks go off at midnight tonight...' He twisted to face me, smiling. 'You'll be able to leave this room- safe in the knowledge that Karol cannot legally lay a hand on you without losing his crown, his kingdom's respect- *and* his future wife.' He wriggled his eyebrows. 'Care to venture a guess as to what's going to happen to make all of that possible, my swan?'

'Oh!' The dizziness came rushing back but it was the giddy, delighted sort this time! 'He's going to ask Ora to marry him? Honestly?'

'Proposal on the gazebo on the lawn at twelve-fifteen,' Kohén whispered, and I almost whooped in delight. 'Wish granted, Lark- you're about to see your first Barachiel queen!' I clapped my hands together happily, and Kohén grinned, nodding to communicate that he shared in my relief. 'So no, I won't risk you going to the masquerade before that has happened, of course, but you're going *after*, and as soon as you're out there...' he smacked my backside playfully, 'the tongues will stop wagging and start clucking again.'

'You really think so?'

Kohén chuckled. 'Well, unless you plan on racing out crying for help repeatedly and throwing knives at me, yes.' He forced me to lie back against the pillows as he traced the line of my lips with his fingertip. 'You will be beautiful, obviously content, healed and on my arm, and none of the damage that had been done prior to that moment will count after you've proven to them that you're not dead or in shackles- I am certain of it.'

'But it will be so late!' I whispered. 'Who's ever heard of someone showing up to a ball *after* midnight?'

'Trust me when I say that no one's going to have a ball until *you* show up,' Kohén remarked dryly, 'least of all- me. And since when has an Eden ball ever wrapped up before four a.m.?' Kohén yawned again. 'You'll have plenty of time to make an impression after his proposal, and my duties- if I still have any- wrap up as soon as those fireworks start going off, so I'll not have to let you out of my sight or grip for even a second. In fact, even with the engagement, I'll still be keeping you a safe distance from Karol and Kohl after, just to be safe...' he yawned once more. 'And so long as they keep their wits about them- no trying to cheat on Ora for Karol, no crying jag and horse thievery for Kohl- everything will fall into place from there. And I don't see why they would try to come between us anyway... I mean, we'll all be officially escorting someone and you'll be required to dance only with me as well, so they won't have a valid reason for trying to separate us anyway.'

'And you honestly believe that that will keep me safe from Karol?' I worried my lip with my front teeth. 'I don't know Kohén- he has my word to come to him and I must honour that. If I could fight him or strike him or scream in good conscience it would be one thing, but if I try that... Lindy and Coaxley will suffer for it, I just know it! Even from this far away, he could hurt them couldn't he?'

'Not before I could warn them darling- that I can promise you as well,' Kohén sighed. 'But yes, I still fear what Karol might do if he gets you alone before then- we both know there are plenty of hiding places in this palace that he could take you if he got it into his head to try and call in that IOU before the clock strikes midnight... but I don't believe he will try anything once he's engaged to Ora which is why I'm all right with you making a late appearance. It's one thing to crave a woman and try to sow some wild oats in your last days or hours as a single man- but to start an international incident over it once you're considered betrothed? To lose his crown? No, he wouldn't be that stupid.'

'*You* would,' I pointed out, and Kohén laughed, pulling me into his side.

'And that's why you love me- and don't you forget it.'

'Because you're the insane-est of them all?'

'And you the fairest- it's a perfect match.'

I sighed, staring at his wan complexion. 'If you believe that everything will fall into place, why the rage and despair?'

He opened his eyes again, and I saw the toll this week had taken on them. 'Because you and I are the only ones that know that I can fix this, and until I can demonstrate otherwise- I have to deal with a shit load of dissent amongst the ranks. Suffice to say that I am too tired to deal with Emmerly in a good mood right now, let alone her, Elfin and Lette in *foul* ones. And as Dulcie just demonstrated, people are getting pretty pissy with me and aren't shy about saying so, so I'm getting foul looks or cursed at every time I turn a corner! And just to add salt to open, stinging wounds, I have to brand those three harem banshees this afternoon so that they will be at liberty to take home the most dashing, loaded, un-escorted men present tonight, and I dread that like you wouldn't believe.'

My heart sank at the idea of not being able to hold Emmerly's hand as she was burned. 'Really? Doesn't that have to wait until after midnight too?'

'No, that's when Karol's chosen few will be released- mine aren't waiting for a wish to be granted or for a birthday to happen... they were free to leave the moment I released them. I only put off branding them until now because I knew they'd have to stay on here for a few days and had other things to deal with in the interim.'

'Like me burning in Hell?'

'Exactly.' He sighed. 'But they need to earn a living now, and they can't do that until they have the silver Companion brand so...' He curled closer to me. 'Actually you know what? You should do it for me. I saved your life so you owe me one.'

I slapped his shoulder. 'Participate in that barbaric ritual? Let me within an inch of that branding iron and I will melt someone's nose- not a female, third-born someone's either...'

Kohén moaned and buried his face into my breast, making me wince when he connected with the spot where my skin had been charred. 'You know I didn't create these customs myself...and the other girls were looking forward to getting their brands, hey?'

'Then why the apprehension?' I asked curtly. 'If you're so sure you're doing the right thing, then shouldn't you feel good about it?'

'Because they anticipate the honour that will come with it- not the pain that I will have to inflict upon them in order to give them said honour. Plus only father and I will be present with the healer that comes, and so they're going to feel as free to be as candid with me as Dulcie just was, and it's not going to be pretty.'

I shrugged. 'Yeah well, you made your bed...'

Kohén looked up at me. 'I did,' he said softly, touching my face, 'but you are in it now, so if I have to stab every person in Calliel with a hot branding iron in order to keep it that way-'

'You're not funny,' I whispered, leaning in to kiss him gently. 'You know that right?'

Kohén's eyes fluttered open, dazzling me. 'Liar. You laugh at all of my jokes- why do you think I want to marry you so much?'

'Because everyone else hates you now?'

Kohén chuckled, closing his eyes. 'Hmm... maybe...but everyone loves you so tell me Larkin...' he opened his eyes and regarded me intently. 'Why *didn't* you run when you had the chance yesterday? Was it because of Kohl?'

'Yes,' I said honestly, and his face contracted with pain, but I smiled gently and brushed his hair out of his face, finding it awkward to do with the cannula still attached. 'And because you're incredibly good-looking.'

He arched an eyebrow. 'That so?'

'Yes. That's all I ever wanted in a man. Someone who would give me beautiful child-' I stopped myself, and felt my stomach tense. Oh God, I'd meant it as a joke but saying it out loud...

'I will,' he promised me. 'I don't know how- I admit that much, but I'll find a way to give you children, Larkin Whittaker. And if not- we'll just take someone else's!' he winked at me while I swatted at him. 'Hey I've got an older brother and a twin so they can carry on the family name while I carry you and the children we kidnap from the villages.' I laughed at that even though it wasn't funny given the 'Given' circumstances that I'd been taken from my mother in, but Kohén touched my lips and whispered: 'There it is again- that beautiful sound. *Told* you I was funny.'

I nodded and snuggled closer to him and when I did my sheet slipped down, reminding me of the precise reason for why I'd stayed with him: not because of Kohl and not because of Karol, but because of the scorch mark that had blistered my skin.

I'd stay in Eden because I'd been branded by the prince at the age of five: right on the heart, and it was only now that he'd released the others that we could finally both make it clear to everyone.

17.

Kohén and I drifted off into an exhausted sleep but it felt as though my eyes had only just fluttered shut when I heard the door bang open again. It was Dulcie- she was returning to tell us that she'd passed on Kohén's message and that his father had had two to give us in return- that Kohén was to get his ass upstairs directly, and that Dulcie was to immediately start seeing to my preparations for the ball.

Kohén tried to protest that both he and I needed sleep if we were going to have the energy to attend a party after the night we'd just had, but Dulcie practically chased him out with a curling wand, saying she wouldn't have Elijah's anger with him on her head and that no one was going to believe that he intended me to go anywhere, so Kohén reluctantly made to leave.

Looking pale, puffy and very unhappy, Kohén turned to me and whispered that he would try to get back and see me before it was time for me to make my own entrance, but that he couldn't be certain that he'd make it, and if that was the case then I wasn't to leave the harem under any circumstances unless it was on *his* arm. I baulked at that, but he reminded me that because I was his and not his father's, I was allowed to refuse to leave with anyone else and could not be forced to do otherwise so I should lock my door behind me if anyone tried, and I nodded eagerly. He then told me that he loved me, promised that our life together would truly start again after midnight and then closed the door behind him- but not before warning Dulcie that I was not to be given any grief, or made up to look ridiculous, and she agreed with a nod and a slam of the door. Then she wheeled my little IV stand out into the main room and over to one of the waxing beds, and I had no choice but to follow.

'Thank God, he's gone at last!' she exclaimed as she began to tear around the spa, flicking on switches for things, and I swallowed and lay down on the bed while she explained that my healer was still a ways off so we had a bit of time to kill before I had to start getting ready, which was a relief. Besides, she said that she didn't have my dress yet- apparently she had to measure me so a seamstress could take in the gown that had been brought to the castle for me, and she clucked her tongue about the difficulty of choosing a nail or make-up colour palette without seeing the dress first, and lamented all of the things that could go wrong as far as hair styling and make up was concerned when she didn't even know what kind of mask I was going to be wearing.

I asked her if she knew if my gown had come from a dressmaker in Janiel- because I had a vague recollection of Lindy mentioning that Karol had asked her to sew me one over a year ago- but she asked how was she supposed to know such things? She hadn't had a single shift in the harem since I'd been brought in and most of the others kicked out, and as far as she knew I ought to have been wearing only a golden toga and a mask if I was expected to go on Kohén's arm.

'Actually that's a good idea,' she said as she traded out my almost empty IV bag for a new one, 'I should be safe if I paint your toes and fingers gold, right? That is the Arcadian colour after all!' I'd done a cross between a nod and a shrug and she'd clucked her tongue some more before telling me to sleep while I could because that was what she was going to do in the other room until the healer arrived. Then she left me alone in that cold space, staring at the wall and feeling sick over the thought of donning a golden toga. It wouldn't draw unwanted attention to me the way that the swan dress had, but it would draw unwanted attention to the fact that I was an official whore now, and if that Lindy had made me a special dress, it would be locked away in my closet until Kohén decided to attend an occasion without me- an event I could only dread.

He promised he wouldn't... I thought, curling up to my side and feeling grateful for the fact that all of the mirrors were at the other end of the room in front of the hairdressing stations, not here near the beds. *If he got out of having to escort someone tonight, he'll be able to do it next time, right? And the time after that, and the time after that... until he's too old to marry and no one cares anymore... right?*

It sounded like the most foolish hope I'd ever had to my sober sub-conscious, but I closed my eyes and tried to let the hope take me over, knowing that the truly foolish thing for me to do would be to stop hoping and wishing and dreaming- knowing that Kohén and I would never amount to anything more than master and slave if I didn't make the effort to believe that more was possible, as fervently as he always had.

*

I fell asleep again and when I awoke, it was because a sleepy-looking Dulcie was yawning and showing someone in. I was shocked to find myself regarding a male healer with skin as dark and luminous as black pearls, and long, straight onyx hair that fell to his hips in a thin curtain. He was as comely looking as he was unsettling, and when he fixed his lilac eyes on mine, the breath rushed out of me.

'Well, this is a first,' he said in an elegant accent, lifting my face and assessing my eyes with a critical air. 'Do you wear contacts, child?' I shook my head to say no, but he pulled back abruptly and blinked, turning to Dulcie: 'See how the hue just shifted! That's extraordinary!'

'Yours don't?' I asked quietly, and he shook his head.

'No they are the same all the time. What causes the shift in yours? Light?'

'I'm told emotion.'

The healer smiled benevolently. 'Yes I can sense you have plenty of that.' He took my hand and examined it while a radiant heat passed through his skin and into mine. 'Power too, despite all of these bumps and bruises and...' he winced as he touched my face gently, 'the black eye... you're not the descendant of one like us?'

I shook my head, even though my insides curdled a bit at the thought of my father. 'No,' I said softly. 'We can trace back my family tree a long way, and there is absolutely no connection to a Nephilim on either side.' *Unless you count the golden man that my mother had sex with because she thought she was with a woman!*

'I don't know if I believe that,' the healer stroked a fingertip down one of my veins, and I watched as it reddened and swelled under my skin, fascinated. 'But it's probably better for you if I leave the matter alone, hmm?' he winked at me and then smiled, shaking his head. 'Truly extraordinary eyes. The hair, the skin...I don't even see any pores here!' he turned to Dulcie again. 'How much of this is your doing? It's incredible work even if she has gotten a bit wrecked over the past few days.' He picked up my lank, greasy hair and frowned at the ends. 'Ugh, split!'

'I can't claim credit for any of it,' Dulcie said woodenly. 'The only enhancement she's ever had have been skin deep, and all of the damage is someone else's doing too.'

'No!' the Nephilim cocked his head at me. 'Lucky girl! Were I attracted to women...'

'She's very beautiful...' Dulcie said, somewhat reluctantly. 'But I don't know if 'lucky' is the correct adjective to use when describing her. I daresay it's those striking eyes that got her into this predicament to start with.'

'And what predicament are you speaking of?'

I looked at Dulcie sharply, and she rolled her eyes and sighed. 'Love... she claims,' she turned away and began to pull out her hair so that she could gather it all up into a ponytail again. 'But unfortunately for her, she is not the first girl to make such a claim in here, and would be the first to have it work out well for her in the end.'

The healer clucked his tongue. 'Don't frighten the girl. She has miles to go, and will need to be brave, not terrified.' He smiled at me, teeth glaringly bright against his dark skin. 'Are you looking forward to tonight, Liberty? I am. In fact, I've come all the way from Rachiel to meet the girl that's inspired such a rebellion...''

I barely heard him, for I'd craned forward to see Dulcie. 'Someone else has fallen in love with a prince before?' and Dulcie laughed, turning back to me. She spoke oddly for she was holding a pin between her lips, but I was able to make out her words.

'Don't you all?'

I shrank back. 'Well... no. I- I don't believe any of the other girls care for Kohén so...'

'Well I'm sorry I over-exaggerated, I'm sure. What I *meant* to say was that in every generation of Companions that comes through here, at least two out of the bunch fall madly in love with their host, and one or two others tend to believe that they have.' She shrugged. 'I will admit, the Barachiel princes have always taken pains to keep the lines between love and companionship clear and Kohén is the first that *I've* seen re-draw the lines all over the place... but he's not the *only* one that has.'

My heart was pounding again, and the Nephilim stroking my arms frowned, giving me the silent command to relax. 'Who was the other?' I asked quickly. 'Tell me, please?'

'Such stories are sixty percent gossip and as this is an old one, I'm sure it is more fictional than factual. Besides, those secrets aren't allowed to leave the harem, remember?'

'A courtesy that no one's bestowed upon me,' I pointed out, 'and look around you- we're in the harem still, so tell me a story! Let me decide what I believe is fact, and what I believe is fictional. What became of her?'

'She was deported to Asiana,' Dulcie said flatly. I inhaled sharply and Dulcie sighed, her eyes softening as she walked back to me. 'Mind you, that wasn't her master's wish. Word had it that she was quite the seductress and had more than one man under her spell, and when the king found out that she'd wrapped the prince around her finger but was also seducing others, well...'

My mouth dropped open. 'Wait... what? She was unfaithful to the prince and *all* she got was deported for it?' I shook my head amazed and a little relieved. I'd been so scared over my dalliance with Kohl! And really, all I could have gotten for it was a relocation! That wasn't so bad, was it?

'Well I'm certain had she been your age she would have gotten a lot worse… problem is, she was only just turning fourteen at the time so she was punished as a child would be-'

'FOURTEEN?' I was beyond shocked. 'The prince was consorting with a girl that was underage?'

'No, he was merely in love with her.' Dulcie lifted her eyebrows. 'It was the two other males that were doing the consorting, apparently, and both would have paid very dearly for it only one escaped, leaving the other to take all of the fall.'

'Sounds like a wonderful girl…' my healer drawled. 'So cunning, so young! The prince really missed out with her, didn't he?'

'The prince was devastated- and never took another lover again,' Dulcie said, and my jaw dropped further. She had to be talking about King Raoul! The only prince to have never married! 'So the laws in the harem have been stricter since. In fact, I believe that was then you all had to start wearing uniforms. Before then, things were a bit more relaxed.'

'That's not fair is it? To punish generations of girls for one girl's mistake?'

'No, but the fallout after it was awful so I can understand why pains were taken to make sure it never happened again. My grandmother held my position within Eden at the time,' Dulcie said, 'she said she was the sweetest girl you'd ever met- but I don't know… I think she knew what she was doing.'

My mind was racing despite the healer's best attempts to soothe me with his touches. I'd only ever heard of one underage girl cheating on her prince before, and that was the same underage girl that had been impregnated by Bastien

Birch. Was it possible that the two stories were the same story?

'Shepherd Birch?' I asked, and Dulcie expelled a splattering cough before regarding me with wide eyes. 'Was this girl found out because she was impregnated by Bastien Birch?'

'You've heard that story?'

'There's a whole book about it!' I said, sitting up again. 'I've read it in the past month. Only I never knew the name of the prince at the time because the monarchs were just referred to as 'the prince' and 'the king' and I didn't know the prince had loved her! Wait, so there was more than one man that could have fathered her child? And he got *away*?'

Dulcie nodded. 'The other male she was dallying with was only thirteen too- a castle staff member's son, and likely not old enough to procreate. Bastien swore that he'd never touched the girl and tried to point fingers at the young boy to get himself off the hook, but the girl was interrogated separately and she rushed to Bastien's defence, swearing that he hadn't taken advantage of her- she'd loved him and she didn't regret what they'd done together because unlike the prince, Shep Birch had been a good, pious man that wanted girls like her to be free to know love as they had.' Dulcie clucked her tongue. 'Well that did it, didn't it? You have one of the accused trying to shift the blame, unaware of the fact that his partner in crime was begging for his forgiveness and a pardon… it made it pretty clear who was dishonest to the core. Add to the fact that Shepherd Birch had been using her as the soapbox he stood upon while preaching that the Given Girls ought to be released, and you had motive too. So it's understood that though she and the other young boy fooled around at some point, it was likely only Bastien got to know her in the biblical sense.'

'God,' I whispered. 'So much was omitted from the biography!'

'That happens often,' Dulcie said, and I thought about the first draft of the family tree that Satan had given me. Had that been fact, or fiction? Oh I hated the not knowing!

'The mother of the boy that Shep had accused immediately high-tailed it out of Arcadia when she found out that her son was likely to get banished anyway, for having had an innocent crush on a girl that had had been less innocent due to her grooming- and children of castle staff have been forbidden from associating with the Given Girls or the crowned princes since.' She nodded at me. 'And I suppose that you are the product of that- you and Kohén both. You are forced to grow up as friends now, and that fosters a bond that will prevent the prince from getting hurt, but one that offers almost no protection to the Companion. I see that he loves you, girl, or believes that he does... but do not be surprised if one day you end up the subject of a cautionary-tale that is passed off as biography when it is really a mostly fictional recount of events that have been distorted by time.'

'I won't be surprised,' I said quietly to Dulcie. 'Why do you think I've been drinking so this past week? I know you think that I'm stupid Dulcie, and in some ways you are right... I was drunk and scared and confused when I gave my virginity to my Barachiel prince, and I was not thinking with my head, that's for sure- only my heart.' I sighed, feeling sleepy and relaxed because my healer had moved to the other side of my bed and was now treating the right side of my body. 'But I gave it away willingly, and I won't tolerate people saying otherwise. I have regretted what I did with every second beat of my heart this week, yes. I have raged against him for not stopping me, and I have raged against myself for my stupidity... but that does not change the fact that every other beat of my heart is for *him*.' I watched as bruises vanished beneath the healer's touch and relaxed more as the tension drained out of my limbs. He plucked the cannula out next and though it hurt a little, he immediately depressed his thumb to the lump on the back of my hand and when he moved it away, it was as though nothing had ever pierced my skin. I didn't know what specific 'ailment' he was curing, but my nervous system was being numbed, that was for sure, and it made speaking my mind easier than it had been all week. 'Kohén wants me to believe that it will work out favourably for us and that makes him stupid too, but I am playing along now because let's face it… if you were in my position, would you want to be smart and aware of how badly your life is going to go for you?' I looked at Dulcie, who was hanging onto my every word while watching the healer trace the handprint over my heart with a glowing fingertip. 'Or drunk, foolish and in love?'

There was a long silence after I'd finished speaking and eventually, Dulcie sighed and said: 'I'd suppose I'd want a long shower, a massage, and the chance to stand my foolish ground on the behalf of the man I loved to my own detriment.'

I smiled at her as the healer moved his hands to my face. They were warm and sweet-smelling and I closed my eyes gently. 'Thank you,' I said. And once again, I meant it.

*

As soon as I'd been healed, Dulcie asked me if I wanted to walk down to the mirror so I could see myself but I told her there was no point- the mirror in my chamber had been broken for days, so I didn't know how bad I'd looked anyway to make a comparison now. Really I was just scared that Satan would make an appearance again, but I must have come off as ungrateful because Dulcie clucked her tongue as she led me into the small massage room, closing me in there with Heath, my healer, who proceeded to give me a deep tissue massage that hurt as much as it helped before lulling me off into another deep sleep. Once that was done, he had Dulcie come in and smooth a rich-smelling mud mask in milky clay over my entire naked body and then she inserted another cannula into my arm and left me there to rest and take in more fluids while impurities were apparently drawn from my skin- alcohol, most likely because the longer it stayed on, the clearer my mind became and the more I hated it.

Where is the tracking device? Where is Kohén? It's almost six! He should have come in by now to check on me, yes? Why did they omit so much from Shepherd Choir's story? How old is Shep Choir if he was there all those decades ago to sort everything out? Where is the tracking device? What if Ora refuses Karol because she doesn't want to be associated with his hated brother?

While I fretted, Dulcie went off to get us all a late lunch and Heath drew my bath using a variety of essential oils that were supposed to help keep me calm. He agreed after seeing to me that I had indeed been suffering from malnourishment, dehydration and anxiety, and that the two had culminated in giving me a panic attack that my body had been too weak to cope with, which had caused my heart to race and then falter. Apparently I would have to take an assortment of nutrients in the form of tablets for days before I attempted to eat a large meal, but before I had my bath I was brought back to sit on my bed while Heath fed me spoonful after spoonful of a cauliflower and truffle soup. I must have looked ridiculous- coated head to toe in white, cracking mud while still hooked up to my drip and wearing paper panties and Heath did smirk once or twice, but to his credit he kept his face as straight as one could while prompting me to open my mouth.

'Miles to go...' he said, giving me another secretive smile and I thought that he and Satan would get along well for their love of cryptic speech, 'but how you'll burn a path.'

I wanted to ask him for a translation but he slipped the silver spoon into my mouth then and I was distracted by it. The first mouthful made me feel queasy despite the fact that I'd been feeling wonderful (perhaps a little too wonderful- I was so drowsy and pliant!) but when Dulcie told me that the cauliflowers had come out of my gardens and would be the last for the year now that the weather was chilling quickly, I ate the next four or five mouthfuls with renewed enthusiasm. It was delicious and I wanted more after, but Dulcie took the rest of the bowl away from Heath and said I could have more once I'd finished my bath.

So into the tub I went, still dragging along my drip, and once I'd settled into the warm, oily water, Dulcie presented me with a glass of chilled ice-water and told me that it was imperative that I drink the whole thing. Not just because I needed the fluids (especially after the massage and mask) but because it would keep me cool in the hot bath and after what she'd seen the night before, she wasn't risking a fever spike on such an important night. I sipped at the water, hating every mouthful but craving more the moment I'd swallowed the last, and watched the water turn as milky as the bubbles upon it in the dim candlelight as the bath absorbed my mud, and frowned as the hand on the clock struck five. What was Kohén doing? Didn't he understand how nervous I would be until he came to assure me that all was going to plan? And that he wasn't being whipped or worse?

The ball starts at eight! What if he doesn't get the chance to check in on me beforehand? Oh, I'll be a nervous wreck until he does!

Dulcie returned twenty minutes into that process and when the door opened, I heard a lot of voices follow her through before it was shut. I inquired as to who was in there and she informed me that the other three technicians had arrived and now Resonah and Rosina were out there getting their hair and make-up done. They would be attending the ball that night but in their golden togas. Elijah was escorting the duchess, yes, and would be unable to dance with them, but they were still prohibited from dancing with anyone else. I remarked that that seemed sad, but Dulcie shrugged.

'They've been in here for a very long time, Larkin. I suppose by the time you reach sixty, you will not mind having to refrain from couple dancing at *one* party.' Then she took in the way I'd pursed my lips (trying not to cry as I imagined sitting on the side-lines and watching Kohén dance with his legal spouse) and she sighed again. 'Look… maybe I'm wrong, okay? There has been one prince that didn't take a spouse because he'd given away his heart to one in the harem before… perhaps that will be Kohén someday. Only unlike Raoul, the object of Kohén's affection may love him back still.'

'Do you really believe that?' I asked in a choked voice.

'No,' she said, and despite myself I laughed. 'But I suppose it's on you two to convince me otherwise. And don't think that I don't want to be convinced, Larkin.' She lifted my foot from the water and began sponging the clay residue off my ankle and calf, warming it as she did with her Nephilim touch and making me reach for the water again. 'I've been doing this job for thirty years now, and all I've been able to think after I've performed every girl's initiation ritual is: I hope *this* is the one that breaks through the glass ceiling.'

I smiled at her wanly. 'I wonder how many of them have thought the same…'

'Most, I suppose.' She smiled at me tightly. 'But you're the only one that has ever come close to making any of us believe that someone *might.*'

'Thank you.' Then I thought of something else and sat up. 'Dulcie… is it true that I have a tracking device on me somewhere?'

Dulcie drooped my ankle and cursed, then went reaching for the other, keeping her eyes off me the whole time. After an uncomfortable amount of silence had passed, she looked up, saw that I was still waiting for her answer and blew out a breath, shaking her head. 'Wherever did you get that idea from?'

'Cherry mentioned it this morning- wait, I suppose that was yesterday morning, wasn't it?' I made a face, then resumed: 'During her tirade against the duchess… whenever that was.' My stomach rolled when Dulcie blanched. 'So… it's true then?' I asked in a small voice. 'Even if I had taken the opportunity to run yesterday morning or a week ago… they would have found me, wouldn't they?'

'I'm not allowed to speak on the subject,' Dulcie said, taking a small brush and scrubbing at the underside of my feet. 'But I can tell you this: if you do have a tracking device on you, I do not know where it is, how it works or who put it there...' she wet her lips and said quietly to my toes: 'Only that you would need to be over two kilometres away from this castle before it would cease to work.' She looked up at me and smiled sadly. 'But you won't be going anywhere, will you Larkin? You're much too.... good.' My mouth popped open as she pulled her hands out of the water. 'I need to get a few more things- you've got shards of glass in your feet for some strange reason.' Dulcie rose quickly. 'Soak them and I'll be back in a moment, okay?'

'But-'

'That's all I have to say on the matter Lark,' she opened the door and held her finger to her lips. 'You have your secrets, and we Nephilim... we have our own. And because we're all equal, why don't you respect my wish to protect myself, as I respect yours to protect...' she smiled ruefully, 'well, that's the eleven-million dollar question isn't it?' And then she walked out, leaving me to literally soak in my own toxins and shock.

Seems like I wasn't the only one in Eden who was too smart for her own good, and that Heath wasn't the only Nephilim as cryptic as Satan!

18.

Once I'd been scrubbed down to what I was sure was my new-born skin I was allowed to get into the shower to wash my own hair and rinse the residue of my soak in the bath off me while the other beauticians finished off the older Companions. I was quick in the shower because I had my heart set on seeing Resonah and Rosina before they left, but by the time I walked out into the main room again, wrapping my hair in a towel turban-style and feeling almost human again, I was dismayed to see just the beauticians left waiting for me. Even Heath had left! And to my horror, the moment they saw me they motioned for me to undress so that they could fit me into a corset and pair of matching underwear that weren't just scandalous- but *humiliating*.

The corset was golden made of a leaf design that showed lace and skin between each individual leaf, but it was fitted so tight that by the time they'd laced me up, I almost had more breasts than I did bottom! And though the same golden leaves covered my intimate flesh on the bikini briefs, they grew sparser and sparser as the lacy fabric stretched for my hips and blended in so perfectly with my skin colour that it looked like I was only wearing a few strategically placed leaves when the light shimmered off them.

'Oh god…' I whispered, covering my face so I wouldn't have to look for my shoes but see only breasts. 'Oh god…'

I knew Kohén was going to lose his fool mind when he saw me in this get-up and I had to admit that I sort of looked forward to seeing his face when he undressed me later (which was bound to happen- I wasn't THAT naïve yet!) but that would be a private moment and *this* was anything but. And when they added lace-topped stockings with a garter belt and delicate, glittering golden heels, my face flamed to the point where Dulcie ordered the pedicurist/manicurist to go get me a glass of water while she pressed her hands to my face and ordered me to breathe and sit and not die again.

I did as I was told, but it took five minutes before I was able to slow my racing heart and lose the flush and even after those symptoms had faded, my mortification remained the same: I wasn't being dressed to be dressed, but stripped and ravaged and they *all* knew it. I was a whore and I could not deny that, for who else but a whore would put more time and effort to how they looked without their clothes on than *with*? And why was this so much more embarrassing now than when they'd prepped me for that awful ritual?

Um, because you were a virgin then but you're a confirmed sex worker now, maybe?

Oh, how I wished Resonah and Rosina had stayed there, because I knew they would have had some words of encouragement or guidance for me that would have a better chance of working than Dulcie's cries of: 'Well, the prince will forgive me for giving him grief after he sees this gift-wrapped apology, yes?' (Not helpful!) but I suspected that they were trying to keep us apart purposefully, and all I could do was wait for the end of my isolation to come.

So wait I did, frozen into a statue of embarrassment and shifting to try and dislodge the irritating way that my belly-button ring was biting into my waist thanks to the corset, while one rubbed stuff into my face, another tended to my nails and Dulcie dried my hair. They'd sat me in front of a mirror but luckily I was angled away from it and I got to keep my eyes closed most of the time while the youngest one, Arial, applied my make-up. I felt incredibly self-conscious to have so many people staring at me up close again, and I was terrified about what they were thinking about me as they worked, so I tried to fill that uncomfortable silence with questions.

Most of them they answered easily enough: How was the weather? Unseasonably cold still and dropping fast. How were the Banished? Quieter than usual but in a way that was unsettling... What exactly did they want? They didn't know-it almost seemed as though they'd broken up into two camps: One that wanted help, and one that wanted to incite mayhem.

But other questions they evaded- especially when I asked if they knew how Kohén was faring, and if they'd heard any news about Cherry? I got a vague answer about Kohén having his own dressing staff so how the hell should they know what he was up to? But they didn't answer the question about Cherry at all, and I noticed a distinctive dip in the mood in the room after I had.

Trying to get back to how carefree things had been a few moments before, I asked Dulcie why she was a beautician when she had such a power... and *that* answer was an interesting one. Instead of saying why, she demonstrated by winding her fingers up in my hair- and then releasing it in a steaming curl. My jaw dropped at that and she'd laughed saying that she'd followed in her mother's footsteps, and her mother's before her. There were other things that she could do, but none that allowed her to leave work for the day knowing that she'd created something beautiful. In addition to that, she only had to work for a few hours a week and then got to live in luxury the rest of the time, unlike her cousin who could do the same thing, but worked long hours as personal assistant to the king of Tariel.

That was an odd story: it seemed like the king of Tariel had allowed himself to become a lot more spoiled than Elijah had, and used his hot/cold blowing Nephilim around the clock for everything from rubbing feet, treating headaches, warming bed sheets and strangest of all- keeping the duchess's complexion perfect and her wine cold. I responded that I hoped he washed his hands often for the sake of the king- but kind of didn't for a laugh of his own, and the ladies beautifying me burst into giggles.

Honestly I actually thought that both vocations seemed like a waste of power, but Dulcie confessed that as far as powers went, theirs were rather limited. It would be different if she were strong enough to generate fire or snow or manipulate the atmosphere of a space as large as a room, but heat and frost via direct contact was all that she or her cousin could manage, and even then, they drained quickly.

'Besides... have you seen my room? It's nicer than Elijah's so it's well worth it.'

'That's not a room- that's a suite,' one of the other girls joked. 'I wish I had your earning power, even if your actual power creeps me out sometimes. Speaking of which- can you not steam so close to her forehead? You're melting her make up.'

I smiled, but started thinking about what Martya and Kohén had said about the diminishing powers of the Nephilim and asked out loud why they didn't go out of their way to breed more amongst themselves, but I'd been surprised to see Dulcie's face become grave again.

'Mixing Nephilim is sort of like mixing spirits... you just don't know what you're going to end up with after- a lovely drink, or poison. That's why the king watches us so closely- it really is better for everyone that our lines remain as pure as possible.'

'Because you're afraid the powers won't go together?' I'd asked, tilting my hair so that Dulcie could access it more easily. 'Or because the monarchy is afraid that they wouldn't be able to control so many?'

'Possibly both. But we don't really want to do it either, and would be wary of Nephilim that would.' She looked around and then shook her head sadly. 'All you need is that one dark power to sneak its way into a pure, very powerful bloodline like the Barachiel one, and the next thing you know...' she shook her head again and unwound another curl that actually burned my forearm when it fell. 'No, we need to be contained, not copulating willy nilly.'

I looked at her out of one eye until the beautician doing my eyebrows whispered at me to close both lest I end up with a monobrow. 'So you believe the dark Nephilim still exist too?'

'I don't know...' Dulcie said, touching a now ice-cold hand to where she'd burned me without me having to ask, before going back to my hair. 'But I do know that we can't risk accidentally reviving a line of them should one remain, yes? Especially not now when all of the feathers are gone and the ability to detect a dark Nephilim is limited to testing blood.'

'Kohén wants the blood tested and then breeding controlled after,' I said, thinking that I didn't think it sounded like a horrible idea. No one knew it, but all of the three Barachiel princes were the product of two Nephilim, and their powers were astonishing. Okay they both came from pure bloodlines but if they were tested first, what was the harm?

Dulcie snorted. 'Yes well that's why the kingdom is never placed in the hands of an optimistic, short-sighted, over-excited seventeen year-old boy, isn't it?' She began pulling sections of my hair up and weaving them together and snickered. 'What always seems like a good idea at the time to them can end up being a disaster for the person they made the spontaneous and exciting decision for, can't it?'

I blushed and was grateful that I had my eyes closed. 'No comment.'

The girls starting debating whether Elijah was a grand ruler or a mediocre one compared to some of the most recent, and I was rather surprised to understand that the humans thought the world of him, whereas Dulcie thought that his father had been superior. It was strange to hear the girls speak of how handsome and charming and kind and fair Elijah was and I longed to pipe up with: 'Pregnant spouse-beating, BDSM and twin-discarding traits *aside*, you mean...?' But even if I hadn't been able to keep my own lips shut, the girl doing my lipstick was doing that for me. Once my mouth was free I told them that they didn't have to rush doing me so and that they could even take a break because my entrance to the ball was going to be a very delayed one, (really I was worried that they'd message Elijah to let him know that I was ready to go much too quickly when it was Kohén that I needed to come for me) but the third beautician shook her head as she blew on my nails.

'You're the last girl we have to do in here, and once we're finished, we've been commissioned to help Ora Camden in the guest wing so we really do have to hurry.'

'Yes the ball starts in less than an hour and she's probably growing impatient.' Dulcie began jabbing pins into my scalp. 'Speaking of which, you'll be all right to dress yourself if your toga arrives after we leave, won't you? Just mind that you don't let it pull on your curls.'

But my toga was the last thing on my mind. 'You're going to see Ora?' I asked, excited to realise that in a few hours, I'd be getting to see Ora too. 'Oh my goodness! Oh... I wish I could go with you!' I tapped my feet together, getting swatted now by my manicurist, Elena, who was in the process of applying a clear gloss to my toenails to seal the golden artwork she'd already decorated them with. I hoped that Ora had taken my costume suggestions- I hoped she looked so gorgeous that Karol would forget my name the moment he laid eyes on her! How lovely would it be if Karol was so stunned by her entrance that he proposed on the spot? I could join the party straight away then!

Dulcie exchanged a surprised look with Arial. 'Wait... I was under the impression that you don't like Prince Karol. Why all the enthusiasm for his date?'

'Because I believe that she'll make him more likeable,' I answered honestly, too happy now to even wince at Karol's name. 'And even if she doesn't, he's likely going to marry her and make her a queen anyway and finally this kingdom will have a female monarch! A sweet, smart, down-to-earth one as well. And after meeting Amelia-Rose...'

'What?' Elena sat up, regarding me with wide brown eyes. 'Amelia-Rose is lovely! I feel awful that Karol didn't give her a second look this time around... and I hope he doesn't marry a republican, ugh! How unimpressive my job would be if I didn't get to tell people that I worked for the royal consorts at the palace?'

Arial giggled. 'If we become a monarchy, you'd have to say you do nails at the Presidents' place,' and the other girl shuddered. I laughed at their antics, but I was a bit confounded by the manicurists' attitude towards Amelia-Rose.

'You *like* Shepherd Choir's daughter?' I wrinkled my nose. 'Why?'

'Because she's sweet and kind and thinks of the less fortunate and...' the girl shrugged then bent back down to do my nails again. 'I don't know, a thousand reasons, I guess, but she's a lot like Prince Kohl too, who I think is an absolute doll. And she's so pretty... never tries too hard to look it either, it's refreshing.'

'I think she dresses like that on purpose- to mislead people into believing that she doesn't have a sense of vanity when really, hers is rampant,' Arial said as she dusted my shoulders with a glittering powder. 'I mean come on... her hair and make-up is always flawless and her jewellery is expensive and one of a kind so a lot of thought has gone into that whole package, trust me. She knows exactly how pretty she is, and more importantly, she knows how to make it look like she *doesn't*.'

'You've become cynical, Arial,' Elena looked genuinely crestfallen.

'No, I'm a make-up artist,' Arial responded matter-of-factly. 'Every time I see her, I see how much effort she's put into looking effortless. In fact, I'll bet she takes twice as long getting dressed as Adeline does, and that the shoes and underwear she's wearing beneath those prim blouses and floor-length skirts are about as raunchy as Larkin's ensemble is tonight!'

'Are you suggesting that she's not a virgin?' Elena asked, looking astonished. 'That it's *all* a front?'

'No....' Arial said, while I mentally nodded my head. 'I'm just saying that for the right crown- I mean, *man*,' she giggled, as did Dulcie, 'those floor length skirts would come off real quick!'

'I don't believe you!'

'Suit yourself,' Arial shrugged. 'I guess we'll see tonight, hmm? I'll bet she's out on the balcony necking with Prince Kohl by ten. Only necking of course- she's not the give away the milk sort, and he is definitely the naïve buy the whole cow sort.'

'You're on!' the other girl cried, while I felt bile rise into my throat at the hideous mental picture. Kohl wasn't mine anymore and never had been so I had no right to get jealous over what he got up to with Amelia-Rose that night... but I was still jealous anyway. Jealous and concerned for him. Oh, I hoped he met someone better! Someone that would have made him their first choice as date, not the consolation one.

But then I imagined Kohl hitting it off with someone prettier than Amelia-Rose, smarter than I and more lovely than Ora and that bile came up again. Okay no, I just had to keep my nose- and my thoughts- out of his love life until I'd had the chance to get over him completely.

'So are you happy that Kohl is taking her to the ball tonight then?' Dulcie asked Elena. 'You said she'd be a good queen, but you also said that she and Kohl made a nice pair too so...'

'I don't know. I'm glad she snagged one of them as an escort for tonight, but I still think she would have been a better influence on Karol than Ora will. Ora Camden is almost as flirtatious and frank as he is- Amelia-Rose would have humbled him, don't you think? And Kohl needs a woman that will bring him out of his shell, and Amelia-Rose might be too gentle for *that*.'

I was beginning to wonder if the beautician had ever actually spoken to Amelia-Rose, but then I remembered that even if she had, Amelia-Rose would have treated her differently to how she'd treated me. I knew all the nasty things she got up to but according to Kohén, Amelia-Rose was an expert at covering it all up. It was a shame, really. I'd adored Shepherd Choir two minutes after he'd started talking! How could he have raised such a strange daughter?

'I don't trust Amelia-Rose either,' Dulcie said quietly. 'There's something almost... fanatical about her zest for God.'

'The Lord,' Arial agrees. 'She calls him 'The Lord' and I agree, it's creepy and smacks of religion.'

'And her obsession with the Given Caste...' Dulcie darted a look at me. 'Not that I don't agree that it should be abolished, or anything, but she doesn't just want it to *end*- she wants the women branded as criminals for it and forced into another kind of servitude. Sorry but I don't think *the lord* would like that very much, Elena.'

'But she would see it ended though- even if the current crop of Given is branded for practicing unholy behaviour... they'd only have two brands, not three- they'd get to stay in Arcadia and they would be the last of their kind.' Elena glanced up at me, looking uncomfortable. 'I'd hate to see you sent off to the Corps Larkin... but I'm a little more contemptuous of those that fight for the right to utilise sex workers, than I am of those that would see it ended!' she shuddered, going back to my nails. 'I'll only ever marry, that I swear! It must be so hurtful to be left at home alone with the children, while the man you want to spend your life with goes off looking for a woman that he prefers.'

'As much as it would hurt to have him up and leave you and your children halfway through their lives, as they used to?' Arial asked. 'At least with joinings you can count on the father staying around until the hardest part of being a partnership is over, while knowing in advance that he may not stick around after.'

'I think it's ludicrous that we'd go from respecting a caste to outlawing it in one fell swoop!' Dulcie said crisply. 'How unfair is that? To be first celebrated then hated?'

'Well, it can be hard to make big changes,' Elena argued back. 'Sometimes outlawing things is the fastest way to drive a change home.'

I saw all sides of the arguments, except Amelia-Rose's, and I was starting to dislike Elena a lot for being a sheep, so

I decided to change the subject all together. 'We'll agree to disagree- about all of it, but especially about Amelia-Rose being superior to Ora!' I squeezed Dulcie's hand after she'd taken the towel off my shoulders. 'Make sure she looks absolutely lovely, okay? No one else can compare to her tonight!'

Dulcie looked at Arial again and they both smirked. 'If we want Ora to be the most beautiful girl at the ball, we're going to need a bigger mask aren't we? To cover certain features up?'

'Good point,' Arial agreed. 'But I wasn't going for real masks- just painted on ones! Now what?'

I frowned at the rude women. 'Ora's stunning,' I said loyally. 'You'll not have to strain yourself to make *that* plain!'

'Ora is lovely, I agree,' a smile was playing at the corner of Arial's lips. 'But you're the one whose face is going to need to be covered in order to allow hers to shine the most, Larkin Of Eden...' she then turned me to face the mirror. 'See?'

My heart constricted with fright at first, because I'd immediately expected to see Satan facing me, but then a moment passed and the woman in the reflection remained pale and golden and... no, not just golden- gold and silver and shimmering, and my heart skipped another beat again as I realised that Satan wouldn't have been able to do nearly as much damage in her form, than I could in my new one.

That's my girl... she whispered into my head, barging in the moment I'd opened the door between my thoughts and hers. *Challenge accepted!*

19.

I was startled to hear Satan's voice but because I hadn't been drinking, I found it easier to contain my knee-jerk reaction to her. 'Oh... my...' I moved to touch the elaborate eye make-up as I silently told her to piss off, but Arial caught my fingers.

'No messing up my masterpiece,' she scolded me. 'It won't look like a real mask if it's got fingerprints in it, would it?'

I swallowed hard, realising that she was right. I was wearing a beautiful eye mask, but instead of fitting me with one, Arial had crafted one out of pearlescent paint and tiny little jewels that sparkled, all trimmed with gold to give it the right shape and depth. It looked like a three-dimensional masquerade mask at first, and yet parts of it had been smudged and faded out to make it clear that it was an illusion, and the way she'd done that served to enhance my cheekbones and eyes even more.

The rest of my make-up was rather plain so the gaze would be drawn to the eyes, and yet my skin looked like velvet and my lips full and glossy without a hint of my old black eye or an exhausted shadow to be seen. I did look beautiful- so beautiful that even I felt a rush of pride, and I knew how foolish *that* was! Especially now that I was back in a room with mirrors!

I love God, I love God, I love God...

'Oh you're much lovelier than Amelia-Rose and Ora combined,' Elena said, somewhat sadly. 'Gosh... what were they thinking when they took away your ability to breed? Kohén may be content, but the kingdom's gonna be uglier for it.'

For once I actually agreed with her though.

'Hush,' Dulcie said quietly, rubbing my shoulder while my eyes watered. 'She doesn't need to be reminded of that right now.'

'Sorry,' Elena said, and she looked genuinely abashed.

'It's my best work,' Arial pronounced. 'Then again, I could probably dump a bucket of rotten tomatoes on your head and you'd still look breath-taking, so if you want Ora to stand out, *you'd* better stay *in*.'

That was precisely what I wanted to do, but Dulcie shook her head firmly. 'Don't even suggest it!' she fanned herself with one hand as she re-arranged my curls with the other. 'If she doesn't step out there tonight, I'm convinced the people in the kingdom will pull this harem apart looking for her, brick by brick.'

I glanced at her and shivered when I felt the curls dance across my bare back. 'It hasn't gotten any calmer out there since Kohén announced that I'd be going?'

'Kohén had his mother announce that you *probably* would be going, but that we had to give you time to recover from the illness that struck you last night so you'll be getting dressed and ready but then having a rest after to make sure that you're up for a late night,' Dulcie said crisply. '*I* know that he intends to take you tonight- I'd wring his neck if all of this work proved to be for nothing, and trust me when I say my neck-wringing *burns*- but the others aren't as convinced, I'm afraid, and will remain suspicious until you've shown yourself. That being said, they have stopped banging on the door.'

Elena frowned. 'Well tell them that she's rested and ready to go then. We could have her out in-'

'No,' I said quickly, sitting down, and was relieved when Dulcie caught my eyes and nodded- quietly communicating that she understood that it was imperative that I not leave the harem until Kohén summoned me. She wouldn't know why of course, but Kohén had obviously found a way to stress the importance that I not leave until he arrived and so long as she upheld that, that was all that mattered. 'No my gown isn't here yet, and I think I should definitely have some more of that soup and give it a chance to settle before I start trying to walk around in these shoes.'

'Of course,' Elena said quickly. 'I saw that bowl of soup before, I'll go heat it for you now so you can relax once we leave.'

'Is Kohén coming to get you himself?' Arial asked, and I nodded again. 'I'd hate to accidentally leave you sitting in here waiting for him if he's expecting us to deliver you out there when you're up to it.'

'No he's coming. But as his escort, there's no point in me going until much later when he's performed all of his master of ceremony tasks, so he won't be along for a while yet.'

Arial frowned. 'But he'll be wrapped up with those tasks until after-'

A knock on the door sounded and Dulcie went over to answer it. I reached over and took a sip from my glass of water, met my reflection again and tried not to wince when I was reminded of how attention-seeking I looked. My make-up was extraordinary, no doubt, but my hair was a work of art too. Dulcie had taken a section and had looped it around my crown in a pretty braid so that it resembled a tiara or a halo, and had left the rest of it out, in long, pretty coils. I should have looked washed-out seeing as how my hair, my skin and even my underwear were all shades of gold, but the sparkles and the occasional touch of contoured shadow defined enough to leave me looking, well, golden.

'What?! But I... can't Karol...? What? Oh, no!' Dulcie exclaimed, and when I looked over at her, saw that she was nodding and waving whoever was on the other side of that door off. 'No, fine, I'll do it! No, I can't exactly let the poor girl suffer, can I? Tell them I'm on my way.' She closed the door and then turned, beckoning to the girls. 'We have to leave right now ladies. Bring the palette and the curlers and take them straight up to Ora's room, I'll meet you there shortly. No dallying, not even for a moment- it's important that you get behind a locked door and quickly. Larkin... are you all right to dress and feed yourself?'

'Of course,' I said, confused. 'But what's going on?'

'Nothing, I'm just needed to heal someone- *again.*' She clapped her hands together, looking anxious. 'Come on girls, hurry! I have explicit orders not to leave Larkin in the harem with anyone but myself so because I have to rush, so do you!'

'But you're not a healer,' I said, standing up and trying not to get knocked over as the girls rushed around me, collecting armfuls of things.

'I am when it's a burn requiring healing...' Dulcie remarked, stepping into a pair of flat, white shoes with an open heel. 'Lark, your necklace and the earrings we have for it to match are right on the counter where you were sitting. Please put them on immediately- it'll be my head if something so valuable goes missing while in my care.'

'Of course,' I said, 'but-'

'A burn?' Arial looked scared. 'Oh my gosh! Please tell me those bastards at the gate haven't started trouble again, not tonight!'

'Well actually they have and that's why you have to get behind a locked door now... but I'm being summoned to deal with a burn that wasn't so much an attack as it was a rite of passage, all right?'

That made me gasp because suddenly, I remembered exactly what would be keeping Kohén away from me despite the fact that the ball hadn't started yet. 'The brandings?' I demanded. 'Oh no! Please tell me that none of my friends are hurt!'

Dulcie held open the door so Elena could race past. 'It's complicated. Kohén had performed two of the brandings without incident, but before they could finish Miss Emmerly, a crisis broke out at the fence. Apparently the protestors started up again and accidentally crushed a small child beneath their feet. Karol was called out to come to her aid directly while Kohén and Elijah were asked to go out there and scare the people back with lightning-' the ground and walls suddenly shook around us and Arial gasped- which I suppose they're doing right now, but although she was in the process of being scalded, Miss Emmerly bravely commanded him to forget about lingering to heal *her* pain and to go to the girl instead. Karol did so and I pray that he got there in time, but Miss Emmerly obviously didn't understand that the second part of the ritual hurts more than the first, because she collapsed from the agony of the quicksilver being applied to the brand and-'

'Oh my god, go!' I shrieked, pushing her out the door. 'No more explanation required, help her, please?'

To my relief, Dulcie nodded and sprinted off and Elena rushed out behind her. I caught the door when I heard Dulcie exclaim out: 'Lock a door between you and the rest of the harem, Larkin. That one, your room, whichever! I doubt the protestors are still going on now that a defenceless child has been hurt and the royals are pulling electricity from the sky, but practice caution all the same!'

'I will!' I cried, and then pressed my hand to my heart, tears welling up in my eyes at the idea of poor Emmerly suffering. I hated that branding ritual- I *hated* it! The Barachiels could do so much good, like Karol racing to that little girl's rescue now, but then they could turn around and brand that same little girl as a whore one day and it just wasn't rational. I'd allowed myself to be talked into a lot of things that I didn't agree with in the past few days, but I'd never be able to un-see how unbalanced things were here in Eden.

That makes two of us, sweetheart... Satan whispered. *Want your very last chance to try and change it? Go back to that mirror and-*

GO TO HELL! I screamed at her, and then started praying to God again as I broke out in a cold sweat. Her voice vanished immediately again but I kept my thoughts focused on god for another fifteen seconds anyway, just to be safe, knowing that this was the eleventh hour of her threatened forty-eight, clearly, and that if I was ever going to give into temptation to her, it would probably be soon. But I couldn't let that happen- couldn't make saving my life a priority over saving my soul.

I was panicked to know that so much was already going wrong on an evening where we needed everything to go right, but I was sober this time, and so I had the clarity of mind to hold the door open with one extended hand while I used the sparkling toe of my shoe to drag the foot of my bed across the doorway until it was what was keeping it ajar instead- afraid that it might lock behind me as so many others had. Praying silently both for Emmerly and the little girl and keeping my eyes lowered and away from the mirrors, I walked over to where I had been sitting, picked up my robe and threw it over my arm before walking over to the microwave where I'd seen Arial put my soup before, following Dulcie's orders to eat to the letter, as I intended to follow Kohén's about hiding in my room. It was unlike me to do exactly as I was told, but I'd been rebelling for years now and it had only gotten me into more trouble so I was determined to step into line now if that meant keeping things under someone's control- anyone's control- even if it wasn't mine.

Bearing that in mind, I balanced the plate in one hand and leaned over and scooped up my jewels with the other, knowing that Dulcie hadn't been kidding when she'd said that she'd be held accountable if the diamond choker went missing, and as much as she'd rubbed me the wrong way that day, she'd been decent towards me since she'd gotten her anger with Kohén out of her system and I wouldn't want her to get in trouble. After all, she was one of the few people in Eden that seemed to know how to maintain a healthy amount of suspicion against our monarchs with an equal amount of respect for the good they had done and I appreciated balanced people like her, Ora and Adeline, who understood that even if something seemed broken and corrupt, sometimes fixing it covertly was a better idea than screaming out the flaws to the rest of the world. Things were not perfect in Eden no... but that didn't mean that they couldn't be one day. Humanity was a work in progress with some sinister origins... so why couldn't we also give the Nephilim race the chance to evolve and grow with some gentle nudging as they had with us? Surely having Kohén's love put me in a position to nudge like no one ever had before?

Once I had all of my things together, I began to hustle awkwardly out into the foggy hot spring area, choosing to leave the door open behind me because I couldn't actually close it without a free hand and because I knew it couldn't hurt to have a bolt-hole, just in case. But I'd only made it two steps to the left before the steam from the heated soup started burning my fingers and so I hurried straight ahead to the pool instead of turning into my corridor, so that I could put the bowl down on the marble edging before the pain could force me to drop it.

Cursing under my breath, I sucked on my fingers for a moment until the heat faded a bit, and then double-checked to make sure that I hadn't melted any of Elena's handiwork but my nails looked perfect- gold flecked and encrusted with tiny diamantés. I sighed and stood up, and then looked at the sparkling diamonds in my hand, smiling gently. They really were lovely and despite how much I'd loathed them when Kohén had first strung them around my neck, I realised now that I no longer thought of them as a collar, but as a promise.

I'll put them on now... I thought, letting my robe slip off my arm as I put the earrings down on the edge of the warm pool, beside my soup. *That way I can alternate hands with the bowl...*

I heard the main door open and the sudden heavy footfalls that followed it the moment I got the clasp of the necklace open around my neck, and though my heart immediately leapt into my throat in a fearful lunge, I concentrated on securing the clasp of the necklace first so I knew it would be safe, before reaching down to grab the robe. If an intruder had found their way in here, then covering the necklace with the robe before attempting to run was definitely the smartest thing I could do! And if I had to run anywhere, it wouldn't be while wearing lingerie!

But then Kohén rounded the corner looking wild-eyed and beautiful and carrying a big cardboard box, and I was so relieved to see him that I only shoved my arms into the sleeves of the robe before I teetered towards him, jubilant, parting the thin cloud of mist between us.

'You're here!' I cried, throwing my arms around his neck and almost knocking the box out of his arms, which was light and easily knocked. I hugged him tightly before drawing back and asking: 'Is Emmerly okay? What about the little girl? I've been so scared, I-'

'All is being handled, and I was on my way back in to check on Emmerly again when one of the servants asked me to bring you your dress.' Kohén dropped the box and wrapped his arms around me, wide-eyed as he searched my face. 'Larkin, you look...' he ran his hands through my curls and I didn't care if he was messing them up, because he was the only person that I wanted dazzled and he looked nothing short of it. In fact, dressed the way he was in a white toga with a gold stripe and a crown of golden laurel leaves, he looked nothing short of dazzling himself and I felt those butterflies coming back.

'You look amazing too,' I whispered, touching his crown and then the golden filigree mask he was wearing over his eyes. 'You look way better in this than I do, actually. Julius Caesar, yes?'

'I thought you'd appreciate the irony of me wearing *your* uniform,' Kohén whispered, smiling up at me for only a moment before his gaze drifted towards my ear. 'But I'll never compare. I... how do you *do* it?'

'Do what?' I asked, touched by how emotional he'd become though I suspected that he'd had a few drinks himself, probably dousing himself with artificial courage in order to get through the branding ritual.

Kohén's voice caught on emotion as he wet his lips, staring down at my own. 'Every time I think you couldn't possibly look more beautiful than the last time I saw you, you find some other way to...' he glanced down at my lower body, and when his eyes saw what was beneath the open collar of the unbelted robe, his gaze darkened. 'God almighty…' he looked pained as he ran his hands down my sides, stepping back so that he could see me better, and I flushed in a good way when he groaned, stepped back into me and pushed my sleeve off my shoulder, letting it fall away so that he could gently kiss my collarbone. 'You'll be the death of me.'

'I had an inkling that you'd approve of this…' I whispered, closing my eyes and grasping his shoulders as his breath tickled my neck. 'You know I'd never wear this for anyone but you, yes?'

'Oh… Larkin… I have to go, but… I…' he raked his eyes up to my face again, and I was amazed to see that they were blue again and misted over with tears. 'I can't do it,' he caressed my cheek, pulling me in against him for a kiss. 'I don't know how to be in the same room with you without holding you!'

'You can hold me whenever you want now,' I reminded him sliding my hands down his chest and biting my lower lip as I ducked slightly to look up into his eyes. 'And the ball hasn't started yet… so why don't you go check on everything and throw about another bolt of lightning or two for good measure while I get dressed, hmm? Then hurry back to me and help me with the fasteners on my stockings- that's the gentlemanly thing to do, isn't it? Helping a lady in need?'

Kohén's brow furrowed as he glanced down at my legs. 'Your stockings are already fastened around those delicious thighs, Lark.'

'I know,' I purred, sliding my hand lower so that I could caress him through his toga and groaning gently when I felt him instantly stiffen in my hand. It was pretty bad timing but I hadn't had him in days and I needed him, so badly! The mask was sexy too- it made him look so mysterious. 'I meant you should come and *un*do them…' I bit his lower lip now and finished: 'We've got twenty minutes until the ball officially starts, and I know you're more than capable of fucking me senseless at least *twice* in twenty minutes…'

Kohén's eyes flew open and darkened once more. 'You want me to… to fuck you?' he swallowed hard, and I almost smiled at the way he struggled with the word. He was all right crying it out in a fit of passion, but he always politely said 'made love' beforehand, and it was a bit cute. Deluded, but cute. '*Now*? Larkin… no… we can't…'

'But I'm almost completely better again,' I insisted, wrapping my arms around his neck and feeling delighted by the way he was trembling. He really *would* thank Dulcie for his gift-wrapped apology! 'I just have this awful, hollow feeling inside and you're the only person in Arcadia that can fill it, aren't you?' I leaned back and pouted. 'Or will you leave me to suffer until midnight?'

That did it! Kohén's eyes flashed and I made a mental note to turn a pout on him every time he resisted. 'The *world*…' Kohén roughly yanked me against him, one hand against my backside, the other around my back. 'You hear me?' his fingers raked across my flesh possessively through the cloth, and I longed for him to strip the robe off me so that I could feel his sparks against my back. 'I am the only person in the *world* for you, Larkin, and I'm gonna remind you of that right now - just to clear up any confusion that there's been of late!'

'Please do!' I whispered, and then Kohén groaned and pressed his mouth to mine in a kiss that was…

Wrong! I thought, eyes springing open. *This kiss is WRONG!* I pulled back immediately, wrestling myself out of my lover's grip, and gasped when I saw first the shock then the comprehension in his eyes. 'You…' I began as I wiped my mouth and the taste of arctic mint toothpaste instead of spearmint away, then looked at the box, back to Julius Caesar and then was struck by the fact that he'd referred to Dulcie as the healer. Maybe she'd healed me and Emmerly, but she wasn't a healer and *Kohén* would know that!

Kohén would… but *Kohl* might not!

'No!' I gasped, pressing my fingers to my mouth as I stumbled back from him, slapping at his hands as he reached for me. 'Not again! Kohl Barachiel, don't tell me that you just allowed me to believe that you were Kohén *again*?!'

'Shit!' Kohl ripped his mask off and threw it to the ground and I instantly knew that I was right. While he'd been wearing it, he'd looked as Kohén would look, but now that he wasn't I could see all the little differences between them that I'd only really gotten to know in the past few days after spending so many moments pressed against my naked prince in my too-bright room. Kohén had a tiny freckle under the corner of one eye, whereas Kohl had a few across the bridge of his nose. Kohl was slightly broader and more muscular, but Kohén had gotten that little bit taller and because he stood taller too he came off as looking older and a lot more self-assured. Kohl's skin was darker and his hair sun-kissed in several strands, but Kohén's hair was darker and glossier and a little bit longer because Kohl's haircut had been more recent...

And Kohén looked at me with love and amusement in his eyes- whereas Kohl was now staring at me looking nothing but displaced.

'Larkin...' he held up his hands. 'I'm sorry, I just lost myself and-'

'*Lost*?' I shrieked, and my voice rang off the marble arched ceiling. 'You think being lost is bad? Try being *dead*, Kohl! And that's what you'll be if he finds out that you- that we-' I cupped my face in horror. 'I can't believe this! Do you even know if Emmerly and the girl are all right, or was that a lie?'

'No they're fine, I saw Emmerly get healed with my own eyes and Karol handed the little girl over to that other new healer as soon as I arrived so he could pick up where Karol had left off, and then Karol went to wait for the ball to start in privacy while he could recover. Kohén's joined father outside now, trying to manage the rebels but I'm sure-'

'Good! Then get out of here before it's too late and pray to God that I can lie to Kohén about this so he never finds out!'

Kohl looked stricken. 'You have to pray to lie to that bastard now? Larkin- HE HAS YOU HERE AGAINST YOUR WILL! The entire fucking kingdom can see that... why can't *you*?'

'I guess she's been looking at things from a different perspective, you know?' a cold voice stated from beside us, and we both whirled to see Kohén- the *real* Kohén- standing there next to Elijah, scowling at his brother hatefully through the light fog. He'd dressed as an Indian Brave and my knees went weak at the sight of him looking so much like Miguel Barachiel had been depicted in the paintings that had captured his first life- but while looking so utterly fatal. 'But you don't understand perspective do you, little brother? So here, let me give you some!'

And before I could even scream, Kohén lifted his hand and shot a flash of blue light across the room, striking his lost, hapless, younger brother right in his golden sash and sending him flying back against the wall.

20.

'No!' Constance's scream rang out at the same time as mine had and we both raced across the room to Kohl's aid. Seeing him hit the wall at least three feet off the ground before collapsing back down like a rag doll had come dangerously close to giving me another heart episode, but I saw that he was getting up before I'd closed in on him and so I pulled up short and allowed Constance to fling herself at him instead. After all, she was apparently the one with medical training, and I was once again the reason why he was in need of it.

'Hey!' Elijah barked at his spouse, watching her fly past with an outraged expression. 'How did you-'

'I slipped in behind you! I thought you were bringing Larkin out and I thought it would look good if we escorted her as a family! Are you all right?!' Constance pulled Kohl up into a sitting position and I moaned when I saw the massive blistering sore covering his right shoulder. 'Can you speak? *Breathe?*'

'I'm functioning...' Kohl groaned, pressing his hand to his wound and turning white when he saw the amount of blood and ooze on his hand. 'He missed my heart.'

'Because I wasn't aiming for it!' Kohén thundered, and I felt his hand latch around my bicep before I was yanked back. 'But if I EVER see you stand within arm's reach of her again-'

'You'll not look at him again unless you want a taste of your own medicine!' Constance raged, and Kohén's eyes bugged.

'It was *my* doing!' I spun around and whimpered when I saw the blue sparks of energy dancing and crackling around every part of my infuriated lover. I held out my arms, making it clear that he would have to go through me before he hurt Kohl again. 'Kohén please, it was my fault, all right? Just like the last time, I thought he was you and I threw myself at him!'

'Don't even try to defend him Lark!' Kohén spat, trembling with anger. 'I wouldn't want your loyalty called into question again, and neither would he!'

I lowered my arms, understanding the implied threat. I wasn't even supposed to be speaking with Kohl yet out of loyalty to Kohén, so defending him wasn't going to help anyone.

'The *last* time?' Elijah demanded, stepping up beside us and look just as angry as Kohén, but without the light show. I'd heard he'd learned how to control the current generated by his temper in his late thirties, just after the twins had been born. In fact, I think he'd learned to do it intentionally because of the twin's birth and because the proof that he'd failed his spouse and unborn child with that temper had been apparent in Kohl's deformities. I was relieved to see him restraining his anger now, but it wouldn't do us much good if Kohén could not do the same. '*What* last time?'

'The first time we met, it was a case of mistaken identity on both parts before their birthday ball,' I said quickly, stepping forward and rubbing Kohén's bare, sweaty and buzzing shoulders briskly with my hands, trying to calm him down. He was wearing only buskin pants, a feathered headdress and war paint around his eyes as a mask and he looked nothing short of sinful. But the beaded, feathery necklace against his chest was shaking due to his rage, and everywhere I touched him sparked enough to sting my palms when the energy crackled and popped against them. 'He thought I was someone else and I thought he was Kohén and it was an innocent mistake-'

'Yes, *innocent!*' Kohén pointed out, still glowering at Kohl over my shoulder. 'He thought you were someone else that night when he kissed you, so it was an innocent mistake then, one that I let slide!' Kohén caught my wrists and jerked them down as he stared into my eyes with his black ones so I'd understand that he wasn't in the mood to be mollified. 'But he knew otherwise tonight, Larkin! Perhaps you did not and you can't be faulted for that, not while he's in a wing he's forbidden from entering while wearing a mask! But *you…*' He stepped around me and this time it was Elijah that helped to hold him back. 'How did you even get in here?'

Kohl groaned and got off the wall, and I didn't know if he was minding his temper because he was in too much pain or because he understood that he'd made a major mistake. 'Someone gave me the box with her gown asked me to take it to her and pass along a message. I walked up to the door to give it to the giant you have posted there but he must have assumed that I was you because he opened the door for me and ushered me in, no questions asked for once.'

'A mistake that you did not bother to clarify because you just couldn't resist the urge to get in here while you had the chance, isn't that right?!' Kohl grimaced and lowered his head, regarding his wound again and Kohén looked to his father, his expression looking even more lethal and his eyes even more blue in contrast to the black stripe he'd painted across his face. 'Do you see what I'm dealing with here? Why I've been so goddamned paranoid-'

'Don't take the lord's name in vain,' Elijah said gruffly, standing taller and looking incredibly distinguished in a sea captain's costume, another old-world fashion I'd never seen outside of a book illustration before. How strange it was that we paid homage to times that had been so troubled! 'I understand your anger, but that doesn't excuse you acting like a heathen.' He then turned to me. 'Did you honestly believe that was Kohén? He made no effort to clarify your mistake? Did he even have the opportunity to?'

I looked over at Kohl but he waved his hand, signalling that I shouldn't bother to defend him again, so I took a deep breath and turned back to Elijah. 'Yes, he had the opportunity to, but I suppose he was overwhelmed so-'

'Larkin!' Kohén snapped. 'You're not helping anyone!'

'I knew she thought I was Kohén!' Kohl burst out, pushing off the wall and striding towards us. 'I kissed her anyway, and I'll do it again until I've kissed some sense into her!'

I gasped as Kohén practically pulsed a bright blue. 'You are very close to breaking our arrangement, little brother-'

'Fuck you and your arrangement, okay?' Kohl demanded, shoving Kohén back when he lunged at him. 'You're gonna tattle on me now? Don't bother, I'll do it myself!' Kohl whirled on his father while Constance rushed over with wide eyes that had been outlined with blue and green gems to match her deep green gown. She was a peacock- jade, feathers extended from her bustle down to the floor, and she'd never looked lovelier or more vexed. 'I'm in love with Larkin, *that* you know! I'd fight to the death for her- that only *Kohén* knows! But the reason why I have not is because Kohén has been blackmailing me into holding my tongue all week, all right? And because Larkin would suffer as much as I have I have accepted the terms... but I won't abide them anymore! Not when I know that she is suffering anyway!'

'Blackmailing you?' Constance demanded, looking to me and I moaned and stepped back towards the fountain, shaking my head. 'With *what?*'

'Kohl, please-' I whispered, but he looked at me and shook his head, covering his wound with his hand before addressing his mother and father at once. 'I unearthed a bible in Pacifica, a King James one.' He swallowed hard and my legs went weak. Oh my God, he was doing this! I looked to Elijah and felt light-headed when I saw his eyes instantly flash an unearthly blue. 'I gave it to Larkin to read and signed a greeting to her within the cover-'

'That is a grievous sin!' Elijah roared.

'And yet it pales in comparison to the ones that have been committed since!' Kohl roared back. 'Kohén found it and a whole bunch of other letters that I wrote to her, expressing my feelings for her, and has threatened to show them to the two of you if I admit...' he looked at me and swallowed hard, nodding, and I collapsed onto the edge of the fountain behind me, moaning into my hands. 'If I admit that I know the truth of how she came to be in Kohén's bed!' He lifted his head. 'She did not give herself to the twin that is now holding her captive- but to the twin that wrote to her and *that* has sealed her fate- a fact that she wasn't aware of until her virginity had been taken already by the first twin while masquerading as the other! She thought she was sleeping with ME!'

Oh no! My nerves were firing off the warning to run but I was too stunned to do anything but watch them all between my parted fingers.

'What?' Elijah asked, turning grey now- and slowly turning to glower at me. 'You-'

'That wasn't it!' Kohén snapped. 'I *thought* she'd already given herself to him prior to that, and I knew if she was found out, she'd be accused of cheating on me and Banished! I wasn't ready to lose her- to the street *or* to the other side of the fence- so I made a point of taking her while witnesses were present so they could attest to the fact that they'd seen *me* doing it, not Kohl! It was for her protection, or so I *thought!*'

'You idiot child!' Elijah stomped over to us and thrust a hand out at me. 'You stained your soul by lying for a girl that had been lying to you and toying with your brother's emotions as well? I knew you were in over your head as far as your feelings for her were concerned but-'

'No!' Kohén shook his head. 'No, I only did that because when she thought I was Kohl- she *ended* things between them completely and apologised...' I squeezed my eyes shut as Kohén bumbled his way through the entire sordid story, admitting his guilt but defending my honour, while Constance crept up behind me and laced her ice-cold fingers through my clammy ones. 'But the moment we... I... I realised she was still pure and I... I have been trying to make things right with her since, all right?' He collapsed onto the stone work beside me and took my other hand, kissing it while staring at his father defiantly. 'She was a virgin that had every intention of remaining faithful to me when I had her, father, and I refuse to allow those facts to be called into question! I also refuse to apologise to any of you for how it all came to pass-' he kissed my hand and then squeezed it tightly, '-when it is only Larkin's forgiveness that I desire, and hers alone! I tricked her into the act of love in order to win her love and save her life- but I shouldn't have. I didn't *have* to- she'd already made up her mind to be faithful to me, before I forced her to change it!'

'Bullshit!' Kohl broke out, and I cringed to think that he was going to throw me to the wolves for no reason, but it was Kohén he attacked. 'You don't want her forgiveness, you want her submission and surrender! You want to force me out of her head and you're trying to make that happen by locking her up in here and dousing her with alcohol, because you know if given an hour of open air and sobriety, she'll realise how poorly you've always treated her and how you've ruined her life and throw herself over that bloody fence anyway!'

I looked to Constance, hoping that she'd be able to offer me or them some sort of guidance before their powers started bouncing off the walls again, but she was staring down at the floor looking only conflicted. I couldn't help but wonder who she wanted to believe more, and was fairly certain that that was a question she was trying to answer for herself.

Kohén jumped to his feet again. 'You know that's not why I keep her in here! There are other factors, remember? Will you ruin her life more in a fit of jealous anger now, Brutus, or can you just shut the fuck up already?'

'Brutus?' Elijah snapped, whirling on Kohl. 'You've read that infernal book too?'

'*No* father,' Kohén said while making a gruesome face, and the fact that he was being honest was clear. 'I have simply heard numerous references to it in other books that I have read- and Kohl's ball gown brought them all to mind.'

'Fuck you,' Kohl said scornfully. 'What would *your* native American name be? Cries-when-he-cums? Kicking-whores? Feather-for-dick?'

'Better than yours, Loses-The-Girl! or is it: 'Wind-in-his-skirt?' Kohén smarted back, and the two boys went at each other but Constance moved between them swiftly, releasing my hand and leaving it lonely.

'Stop it! And tell me, where is that book?' Constance finally looked to me. 'Larkin, is this the secret you mentioned having to keep from me? Is that Bible all that is at stake? But no...' she frowned, pushing the boys away from one another. 'Kohén just said that there's something else-'

Oh God...

Kohén looked at me. 'You told her? How? When?'

'After she struck me! That is when I found my voice again, okay? Only I told her that she needed to stay out of matters because she could only make them worse!' I didn't know if he'd believe that or not, but he looked somewhat assured so I plunged on: 'I asked her to encourage Kohl to find happiness and to not antagonise you or anyone else on the matter because she didn't understand how badly things could go wrong for us, and wouldn't have to if she just let things be!' I turned to Constance. 'And no that is not all that is at stake but my lips are sealed on the rest, and no, I have no idea where the Bible is. All that I know is that Kohén promised that if Kohl played along this week, he'd give the book back to him as soon as he boarded the ship to Pacifica so that he could dispose of it himself. It was a peace offering- blackmail that went both ways.'

'Where is it then?' Elijah demanded of Kohén, holding out his hand. 'We must burn it, immediately!'

'You'd cover for them?' Constance asked, shocked but eager.

'You *wouldn't*?' Elijah demanded. 'Have you not seen the state of things out there woman? Our boys will be flogged for the lies and secrets they've allowed to fester behind these closed doors, but I won't have Karol's birthday or Eden's name ruined by their shenanigans even more than they already have been! God probably wouldn't approve of it, but he wouldn't want poor Karol ruined by any of this either, would he?'

'I agree,' Constance said quietly, nodding and squeezing his shoulder. 'I don't like it, but I agree. Karol is an innocent in all of this and I won't see him suffer.'

Kohl snorted but Kohén diverted attention from him by saying quickly: 'You don't have to destroy the Bible- I already have.'

Kohl laughed bitterly. 'You wouldn't have destroyed that- you've just hidden it away so you can hold it against me forever!'

'Actually no, though fuck you for believing that wasn't my right!' Kohén looked back to his father. 'Larkin told me that she loved me last night and that made me realise that I didn't need to fear Kohl stealing her heart anymore... so before I came to see you to barter my way out of the date with Amelia-Rose, I burned it and any hold that I had over him, but neglected to mention it, just to be safe.' He turned to Kohl again, as I felt something inside me unravel-something good this time. 'I burned it so I'd never be tempted to use it against you again, because I knew that it wasn't godly to hold onto it so... and *this* is how you repay me?' He shook his head, eyes slitting. 'I hate you. Just thought I'd say that now in case that fact wasn't already plain.'

'Oh, it's plain...' Kohl said, but with less fire in his own blue eyes and understandably so. If Kohén truly had burned that book, then he'd earned some of the feathers in his headdress- that was for certain. It made me feel better about him but worse for poor Kohl, who looked only like a young man could look after losing a love, a brother and a best friend all in one week.

'You really burned it?' I asked, and Kohén nodded, touching my braid.

'The ashes are in the fireplace in my room- my attempt to earn a halo like the one that you are currently sporting.' He turned to his father again while I pressed my hand to my heart and sobbed. For once, I'd been a good influence on someone here! 'If you go in there, you'll find a corner of a page intact to prove it.'

'I don't care to see it,' Elijah said rubbing his forehead. 'I always thought the hysteria over that thing was a little overwrought, but the only three people in this palace that have touched it have apparently acted with nought but darkness since doing so, and I will not lump my own soul into those ashes.' Elijah motioned to me to stand up and I did. 'And speaking of souls... Larkin of Eden...' he cocked his head and stepped closer to me, eyes drilling into mine and I shivered: This was it! The moment I had been dreading for years! Had Satan's warning concerned Elijah's punishment? Would he do something to inspire me to take my own life now?

Keep calm and breathe! He knows about the affair now, but he knows the truth to it too which is a blessing!

'You have caused a lot of chaos in here- do you deny that? Writing letters to your master's brother was out of line, as was accepting that bible- and conspiring to sleep with the wrong brother just so you'd have the chance to run...' he sighed. 'There really is no end to the list of rules that you have broken, is there?'

'No, your majesty,' I said, my voice breaking, 'and I also know that the rules that your sons have broken were because of me too, so if it's all right...' I glanced from Kohén, then Kohl, then back to the king, deciding that I was sick of crying to Satan for help, and so I would do whatever it took to get into Heaven. And if this truly was my last night on earth, then I was running out of time to atone for my sins and forgive myself- to reverse the damage that I had done to the two boys, whose only sin had been to love someone that did not deserve it. 'Punish me for what they have done wrong too, please?'

I didn't think it was possible to silence four Barachiel's at once, but my request was met at first by only that, stunned silence.

'What?' Kohén whispered after a moment's pause, coming up to my side and trying to twist me to face him.

'Like hell!' Kohl exclaimed, earning a look of recrimination from his father once more.

'Larkin!' Constance hissed. 'No, you-'

'You are the one that first brought it to my attention that I am a horrible influence on your angelic sons, and I hate myself for it every day. So please...' I pressed my hands together in prayer, begging Elijah to do me this one good turn. '*Please*- if they are to be whipped, assign their lashes to me as you threatened to do yesterday. I'll take every one, and gladly and pray that each sting absolves a little piece of me.'

'No, don't accept that, father!' Kohl rushed forward.

'No, I'll take them!' Kohén cried, tugging on his father's arm. 'Don't hurt her- I can't bear it! I've already hurt her more than I can stand!'

'Shut up, both of you! You think I'd whip a girl when the entire country is watching me to see that she's being treated well? No. Well, not yet.' Elijah turned back to me. 'Go put your dress on Larkin and dry your eyes. You want to atone for your sins? Then you'll do it now by marching yourself into that ballroom and acting as madly in love with my son as you claim to be!' He raised an eyebrow and drawled. 'Just one of them though, all right? Preferably Kohén.'

'Father!' Kohén exclaimed as I blushed beet-red, but Elijah rolled his eyes.

'Please,' Elijah lifted his hat off his head and wiped sweat off his brow, looking at me and shaking his head. 'If I don't laugh about it somehow, I'll cry.'

I pressed my hand to my chest, astounded that the king was being so... gracious. Sure he had a lot to gain from presenting me to the palace alive and well, but he could have done that by whipping me and then having me healed too, but he was choosing kindness- kindness with a hint of sarcasm. 'That's *it*?'

'Until you piss me off again, yes so I wouldn't look so relieved- you have quite a habit of pissing me off!' Elijah turned around, picked up the box, dragged a golden gown out of it and threw it at my feet. A smaller, thinner package with an envelope pinned to the front of it fell to the misty floor too, but my eyes were fixed on Constance as she rushed to collect the dress, looking relieved. 'Go on- put it on… you're not helping matters dressed as you are, as Kohl had already demonstrated…' He ignored the dirty look that he earned from both twins and went on, motioning for me to cooperate with his spouse. '*If* you perform as well as you need to tonight- as you've been trained to do at the expense of my purse and my patience- I will pretend that none of this has ever happened.' Constance immediately dropped to help guide my feet into the dress and I rested my weight on her shoulder as I lifted one foot, too stunned to do anything but comply. 'But if you do not convince the world that you are the luckiest Companion in the world, then all three of you will be whipped after-' he pointed to Kohl, 'including *you*. I swear kid, I understand the temptation of course… you are a Barachiel and she is rather enchanting… but if you so much as look sideways at her while on Amelia-Rose's arm tonight know that she will suffer twice as much as you will, got it?'

Kohl nodded, keeping his eyes off me and on the king. 'Yes father,' he said. 'I'll be the perfect son as always- the one you're *so* very proud of.'

'Don't get sarcastic on me kid,' Elijah growled. 'I've already hit my tolerance level for disrespect and ingratitude as far as the three of you are concerned! One more incident- one more filthy look or cursed word- and you'll all regret it!'

'Oh my gosh…' Constance's hands were white-knuckled and shaking as she drew the dress up my mid-section, but she looked up at me with those ice-blue eyes. 'Larkin this is gorgeous… did you order it in advance?'

'I've never seen it before,' I said, confused as she walked around me to smooth the bodice into place and then zip up the back. It fit me perfectly and was truly a work of art, because the entire bodice hugged the curves that my corset had provided me with (I'd thought it odd that I'd been measured after putting my underwear on!) and had been embellished with golden feathers! Not fluffy ones that gave me that duckling/ swan look, but smooth ones that appeared to have been hand-cut from glittery satin, and them glued to the structure of the gown beneath in layers! They lay like scales- flat and shimmering and in crazy patterns that were only obviously when you looked up close, but appeared as one smooth layer of fabric when I softened the focus of my eyes.

Most of the feathers were fake, but a few real ones had been added to the low-cut sweetheart neckline so that their fluffy tendrils moved like whispered breath had stirred them, and the skirt that Constance pulled up my pantyhose next has been made of the thinnest, softest golden fabric that I had ever touched! It was translucent like chiffon, but felt as soft as rose petals and had the consistency of tissue, and despite the fact that I could tell that at least six layers had been used to make the skirt appear opaque, there was barely any thickness to the fabric at all and the feint breeze stirring the skirts made them shimmer and dance. I shifted my weight when Constance tried to un-snag a part of the skirt from the clasp of my shoe, and a slit appeared in the skirt, revealing my opposite leg almost all the way to my upper thigh.

'Extraordinary…' Elijah said, then looked at me and shook his head, smiling ruefully. 'My sons were all done for the moment you were walked through our gates, weren't they, little Lark?'

I blushed while Constance peeled up the bottom of the corset in order to slip the band of the skirt beneath. I couldn't work out if it was the most scandalous dress I'd ever seen or the most demure, but one look at Kohén's face confirmed that it was certainly the most beautiful. 'Kohén…' I desperately needed another sip of water. 'Did you order this?'

Kohén raised an eyebrow. 'You would have worn it every day of your life if I had known of its existence.' He took my hand and stepped back from me, shaking his head. 'Are you a swan again?'

'I don't think so,' Constance reached over, picked up the second bundle, read the note that had been pinned to the front of it- and then handed it to me. 'Look.'

'Pull the bow?' I recited, confused, and then saw that there was a golden bow wrapped around the second bundle. Kohl took the other item from her, shot me a look and then stepped three paces back from us before pulling on the bow.

'What are you-'

'If it's a bomb or something, it's best that the irrelevant brother opens it, yes?' he smiled grimly at me, and my heart broke for him.

'Kohl...' Constance said, moving to walk over to him, but he held up a hand and pulled the bow and we all flinched and gasped as the package exploded- not in smoke and fire, but into a pair of long, elegant golden wings.

I pressed my fingertips to my lips, moved because they were stunning- heartsick because I did not deserve to wear them.

Someone had made me into an angel- someone who clearly didn't know me at all.

21.

'Well!' Kohl shook his head and then walked over to me, motioning for me to turn around while he held open the shimmery feathered wings. 'How's that, hmm? She's accused of being the darkness tainting us all, and yet someone clearly thinks of her as the only angel.'

'You're not pinning angel wings to *my*... angel.' Kohén snatched the feathers from Kohl who raised his hands in surrender and then I felt his fingers tickling the lower half of my back. 'They attach here...' he said, and I felt a click as a button snapped shut, and then the press of his lips to my cheek- a kiss that I was sure was supposed to get more of a reaction out of Kohl than me, for I could feel his heated gaze scorching a trail over my shoulder and into his brother's face across from me. 'And you truly are an angel, my love. Never have you looked so glorious- and never have I felt so blessed to have you in my life.'

But I was barely listening to him, I was staring down at the dress and reflecting upon what Elijah had said- about me having done all of his sons in. He'd only been thinking of the twins of course, but there was a third Barachiel that had been corrupted by his desire for me, and hadn't that same Barachiel asked Lindy to design me a dress for his ball? I'd asked her to sew me a duck costume and hadn't thought about it since but now, my toes and fingertips were beginning to feel, well, numb, and it was a numbness that was spreading through me. I looked up at Kohl, frowning. 'Who gave this to you? Didn't you say that they had a message?'

Kohl looked confused for a moment, but then a light came on behind his navy eyes and he nodded. 'I don't know who it was- there are a whole bunch of servants running around the palace. But I believe I saw her at the last ball we attended- a pretty dark-haired girl.'

Gabby- Gabby or Satan. My blood felt cold. 'And the message?'

Kohl frowned again and then said: 'Tell Larkin that the designer and her family cannot wait until they see her in it! And thank her for the surprise invite!'

The world tilted so sharply that I actually swayed and had to cling on to Elijah of all people. 'The designer...?' tears filled my eyes. 'And her *family*? Oh God!' I whirled around, grasping at Kohén. 'Lindy!' I hissed, and he leaned his head forward, like he was about to fall over. 'She's here, Kohén! Lindy's here! Her family too, oh *God!*'

'Glad tidings indeed!' Elijah boomed, patting my back, misconstruing my horror for jubilation. 'You were rather close with the Trevassé family, weren't you?'

But Kohén did not need to be told that it was the worst news I could have been given. 'I... he...?'

I nodded. '*He* ordered this, Kohén! He brought them here! I...' I looked down at the envelope in my hand and with a thundering heart, tore it open until I saw the card inside. It was on a piece of the palace's official stationary, and the script was too perfectly composed to have been from anyone but the crowned prince:

Dear Larkin.

I'd rather hoped that we'd be meeting at midnight tonight to tear up your contract along with all of the others before enjoying a private celebration for two, and though circumstances have changed, my desire for you has not. It may appear that way, but you would be foolish to believe that anything would prevent me from taking you in my arms at long last. I have fallen silent and I have kept away- but only physically for the sake of keeping up appearances, Larkin. Inside my body I am screaming for you and reducing that harem and anyone who tries to stop me from getting to you to rubble. Were it not for my desire to maintain some dignity as far as my family name is concerned, I would have done so already!

But dignity can be restored in the Barachiel name in many ways, and we cannot be watched every second, despite what they all believe, so you will come to me before midnight, or I will come to you. That is not a threat, sweet angel- but a heartfelt promise. And Barachiel men take promises awfully seriously, so I beg you to keep the one you made to me- and your gratitude for all I have done to you- at the forefront of your mind when you ask yourself what I mean to you and what I still could, because birthday wishes can only be granted after the candle has been blown out- and the candle I hold burning for you could withstand an electrical storm and a monsoon, my love- so it can most certainly weather those that would oppose it!

So fight for me the way I am fighting for you. Slip your beautiful being into this beautiful gown and then come celebrate my birthday with me, your dear friends, and the Blue-Collar family have travelled across the country to tell you how much your sacrifice meant to them, and know that I will be counting the seconds until you arrive-

... and that I will remain the most eligible bachelor in Calliel until I have had the chance to capture you the way you have captured me.

Sincerely,
Prince Charming.

The world was spinning by the time that my eyes traced over his signature, and I cupped my hand to my mouth as Kohén snatched the paper from me and stormed across the room, getting distance from our audience so that he could read it in private. Too numb to even cry, I watched Kohén's eyes trace Karol's elegant cursive, and saw the actual moment when his mind snapped. He let out a bellow of indignation and then turned back to gape at me, astonished.

'What is it?' Constance demanded, watching Kohl lope over to Kohén, asking to read it too, but Kohén held him off, making it clear that he had not even finished yet. She made to follow but I held her back and watched as Kohén handed Kohl the letter at last and then turned around to start screaming and cussing so loudly that I cringed at last and shrunk into myself.

'What is going on NOW?' Elijah demanded, but neither twin answered him so he looked to me. 'Larkin, who is the gown from?'

Thinking quickly and all too aware that Kohén would not be capable of doing the same for quite some time, I looked down at the sheath of paper that I still had in my hands that Karol had included- an invitation to the ball. It had the Barachiel family crest at the top- more 'official' paper, and when I turned it over, saw that the reverse side had the same. An idea grew from a theory and then it became a plan as I realised that the only way to get myself or at least- Lindy and Coaxley- out of this mess, was to repeat the behaviour that had gotten me into it in the first place. I would strike a deal with the most powerful man in the world to get me out of debt to the second-most powerful man in the world. Neither of us would like it, but we both needed it to happen in order to get what we wanted. So, swallowing back bile, I looked up at Elijah and asked:

'How badly do you want me to go to that ball, your highness?'

Elijah looked non-plussed. *'What?'*

I pointed at Kohén. 'He's about to forbid me from attending, and I have to do as he asks. I do not want to go now either, would gladly taking a whipping for refusing and fear that if I do I will only be able to go as a hysterical mess- but there is a way that you can calm me down and possibly even placate him.' I handed him the piece of paper and then pointed to the leather bag that he'd brought along with him. 'Do you have a pen in there?'

'I do but-'

'Get it,' I said quickly, and though the king looked like he was about to protest, both twins were now cursing and arguing and snatching the letter from one another's grasp, and so he sighed and took the pen from Constance, who had already fished it out.

'Larkin, what's going on?' Constance asked, staring at the boys, stricken. 'What is this new crisis, child?'

'This is a solution to a crisis, but only if you act quickly.' I motioned to the paper, which Elijah was holding rather stupidly. 'I will go to that ball and I will win Arcadia's trust back, but only after you have secured mine. Right now, this very second, you need to write a pardon for me.'

'Why?' he barked, but was already kneeling. 'What have you done?!'

'A pardon for me to gift to *another*,' I pointed to the paper again. 'Write: I King Elijah the second of Arcadia, do solemnly swear...' I paused, holding my breath as the king first stared at me and then began to write, 'to pardon Lindy and Coaxley Trevassé of their crimes against the crown...'

'Crimes?! Elijah demanded. 'As in *plural*?'

'Coaxley? Larkin... whatever are you *talking* about?' Constance was staring at me like I was an alien being. 'Those two would never hurt a fly!'

'I know that,' I said quickly, 'but they are criminals by Arcadian law all the same, and I will have them pardoned before their sins can come to light, or I will go out there and scream everything that I have not told you two!'

'Larkin-'

'The dress is a warning- a threat against the family of the designer, and I'll not speak another word about it and what that means for me, this family or hers until I know that they will be pardoned for their behaviour as quickly as Elijah has pardoned his own kin- because we are all equals, right?'

Constance burst into tears. 'You've kept so much from me Larkin! I thought we were confidantes?'

'I have kept a lot of things from a lot of people,' I said pointedly, silently reminding her about the secrets of hers that I had in my possession. 'And now that you know only of the existence of two of them, can you not understand why I stay hushed on the others? They're all vile.'

'Fine!' Elijah shook his head, writing fiercely. 'This is disgusting behaviour- a man of God, covering up sin after sin and for what? To save a bunch of ungrateful bastards that insist on sinning! What I ought to do is write this entire family off and see if Ewan and his children could fare any better upon this throne!'

He was right, but he wouldn't do it. Like Miguel he was determined to do what was right- but just as pre-disposed to do what was wrong.

'Sign it,' I said quickly, leaning over to peer at it to make sure he'd written what I'd dictated, verbatim. The moment his signature slashed down the page I blew out my breath and nodded. 'Thank you. Deliver that unto them and the moment they have it, I will walk out that door with a smile on my face.'

'Deliver what?' Kohén stalked back over to my side, looking from me to his father. 'You're not going anywhere Larkin, and you couldn't possibly want to! Not with all that's at stake!'

'I have just erased most of what was at stake,' I told him firmly, pointing to the declaration. 'Your father has pardoned Lindy and her family and once they have it, I will be able to walk out there safe in the knowledge that refusing to follow the instructions in that letter will not ruin their lives... and what is left of my faith in mankind.'

'You'll be able to walk out there safe in the knowledge that the crowned prince has been decapitated and his head run through on a spike!' Kohén spat, taking me and forcefully sitting me down on the edge of the pool as his family gasped. All but Kohl of course, who was nodding in agreement. 'He thinks we ought to fear his temper? Ha! Once I'm through with him, he won't have the strength to cover a blemish let alone get an erection-'

'He won't touch me if I refuse him!' I cried. 'He wanted me *willingly,* Kohén! He will lash out at them when I make it clear that I am anything but willing, but he won't be able to hurt them once your father has absolved them, so-'

'He will *so* touch you!' Kohén bellowed. 'Or he believes that he will!'

'Karol?' Constance pressed her hand to her forehead. 'You're talking about *Karol* now?'

'Yes mother surprise surprise- he's as fucked up and corrupt as the rest of us- only more so. But don't let that make me the lesser of two evils or anything... I know how much you like believing that I am the *only* horrid one!' Kohén turned straight back to me as his mother recoiled back into her spouse's arms. 'Honestly Larkin... how could you receive a letter so sinister and loaded with double-entendres and walk away believing that all that is good and light will triumph in the end?'

'Because that is the whole point, isn't it? This is a family that has descended from angels!' I hated Kohén being so angry with me, but I hated how jaded I had become towards the world more and desperately needed something to change- to believe that something could change. 'You want me to believe in the best of you! So let me believe in the best in *him*!'

'But you're only saving your friends with that letter,' Kohl pointed out, arriving at my side and resting his hand on my shoulder. 'What about the other things he hinted towards doing to spite you? Marrying Ora? Releasing the others like me? No I agree with Kohén- you need to stay away from him until midnight, and under lock and key. Karol talks a big game but he's trying to scare you by making threats that he himself would be too scared to follow through on, and if you fall for it and go out there you will walk right into his hands! He says he will rip the harem apart? I say let him try! But he will have to contend with both of us *first,* and then explain his sudden renovations to the rest of the kingdom that will surely be gawking!'

'And Ora,' Kohén said quickly. 'I overheard them talking about their dream weddings this afternoon- planning and plotting about drama and beauty and making it the biggest event of all time! Do you honestly believe he'd shatter the heart of Rabia's most beloved child by doing anything as gratuitous as what he has hinted towards?'

'WHAT ARE YOU TALKING ABOUT?' Elijah thundered, and Constance jumped, pressing her hand to her heart. 'What has Karol got to do with any of this?'

'He wants her, father!' Kohén leapt up and shook the letter in his fist. 'And what's worse, he believes that he has the right to have her and is threatening to do whatever it takes to bring that to pass! The gown is from him, the letter is from him, and it contains orders for Larkin to come to him before midnight, because only once she does will he follow through on his birthday wish and propose to our first future queen!'

I moaned and covered my face while Kohl rubbed my back and once again, Kohén forgot to be jealous and crazy over him because he had someone else to focus his ire on.

'Father has to know, Larkin...' Kohl whispered. 'He is the only person that can settle this matter.'

But he couldn't- I knew Elijah wouldn't. He'd be so furious when he learned of what I'd promised Karol and why I had, that I knew that there was a reason why Satan had predicted that my life would end this night: because it was fate. I knew I'd done wrong when I'd gone to Karol the year before, and I'd known that every day that had passed without anyone finding out about it all had been a stay of execution... but I'd known that eventually, the truth would come out and I would be ended as a result.

Satan hadn't been trying to scare me, she'd truly been trying to warn me. One of the Barachiel's was going to kill me by the end of this night, and even if they didn't, I would be left with so little to live for that I would kill myself.

22.

'But Larkin is not permitted to go with another man, so why would Karol believe that she'd break a law to-'

'Larkin promised she would, okay?' Kohl said quietly. 'In a moment of desperation and in need of his assistance to get Lindy and Coaxley out of Arcadia before their third-born child could arrive-'

'*What?!*'

'She went to Karol and offered him what she knew he wanted: her. She'd said she'd come to him *freely* the moment she was released, and in exchange for that, he would sneak her friends out so that they could live in a country where it wasn't a crime to have three children!'

'Karol would never accept that offer!'

'Or break such rules!'

'But he did!' I snapped at his parents. 'He got them out and is determined to make me keep my end of the bargain even though I don't get to walk free at all now, and never will!'

'Why would you offer him such a thing, Lark?' Constance asked, mystified. 'You wanted out of here so badly! And you've made your dislike of our eldest son obvious! Why break so many rules for him?'

'Because I was so angry and scared at the time that I didn't care about my own future anymore!' I shrugged. 'I might have made it through the series of disasters that pre-dated my chat with Karol, but I received a letter from Martya that very morning- one she'd hidden before leaving- warning me that Elijah had threatened her privately- threats that he said would come to pass in that awful dungeon room.' Constance blanched and Elijah's eyes flashed but I went on: 'She told me that she feared for my life, and said that if I didn't hear from her again then I should assume that something awful had happened to her, at our king's hands.' Elijah finally crackled with rage, but I lifted my chin and met his eyes when I said: 'And I never heard from her again, your highness! So tell me... what would you have done in my position, hmm? Trusted you- or turned your back to God?'

There was a scuttling sound as Constance swooned into Kohl's waiting arms, and now that I'd finally unburdened myself of that revelation to the king's face, I was tempted to do the same.

'Constance!' Elijah took after his wife, lifting her face so that her fluttering gaze would meet his, and moaned when he saw her recoil in horror. 'No, don't you believe her, it's all lies!' Elijah turned back to snarl at me as his wife covered her face with her hands and sobbed, and his sons looked at him with matching expressions of horror. 'Martya's death was a freak accident!' he snapped at me. 'She filled your head with paranoia and then somehow cursed herself! I never touched her!' He looked back at Constance and kneeled before her, taking her hand and patting it and I smirked to see him drop his indestructible façade for once. 'Darling please... I admit that I threatened her so, but I didn't follow through with them! I was furious with her when I found out that that panacea was a fake but before I could contemplate how to punish her for it, she was dead and Karol had already unearthed the missing ingredient anyway! We were at sea together at the time-you have to believe me!'

'Oh Elijah...' Constance shook her head sadly, looking away as she wiped at her tears and allowed Kohl to stand her up again. 'You ask for the faith of a devoted wife, but you ask of it from a woman that has been forced to stand aside and watch you go into that dungeon room time and time again?' She stood back, hugging herself. 'I'm sorry. Like Larkin, I want to believe in the best in all of you, but you have all robbed me of that right this very night.'

'And Karol didn't find the missing ingredient either, father,' Kohl said softly, and my heart skipped another beat as he proceeded to fill Elijah in on all of those sordid details wile I moaned behind my hands. He made me come off as a hero for saving someone other than myself, but it didn't change the fact that I'd gone behind Elijah's back!

Kohén breathed in sharply when Kohl had finished. 'You knew so much? For that long?'

'When do you think Larkin and I connected, big kahuna?' Kohl asked. 'You went out the door on her sixteenth and she went out the window where I was waiting with my gift for her.'

'A jar of fireflies that he released for me,' I said softly, closing my eyes and wincing in pain as I remembered how much Kohl had meant to me that night- and how much I'd hurt him since.'

'Fantastic!' Kohén stood up and threw up his hands. 'Once again you sweep in and play the romantic hero at your leisure while I was the one juggling my responsibilities and affection for her, trying to make it all work!'

'Blame me all you want for what has gone wrong between you since, but the reason why she did not run that night and hurl herself over the edge of the tidal fall was because I was there for her when you were not!' Kohl made a disgusted sound and turned to me. 'I'm sorry, Larkin but tonight... I can't help but think that you would have been better off if I hadn't been there to stop you. And that I'd followed suit.'

'How dare you decide what her life and happiness with me is worth?' Kohén snarled. 'She is MINE! And she was never supposed to be yours! She wouldn't be in this predicament if you had just stayed on that island where you belonged! You tried to take what I had and I fought back for it and here we are. I agree it's fucking awful and that she is the one that has suffered the most for it, but I will not shoulder *all* the blame for it!'

'Both of you shut up!' I said, standing up and putting my hands between them when I saw Elijah gnash his teeth in anger. 'This is my fault, all right? And passing the buck of blame won't fix anything but make me despise you both!' I looked at Elijah and shook my head. 'Karol's been after me since I was fifteen, and the twins since I turned sixteen. I

knew there was no way I was getting out of here as a virgin-
'

'You were never supposed to-'

'I know!' I screamed, cutting the king off. 'But I couldn't tell *them* that, so I worked on plans of my own! You cannot educate a woman two hours a day on how to use feminine wiles to improve her station- and then punish her for using them to *improve her station!*'

'Touché...' Kohl muttered, smirking at me.

'Karol has been after you for that long?' Constance demanded, and I nodded, without taking my eyes off Elijah's. 'Oh, God, I can't keep denying his sinful nature, can I?' she looked to her spouse. 'Our boys are afflicted, Elijah! This harem nonsense must stop!'

'They're not afflicted, but infected- by her!' Elijah tore off his captain's hat and advanced on me. 'Who do you think you are? All along you've led me to believe that you were in love with my son, and yet all along you were manipulating all three of them into finding a way out of here! And to go over my head like that... to ask my son to help your friends cover a crime? It's deplorable!'

'But it's also something you've just proven that you will do without hesitation to save the people that YOU love from disgrace!' I screamed. 'Lindy and Coaxley are the only people that have ever shown me kindness without expecting something in return and I am NOT sorry that I got them out of here! I am glad- *glad* that I have made it possible for their child to grow with a mother and father who love them and not tossed to the wolves here!'

'Oh Karol...' The duchess was wiping at tears. 'I just can't believe that he would make such greedy arrangements...when I see him I'll...'

'That is *your* fault, duchess because I warned you, remember?' my voice broke. 'I came to you that day in the garden and tried to voice my fears, but you cut me off cold, saying that your sweet, eldest boy wouldn't mean anything real by his flirtations, remember? But that promise had been made well over a year before then, and Karol took every opportunity he could to remind me of it after, even on Tuesday after he freed me! Cry if it makes you feel better but it changes nothing- your eldest son isn't prince charming- he's a *glutton!*' I took the letter from Kohén and handed it to the king. 'You don't have to believe me, but there is a signed declaration right there in his hand!'

'It's all true,' Kohl said simply. 'And the only reason why Kohén and I haven't torn one another limb from limb this week is because we decided to unite against him.' He glanced at me sadly, and he was truly an angel. 'To protect the girl that we both love, even if only one of us is capable of being loved by her in return.'

'Oh no... oh no...*no!*' Constance sank to her knees and held her head in her hands. 'What will become of us? Surely, this family is as evil as though we were Satan's spawn!'

'Do not use her name in here!' Elijah snapped, still staring down at the letter.

'Why not? She is everywhere! And it is our fault!'

'Not in our hearts, she is not!' The king looked to me, and every muscle in his face was tight and hard and without emotion. 'So you believe that pardoning Coaxley and Lindy will restore your right to finagle your way out of the deal you made with the crowned prince?'

'She's not denying him because she's not a woman of her word or trying to finagle anything- she's denying him because her word is not hers to give anymore, thanks to Kohén,' Kohl said loyally. 'And I don't think Kohén's going to agree to let Karol borrow her any time soon without starting World War four first.'

'Is that true?' Elijah looked to Kohén. 'You will refuse to escort her out there even now that she has this pardon, because you fear that Karol will risk everything to have her anyway?'

'Everything that he currently has,' Kohén said crisply. 'I was willing to let her go out earlier before, if you'd agree to keep T'are at her side until I am done with my duties. But that was before I saw that letter...' he shrugged. 'So, no. Unfortunately, though there is a punishment for touching another sibling's Companion, it's never happened before so the rules say that the offenders will be stripped of their own Companions and whipped... and what does Karol care? He's already released them!'

Elijah furrowed his brow. 'That's incorrect- any man that touches a Prince's Companion will be branded as thief, and if the offender is another member with access to the harem, they can be disinherited! That law is there to protect the girls and uphold the fact that they are Companions to one Barachiel and one *alone*!'

Kohén sat down beside me and pulled me to his side. 'Only after they have been branded in gold father and declared a permanent resident of the harem, and Larkin is not. Therefore, she isn't protected by that-' he stopped talking as my heart skipped a beat and I heard the king exclaim:

'Then brand her! Brand her in gold and you'll never have to look over your shoulder again- not to your twin, and not to your eldest brother! It will solve all of our problems! Look-' Elijah kicked the leather satchel across the ground to Kohén's feet. 'I have everything you need to do it, right in here. Brand her Kohén and you will never have to worry about losing her again.'

My lungs expanded on what felt like acidic air. It would solve all of their problems, all right... but it would also make it impossible for me to make another move in life without Kohén's written consent. Other favourites had fared okay after getting one before- but there princes had usually released them anyway, whereas I knew that would never be the case with Kohén. The silver brand that my friends had gotten earlier that afternoon declared what caste they belonged to- but mine would declare *who* I belonged to, *forever*- and my owner would never let me out of sight ever again.

S.K MUNT

And I would die if it were fastened to my flesh. One look into Constance's anguished eyes told me she knew that, and my answering one said goodbye.

'No,' Kohén said simply, shaking his head and pulling me closer, but I'd already turned to ice. 'I have vowed to Larkin that I will never brand her. She is here because I love her, and she will stay because she loves me- and *that* is what will keep her here- not a scalding iron!'

'You cannot be serious!' Elijah raged, kicking the bag again so that a velvet box fell onto the floor. 'Do it, and let's end this! We could be out in that ballroom in mere moments!'

End me, I thought, feeling as though I were already fading away. *It will end me...*

'No we could not, because Larkin won't go!' Kohl shouted, getting to his feet. 'You will ruin her forever father! You will be forcing Kohén to break the only promise that he has a hope of keeping towards her- to earn her love, not steal it!'

'A promise that needs to be broken so she learns her fucking place- which is at his side whether she LIKES it or NOT!' Elijah reached down for the box but Constance reached forward and snatched it out of her hands. 'We have looked after her for twelve years! Now, it is her turn to take care of you!'

'Elijah think!' Constance cried. 'I know you are furious, but think of how this girl has suffered because the men in our family are obsessed with her! Is it not enough that she has had her virginity stolen from her, been locked up in this hell hole for a week and starved to the point of heart failure- now you'd make her worst fear come true and jab her with *fire* as well?

'She has fed their obsession with a series of outfits, exploits and promises that even *I* would find overwhelming!' Elijah cried. 'You've said all of this yourself time and time again, and now finally when I agree with you- you decide to act like a mother for once?'

Constance slapped him. 'Act like a *father* for once, instead of a king!' her icy eyes flashed as Elijah cupped his face and gaped at her. 'You are the one that has taught him that woman are there to serve the purpose of friend or lover but never both! Go out there, drag Karol in here by his earlobe, bring him to a heel and make him sign away Larkin's IOU NOW!'

'So he can make a scene? Throw himself at her? Refuse to marry Ora and fuck up everything else for us over this bloody child?'

'You'd better!' Kohén raged. 'If you want Larkin out there looking happy and content than you'd damned well better!'

Elijah whirled on him. 'I am trying to give you what you want- I am trying to give you ALL what you want but you are never satisfied! You've asked me to break so many rules and look the other way on so many infractions tonight, but I will comply no more- I am a man of God and I will do only what is just, fair, lawful and deserving!' He pointed at me. 'Brand her now, and ask for her forgiveness after. Spend the rest of your life making it up to her if you will, but remember who you are and what she can never be to you!'

'An equal?' I croaked.

Elijah looked at me with flat, unmoved eyes. 'Exactly.'

I lowered my face, and the flag.

I should have taken Satan's hand. It would have burned less than putting my heart in the hands of a man of god.

'No!' Kohén sounded like he was about to cry and Kohl had wrapped his arm around me and was whispering that he wouldn't allow it to happen, but I couldn't feel his touch or hear him through the roar of fire in my head and Kohén's hollering. 'You need her to redeem us, not damn us! If we brand her, she will run out there blistered, bloody and teary-eyed!'

'No, she won't.' Elijah held up the IOU. 'Not if she wants this delivered to her friends.'

'Elijah…' Constance sounded beside herself and I lowered my head further until I could feel the mist shrouding my face. 'How could you? She asked for that before you knew of any of this.'

'And now that I know why, I understand that it is not something that should be handed over so easily, and that's what makes the difference between being a love-struck adolescent and a king- the ability to think a deal all the way through. Larkin will take the brand and thank us after, then go out there with a smile on her face and a spring in her step, or I'll have that third-born child deported and its parents Banished!' Elijah stepped back and I felt as though he'd crushed my heart under his heel. 'You have exactly five minutes to brand her. When I return with her healer, it will be Karol. We will have a nice little chat about how we're all going to get along from now on and then we're going to put all of this behind us.'

'I won't allow it to happen.' Constance said, and I heard her skirts rustle as she stood up. 'Elijah I-'

'No, you won't *allow* it to happen, you will do it yourself. And once you have proven that you have what it takes to be a wife: devotion, respect, submission and faith… I will make you one.'

I looked up now, jaw dropping, and saw that Constance had cupped her face. 'What?'

'I will propose before the fireworks, and leave Karol to do the same to Ora after.' Elijah lifted her free hand and kissed it, and I saw her sob gently. 'You want to do the right thing, don't you my love? Make the girl you care so much for belong here- so that you can watch over her forever without ever again fearing that she will come between your sons, or put their souls at risk.' He stepped back, looking at all of us, but his final gaze landed on Kohén. 'You have five minutes. Work as a royal family ought to for once, or you can all kiss the chance of ever having a title goodbye. I will promote Karol's firstborn son above you both…' he glanced at Constance, 'and kick you to the curb the moment these two turn twenty-one. If they make it that far!'

'Because you know it will be a son, right?' I croaked, glaring daggers at him. 'It always will be, won't it? You'd kill it otherwise, like you killed Martya!'

Elijah shook his head. 'I didn't touch Martya so your accusations don't penetrate my heart. And I always wanted a daughter Larkin, but sadly, I did not get one and it was through no fault of my own.' He glanced at his wife once more and smiled gently. 'A fact you can remedy right now, my lovely queen. Just think- by morning we could have both Larkin and Ora committed to staying here with us forever!'

'I wouldn't be your daughter!' I hissed. 'I'd be your possession!'

'Same thing.' He began to saunter away, balling up Kohl's letter and throwing it over his shoulder. 'Only the prince gets a harem, Kohén, remember that! Follow your heart and watch it break, for she will be sold to Yael if I return here and find her unbranded, and you will get a nice little duchy somewhere bereft of electricity in lieu of a crown!'

'Sit down, Larkin,' Constance said as we heard Elijah's footfalls begin to fade. 'You wanted a queen? Well, you're about to get one.'

'That's my girl!' Elijah remarked, and then the mist that had parted for his exit closed up around him, leaving me in the room with two people that had everything to gain by making my worst nightmares come true, and one who had everything to lose- again, but no way to fight against that.

And not a mirror to be seen.

My time was up.

23.

We all remained frozen until we heard the door slam shut behind Elijah, and though tears were running down Kohén's face, he took my hand and led me back to the edge of the pool. 'Sit down, sweetheart,' he said huskily. 'We'll make the preparations, but we'll not actually brand you until we hear him come back in. That way, you won't have to suffer the pain for more than a second, and Karol will have to witness what he has done to you.'

'What *Karol* has done to her?' Kohl demanded. 'Are you serious?'

'We would have made it through this night if you'd kept your hands off her, but you did not so don't even try to turn this around on me again!' Kohén spat, rubbing my hand gently and leaning in to rest his forehead against the side of my face. 'I'm sorry, my love. I'm so sorry. But I have no choice!'

'Oh you have a choice- choose to let her run with Kohl *now*, son!' Constance cried, and we all rotated to look at her with shock. She'd pulled the brand out of the bag but pointed it towards the passageway instead. 'You have five minutes- they can get to the stables in five minutes and put some distance between them and this place!'

'What?' I asked weakly. 'You're not going to brand me? But Elijah offered you-'

'Something that doesn't seem as grand as it once did,' Constance said quickly, waving her hand. 'I wanted to be married to the love of my life, not the bastard that did what he did to Kohl and then swaggered out of here like he was the *second* second coming just now!' She came over to me and lifted me up, pulling me into a hug before pushing me towards Kohl. 'I'm sure he'll make me regret it, but not as much as I'd regret branding you so go! Go now!'

'No!' Kohén reached for me before I could thaw out and yanked me back to him. 'She can't go, and not with him! They'll be caught!'

'These are two of the most intelligent young adults in the world, Kohén! They can find a way out of this together! And if you love her as you say you do, then you need to let her go!'

'SHE'S NOT GOING ANYWHERE!' Kohén hollered, pressing me to his chest and sparking and shaking all at once. 'I love her! I can't live without her! And I know you're not doing this for her sake, but for HIS! Just like you've always done!'

'Kohén, no! I am doing this for your soul!'

'Bullshit!' My Indian Brave was furious- and not brave at all. In fact he was trembling. 'You couldn't give him a crown, but you'd give him the very thing that I've built my world around and buy yourself some peace with it, wouldn't you?'

'At least I'd take her instead of the crown!' Kohl growled, yanking for me. 'Let her go, Kohén! Open your fist before the firefly loses her light! If we run we will be blamed, your fury will be clear, father will consider you allied against us again and we'll both get something we want!''

'Do you think I want that crown without her? Do you think the king will hand that pardon over to Lindy and Coaxley if he comes back here and discovers that she's fled? And think of the uproar from our people when they discover that she felt the need to flee! You won't leave me with a crown- but with ruins!'

'Our people are entitled to roar over injustice and it is your job to listen to them until they have lost the urge to revolt! We are supposed to be serving them, not using them as servants!'

'No, Kohén's right!' I whispered, pulling away from Kohl. 'Thank you for thinking of me, but I won't save my own skin if it causes them pain. It would make everything I've done for nothing!'

'Everything we've done *together* Larkin!' Kohén turned me to face him. 'We're an us, surely that won't change because I have to stand aside and allow my mother to do what my father has ordered?'

I lowered my eyes. 'I love you, Kohén...' I swallowed hard. 'But I have already told you what I will do if I am branded, and that has not changed.'

He gasped. 'You'd... you'd die?'

I said nothing, merely stared at the floor.

'And I'd take whatever you've threatened to do to me if she does, and with pride,' Kohl said coldly. 'Let her run Kohén, or you will lose us both anyway!'

'You're bluffing,' Kohén's voice cracked as he forced me to stare up at him. 'You wouldn't! You love me! Our love is worth living for!'

'Our *love* is, but my servitude to you is not.' I sat down on the edge of the spa and twisted, presenting Constance with my left shoulder. The weight of all of the reasons why I could not run weighted down on me, caused me to sink to the ultimate submission. 'Do it,' I said softly. 'I will not fight you or blame you, your highness- seeing you crowned because of me is the only wish I have a chance of seeing granted now anyway. All I will ask after is that you let me sleep alone tonight.'

'So you can hang yourself? Never! Kohén, look at her!' the duchess cried. 'Look at what your love has reduced her to! A subservient, terrified, resigned shadow of the girl she once was! Let her run and get that pardon to Lindy and Coaxley yourself! Together we will find a way to save them for her!'

'Oh so now we're a team?' Kohén snorted and wiped at his eyes. 'Great. All I have to do to earn your respect is give up everything, and all Kohl had to do to get it was break every law that he had the chance to! Ha!' He lifted his hand and a stream of blue fire shot across the room and hit the end of the brand, making it glow orange immediately. Constance dropped it in shock, but not an electrical shock, thank goodness, and before she could back away more than a few steps, Kohén lifted it up off the ground by the stem and thrust it back to her. 'We can only have three minutes left! Do it mother! Do it *now*!'

'No! Don't do it mother!' Kohl panted. 'I will go and find a way to barricade the door and buy us more time to talk some sense into him!'

'You will do no such thing!' Kohén cried, whirling after him, but Kohl had already vanished into the mist. 'All you are doing is delaying her access to a healer!'

'To Karol! He is delaying *Karol's* access to her!'

'This glyph will do the same!' Kohén wrapped his arms around me and then turned my face into his shoulder. 'Do it now, mother, because if my older brother walks in and finds her unbranded, every drop of blood that is spilled after will be on your head instead of a crown.' He looked at me. 'I'm sorry Larkin... you can't run from this place and expect to disappear. I never told you this before but-'

'There's a tracking device inside me,' I said sadly, and I heard both Kohl and Constance choke on shocked cries as his eyes brightened, not with happiness, but surprise and sadness. 'I know. Cherry told me. Why do you think I've been so compliant?' I rolled back my shoulder and stared at the duchess. 'Go on,' I said gently. 'I already know how this ends, Constance. All you're doing is delaying the inevitable.'

The duchess sobbed and looked at me, and I saw the branding iron shaking in her hand, still bright orange- bright enough to hurt my eyes. Weeping but nodding as I saw her ask her permission to do the unforgivable in her eyes, I turned away from Kohén and opened my shoulder to her once more.

'You'd better get it on the right arm,' I said softly, sniffling. 'I mean the left. I wouldn't want to have to go through this twice.'

'Lark...' Kohén turned so that he had one foot in the water, straddling the edge, and then pulled my hair slowly over the other shoulder and out of her way. 'I love you,' he kissed the back of my head. 'I will love you forever and I will find a way to make you happy despite this.'

I smiled sadly. I believed him- and actually felt for how much he was going to hurt, because the girl he loved was going to be dead by midnight before she could be forced to bow even more before her prince.

'Go on mother,' I heard Kohén sob as he kissed the back of my hair again- my halo- and heard my wings rustle against his feathers. 'You know that you must.'

Constance sighed, and tear tracks were streaming down her face. 'I know,' she whispered, 'because if people weren't branded as whores, who would be able to tell the difference between them, and royalty, right? So I will do it...' I closed my eyes and cringed when I felt the heat of the brand draw closer to my skin. Kohén was holding his breath, but I had not taken one in a while and didn't care to. 'I will brand the whore and make myself a ruler, at long last- one that has earned that title, right?'

'Just get on with it...' Kohén said wearily. Kohl was shaking his head and begging me with his eyes to run still, but I closed my eyes, knowing that I could not bear the burden of his pain now. I had too much of my own.

I love God. Please, take me into Heaven once I have taken this penance? And watch over these Barachiels, please? I refused Satan for you! Please, do one thing right by me, just one!

And then Constance thrust forward the brand, and Kohén was the one screaming. 'You're the third-born, Kohén Barachiel!' the duchess screamed, and I gasped as Kohén leapt to his feet, knocking me over onto my hands and chest on the side of the pool. 'Not Kohl, YOU! No one in this room believed that changed the worth of a person but *you* do, so BURN for your lowly status!'

Feeling like this had to be a nightmare, I craned my neck around and screamed when I saw that Kohén was yowling in pain and grasping at his chest, but Constance was still grilling him- still driving him back onto the foggy floor. He landed on his rump and then his back and yet still she pushed it into him, and my nervous system was shattered by the sounds of his screams.

'Oh, Constance *no!*' I cried, pushing up and awkwardly rising in my heels, but she was stabbing at him like a madwoman, trying to burn him elsewhere and everywhere while he bellowed and smacked at the side of the stick, attempting to knock it free before it could get him again. 'I know you're hurt and angry but this isn't the solution!'

'It is the only solution! Look at him writhe- look at him get what's coming to him for once!' Constance screamed as Kohén feebly sent a jolt of blue light her way, striking the end of the stick again and then travelling up the length of the rubber coated handle. That rubber would have prevented the electricity from earthing out but she dropped it anyway, then realised her error and scrambled after it again. Kohén lunged for it but the closest end to him was glowing brightly once more and he shrank back when she lifted the handle off the floor and advanced a second time.

'Constance stop!' I threw myself at her, hugging her and causing her to drop the stick in fright. It landed dangerously close to her feet and the long skirt of her gown but I drew her back, keeping her arms pinned. 'Please stop! Please! You've done what you set out to do! You protected me! Please...' tears were running down my face and when I pressed my cheek to hers, I felt her tears and heard her haggard breathing. 'I can lose any one of them to the darkness mother, but not you,' I whispered, kissing her cheek. 'Please, stay with God and with me!'

Constance doubled over, sobbing. 'It's not enough... it's not! He should die!'

'Mother!' Despite the fact that she'd just tried to impale him with a heated element, poor Kohén still had the naivety to look shocked by her declaration, and I saw my sweet five year old friend in his tear-filled eyes and shattered countenance again. 'What's come over you?'

'I'm suffering honesty, like the rest of you! Too little too late I know, but at least the secret I have been keeping for so long has the power to make things right once revealed!' She pointed her finger at him. '*You're* the third-born, Kohén, and I'm going to tell EVERYBODY! I'm going to scream it from Miguel Barachiel's cottage by the ballroom, and see your brother crowned as the next in line while YOU rot in the corps!' she laughed harshly. 'Unless you can find a brothel that will take a male escort that wouldn't know how to seduce a woman without cornering her first!'

'You're lying!' Kohén winced and tried to touch his chest and I felt my fever returning at the look of horror on his face when he glanced down to see what damage had been done. The Companion brands- a simple glyph untranslatable to any other culture or language within a circle- was only supposed to be kissed against the skin and for the briefest of seconds, and the longevity of the scar was dependant on the metallic powder being used to harden and set it after. But Constance hadn't done the job as carefully or as gently as required, and when I looked down at the end of the branding iron, I saw that clumps of skin and feathers had become stuck to it- from where she'd partially melted his necklace into his wound. It wasn't a pretty symbol anymore- it was a gaping, bloody misshapen welt in her son's perfect chest, and even if she hadn't penetrated his heart physically, her words had certainly inflicted the kind of wounds that Kohén would never be able to recover from. 'You have to be lying! You-'

'I'm not! You're not the rightful heir to the Pacifican throne and though I have been motivated to keep that fact to myself since the day you were born, I cannot let you brand her: you're not going to brand any companion in gold- ever- because YOU NO LONGER HAVE HAREM ACCESS! I will see you stripped of EVERY entitlement you've ever been given! Including Kohl's right to be released tonight too! You have not earned that with the other fourteen, and you will stay in Pacifica and out of my sight until you are twenty-one or I am DEAD!'

I moaned when I saw Kohén's face crumple. He'd already been in absolute agony and struggling to keep his balance, but when she denounced him, he fell to his hands and knees once more and shook his head. 'It can't be true…' he croaked, and I released the duchess and ran to him, knowing that the only person in the world that had a hope of comforting him now, was me. 'It just can't be…'

'But it is!'

'Constance, *enough*!' I guided Kohén up until he fell back against the side of the pool and then cupped some water in my hand, letting it trickle and sizzle a path down his chest. He hissed and ground his teeth together, but his hand cupped my knee and squeezed it gratefully, and I knew no human had ever needed anyone as much as he needed me right then. 'You have shocked him and hurt him and scarred him- do not torture him too! He didn't know, remember? You cannot punish him for the secret that you and Elijah have been keeping!'

Kohén's eyes widened and he looked at me, stricken. 'Lark… you *knew*?'

I nodded and sniffled, distraught now that I'd seen the damage to his chest up close. I plucked a blackened, shrivelled feather away from his peeling skin and cupped another handful of warm water, irrigating it as best as I could until Karol could arrive and give him the treatment he needed. 'She told me in Pacifica, after I found you with…' I screwed up my face, not ready to admit than instead of using the information to force Constance to make things right, I'd used it hoping to get myself out of there- with Kohl. I'd tell Kohl that in private to help him understand, if I ever got the chance to, but could not bear to blurt it out now and strike Kohén again. 'She did not mean to tell me, but she did. And I…I'm sorry Kohén. I didn't think you should ever find out, not even this way.'

'How?' Kohén turned to his mother. 'How is this possible?'

The duchess had the brand in her hand again and was staring at Kohén's wound, eyes still dilated, face a serene mask that I knew was the result of shock or possibly even peace. Hadn't she waited her whole life to get this off her chest?

'The first child arrived was damaged,' she said simply, staring down at the poker. 'The second... perfect. I did not care, I loved both of my beautiful baby boys...' her voice caught. 'But your father could not stand to see the result of his abuse of me reflected in the next in line, so he told others that the perfect child had come out first.'

'No!' Kohén's mask was sliding down his face, making his tears look black but not diminishing his beauty in any way. 'You couldn't have done that! Not you, and not father! That's sinful! More sinful than anything any of us have ever done!'

'And I have paid for it with a stain upon my once-perfect soul,' she paused, smiled oddly, still staring at the glowing disc at the end of the stick. 'Perfect... isn't that a strange word? I don't know if I've ever come across anything perfect that was perfect, inside *and* out. Everything is flawed...'

'As God was,' I said gently. 'Constance I know you're upset, but Kohén needs a healer-'

'*Kohén* needs something?' Kohl strode through the fog looking downright dangerous. 'You just announced that my entire life has been a lie, and that I have been denied every birthright I deserved, and that I have spent my life breaking rocks and sifting through ruins while being treated like a third-class citizen, but what we're going to talk about next is what *Kohén* needs?' I flinched and Kohl glared at me. 'I won't say that I can't believe that she and father would allow this to happen to me! To keep this secret from me for so long and let me suffer for THEIR shortcomings... but *you*, Larkin?' Kohl looked winded. 'How could you have not told me that I was living someone else's life? That I deserved *more*?'

Who doesn't deserve more though? Why should I have told him anything, when he already had so much more than I?

His imaged blurred as tears filled my eyes. 'Because you were *already* more, Kohl...' I whispered, and heard Kohén moan on the ground beside me. 'I'm sorry, I knew you had a right to know, but I thought you were so much more perfect than any of us because you didn't. Because you *worked.* Because you treated others as equals- and fought for what was right even while suffering every injustice as I had.' I swallowed hard. 'I didn't want to see you trade in your halo for a crown- not when I knew that you were the kind of man that would find a way to have both- who would feed the Banished before he would fatten the nobility further.'

Kohl's eyes lightened immediately. 'You did love me, then?'

I nodded, shaking tears free. 'As you were. I gave you up because I knew I would ruin you... as Kohén and I have ruined one another.'

'He *has* ruined you,' Kohl's voice was strained. 'A tracking device? Really? And yet you tend to him anyway?'

'The tracking device has been around for generations- could no sooner prevent her from getting one than I could stop her from being sucked into this system,' Kohén said feebly, and I silently cursed him for having eyes so blue, features so appealing, and a body that twisted itself into delicious patterns as it writhed beneath me. 'Why do you think I went to such lengths to get her to fall into line? I could not bear to see her hunted like an animal!'

'But that's exactly what you did,' Kohl said, then looked at me, distraught. 'He's not your true love, Lark, he's your keeper!'

'What should I do, Kohl?' I asked, weeping gently. 'Kill him? Kick him while he's down? Laugh at his pain?' I sniffled and shook my head. 'This palace does not need more spite and anger and vengeance- it needs more *light*.' I touched Kohén's face, then looked up at Kohl. 'If I can forgive him for what he has allowed to happen to me, then you can find a way to forgive him for what happened to you- to forgive the boy that once leapt into the ocean and tried to swim to Pacifica on your behalf, surrendering the crown that you have convinced yourself that he stole from you in your current anger.'

'I know he didn't steal it,' Kohl said, looking down at Kohén, whose eyes were practically rolling back into his head from the pain. 'But I know he wouldn't willingly give it up now if he had the choice, the way I gave *you* up once.'

'Brother, if I can't have Larkin... then I don't care.' Kohén winced and bucked as I plucked a thicker feather from his wound. 'Take my crown! Take it and do better than I would have, and better than that corrupted Karol and king will!' Kohl's eyes misted with tears, and Kohén touched his hand to my face. 'I don't care if I get shipped to Pacifica- I don't care if I end up in *Asiana*, so long as you tell me that the paths that we both take will intersect again once we are both free and redeemed?'

I almost laughed. 'Downgrade from prince to Blue-Collar bum? No thanks. I think I'll pursue T'are next. He's very muscly, he already has a trade and he doesn't talk shit like you lot.' Kohén tittered, and we exchanged a smile. I didn't know what would become of us, but I did know I'd make him push Lady Liberty by hand across the country before I trusted him with my affections again!

'Larkin's path is none of your business, and I commend her for not kicking you in the balls for you even suggesting that she look your way again!' Constance cried. 'She's leaving this continent as soon as she receives a pardon from a soon to be VERY apologetic king and I hope she never looks back! And I am putting an end to this ball nonsense right now!' she threw the brand behind her. 'Karol does not deserve a ball and he does not deserve Ora! What he needs-what you *all* need- is some good old-fashioned parenting! To learn that consequences and spontaneity go hand in hand! Let the kingdom watch us drag you all out there by the scruff of your necks and shake you, and we'll win their respect back faster than with marshmallow wine!'

'Parenting? From who- *you*?' Kohl turned on her, and I saw her shrivel back when he laughed harshly. 'You're funny! I always knew you were beautiful, weak, spiteful, overwrought and over-dramatic, but I did not know that you had such a sinful sense of humour!'

'I think it's funny that you take an exception to her maternal instincts despite the fact that you benefitted from them *twice* as much as I did...' Kohén groused, but no one responded to him.

'Kohl!' Constance's face creased, making her look her age for the briefest of moments. 'I know you're angry that I kept this secret from you but doesn't it count that I'm making things right now? Don't you understand why I've always fought for you so?'

'Because you felt guilty!' Kohl snapped. 'You didn't do the things you did to make me feel better- you did it so *you'd* feel better! If you'd cared about me the way a mother should, you would have protected me from my father's vanity! But you hid behind him and let me take the fall! So don't scoop me up from rock bottom now and call it *parenting*!'

'This isn't rock-bottom!' she protested. 'Your life has only just begun!'

'Seventeen years after my twin's did!' Kohl reached down and picked up the brand, wincing when he too saw the stuff stuck to the glowing tip, then dragged over the satchel with his foot, preparing to pack the awful stuff away. 'I get the crown but I've already missed out on the education, the dancing lessons, the dinners with important people, the harem, the balls, the *birthday* cakes! Who's going to take me seriously, stepping into Kohén's shoes that have been stretched by advantages while I was barefoot and knee-deep in pumice stone? Kohén's first job as a prince was to cut the ribbon on the library, but what will mine be?'

'Whatever you want, Kohl,' I said softly, smiling at him. 'And knowing you, it will be something wonderful.'

Kohl's face softened. 'You still have faith in me being able to do this? To be a prince... maybe one day a king?'

'Of course! You'll always count on my support, no matter what, Kohl, I swear it,' I said, helping Kohén up onto the edge of the pool so that he could sit. 'But what you need most of all is to have faith in yourself-' the doors started rattling in the distance and all of our heads whipped around to stare down the misty corridor.

Oh God! Time's Up!

'Shit!' Constance said, moving to pick up the scattered parts of the brand bags. 'This is going to get ugly before it gets prettier. Kohl, help me hide the branding gear until I've talked sense into your father, okay? We can't remove the barricade until this is hidden- just in case he does something rash in the heat of the moment.'

'Something else I'd suffer for seventeen years more, no doubt,' Kohl grumbled, but he moved to pick up the still-glowing stick anyway. 'Larkin, perhaps we should hide you too, just for a few minutes.'

'If you think that's wise,' I said, smoothing my dress and then touching my hands to my face and pulled them back, expecting to see them blurred with paint, but to my surprise, my mask had either remained intact or had already been completely washed off by my tears.

'Good idea,' Constance said, bending to put the jar back into the bag. 'Is there anywhere in here that we can take her, where your father's key won't work?'

My heart contracted- if someone suggested the dungeon than I'd scream!

'There is,' and then Kohl lifted his hand and backhanded his mother so hard that she didn't even have the chance to scream before she was thrown into the side of the pool- but I did, and I screamed loud and hard.

Still, my hysteria was not enough to mask the crescendo of sickening cracking sounds that her bones made as they snapped and splintered against the hard marble, and the tears that flooded my eyes were not yet thick enough to spare me the sight of the blood that exploded from the side of her beautiful head as it split against the stone wall. Kohén let out an all-mighty shout and jumped to his feet, but he and I never had the chance to fend off what came next, for we had been too naïve, both of us, to understand just how much damage we had done to Kohl's once pristine soul. 'And that's where we will be locking up your body, you heartless, conniving tramp!' Kohl finished, and then turned to me, gripped my wrist and yanked me to him. 'I'm sorry, Larkin,' he whispered, 'but mother has left me no choice!'

And then the red-hot brand was being forced into my shoulder- at the hands of the angel that I had been too distracted to see plummet to earth and directly into Satan's embrace. She'd warned me about it though, hadn't she? She'd said it was too late to save Kohl.

I thought she'd meant his life but clearly, she'd been referring to his soul.

24.

I fell to my knees, so overcome by the pain that my vision blurred and my mind spun in erratic circles, but Kohl was grasping my elbow painfully and holding me up so that my shoulder would not lose contact with the instrument searing into my flesh, so I pressed my hand to my thrashing heart and screamed as I never had before.

'Have faith in me, like you swore you would!' Kohl rasped, 'and I swear this will get us both to where we need to be!'

Constance! Kohl! NO! No this has to be a nightmare! I prayed to wake up but the burning went on as it had in my fever dreams, incinerating me from the inside out. I ran out of breath to scream with and yet my mouth remained open in a howl of despair and just before I reached the point where I knew the agony would make my heart fail, the brand lifted and I was released.

Kohl branded me! Not the corrupted twin, but the angelic one! Oh GOD!

I fell hard, crumpled and straining away from the inescapable pain, and though I could hear shouting, I could not make out a word of it for the way the blood was rushing around inside my head. I opened my eyes though, and when I found myself staring at Constance's slackened, blood-streaked features, immediately wished that I hadn't.

'No!' I whimpered, straining for her. 'Please, *no...*' I squirmed closer but my arm throbbed at the movement and I rolled onto my other side, howling in agony- both from the pain in my shoulder and the pain in my heart that I knew would never abate now that my mother was gone. The brand wasn't pressing against me anymore, and yet now it felt like it was being shoved more forcefully into my flesh, and little circles of blistering heat were radiating out from the injury point in ripples now, ripples so intense that they made every muscle in my body seize up as they washed over them. How had Emmerly withstood even a moment of this? How had Kohén taken it in such a tender area? They were braver and stronger than I! I loathed Karol and yet I would have wept for joy to see him saunter into that room now if it meant the end of the pain! Or Dulcie!

But you won't see him or Dulcie sauntering to your rescue, because that door has been barricaded, remember?

There was a sudden movement then and I cried out when someone stepped on my open palm. My eyes flew open, first so I could see the mural painted on the ceiling above me, then so I could see and Indian-Brave, bloody and red-faced hurl himself at his Roman reflection and smash him to the ground, just above my head and beside Constance's corpse. I twisted and felt a surge of hope when I saw Kohén straddle his brother, pull back his fist and then strike the boy beneath him hard and sharply across the jaw, but the movement must have agitated the wound on his own chest because he curled up slightly, groaning after he'd thumped his target only once.

Kohl had not been trained to fight as Kohén had, but he had learned how to fight dirty evidently, because he struck out, jabbing two fingers directly at Kohén's chest. I could not see where they hit him, but Kohén's roar of pain was a good indication that he'd found the only weakness his brother had and I winced in sympathy. Then before he could recover from that, Kohl sat up and threw a clumsy punch into Kohén's face, sending his brother toppling to the side. Kohl had a line of blood trickling from his nose and his upper lip where Kohén had split it, and although Kohén did not bear similar injuries, he looked pale and sweaty and almost out of his mind with horror as he thrashed, trying to sit up but sliding in a pool of his mother's blood.

'You killed her!' Kohén got onto all fours and crawled to his mother, taking her hand but it was limp and sitting at a strange angle and his face crumpled as he bowed to kiss it. 'Mom... mom I'm so sorry! I'm sorry I wasn't enough for you! I tried mom!' he howled and buried his face in her splayed dark hair, sobbing. 'I loved her... I loved her because you told me that was important, once! To love! To love with all your heart...' he twisted back to his brother, face unrecognisable in his grief. 'What have you done, Kohl? *What have you done?*'

'Kohén...' I croaked his name and pushed up, but I wasn't strong enough and a fresh wave of throbbing almost had my face smashing into the marble floor. I managed to land with my head on my forearm, but before I could push up again, I sensed movement beside me. The same hand that had dropped me so unceremoniously before now coaxed my up gently from the floor using my good arm, and I sobbed when Kohl wrapped himself around me and kissed me so sweetly that it was like Kohén had actually knocked the evil straight out of him. Kohén looked up and saw us and his face spasmed with rage but I lost sight of him in that same beat.

'I'm sorry, I do mean that- I never wanted to do this to you....' Kohl kissed my blubbering lips again and then cupped my injured shoulder with his other arm- and suddenly it felt like he'd put out the flames with acid. 'But it's the only way we can be together now, Lark.'

I twisted my head to the side, screamed, and then looked down at his hand and saw the golden powder spilling from his palm and over my ruptured skin. All at once I hated Kohl Barachiel as intensely as I had once admired him. And what was worse- I remembered that he too had warned me that this might happen, just four nights ago.

'But I can promise you, that you would have been the only one, and that I would have spent the rest of my life making it up to you-you and your golden brand.'

'You would have...?'

'On the night of my sixteenth? The way you looked under those lights darling... I would have trapped you like the firefly that you are, and would never have let you go, even after just that one kiss. I'm sorry, but it's true.'

'Don't be sorry-that was sort of romantic.'

'But mostly psychotic,' he'd smiled tearfully then, 'and it speaks volumes about a Barachiel man's sense of entitlement...'

Indeed it did, and yet, I'd convinced myself that he'd been exaggerating- to my own detriment. I'd even called it romantic! So close! Once again I'd been so close to escaping this place- this life- and once again I'd had a door locked and slammed in my face only this time, that door would lock me away from the world!

Though I was used to growing angry with myself for doing stupid things that led to me being cornered, I was unprepared for how volatile my anger would feel when the cornering had been done by somebody else. If I could move, I would have clawed his face to shreds!

'No!' I cried, and my knees went weak again as the pain flattened me. I'd always dreaded what this moment would be like and was dismayed to discover that it was infinitely worse than I had feared. The pain was intolerable in itself, but the betrayal cut me like a blade. 'Kohl no! And *why*?'

'Because I-'

'Let her go!' Kohén suddenly smashed us apart and though I knew he'd meant well, he only agitated the agony further with his rough intervention. I screamed again and then bit into my own fist, staring down at the brand on my arm with absolute horror. It had mystical properties that powder, and as I watched, fascinated and horrified, the excess powder fell away from my healthy skin but melded to my still-searing scar, hiding the blood and gore and char and leaving a glistening, metallic insignia on my flesh. It was as three dimensional, hard and shining and perfectly engraved as a gold coin- which seemed fitting, because it was a kind of currency unto itself. But unlike a pouch of gold coins or my necklace, this could not be traded or sold- I'd been deemed invaluable and worthless, all at once. That, I knew and understood, but what I did *not* know was who I belonged to now?

Not to yourself! My sub-conscious cried as I collapsed in every way. *Never again to yourself!*

'Larkin!' Kohén had sent Kohl staggering backwards against with another punch and now he tenderly grasped the elbow of my burned arm while tightly grasping the other and gaped at the brand, looking as lost as I felt. 'Oh... baby! I can't believe he did this to you!'

I would have agreed but could not open my mouth for fear that I would start screaming again and never stop. The powder sizzled against my wound as it sealed it with the potency of acid.

'What *you* were about to do to her, you mean?' Kohl snarled, swaggering back while spitting out blood. He saw the bottle of champagne that Constance had brought in with her, paused to rip off the foil top and then popped it across the room, missing Kohén by one premeditated inch. 'I guess identical minds think alike!'

'I was going to brand her because I thought I had no choice!' Kohén growled, shaking his head in disbelief. 'But as soon as I was cast off my throne, this palace lost any right to hold her here, you idiot! Didn't you hear a word that mother said? She was going to get her *freed*!' He wiped tears from under his eyes, smearing his dramatic make-up further and then looked over at his mother's body again with a desolate expression. 'Before you killed her, that is. I think I must be in shock, because if I actually believed that what just happened actually happened...' he turned back to his brother with slitted eyes. 'You'd be dead.'

'Well I don't have any intention of killing you, so dial back the psychotic rage a bit while I organise my thoughts, okay?' Kohl held the champagne bottle to his eye and squinted. 'I had my ducks in a row a minute ago, but now you've gone and scattered 'em. Damn, you can throw a hook! I can barely see out of this eye now. Not that that's anything new...'

Another wave of pain crashed over me and as I doubled over and was caught by Kohén, I managed to catch a look at Kohl's face and was amazed by how unconcerned he looked. Who was this sinister, carefree man? Where had my angel gone?

'I forgot that you missed out on self-defence classes...and I officially don't care anymore,' Kohén drawled, 'but if you're feeling off balance, I'll happily even the other eye up for you so you don't have to go back on the patch? I'm going to roast you from the inside out once Larkin's safe from you anyway but-'

'Shut up, and listen to your big brother, okay *little* Kahuna?' Kohl closed his eyes and chuckled, while Kohén crackled around me. I had a feeling that he was crackling hard enough for it to be stinging me and yet the pain still radiating down my arm and through the rest of me was still too overwhelming for my senses to hone in on anything else. 'Huh, *little* Kahuna. That's going to take some getting used to...'

'I'm not listening to another second of your psychotic blather!' Kohén exclaimed, scooping me up in his arms. 'If you're going to try and kill us then go right ahead and-

'I told you, that's not my intention! But I will if you take another step towards that door before hearing what I have to propose!'

'Fuck you and your proposals-'

'No fuck YOU!' Kohl thundered. 'Electricity and water don't mix, remember? I'd hate to see you swept away by a wave of my generated anger, while crackling with the girl we love in your arms! Talk about a *waste*!'

Kohén had been stalking towards the door with me in his arms but now he froze and I sobbed. How could this not be over yet? How could one corridor continue to be the difference between joy and desolation for me?

'Thank you,' Kohl cleared his throat as Kohén slowly began to turn back around. I felt him straining to get his surge under control, but he was trembling with far too many emotions for him to be able to do that anytime soon. 'Now, Mother said that she was going to try to get Lark free, yes? But I think we both know she was going to fail.'

'Don't tell me what to think! You haven't been promoted above me yet, *insane* Kahuna!'

'And I don't plan on being promoted above you...'
Kohl said casually, and even I flinched in surprise at that.
'That's the whole point.'

'*What's* the whole point?' Kohén was trying to sound
like he didn't care, but I could feel his heart pounding
against my good arm, and saw the triumph in Kohl's eyes as
I was rotated to face him again.

Oh what? What now?

But Kohl wasn't looking at my eyes- he was looking at
every part of me but my eyes, and his gaze was a heated
one. 'She's in high demand, our Larkin, in Eden *and* outside
of it...' He paused to take a swig of champagne and then
began to saunter towards us. 'If I hadn't branded her just
now, father would have done it anyway and would have
snapped mother's spine as I had if she'd tried to straighten it
against him, regardless of what she thought! And don't give
me grief about disposing of that heartless nitwit- you think
she would have shed a tear if *you'd* died tonight? Damn, she
almost exterminated you her*self*! Calls herself a mother,
she's a son of a bitch if I ever met one- and I've met *plenty*.'
Kohl tilted back the champagne, took another mouthful,
gargled it and then spat it out on the floor near his feet in a
spray that was tinged pink by his blood. 'Nice,' he looked at
the label. 'This is the good stuff, isn't it? I suppose you've
come accustomed to gargling with it, while I've had to do
the same with seawater?'

'I'd take seawater in my mouth over champagne every
day and don't try to play your tiny violin for yourself now!'
Kohén snapped, while I gritted my teeth and wondered if I
had a chance of wriggling out of Kohén's grasp and making
it to the front door so that I could let Karol in before I
fainted. I didn't know how it was possible but instead of
ebbing away, the pain from my brand was increasing! So
much so that I could barely focus on anything but it, and
what Kohén said next sounded like it was being babbled
underwater:

'You've had my sympathy since the minute I was old
enough to understand what would happen to you when you

turned five, but that's done with now. Larkin's desirable yes and her future was sketchy at best a few moments ago, but you branding her won't improve her life, only ruin it further, and mother...' He guided me further back, sitting me on the edge of the pool. 'What the fuck, Kohl? No *really*: what the fuck?'

'She had to go!' Kohl reached out and pressed the bottle of champagne to my wound and even though I bucked and squealed at the pressure, I understood that he'd done so to help me when Kohén kissed my forehead, told me that the frosted glass would take the edge off the pain, and then held me more tightly so that I could not struggle against it. 'You heard her- she was going to scream the truth about our birth rights for everyone to hear and she wasn't going to be talked out of it!'

'Why would you want to talk her out of it? It makes no sense! All you've ever wanted was to trade places with me and now that my life is handed to you on a silver platter, you expect me to believe that you'd turn it down?'

'I would, and I will!' Kohén snorted and made to leave again but Kohl's voice became insistent as he stepped forward: 'I don't want to be the second-in-line in a monarchy, Kohén! I want to be the general of Isthmus! I don't want to answer to father, I want to work with someone that I actually respect, like Atticus! I know how to organise men and get work done and oversee large projects and deal with islanders and Blue-Collars and God, even criminals, but after spending three days with Amelia-Rose I can tell you that I couldn't take a week in your stiff, polished shoes in the noble circles! And even if I wanted to I'm not being close to ready yet, and I won't be thought of as the inept twin that was handed a title that he cannot handle-Ssh...' Kohl whispered as I mewled, and then I felt the champagne bubbling and spilling down my skin and I shrieked. 'It's almost over, Larkin, I promise.'

'A Barachiel promise!' I gasped, bucking against Kohén's hold on me. I didn't have the strength to strike

Kohl but I would try! 'That's as good as Satan's! Actually no… Satan occasionally does what she says she will.'

Kohl raised an eyebrow. 'Close with Satan now, are we?'

My eyes rolled back into my head when the throbbing began to intensify again. 'She lives in my mirror! She talks to me all day long!'

'Jesus Christ…' I felt a cool hand smooth my hair away from my clammy neck. So hot! I was frying me from within! 'She's scalding to the touch and talking crazy. God Kohén, has she lost her mind this week? I guess she must have, to have been staring at you with that vacant, purple gaze despite all you'd done to her…'

Get your hands off me! Both of you!

'Her eyes were lilac before, not purple…. and probably never will be again thanks to you, so finish what you were saying or let me open the door!' Kohén sounded like he was on the brink of tears again. 'She doesn't need champagne and smart remarks- she needs a healer!'

'And now that I've branded her, she can get that and everything else that she wants- and so can *we*.' The cold, wet bottle moved from my arm and I felt warm lips press near to my burn. I felt Kohén stiffen while I gnashed my teeth again and bucked- the heat of his breath was too much! 'If you agree to stop fighting me for her... and share her instead.'

'What?' Kohén's voice pitched. 'Are you out of your *mind*?'

I'd been prepared for Kohl to suggest trading me back for the crown, but nothing could have prepared me for that and I sucked in a breath and sat up. 'You stupid, fucking, worthless piece of-*mmph*!' my eyes bugged when Kohl slapped his hand over my mouth, but I used my teeth to nip at the palm of his cool hand, pinching the skin between it just as Kohén jerked up his elbow, striking Kohl sharply in the underside of his nose He grunted, shook his hand free and then roughly tore me from Kohén's arms.

'Hey!' Kohén lunged for me, but Kohl wrapped his arm around my shoulders, pinning them to my ribcage and kept the other clamped around my mouth. He squeezed my wound as he squeezed me and Kohén took one look at my face and held his hands up. 'Stop! You're hurting her! I won't try and take her back just don't hold her so tightly-'

'See that's what we *can't* have!' Kohl snapped. 'I'll hand back the crown but I will not regard you as my better, not in any regard. You won't be ordering me around! You won't go on assuming that you have some sort of bond with her that I do not- that you have some *right* to her that I do not! If we're going to do this then we have to be equals in all of this; we play nice, or *you* don't get to play at all!'

'*Play?*' Kohén tore at his hair. 'What are you talking about?' he pulled his headdress free when he realised he was still wearing it then grimaced, pressing his hand to his own sore which obviously wasn't troubling him the way mine was still debilitating me. 'This isn't a game! We're not children fighting over a toy-'

'We fight over everything, and we always will! Unless we take her advice at last, and start working as two halves of a whole, like we were supposed to?' Kohl kissed the side of my head and then inhaled my hair but then jerked back, leaning away from me when I began to gag, letting me twist slightly in his arms so that I would throw up on the floor not on him. 'Shit, breathe baby... you don't want to soil that lovely gown...' he rubbed my back and I gagged again but nothing would come out- I had nothing in my stomach to throw up anyway. I moaned and he sighed, lowering his voice. 'I know you don't believe it right now and I know that Larkin is wishing me a speedy death... but I love her, Kohén, and I know that she loves me. She doesn't feel it right now, but she will- she could forgive both of us if we spend the rest of our lives atoning for what we have done to her.' He pressed his next kiss to the top of my shoulder, just like Kohén always had and practically purred. 'She loves you too. I fear it's a product of brainwashing, but it's real enough to her for it to resonate with me. It's not an ideal arrangement that I'm suggesting because it was up to me, she'd never be forced to endure *your* embraces again, and I know you're going to baulk at the idea of letting me have equal time with her... but that is exactly what I'm suggesting!' He tilted my face up while keeping my mouth covered. 'Let's stop fighting over her and start fighting for her, and everything that she dreams of! Alone, neither of us have the power to make any of her dreams come true or to stand against father, but together... we'd be unstoppable.'

What? NO! Kohén NO! Don't you even consider this! I looked up at Kohén and shook my head, weeping and feeling immensely relieved that he looked as horrified as I felt. My stomach was still cramping up painfully and I was melting from the inside out, but the urge to vomit had returned to be the urge to die.

'You want to share her... as in... *actually* share her?' Kohén recoiled, face wrinkling. 'Out of the question! I'd concede to let her go and see which one of us she wants, and even give you the chance to freely win her heart again, if that is possible... but anything else is-'

'She won't choose one of us, Kohén, not if she's given her free will back! We've both done too much to hurt her! She'd take death over a life with either of us now and gladly, which is why I branded her- to take the choice out of her hands again- and that's *exactly* the way she likes it.' The arm that was wrapped around me retreated, tugging on the necklace gently and then dropping to trace a line across my collarbone. 'Don't you Larkin?' Kohl nibbled gently on my earlobe as I moaned in horror, and when he slipped his finger into the top of my cleavage, I shuddered. 'You don't want to like it, but there's darkness in you- a craving to be ultimately possessed. Those books you loved so much... they were all about women that were stronger than steel, until the right man came along and tamed them. And that's you, sweet swan. Like a wild mare, you don't want to be ridden... but when you are ridden right... oh, how you gallop!'

But the only thing galloping was my heart rate and body temperature and to prove it, I gagged again and this time, Kohl let me go.

25.

'Kohl leave her alone!' Kohén looked sick, and his sparks were beginning to crackle as far as a foot away from him as Kohl pulled back my hair so that I could throw up without wrecking it. But once again, nothing came out, and all I could do was sob and gasp for air. 'This is despicable!'

'No, it's what she *wants*,' Kohl pulled my hair behind my head to straighten me up again now that he'd deemed it safe once more and suckled on my pulse so hard that I cringed and tried to squirm away from him. But he slapped me quickly right near my brand and I screamed, knees weakening. 'She's a complicated girl, and isn't that part of her appeal?' I felt him tug hard on my zipper and suddenly, my bodice and wings were falling away, revealing the corset beneath again. 'She rebels against the concept of women being dominated by men- of being treated as inferior to anyone- and yet she can't help but be attracted to the men that manage to overpower her anyway. By fucking her without her consent, you became that kind of man, and by branding her today, I joined you. It's the same with Karol- he had something to give her and she knelt before him and begged him to do so. Don't you get it? She never wanted to preserve her virginity- she wanted it taken from her! She just wanted someone to understand that without her demeaning herself by asking for it!'

I called him every name under the sun and jerked and twisted in his grasp but he only held me more tightly.

'I wouldn't have believed it but when I saw how she melted at your touch that night... when I saw how she came again and *again*-' My face flushed so hot I knew my make-up had to be melting off now. Fuck the Barachiels- all of them! Their ability to twist their evil deeds to make it seem like they were answering the demands of others was their greatest skill and most fatal flaw. 'Oh, how I enjoyed watching that! I was devastated, but I haven't been able to sleep since. Of course it's not you I see her riding in my head but me, and that's something that will help you get through this Kohén... see *your* hand on this delicious breast...' He cupped me through my corset and squeezed greedily, and my fever spiked again. It wasn't lust I was feeling, far from it, but all Kohl heard was my muffled gasp and suddenly, I felt him hardening against my rump. 'See *your* fingers, seeking entrance to-'

'Stop!' Kohén stepped forward before Kohl's hand could slip under the slit in my skirt, shooting a tiny spark that bit into the back of his brother's hand, making it twitch and smoulder while Kohl gasped behind me, and I sobbed in relief when he stopped pawing at me and started shaking it out and cursing. 'Just stop! I won't agree to this! This is my worst nightmare you're suggesting, not a solution!'

'It is the perfect solution!' Kohl snapped. 'We both get her this way!'

'*What* way? I don't see how any of this has a hope of-'

'You stay on as the firstborn twin and we never reveal that we know otherwise! We tell father and Karol that mother refused to brand her so we did it instead! We tell them that she bolted, hide her body until we can find a way to toss it outside to the Banished, and let *them* take the fall for her death after! Father will only care that Larkin is still beautiful and willing to put on a brave face out there tonight- because you and I have agreed to make amends for the sake of the family- and then when I board that boat to Pacifica- probably later next week now because we'll have an important funeral to attend first- you and Larkin will come with me! You can request to be provided with a house on Isthmus, and then ask that I be accommodated there too once it has been built, seeing as how we will both have titles there, General and Prince! We will each have a private chamber of course, and as far as everyone knows, she will dwell in her own personal harem within for *your* benefit... but two keys will be cut to fit the lock on her door and we will *both* be at liberty to use them!'

My stomach sucked back against my spine as Kohén's jaw dropped. 'You cannot believe that will work! All you have suggested is dependent on Larkin playing along and she's not that fucking good at acting-'

'It will work, and it will work beautifully, and if Larkin values the lives of Lindy and Coaxley and their sweet little third-born girl, then she will keep her mouth shut but her eyes sparkling on the matter until the day they die- of natural causes, of course.'

I'd probably been foolish to believe that there was a chance that Kohl would snap out of this evil mood of his sometime soon, but I had, but that threat passing his once-sweet lips broke me and I wilted.

'What?' Kohén demanded. 'How? Father has pardoned them!'

'In theory- but he won't hand it to them until he's seen her brand, and that means we'll have the chance to swipe it back yet.'

I shimmered with loathing- every nerve ending hissing like snakes, and turned away from him again. *Just let me die! Satan please... I beg you! Let Kohén strike out in rage and shock me by accident! Let the pain make my heart fail! Do something, anything, if it will make this nightmare stop!*

'You're sick,' Kohén bemoaned. 'Turning her kindness against her like that.'

'It's nothing that hasn't been done to me! And it's not something that I intend to have to use against her, once you agree to my demands- and I know that you will. No one will know that I am seeing to her needs as well, of course- that will be *our* little secret,' Kohl reached into the cup of my corset and caressed my right breast and I saw Kohén's face turn ashen. 'She will pretend to have issues with it at first, but we will do all that we have promised her and more, Kohén-' he tugged on my nipple and I whimpered, 'and she will learn to forgive us and make her peace with her new lot in life. Just imagine it, Larkin...' Breathing heavily, Kohl rubbed his hand over my mid-section and then squeezed my hip while he scooped my breast out of the top of the corset.

'You'll have cotton fields that will stretch to meet the horizon, a library full of every book that you could ever dream of reading, your freedom to swim and run and sunbathe and climb trees and surf... and access to not just one of the men you love, but *both*. You will not have to feel guilty for giving into your attraction to me, because you will have Kohén's blessing to do just that, and you will not have to fear losing your best friend- because he will most likely be fucking you every second that *I* am not.' My skin blistered in gooseflesh that did not feel cold but boiling hot, and when Kohl saw the little bumps, he chuckled. 'See?' he looked up at his twin, who was gaping at us, astonished. 'Just the *thought* of getting serviced by the both of us has her hyperventilating.'

'I think the fact that you've lost your mind is what has thrown her here!'

Kohl sighed and moved to my other breast. 'Why is it so crazy? There are two of us, two of *these*...' he twirled my left nipple between his fingers and ground his hips against me again, breathing lustily. 'Two beautiful places that we can kiss at once, two beautiful legs to spread, two sweet hands to hold...two ears to whisper dirty things into...' his hand slid into my skirt again, 'two tight, warm places that she can be taken- simultaneously if she's so inclined...' My muscles seized up as Kohén's mouth dropped open in astonishment. 'Have you had both yet little brother, or is there a virginity left that I can claim?'

Oh God NO! Why isn't anyone pounding on that door anymore? T'are, help me!

'N-no... I wouldn't...' Kohén stammered, but he was staring at Kohl's hand, fascinated- and not at me, 'she wouldn't...'

'But she will... she'll ask for it, Kohén, and if you won't give it to her there, you'd better fucking believe I would...' Kohl squeezed my backside and I felt my tears streak down my face again as he chuckled. 'Oh don't look so horrified- I know you've considered it, and I know she will.' Kohl smacked my ass lightly and then went back to stroking my breasts. 'And look, I'm not *completely* overcome- I am aware that what I am suggesting is rather manipulative and immoral... but I only suggest it because I know in my heart that Larkin wants to be with us both, and it's only a matter of time before she admits it to herself and makes her peace with it all. Then, we will be able to lift the threat from Lindy and Coaxley's head and she will stay anyway, not because she has to, but because she will know that we can make her happier than anyone else can.'

Kohén's eyes searched mine as he stepped forward, and I was horrified to see that his sparks were diminishing as his eyes were darkening. 'Is this true? On any level? Would you be able to-'

'She's not going to agree *now*, you idiot!' Kohl snapped as I began to writhe and fight him, not caring if I agitated the pain anymore because the heat overwhelming me was making every part of my body burn as fiercely. 'She needs to be convinced and that's going to take some time, but *I* don't have the time to convince *you*! We have to present a united front against father and soon, so agree now!'

'I can't!'

'You can! You can give her so much! We'll open an orphanage there and we'll collect third-borns and she can raise them! She can give them all the advantages that we gave her, without them having to sacrifice anything for it! We'll make her the queen of Calliel, even though she'll never have the title she'll have the respect and admiration of all, and we will get it too, for having treated her so kindly!' Kohl was hyperventilating with excitement as he explored me. 'And just think of the opportunities it will present us with! We can both take spouses and never have to worry about how we feel about them, because our needs will be met by our true love! We can have kids, and she can feel like a mother to them as well as the others! We'll choose spouses that will adore her as we do, as *most* women in Calliel do right now, and force them to treat her with the kindness that our mother didn't bestow upon her until it was too late!'

'You keep saying *we,* and as beautiful as some of the pictures you are painting in my mind are, I cannot stand that 'we'! I love her too much to share her!'

'Enough to let her go?' Kohl demanded, cupping my breath and squeezing it hard again, causing the flesh to bulge between his fingers. 'Enough to never have her again?' His fingers slipped into the front of my skirt and yanked it back over my hip, baring one leg and garter. *'Ever?'* His hand snaked around my hips and caressed my golden panties through the part he'd made in the fabric, and I closed my thighs around his hand, making him chuckle once more. 'The heat coming off her, Jesus! What's it like, Kohén? Tell me... sinking into this...? *Is* it heaven?'

I was weeping freely now, but when I looked up at Kohén, was gutted to see that he still wasn't looking at my tear-streaked face, but between my legs where luckily, I was numb.

'I...'

'Was it worth it?' Kohl breathed, groping me hard enough for it to hurt and thickened against my back. 'Tell me that having her wasn't worth what it did to your soul, and I'll let her go.'

Kohén's face contracted. 'Stop...' he whispered, but he stepped closer, eyes drifting across my breasts now. 'Please... don't make me do this...'

'Was it *worth it, Kohén?*'

Kohén dropped his face into his hands and shook his head. 'Fuck...!'

'Kohén! Man up!'

No! Stay a boy! My sweet boy! The one that gives me butterflies! I sobbed when I felt my panties tugged down crookedly beneath my skirts, allowing Kohén a glimpse of my intimate flesh.

'Look at her! Look at her, and tell me that I don't have heaven in the palm of my hand!'

Kohén peeked between his fingers, roared and sent an arc of blue light streaming across the room. At first my heart leapt to believe that he was going to fight for what was right, but the energy hit the water of the pool behind us and sizzled as Kohén dropped to his knees at my feet and plunged his face into my thighs, tickling me with his hair and repelling me with his surrender.

'She's heaven!' He glanced up, but not at me- at Kohl who was leering down at him over my shoulder. 'She's heaven and now that I've been to Heaven, I can't exist outside of it.' He swallowed hard and squeezed my rump, kissing the inside of my thigh as I closed my eyes and expelled all of my hopes and dreams in one breath. And as the oxygen left me I imagined that my soul was leaving me too- that my life was leaving me. They could do what they wanted to what was left behind but I would not be there, I swore it. 'I agree to your proposal,' he rasped haggardly, and their dual body temperatures became a conflation that immediately began to smother me. 'Tell me what I have to do to make it happen!'

Kohl sighed in relief. 'Go take mother's body to Larkin's room, lock it away and then hurry back here.'

'Me?' Kohén paled. *'Why?'*

'Because I'm not letting Larkin out of my grasp until I know you're not going to try to shock me, that's why! And because if you're in this, you're all in; as culpable as I for her murder.' He nodded towards the corridor. 'Try not to leave a trail of blood, and stuff her in Larkin's closet if you can. If our little swan plays along, we'll find a way to get mother's body out her window and onto the lawn. But if Larkin tries something smart- we'll tell them that she did it, and let the ungrateful bitch hang!'

I'm not here! I'm not here, I'm not in this. I am somewhere else, floating away.... no, not floating, sinking. I don't want to go to Heaven if it is filled with people like this that god has forgiven- I want to go to Hell, so I never expect kindness from anybody ever again! I can bear the cruelty, but not the shock of it.

'Then what?' Kohén breathed as he nuzzled my thighs, and the fact that he had not baulked against the suggestion of disposing his mother's body made something slither around inside my stomach. Like a switch, he'd turned off his humanity and now I followed suit, closing my eyes against his face. I'd die for killing Constance- gladly. Especially if that meant I'd get the chance to raise hell first but ripping off one Barachiel's cock with my perfectly manicured fingernails and forcing it down the throat of the other!

'Come back here, and then we'll seal the deal- inside of her,' Kohl removed his hand from my mouth but I let my head fall forward as he pushed me to my knees in front of Kohén, holding me there by my shoulders. My head was spinning so I bowed it and allowed my heavy curls to drape forward, veiling me.

No! Now? Right now? Please God NO!

'What?' Kohén's breath was on my face and hair and so I turned away from it, sickened by his proximity. 'Now? We haven't time!'

'We'll make it. You think I'd trust you to keep your word so easily? No, I'll believe that you'll share her only once you have. Do as I have asked and we'll have her now- *together*- and *then* we'll join the party. And according to that clock over there, it's only just begun.'

'But-'

'Deal with the cold body, while I warm up the hot one further. We're two halves of a whole, remember?'

'Fine!' Kohén snapped, rising to his feet and taking my hand in his. 'But let's take her into the dungeon room first, okay? That way we can tie her up and won't have to worry about her hurting us or herself until we've... you know...'

'Not a bad idea,' Kohl said. 'Isn't there a way to tie a woman so that we can both have her at once?'

'There is, but you'd better be gentle about it,' Kohén squeezed my hand and knelt before me while I stared at his hand, horrified to know that he was doing exactly as Satan had predicted he would. 'Larkin, I-'

I spat at him, inured beyond repair. My mouth was too dry to work up much moisture, but the gesture had the desired effect anyway and he recoiled.

'I'm doing this for you!' the lusty moiety that I had once held up onto a pedestal cried, reaching down and hoisting my chin up so that I would have to look up at him. 'It's us, or Yael!'

'I choose Yael!' I croaked, struggling against Kohl while glowering at Kohén, but Kohl secured my hands behind my back with one hand, pulling on them tightly enough to set my arm on fire once more. My head spun from the pain and I lowered it again, willing a loss of consciousness as I whispered: 'I choose *Yael*...'

But I'd never meant my hateful words towards Kohén, and so I could not blame him for not believing them now. 'You love me!' He cupped my face and began to kiss me passionately while behind me, Kohl laughed and pushed me forward, encouraging the contact. I tried to turn my face away from him but he only kissed the skin he was presented with instead before drifting down to my breasts, moaning before Kohl began to knead them from behind. 'And I love you...' Kohén's hand slid up my thigh, 'I told you I'd do anything to keep you Larkin-anything! The fact that you've never understood how much I meant that is *your* mistake, not mine!'

It was and I sobbed because he was right. If I'd ever understood the depth of his obsession with me and where it would lead me, I would killed myself years ago.

'That's it...' a second set of lips began to slide across my back, and then fingers were slipping against the crotch of my panties from beneath- fingers that knew exactly how to manipulate my body. I couldn't believe that Kohén was initiating this! How could he been so jealous of me for so long only to stoop to this in the end? It made no sense!

'Kohén, stop!' I gasped and tried to move my hips away from them, but Kohl's slipped from my breast and caressed me somewhere even more private and I shrieked, only to have Kohén muffle it with his mouth once more. '*Ow!*'

'One of us is going to have you here...' Kohl whispered into my ear, 'you decide which- and take your time- I could explore both options for hours.'

'Don't,' I felt Kohén smack Kohl's hand away as he pulled back from the kiss he'd been a sole participant in. 'As eager as I am now, I can tell she's not ready.'

'What?'

Kohén relaxed back onto his heels. 'I just investigated and there's no way we can do this yet without hurting her- trust me, I know what I'm talking about. It's no fun when they're not into it, and we won't be winning her anything if we try to force matters, let alone her heart.'

'Fine,' Kohl's hands went back to my hips. 'You need to go deal with the body first anyway-and maybe bring the rest of that champagne back? Got her in love with you again- might work for me too.'

'It won't!' I protested, hanging my head as I shook it. 'Both of you please- don't do this! I know I'll never want this! You're not devising a way to keep me forever, but to lose me faster!'

'You'll change your mind,' Kohén whispered, sounding hurt and a million miles away to my unravelling mind. 'I'll earn those lilac eyes again, Larkin- no matter what it takes.' And then he turned and walked away, lifting his mother's body from the floor and staggering off through the mist with it, taking my will to live in this world a second longer with him

26.

'We have to be quick, brother!' Kohén called over his shoulder. 'If we don't see to our burns soon, they may not get the chance to be healed as completely as we would both like. And I really don't want to see Larkin in pain for a second longer, so take her down to the dungeon and then take your dress off so we can get this over with!'

Ha!

'Oh, I'll be quick,' still holding my hands behind my back, Kohl reached around me and began to pull my skirts back over both hips now, clearing a wider path. 'And from what I saw, you will be too- despite having apparently had a lot of experience!'

'Fuck you Wind-In-His-Skirt...' was Kohén's fading, laboured response.

'Nah... I have someone prettier in mind...' Kohl's hand slipped under my chin and twisted my head back so I had to face him, and his eyes were blazing. 'Thank God he's gone at last...I needed us to be alone, darling, don't you see?!'

'What?!' My heart lifted and my hopes spiked. Had this all been a ruse? I sat up taller, wondering if the duchess was playing dead or if my brand was fake, but before I could realise what a reckless, pitiful hope that was, or ask if he'd had this planned all along, Kohl guided my face closer to his and nipped at my lower lip.

'Well, our first kiss ought to be in private, don't you think?' His eyes were still dilated- black as original sin. 'And this is what this is- our first, *true* kiss.'

'*Mmmm-*' But all too suddenly he was kissing me hungrily, scraping his lips and teeth and tongue against mine and I was yelling but his mouth muffled my distress. Growling he tugged back on my hair when I tried to close him out and raped my lips a second time while his hand slipped down to rip the slit in my skirt all the way to my hip.

I'm not in this! I'm not here! I am far, far away! I thought as the dizziness increased and the sounds that Kohl was making began to lose clarity. He palmed and then mashed my breast once he'd found it again and the metal boning poking out the top of the garment dug into the soft undersides of it, making me whimper.

Ow, ow, ow, ow, OW! I'm gonna get his balls into a vice with teeth and crank it for this!

'So beautiful... heavy... soft...' he moaned as I made a hideous face and tried to deflect his kisses. 'God, I don't know if I'll make it down to the dungeon!' He tried to keep my lips under his but he was much more interested in what my breasts were doing and so I ended up getting licked all around my mouth which was awful and kind of shocking. I'd already known that I'd get no pleasure from his touches, but Kohén was an intuitive lover, like his eldest brother and father were rumoured to be, so I'd always just assumed that Kohl would have inherited some of the skills that kept the women in the Barachiel harem grinning year-round.

But evidently that was not the case. Kohl poked and pinched at me with the hands of someone that was used to handling rocks not flesh, so not only was the experience horrifying and mortifying- but painful and almost funny. He was so into it that he didn't even seem to notice that I was taking the attack the way someone would tolerate being licked by an over-zealous dog: straining away and bubbling my lips to get rid of his excess saliva.

Down boy! I thought. *Ugh, someone get this pup a fucking chew toy already!*

'Oh Larkin...' he dropped my breasts and reached between my thighs again. 'Look at you! Twenty-four hours ago I believed that this would never happen but just look at you- spread open for me, ripe for the taking... and *perfect!*' he breathed, spiking a finger inside my bunched panties, making me gasp and twist away from it. 'Mine!'

'Ow!' I yelped, trying to rise up so that I could clench my thighs together, but he smacked my rump and pulled down on my arms so that I sank onto my haunches more heavily, my thighs widening by default. Two fingers jabbed at me now and I hissed, straining upwards again and arching my back, trying to free my hands from his and escape the blunt impalement at the same time.

But there was nowhere to go. I went limp and cried instead, shaking my head and wishing that I could turn back time, because if I could, I'd go back to the night that Kohl and I had pleasured one another with a flower- and sodomise him with a broken tree branch!

'You're so tight! My brother must have a pin dick!' Kohl remarked as he had a go at pinching my labia together, blessedly retreating from inside me for a moment.

'No... you're not *that* identical!' I spluttered. 'I've just withered up since you started touching me!'

Kohl sucked at his teeth and tugged on my arms again, biting my earlobe hard enough to draw blood. It should have hurt and yet that other pain was still too all-encompassing for me to feel much else, and when I looked at my shoulder I actually chuckled, understanding why at last.

Understanding that I wouldn't have to commit suicide this night- because I was already dying. And thankfully, I was apparently the only one that knew that.

'I think mother's been a bad influence on you!' he snarled, grinding himself against my tailbone. 'Or maybe you've just been reading the sort of books that a young lady oughtn't read, hmm? They've given you a smart mouth! Perhaps *I* was the bad influence all along.'

I cackled, deciding that if I truly was going to go out, I'd go out with a bang. 'You haven't the self-possession to influence a mosquito, Kohl Barachiel!' I panted through clenched teeth as the pain in my arm hissed and bubbled up my shoulder and into my head. 'Isn't that why we're here? No matter how many leg-ups you've had to escape your caste, the only reason why you've got anything going for you at all is because you had a friend pull some diamond strings for you, and a big brother that took sympathy on you!' I snorted. 'Wait, that wasn't even sympathy. Karol only released you to impress *me*!'

'Diamond strings?' He wrestled my arms roughly, making me gasp. 'What the fuck is *that* supposed to mean?'

'You didn't earn Atticus's respect- *I* did. He wouldn't have trusted you and your wet blanket Nephilim tendencies enough to run a quilting bee, let alone a community if *I* hadn't asked him to as part of my conditions to move to Pacifica one day!'

Kohl released my arms and pulled back on my hair, practically bending me in half at the spine so that he could glared down into my face. 'What?'

I narrowed my eyes at him. 'I even had to beg him, you know that?' I folded over my lower lip. 'Please Atticus... you're the closest thing to a father he has, act like one, and give him a chance, *please*? For *me*?' I wriggled my eyebrows, dropping the pout. 'Hardest sell of my life, seeing as how he's gay. You really need to get your impulse control under control, you know that? If Yael hadn't been trying to outbid him, Atticus might have given up on attaining me if it meant binding himself to the useless twin!'

It was the cruellest thing I'd ever said to anybody, and I saw the hurt hit hard. 'You're lying!' Kohl was turning white and his erection was deflating beneath me. 'You're just trying to emasculate me so I won't be able to perform!'

I shrugged and even that burned. 'What do I care if you screw me or not now that you've screwed up my life? Kohén's twice the man you are, *itty bitty Kahuna.*' I lowered my eyes and smirked at his attempted erection, and saw it wither further under my disdain. 'So long as he still gets a go, I'll find a way to climax. And for a whore like me- that's all that *really* matters! In fact- you take the other virginity, okay? That way, I won't have to worry about it *hurting.*'

His balled fist hit me hard in the solar plexus and I grunted as the wind was knocked out of me. 'Bitch!' Kohl slapped me hard a beat later, and I twisted away from the ringing in my ears and nose-dived headfirst into the darkness that was rushing up to me. 'I'll make you regret every hateful word you've just said to me!'

'Not as much as I already regret every kind one I ever said...' I slurred, pressing my roasting cheek to the floor as the fog closed over us- over *me*. 'And I never should have said them- you never loved me anyway. *Neither* of you did...'

'Because we can't let you go?' he croaked, shaking me. 'That's what you're basing your diagnosis on? That for want of you, I'd give up my soul? That's not fair! I cannot love you or have you in the regular way and neither can he, but we've done the best we can, so don't throw your very predicament at us as proof that we don't love you! The fact that you ended up here was proof that your *parents* didn't!''

That stung, but it was an old wound so I let it go. 'There's more solid proof that your love is a lie than that...and I'm boiling alive in it!' I swallowed hard, trying not to scream as more flames licked a path through my shoulder, across my heart and to the other side, making my fingers twitch. 'And I want it to...' I bit my lip and spasmed as another flash-fire rushed through me. 'Oh god...I can't breathe...! Thank Satan, I can't *breathe*!'

'Larkin?' Kohl sat up straighter. 'What's going on with you? I didn't hit you that hard! Are you sick again?'

'Please let this be the end of it!' I whimpered, and my vision began to blur. 'Please! I don't want to have to feel my heart so take it, Satan! And damn God for... for... forsaking...'

'No!' Kohl gasped. 'Lark, stop saying such things! Kohén! Kohén she's becoming delusional!'

'Kohl?' I heard rapid footsteps. 'What's going on? You were supposed to take her down the back-'

'Something's wrong with her! I think her fever has returned!'

'What? Oh, Hell!'

'She's breaking into a sweat, and she's babbling... renouncing God, and thanking Satan for the pain she's in! Saying she can't breathe and doesn't want to!'

'That damned fever's back? Shit! That almost killed her last night!'

'Almost doesn't count!' I sobbed, struggling in Kohl's arms- agitating my wound as best as I could, knowing I needed to finish this before they could get a healer in there! 'You almost loved me... but not enough, so it doesn't COUNT!'

'Why does you getting sick mean we don't love you?!' A hand was pressed to my forehead and then jerked away. 'Ow! She's-'

'It doesn't!' I panted, gasping. My heart was racing, but I allowed it to gallop off without me, because I didn't want it any more- just its power for as long as I could stand it, to pump my poisoned blood through my veins until my entire being was flooded with liquid fire, like kerosene had been mixed with water and then set alight. 'But this time you made me sick, and thank god- THANK GOD- this time, there'll be *no* reversing it!'

'What? What are you-' Kohén sobbed and knelt beside me and when his hand closed around mine, it was too much body heat for me to bear. 'What's *wrong*?'

I opened my eyes and smiled at him- a watery smile that I hoped was dull enough to let my hate shine through- hate that wasn't diluted by even one drop of love, not anymore. I was burning and my soul and heart had been incinerated for it, leaving me with nothing to love a Barachiel with. Nothing to fight for Lindy and Coaxley with. Nothing to accomplish, but causing them pain before I surrendered to my own.

I craned my neck to look at my shoulder and laughed when I saw the veins around my brand that had seemed prominent and swollen a few moments before had continued to swell- travelling all the way down my arm to the back of my left hand, which was balled into a fist to counteract the agony. My skin was tight and white around them in some places and flushed red in others, and in the two seconds that I watched, I felt the veins on my right arm began to thicken as my blood boiled there as well. It didn't look right- it looked evil, and was clearly symptomatic of the kind of illness that couldn't be cured which was exactly what I wanted. Satan had said I'd needed her to escape here alive and maybe she was right, but death was still an escape and I yearned for its swift arrival, even if that came hand in hand with sheer agony.

The twins hadn't seen this coming because they'd been looking at things about me that mattered more to them than a useless shoulder, but *I* had, and I was so relieved to know that my beauty was being morphed into something monstrous due to their negligence that I could have laughed in triumph. I wanted those poisoned veins to swell under my face, to burst and soak my hair when they erupted and that was what this was all leading up to, I knew it; an eruption, and after too many years of fighting for them I finally gave up- released my fists and let the rage and despair course through me; I let myself be ugly.

This wasn't *my* fault. I did *not* deserve this. Time would *not* absolve them of what they'd done to me or heal the pain, and I would not remain in Eden for the rest of my life- because I was leaving *now*. Kohl, Cherry and Dulcie had accused me of being brainwashed into believing that I was happy here and I'd disagreed- how could it be brainwashing if I'd longed for the lie myself? If I'd been a willing participant in the sham? But I knew now that brainwashing wasn't a recent affliction but an ancient one: I'd been conditioned to believe that this was where I belonged and that Kohén was who I belonged with since I was five, and being aware of the fact that that was being done intentionally to me had convinced me that I was above falling for it, and that I was staying here because it would eventually pay off for me if I played my cards right.

But I'd fallen, and I'd fallen hard, and the twins had fallen with me. I'd not thought clearly since the day that Karol and I had first ended up in that pool together- since I'd looked in the mirror and had seen a swan instead of a duckling. I'd stopped fighting against the system then and had started fighting with it, trying to find a way to make my world co-exist with theirs, but that simply wasn't possible. Equality on earth would never be possible so long as the person in charge believed that they were entitled to more than another.

I wasn't a third-born, I was a person! I wasn't a caste- I was so much more than that or at least, I had been once. They'd treated me like a toy and had shattered me like one and I would not leave this earth until they understood that a butterfly or a firefly or even a diamond could be closed in a fist and expected to remain beautiful after.

'Look me in the eye, *both* of you...' I slid that smile back to Kohl, 'and tell me how to men that are madly in love with a woman...' the fog closed in, but it was thick enough to choke me like smoke now and I welcomed it, 'can forget that's she's allergic to gold before they burn it into her bloodstream?' I saw their expression shift from confused, to horrified to understanding before I let my eyes close and actually felt my blood bubble like sulphur as a sudden buzzing in my head became a scream.

'Oh no! Oh no, oh NO! She didn't-'

'We for*got*!'

'The gold! There's real gold in that powder, Kohl! You poisoned her!'

'You were going to let mother poison her! You spend every second of every day with her! If you didn't think of what the branding would mean for her, why should I have?'

'I never thought of it as being real gold but- she needs Karol, now!' Kohén sounded hysterical. 'Her arm! Look at her arm!'

'She's known about that allergy for weeks now! Why didn't she mention it earlier? That would have saved her from this all together!'

'Because she didn't want to be saved, oh Larkin...!' hands scooped under me. 'No baby, no! This isn't how we're supposed to end! We weren't *supposed* to end, ever!' He shook me. 'I was lying, Larkin! I wasn't going to let him share you, are you kidding?' he shook me again. 'I was just playing along to buy time!'

'What?!'

'I was waiting for you to undress or take her down the hall to tie her up- to release her for just one second- so I could kill you where you stood, you psychotic son of a bitch!' My hair was smoothed away from my face. 'I didn't hide mother's body Larkin I lay it in the hall by the door so it would be the FIRST thing that father and Karol would see when they came in! I would have opened the door too, but he started screaming-'

'You were double-crossing me?'

'Of course I was, you sick mother fucker! I'd never share her! You're lucky you survived touching her skin for this long!'

'But you touched her with me! *You* groped her-'

'I tested her, dammit! You both claimed to have loved one another once, and I was temporarily thrown by it! So I inspected her, okay? I let her go to you for one moment so I could see if she reacted to you as she does to me but she did not and I knew I'd been a monster to let the charade go that far!' Kohén sobbed, shaking me more violently. 'Baby please, I just wanted you to have what you wanted! I wanted to see if the dream might be yours- the orphans, the books, the house by the ocean… the two of us, united! I didn't want to do it and I should have known better but I was so jealous and scared and-' his voice cracked. 'I lost my faith in us. You made me lose faith in us, Kohl, and now she's dying!'

'I ought to kill you where you stand!' Kohl bellowed.

'DO IT!' Kohén raged, and I felt him crackle around me. 'I don't want to live if she does not!'

I heard what Kohén was saying- heard the words that ought to have flooded me with relief, but my blood was lava and burned off any emotion that they might have evoked before they could resonate with me. His admission changed nothing- I was still dying because he'd broken his word to protect me from that brand and he would not get my forgiveness to ease his conscience with.

I'd known that the golden brand would give me an allergic reaction, had known and had kept that fact to myself knowing that I wouldn't be led out into that ballroom while covered in a violent red rash- but I had not known that it would burn me from the inside out like this. I was grateful that it was though, saving me the trouble of doing myself in, while bubbling away at my humanity like acid. I'd wanted to love God in the end but I did not and could feel no guilt for it now. I hadn't wanted to go to Hell, but I was getting there due to the decisions that others had made- not by making decision of my own violation- and I was at peace with that too because my indifference towards my soul had freed me from the mortal, emotional trappings that had been caging me in for life!

Besides, I'd managed to find a way out of there without taking Satan's hand. I wasn't much, but I was stubborn, and a smile twitched my lips when I realised that I would have had it all if I'd set my mind to it; the cotton fields, the library, the adopted children... the Rhett Butler of my dreams. I would have made it all happen, had I been given the freedom to do so.

'I-OW!' I felt Kohén seize up and stumble. 'What was- *ow*!' a slapping sound, we spun around.

'What are- hey! *Ow*!' another cry. 'Kohén, did you zap me?'

'No! Something's stinging at me too... I... oh my GOD! Wasp!' Kohén stumbled again and I felt my shoulder flare with more bright pain as he hit the ground and let me roll out of his arms. 'WASPS!'

Kohl let out what could only be a shriek of fear and that's when I heard a piece of that buzzing in my head break away and zip past my ear. My eyes flew open when I realised that there were truly wasps in the room, and focused on one as it blurred past. I shouldn't have been able to see it given how out of my head I was, and for how the room was flashing as Kohén sent balls of energy hurtling at his tiny assailants, making the fog flash and crackle, but the wasp was glowing faintly the way a generic one oughtn't and I smiled as I realised that these weren't regular wasps, but manifested ones. And they were filling the air! My back was to the fireplace and I pushed up weakly and looked to my left, whispering her name when I saw her and smiling tearfully:

'Constance…'

My mother looked at me and smiled through bloody, cracked teeth and I knew in that moment that she was my mother and not theirs. She'd crawled out of the corridor and had come to help me, even though it was clear that she was beyond the point of being helped herself.

'Too little, too late again, I know Lark…' she lurched forward and collapsed, landing on her hands and knees and crying out in pain when her shattered right arm went out from under her, but before I could drag myself towards her, she curled back her left hand like she was throwing a ball and then let another handful of winged, hissing creatures fly across the room and to her boys. 'But what the Hell!'

And that was when the entire world began to buzz with her bright, light Nephilim energy.

27.

The boys must have known that there was no escaping a cloud of wasps but they were almost as stubborn as I was and so they fought hard. Kohén was dancing around, alternating between crying out my name (he'd lost sight of me in the thickening air) and sending out bolt after bolt of energy until he apparently had the sense to throw a shield of energy out and away from him, causing any of the winged creatures that came near to him to fry when they hit it and full to the ground while he bent low and tried to cross the room, angling towards the open spa door.

Kohl had hit the deck and was attempting to use the mist like a shield and unfortunately the low position he assumed almost immediately allowed him to spot his mother across the room beneath the blanket of mist that was about knee-high and thickening due to all of the activity in the room. He let out a shout of discovery when he spotted her and then the cloud of stinging insects that she sent wafting his way, and immediately pushed up off the ground and began to stagger backwards from it, running into the side of the spring after having travelled only a metre or so. He grunted and almost lost his balance and the swarm closed in on him, but at the last minute he twisted around and half-dove into the water awkwardly, generating a huge splash that slopped over the sides.

'Go Larkin, *now!*' the duchess croaked at me but I could barely lift my head up let alone contemplate running. Besides, there was no point.

I looked at her and shook my head. 'I'm done for...' I gasped. 'My nickel allergy... the brand... it's poisoning me.'

'No,' she gasped, and began to slither towards. 'No, that can't be true!'

'I can't move...' I confessed, and then moaned when another rush of heat overcame me, tearing at my skirts, trying to get the too-warm fabric off my legs before I burst.

'I'm burning up! Go let Karol and Elijah in if you can... let them see...' I bowed forward again, saw my bared breasts and grimaced, using the energy I had to try and stuff myself back inside it before she got to close to me. 'Let them *all* see...'

'Demon!' Kohl leapt out of the water and arced his hand through it while thrusting the other in his mother's direction. His face was already swelling up in several places from where he'd been bitten, and his burn wound from earlier was leaking watery blood down his near-transparent toga. 'Bitch!' His water spray dissolved a lot of the mist, but he dropped that hand and swiped the other now, craning his head to look for his brother. 'It's mother causing the wasps!' he roared. 'Kill her Kohén, and make it count this time!'

'No Kohén, don't!' I mewled, but I couldn't be sure if he'd heard me. He was almost at the other side of the room then but he stopped abruptly ducked and turned, searching through the mist.

'Larkin!' he began to barrel forward, sliding the last few metres so that he could take my hand. 'Larkin come on, we have to get out-'

'Get away from me!' I screamed and that was when I heard Kohl yell out something indecipherable. I looked up when the roar expelling from his lungs became thunderous and shrieked when I saw that he was somehow manipulating the water in the spring to his will. As he lifted his hands in a beckoning motion, the water was rising to the height of his chest and leaning back like a curling wave, forming a transparent wall between him and the rest of us. He looked first from his mother then to me as though deciding where to send the hilt of it first, but his eyes snagged on Kohén's as it extended to mine and with a victorious shout he motioned his hands forward, directing the wave *our* way.

Unaware that any of this was going on, Kohén had managed to grasp my wrist and was attempting to drag me to my feet while I pulled back and away from him, and when I saw that his charge had tripled in ferocity, I understood that if I didn't break his hold I would die as a result of their combined powers and not their foolishness and that was horrifying to me after having lost so much!

'*No!*' I hissed, curling away from him and causing him to overbalance my way, and he would have hit the ground on my lap if Constance hadn't taken that moment to make him a priority for the first time in her life. Or rather, the first time since she'd lied about which twin had come first.

'Kohén drop your charge NOW!' she bellowed in a voice more authoritative than any I'd ever heard her use before and it had its desired effect on her only obedient son. Kohén's eyes bugged and he jerked his head her way, seeing her at last, but she was looking behind him and at Kohl and that forced Kohén's gaze to follow. He saw the wave the moment it smashed against the ground three metres from him, looked down at himself, over at me and with a grunt of exertion, twisted sideways and dove across the room. He moved far too fast for any human to be expected to move and survive, coming down at the marble floor at a horrible angle while still sparking madly, but at the last moment he curled his body into a ball and rolled swiftly, landing on his feet and taking just the smallest fraction of time to bounce before he dove into the open door of the spa. I couldn't care less whether he lived or died now that he was away from me, but part of me was still rather entertained by his athletic antics.

The wave hit me then, but it was too shallow to do anything but push me back closer to the fireplace that was set between the two spa doors, and practically harmless without the threat of Kohén's electricity near to me, but it was warm water and repugnant to me for it. I howled as my fever spiked higher and the weight of my skirts grew heavier and more oppressive, but I heard a smash a beat later, and looked up to see Kohén fling himself onto the metal bed frame that I'd dragged across to hold open the spa's door. The water swooped across the floor beneath him a second later but he got his foot up onto the mattress on time, so it flowed harmlessly past him and down the other side of the corridor, dwindling to a trickle before it reached the first door on that side.

'Get her!' Kohl yelled then, and Constance and I looked at each other, wondering which her he was referring to. 'Kohén-'

'Fuck you! You tried to kill me!' a bolt of lightning ripped the room in two, headed straight for Kohl, but Kohl had started retreating and jumped backwards out of the spring just as the electricity hit it with a mighty *crack*. Water hissed and bubbled but Kohl was already racing around the side of the spring towards Constance *and* the way out, drawing up another armful of water as he went.

'You were going to try to kill me first!' Kohl wheezed. 'Now you cry foul? Eat shit!' He didn't have the time to manifest a wave as wide as the last this time, but he backhanded it and sent a solid stream shooting Kohén's way as Kohén sent out a second bolt. The two forces hit one another with an explosive hiss, but the only damage done was to the fog, which dissolved like someone had taken a bite out of the air. Spent, the boys both swooned back as their powers did, gasping in lungful's of air.

They're weakening! But not fast enough! All it will take is one look at Constance or I to revive either! I must act now!

I whimpered, trying to sit up and grasp at the fireplace, determined to get to and shield Constance's body with my own even if it was the last thing I did, but I saw Kohl stumble again just as a gentle zing erupted from Kohén's direction. I looked from one faltering twin to the other and was able to make out what looked like dozens of tiny welts on their bared skin as each half-collapsed again, clearly trying to get up to fight but most certainly failing.

The wasps! I realised, looking around the room. There were barely enough left after the electricity versus water showdown (I'd seen how quickly Constance's manifestations could be dissolved in Pacifica when it had rained on her) but they'd already done a lot of damage to handicap the twins who were now falling prey to their own allergies, and I knew that if Karol didn't find a way in here soon (was that banging on the door I could detect over the blood rushing in my head?) they would be done for. In fact, there was a good chance that they were done for anyway. Hadn't the last attack stopped Kohén's heart?

Where is Elijah? Why are he and Karol taking so long? Surely they would have been able to break down the door by now!

'Run, Lark…' Constance wheezed, crawling my way on her elbows again. 'Mine won't be as potent as the real thing, and I don't even know how allergic they still are now that they are grown… this might be the only chance you'll get so run now! the people on the other side of the fence will shield you!'

'There you are!' came Kohl's infuriated shout, and I screamed out a warning when he appeared out of nowhere, grasped Constance by the hair and jerked her off the ground. 'Dark Nephilim!' he raged as I threw myself forward but landed facedown, burning up on the inside.

'What's your excuse?' I heard her gasping for breath. 'Rapist!' she went on. 'Double-crosser! Ungrateful little-'

'You can't rape a whore!' Kohl screamed then, reaching into his toga, and I shrieked first in outrage, then in terror when I saw a long, thin blade emerge in his fist and come striking down at his mother's shoulder. I didn't see it pierce her but her eyes bulged in their sockets as blood sprayed out of her mouth, and that was it for me! I grunted, arching my back as sympathetic agony made me feel like I'd been the one ripped open.

No!

Yes! Hissed another voice that I knew was not mine, and suddenly I wished that the spring was full of mirrors so that I could drag Satan forth and let her end Kohl the way he had just ended his mother. But there were none so I could do nothing but boil in everything that was evil and gape as Kohl yanked the blood-covered blade out of her back while mine throbbed in sympathy. The duchess flopped facedown with another sickening crack in a pool of her own fresh blood, and I felt my heart thud one final time as I opened my mouth to scream and throw myself at her murderer. Killing her the first time had been heinous enough, but *twice*? No! I was dying and he was going with me, and all I could hope that Hell would be expansive enough to ensure that I never had to see him again!

But suddenly I was bursting into flames instead and hurtling back- and away from him! For a moment I thought Kohén had finally 'gotten' me, but it took only a blink of shock for me to realise that like a dragon, I had just released not breath and voice- but *flames*!

'*Whaaat????!*' I thought, clinging to the wall behind me as the pressure of the release knocked me backwards, but I hadn't the mental capacity to wonder why or how, only to scream more as everything that I had ever wanted to shout at God, the Barachiel's and everybody else that had ever hurt or scared me poured out of me in a fireball so bright that it blinded me. *Oh God!*

Flames as hot as my rage, as swift as my sudden hatred for Kohl, and as damaging as any bolt of lightning could have ever hoped to be shot out of me like a solar flare bursting forth from the sun and blasted Kohl so hard that one moment he was there and the next he was imbedded into the plaster of the wall some ten feet behind him and screaming as his hair caught on fire. The flames vanished then and I fell forward on all fours, panting as a cloud of steam gushed out of me.

'Larkin!' I heard Kohén crow from behind me, but I couldn't do anything but stare as Kohl fell out of the wall and flopped into the water puddling beneath it, rolling and howling in agony as the flames were snuffed out. All of that would have been overwhelming enough, but no sooner had Kohl begun to simmer and moan, then I realised that my fever had broken as clearly and sharply as my water jug had that day when I'd hurled it at Satan!

'Oh… *oh*!' I twisted my neck and arm, gaping at it and feeling a shiver of some potent but unfamiliar emotion when

I saw that although the brand was still there, the skin around it had healed perfectly, and the bulging veins had vanished, leaving my arm smooth and golden once more. I touched my face and felt that although it was still sore from where I'd been struck, wet from sweat, misted with water, slick with tears and decidedly warmer than normal human skin ought to be, it was no longer an intolerable flush emanating from my core. I stretched out my hands- fisted them then spanned my fingers before fisting them again, and though my left one still ached from where Kohl had trampled it, they no longer felt weak or exhausted- but the opposite! In fact, I felt like I could crush anything and anyone with those hands!

I'm... I'm alive! I realised, rubbing my lips together and swallowing, amazed that although I could taste something different, I didn't feel parched or sore- or burned at all! And my fever really was gone! One moment it had been like a dense cloud of pure humidity had been closing in on me, and the next it was like the world had fragmented and then come back together in perfect alignment, allowing a breeze to find its way to me again and revive me. *'How?'* I whispered, and then a memory came back to me as clear as if it had happened seconds before. Of me kneeling before Eden's fence, with my mother kneeling on the other side of it.

'Oh, mother... I wish I were a Nephilim- a healer! I'd come home, I'd touch father's heart...'

'Are you sure that you're not?' my mother had asked. *'You could do so much for me, if you were! Maybe you just haven't found your power yet! They say it usually takes a severe emotional prolapse to-'*

'There's nothing there!' I'd cried. *'I've know every kind of emotion there is- I have been at my lowest, and my happiest...'*

But I hadn't. I thought I'd had, but at the age of sixteen, I'd scarcely understood the words loss, anger or pain. But I knew them now! Oh boy, did I know them after this night!

And evidently, that brand had been my trigger, or at least, my 'allergic' reaction to gold had been and now I knew- there was a reason why I couldn't feel fire's heat until I came into contact with it, and why things grew easily from my touch in frozen earth! I couldn't touch electricity without being shocked, or affect water the way Kohl could or heal anyone- but I *could* breathe fire and live, and that made me a Nephilim, all right! That made me my father's child- the father I'd never met... and *that* terrified me. My head spun with thoughts that were clearer than any I'd had before, and sparkled despite the pain associated with so many of them. I'd never seen a fire breather before- if that was what I was.

I am a dark Nephilim! That's more than being a third-born, and more than a whore, but is it better than being either? No! They'll kill me faster!

'Lark, you're an angel!' a hand touched my bicep and I flinched, spun and shrieked, slapping at Kohén's hand and then jumping when I saw five flares shooting out of my fingertips and burning an arc of clarity into the mist and smoke. *'Shit!'*

'Don't touch me!' I hollered as my Indian Brave fell back onto his backside and gaped up at me, obviously terrified. I stared at my own fingertips for a moment, shocked a second time to see fire seething from them without causing me pain or deformation, and had a flash memory to the day before when they'd done the same thing. I'd thought it had been spilled kerosene that had caused them to catch alight like that when Constance had swiped the torch from my hands, but what if this fire had been trying to escape me in a panic even then? What if it had been trying to escape me my whole life, and I'd repressed it, or had allowed others to? My fevers, the way I flushed so hot whenever I was upset- the way that heat often felt like it was smothering me from within... had that been my fire just begging to be released all along? I remembered Karol and Kohén inspecting me that dreadful day- remembered the comments I'd heard then and since about how hot I was on the inside- how I burned them in a way they enjoyed...and my teeth clenched together. No wonder I'd been repressing my heat! It had been one more thing that about me that they had made me feel ashamed of!

I looked at my primary oppressor, Kohén, and sneered. He was covered in welts and deformed by them and I liked it- I wanted him to look as ugly on the inside as I knew he was within. 'Don't touch me ever again, don't look at me don't THINK of me Kohén Barachiel, because I hate you! I am NOT your angel I am-'

'*An* angel! You are *an* angel!' Kohén pointed at me and I ducked, presuming he was about to hurl his own firepower back at me, but as I ducked I heard the rustle, and that made my heart skip a beat, to think that someone was sneaking up behind me. I twisted as he clarified: 'Not just *my* angel, but an actual winged creature! *Look!*'

I'd spun to see if Kohl as sneaking up on me, and I saw the blur of white as I did, and heard a more pronounced rustle. I looked up, following that white blur to several inches above my head and my lips parted in astonishment when I saw what Kohén had- feathers as tall as I was extending from behind me.

No! How? Oh...oh, does this mean that I am good? Can it?

'Oh Larkin...' Kohén breathed. 'You're the most beautiful thing I've ever beheld...'

I curled in my shoulders, scared at first, but they moved with me and fascinated now, I lifted my hand, tentatively touched the softest, purest thing I had ever seen, and *shivered* as pleasure raced through me.

I am an angel! Oh... no WONDER Satan wanted me so badly! I'm not just a Nephilim, if I have wings, I could be the most powerful one left in existence!

Panting now, I reached behind me and felt the place where the wings had sprouted from the centre of my back and understood why I'd felt pain when Constance had been stabbed.... because that was what had caused the wings to erupt from deep inside me! They felt sore around the base, but it wasn't much more than a burn, and a burn I could cope with if it meant I could fly, right? Because if I could fly, it meant that I could fly far away from here, and never look back! Not even with... I looked at my brand then and my eyes slitted.

On second thought... no I can't cope with being burned...
Swallowing hard as a lump of anguish formed in my throat again, I looked over at Constance's lifeless body then and

sobbed to see the pool of blood growing around her beautiful peacock dress. When we'd first met, I'd truly believed that we'd lived utterly opposite lives! That we'd never ever get to stand on common ground! But she had had wings once too- we'd *both* been birds, we'd both been locked in gilded cages due to our foolish hearts- and we both had suffered for it. Too in love with our chosen Barachiel's to leave when we should have- but too adored by them to be released. *And I think it's time that Kohén understands just how excruciating being trapped by fire can feel!*

I sighed and my wings drooped. My body had begun to heal, yes but my heart... my heart was cinders. I wouldn't be flying anywhere, unless it was to find a greater height to fall from.

'Larkin... God Larkin... I knew it.' I heard Kohén's voice break, and the water slosh beneath him as he crawled towards me. 'You're not only the most beautiful creature that has ever walked the earth, but the most heavenly. And I love-'

I hissed at him as a shudder ran through me, wiping my tears from my cheeks as I slowly pivoted to regard my captor once more. Releasing the flames and developing the wings had cooled me and had even granted me a temporary sense of elation, and yet the worst parts of my reality had not changed for those developments, and it was with an aching heart that I realised that my fate hadn't changed either, and I didn't desire it to. I was going to get free, yes, but I wasn't going to live beyond that.

I could not. Not in *this* world.

Just like that, I felt the shadows that had been building over me all day fall out of the sky and crush me once more. Kohén blanched and drew back, and I thought that it was because he understood that I was about to go boil him alive until he finally understood what fear and pain meant- but then I felt that shadow descend further, looked back over my shoulder in Kohl's direction again- and moaned when I saw that my beautiful, perfect feathers were turning black now.

Constance was wrong, I thought. I hadn't been born as a dark Nephilim, but I *had* become one within Eden's walls. Had I ever been the bad influence? The negative energy? I didn't supposed it mattered now. All that mattered was that I made damn sure that no innocent girl was ever treated as I had been again!

'Y-your tears...' Kohén was moving back further, and his adoring gaze was gone. 'You're... you're crying...' he looked stricken as he whispered the admission: 'Blood. Oh... oh God! Lark-what have I done-'

'The unforgivable!' I screamed, then lifted my hand and sent a flare across the air like a meteorite, hitting the base of the chandelier above him and making it swish and, tinkle and groan. Kohén looked up at it, paling further, as the little crystal cups in it began to slosh and then burst into flame as the kerosene was ignited, just as Satan had done at his sweet sixteenth ball. 'The unholy! The unthinkable! And there is no redemption for any of it, so burn in your love for me, Kohén Barachiel! *Writhe!* For it is the last heated touch you'll ever know!'

And then the chandelier fell from the ceiling and crashed on top of him, its heavy golden frame forming a cage around him now, and to make it clear how guilty I did *not* feel about it, I turned away before he'd started screaming, stabbed my delicate golden heel into Kohl's gut as I stomped over him, and laughed when I heard their identical screams rise behind me.

Better not let them die a slow death... I thought idly, trailing my fingers along the gold-leafed wallpaper along the corridor on my way out, and breathing in the smoke deeply as they ignited. *That would just be evil!*

'I knew you'd be able to do it!' a voice cried, not inside my head but from beside me as I passed a mirror. 'I prayed that you would, but my prayers haven't been answered for a very long-'

I whipped the mirror off the wall and let it shatter against the floor. I didn't need her help condemning myself or an audience-that was already done!

Now it was time to dance with the true devil.

28.

I heard the banging the moment I was within a few metres of the harem entrance, and although there were long cracks splitting the wooden surface of both double doors, I could see that they hadn't been successfully kicked in because clever, shrewd little Kohl had kicked down the door of the first rooms on either side, dragged out a long chaise lounge and then had wedged it between both entrances, holding it almost flush to the threshold. Clucking my tongue, I went into the first darkened room (why hadn't I gotten a velvet chaise? I would have loved reading on that!) and pushed the heavy daybed back across the corridor and into the left-hand side. I didn't move it all the way though, only half, and then stood back and let whoever was trying to gain entrance open it for me.

Boom! A crack of what sounded like thunder shook the walls a little and I gulped, too discombobulated to know if that had just come from one of the boys behind me, or from outside. Either way, I needed to get away from anyone that had the power to do that!

'You kick like a woman!' I taunted whoever was on the other side of the door, cupping my mouth with my hands to amplify it, and then grinned when a second later the doors burst open. The left handed door only moved a few inches, but the right-hand side came in so fast that it rebounded off the inner wall, blocking T'are's entrance as soon as he lowered his foot and attempted it. He looked flushed, shocked and then horrified when he saw me, and taking advantage of his bewilderment, I grasped the door and flung it back, then readied myself to burn off his eyebrows.

'Your wings!' he whispered, looking forlorn. 'I thought they were going to be white!'

It was like someone had hit me over the head with a house and I teetered back, gaping at him.

'*What?* You…?'

'Yes I knew!' he said quickly, glancing behind me and frowning when he heard and saw evidence of my battle with the Barachiels. 'You'd be surprised how many of us have been waiting to see your feathers at long last, Larkin Whittaker!' His gaze was now troubled as it slid back to me, and then assessed my wings again. 'I had anticipated white plumes, but the black ones are equal to white in loveliness, are they not? Lovely and well-earned, I suspect.'

'I don't know what you're talking about, but you need to get out of my way!' I cried, curling my fingers warningly, but the flames spluttered and went out as though someone had blown out birthday candles, and my heart skipped a fearful beat when I remembered what T'are could do. A translucent haze was swirling around him like a wind now and though it was not hurting me, I could not summon up my defensive heat in his presence. Another thunder crack sounded and now I knew that it had come from outside! I prayed that it was weather, but I doubted it.

'I thought you girls were trained to be well-mannered?' T'are asked, arching an eyebrow at me, and before I could move to dart past him, he stepped out of the way and lifted his arm, motioning me through. 'All you ever had to do to be free of this place was *ask* me to stand aside, my lady.'

I burst out of the room and into the little nook under the stairwell before whirling on him, shivering when I realised how drastically the temperature had decreased over those few feet. The heat from within the harem had been unbearable, and the contrasting chill in the corridor outside of it was almost as bad. 'What's that supposed to mean?' I hugged myself, rubbing my bare upper arms briskly to warm them. 'Are you saying that I wasn't really a prisoner here?'

'Not on my terms,' T'are said and I almost laughed. Or at least I would have if I weren't so busy sucking in lungful's of chilled, free air while trying not to cry.

'Well if you intended to let me pass, why didn't you just say it?' I demanded tearfully, lifting my skirts and wringing them onto the floor. 'I've been going out of my mind in there!'

'I was given my orders, and you yours,' he said, and I scowled at him, thinking that he and every other cryptic bastard in this castle could go to hell. 'But if you cast your mind back to only yesterday morning, you might recall that I urged you to leave before I realised that you had the duchess with you, and made no move to thwart your escape when Chérrine was begging you to leave with her.'

'Chérrine? *Cherry?*' My surprise knew no bounds. 'You were in cahoots?!'

He smiled. 'It's a little more complicated than that, Larkin Whittaker but yes, she's been doing as requested by the same person that has been instructing me on how to act for a very long time.'

'Satan?' I demanded, and his eyebrows rose in shock.

'What? *No!* Why would you even joke about that? I am a light Nephilim, Larkin, not dark! As *you* are!' He stepped forward, wiping a tear from my face and then looking down at the blood smeared on his fingertips after sadly. 'Well, as you will be again.' He looked back up at me. 'So long as you still have feathers, there is a chance that your soul will be saved-'

'Don't talk to me about saving me! It is the least of my concerns!' I was thrown to learn that there was someone else pulling strings on the palace's Nephilim employees, and had no time to stand there and debate right and wrong. 'Tell me who you have been taking your orders from, and why! Because if you intended to let me go free, it certainly isn't just Prince Kohén that you've been answering to, is it?' I wanted to bolt for it, but I knew I could not until I knew where it was that I ought to be going and where I needed to avoid going, so I took a moment to compose myself while I wrung as much water out of my multi-layered sheath skirt as I could. It was almost completely transparent now, and I wanted to rip if off and be free of its sudden weight, but I was only wearing my corset and panties beneath it so I didn't dare. I hated the fact that I was half-dressed, but the corset wasn't that much more revealing than the golden bodice had been so I made sure that I was tucked inside it as decently as possible and then decided not to care about what anyone thought.

'No. It wasn't just from Prince Kohén, and I suspect that I may never take orders from him again, by the looks of that place!' T'are stepped back up to the door of the harem and looked inside. 'What's going on in there? What *happened* to you?'

'The princes and I had a rather heated argument!' I spat, earning a smirk from him. 'One that I won, and must now disassociate myself from so tell me, what's going on out *here*?' I looked around the empty hall, puzzled by how normal everything seemed, only feet from where I had just created Hell on earth. I could see in the reflected glass of the front wall that there were hundreds of people in the throne room beside us, glittering in their costumes and chattering loud enough to be considered overwhelming. None of them would be able to see me on the other side of the wall given how dim this alcove was compared to the foyer, but with so many milling about, I knew it was only a matter of time before one of them peeked around the corner. Why weren't they in the ballroom where they belonged? 'Elijah was supposed to be back at eight on the dot with Karol-'

'The guests have been told to wait in the throne room until the threat has passed,' T'are said quickly. 'And I have been told to stand guard here- as per usual. First by Kohén then, the king.'

'What threat?' I asked, craning my neck to see if I could spot Ora, or Lindy. 'The Banished? I thought they'd been subdued already!'

'I don't think they'll ever be completely subdued, Miss Whittaker, not until they're satisfied.' He pointed down into the seldomly-used corridor behind us that led into the wing of servant's quarters beneath the Monarch's suite. 'The king came back a few minutes ago, found the doors barred and then dashed off in search of another way in. But then Amelia-Rose intercepted him and informed him that the Banished and the Sequestered started attacking the fence again and he has been out there since, trying to scare them off with repeated cracks of lightning while herding bands of my Nephilim associates and his guards together so that they could get the guests out of harm's way while barricading the castle.'

'Sequestered?' I spluttered. 'Who are The Sequestered?'

'They're the Banished, as far as the nobility are concerned,' T'are said, and his eyes darkened with anger. 'But they are something else entirely- and it is them that you must find your way to now!'

'What?' I demanded. 'No! I do not know them, and I cannot waste time getting to know them! This place owes me a debt or two and I must see them repaid!'

'I don't know exactly where they are-'

'But they're not upstairs?' I asked, pointing to the monarch's suite, knowing that I needed to find that pardon before I left, but that I could go for my contract- all of the third-born contracts- before I had to look for the king if the opportunity arose.

T'are frowned. 'I haven't seen anyone come past here for quite some time, but there's another entrance so either or both *could* be...' He pointed back towards the ball room. 'But as far as I know, Karol is in the ante-chamber off the ball room, recovering from the healing he had to perform, waiting for Kohén to fetch and present him while probably completely oblivious to all that is going on out here, and his highness is out on the lawn with both Sheps, Amelia-Rose and Prime-Minister Hartley, trying to get things under control.' He stepped forward, looking me over. 'Miss Whittaker... what was Prince Kohén wearing tonight?'

'Not what you thought he was wearing,' I said quickly, giving him a pointed look that made him grimace. He opened his mouth to start apologising but I held up my hands. 'Never mind all of that, what happened, *happened* and now we all must live with that- or die trying.' I pressed my hand to my forehead and looked down as I thought things through, before looking up at him again, curious. 'Regardless of the fact that the royal family is not home, I still need to call on them and fetch something that they have of mine...' I cocked my head. 'Are you attracted to women?'

His pale brows pulled together. 'Excuse me?'

I motioned to myself. 'If I needed to flirt my way into the crowned prince's office-'

'It would work on any red-blooded man with a key, Miss Whittaker,' T'are said quickly, smiling and blushing a little. 'But I do not have one, so it would be a pointless waste of your time. Like this one- it has bars running through it, so it's practically impenetrable without that key, even for me.'

'Define *practically* impenetrable?'

Another quick grin. 'Got an axe handy? Perhaps a battering ram?' He nodded towards the throne room. 'The power to make us invisible and silent so the entire bloody city doesn't come in here to see what the racket's all about while we use them?'

'Shit. No, I don't...' I looked upstairs again, wondering if I should just cut my losses and get the hell out of there. Who needed a piece of paper saying that I was *legally* free, if I was physically free already?

But I did need it- seeing that contract torn up was all I'd dreamed of since I'd turned thirteen and had learned what was to become of me due to it, and it was the only dream that I'd ever had that was still salvageable. Besides it wasn't just my contract I wanted to tear in half- but the other fourteen that were due to be released that night and probably would not be now, thanks to all of the mayhem I'd caused. My brand would limit me forever no matter what I did or where I went, but those contracts, I knew, could be broken by being lost or destroyed, and I intended to make that happen now no matter what it took, especially seeing as how I no longer had to worry about the consequences I'd have to face after for it.

'Where's the other entrance?' I asked, trying to remember if I'd seen a fire escape or anything upstairs leading down into the laundry rooms below. I knew I should just run back into the harem and slip one of the other's rings off, but the idea of going back in there... no. No I could not. I did not want to see what had become of them, and could not risk that Kohén or Kohl was still alive in there and looking for payback. 'Maybe I-'

'No! Miss Whittaker I'm sorry but if all you've said is true then you need to stop worrying about getting upstairs, and start worrying about getting over that fence!' T'are grasped me by the shoulders and rotated me so that I was facing into the deepest corner of the corridor where the servant's passage was. 'Get onto the lawn and run for it! Look for Chérrine or-' a massive crack exploded from behind him, and both he and I whirled to see a beam of lit timber fall through the roof of the harem and crash into the fog, smoke and darkness shrouding the floor, not far from where I'd left Kohl spluttering in a puddle of his own making. People in the room next to us began to scream, and when I heard one from within the harem- a female one- my heart faltered.

'Oh! That was Constance! If she's not dead I have to get back in there-'

'You won't be going in there ever again, my lady!' T'are shoved me roughly back and I smashed into the bust of Miguel Barachiel, knocking it onto the floor. He bowed. 'I mean no disrespect, but I have orders to guard you with my life and I *will* honour them!'

'I can't leave her to die!' I said, wincing at the split, marble head and wondering how expensive that had been. Damaging it had probably been more costly to my soul but as my feathers demonstrated, I was already in a grievous amount of debt as far as that was concerned anyway, and was running out of time to fix any of it.

'Why not? She's left you here to rot all these years!'

'No!' I surged forward again. 'No she is GOOD! She is Nephilim too, T'are, and she has been trying to help me! I left her with them, believing her dead at Kohl's hands, but if there is a chance that she can be-' I shrieked and ducked when a buzzing black cloud swarmed towards us, pulling T'are down too.

'Oh my God!' T'are crouched but craned his neck watching the cloud of insects swarm above us, wings clicking, stingers vibrating. 'Is that *her* doing?! The duchess is truly a Nephilim?'

'Yes! The locusts were too! But she is light, T'are! The plagues were her way of punishing Elijah for his treatment of- *oh*!' I spat and tuned my face as I copped a wasp in the forehead but it hadn't stung me, merely collided with me. T'are's energy swirled up as he gaped at the spectacle, and as though they'd hit an invisible wall, hundreds of insects- locusts, bees, wasps, mosquitoes and even dragonflies turned into dust that rained down upon us. I shrieked again as did he and scurried back under the little alcove that I'd sought solace in before, but the majority of the swarm had already cleared us and were arcing around the stairwell towards the throne room, and the last were still in sight when the screaming increased again. T'are and I looked at each other, panting and panicking, both knowing that pandemonium was about to break out!

'I'll go pull the duchess free if I am able! If you swear that she is good!' T'are began to pull me to my feet, wincing when he saw my brand. 'And then, I will meet you outside!'

'She is!' I swore, shaking the powder off and watching the remnants of the duchess's magic sparkle across the floor, like the gold in sand. 'Please T'are, even if she has perished, I beg you to bring her body out with you! Do not pause to assist Kohén or Kohl- they will not be able to stop you with your power, and are far too weak from the stings of the wasps to fight you with any human strength either!' I glanced into the harem, feeling a smidgen of my humanity creeping back in to think of Kohén burning alive in a golden cage. I sobbed. 'That is... that is if they are not dead already!'

'I'll go!' T'are did not turn to farewell me. 'But you must too! Run, Larkin! So much depends on you getting free of this place! Run and I will follow!'

'Fine!' I cried, even as my gaze flitted from the marble stand that Miguel's head had been on, to the innocuous-looking double doors above. If it was a battering ram I needed, then problem solved! 'But do not take orders from Kohl if he has recovered!' I called after his retreating figure, praying that he would survive this awful errand. 'He may be the true firstborn twin, but he committed regicide this night and-'

'What?!'

'Oh my God!'

I whirled and then retreated to see that Elijah and Amelia-Rose had entered through the servant passage while my back had been turned, and were now staring at me with astonishment. Well, Amelia-Rose was staring at me with astonishment- Elijah was falling to his knees, clutching at his heart. I looked after T'are, but he was already halfway along the corridor and being absorbed by the flickering shadows and I would not call him back if that meant that Constance would die. Surely I could handle these two alone?

'Kohl killed Constance?' The king looked grey and suddenly decades older as his face spasmed in anguish. 'No Larkin, no! *Why?*'

'Oh my goodness…' Amelia-Rose looked sick. 'You dressed as Satan? That's the most inappropriate costume I've ever seen! And Satan had black ringlets, not golden ones! How stupid are you? It was just an excuse to wear bloody tears and get around in lingerie wasn't it, you twisted little shrew?' She crossed her palms over her chest and lowered her head. 'Oh lord, please have mercy on this poor, damned girl…'

My mouth popped open. She thought I'd made myself look this way for ATTENTION? I scanned her, frowning to see that she'd dressed as a man or rather, in a tight-fitting costume that resembled a suit of armour, but with a stretchy fabric embellished by sparkling steel. She had a sword in one hand, and her long burgundy hair swept up into a harsh bun and only natural-coloured make up with a gleaming chrome eye mask. As Arial had mentioned earlier, she'd dressed in a way that suggested that she had not attempted to come off as attractive- not in the traditional sense anyway- and yet the costume was plastered to her every curve, showing how muscular her figure was, how wide her hips were and how prominent the gap between her thighs was. Child-bearing hips, that's what men called them, and the way she walked made it clear that she knew it. 'Who are you supposed to be?' I snarled. 'Joan Of Arc?'

Amelia-Rose's grey eyes flashed like thunderheads behind that mask. 'Yes, actually. A saint… as opposed to a sinner. An ensemble I'm sure, that *you* would not be able to pull off.'

'And one that none of the princes would be inspired to pull off you either,' I shook my head, smiling cruelly as he features hardened. 'Oh Amelia-Rose… how inept a predator you are! One cannot hunt royals with a sword- not in Eden anyway. The Barachiel men like their women submissive in skirts and screaming for mercy- not telling them what to do.'

'Larkin!' Elijah scrambled forward, tugging on my skirts as tears ran out of his eyes. 'Tell me what happened to Constance?'

I felt a flash of heat and kicked at his hands, snarling. 'She would not brand me! She was buying time for me to make my escape! When Kohén insisted on following through with your orders, he refused to let me escape with Kohl and so she branded *him* and screamed the truth- that he is not the next in line! That you lied about the order that they had arrived to the world in!' Elijah pressed his hands to his forehead and gaped at me from beneath him, cringing at every sentence I uttered as though each were a physical blow. 'She branded Kohén as a whore right over the heart and said that she'd find a way to make you release me because you no longer had a claim on me, and that Kohl would not inherit me, because new virgins would have to be groomed for his delayed gratification- an entitlement she was certain he would refuse, seeing how *good* and *kind* Kohl was!' My voice cracked. 'But Kohl threw her against a wall, shattered her bones, stole the brand from her hand and branded ME in her stead! He turned on me, then tried to convince Kohén to keep all that she had confessed a secret! Said that he would go on pretending to be the third-born, if only Kohén would agree to move to Pacifica with him and forge a home together there where they could share *me* behind closed doors! That way- they would both get what they deserved and desired, you see? And *your* respect!'

'No!' Elijah shook his head as Amelia-Rose gasped behind him. '*No!*'

'Yes!' I kicked at him again as he reached for me a second time, feeling my hatred mounting all over again. How dare he gasp and cry, over consequences that he had brought to pass? 'He barricaded the door and made Kohén drag the duchess's body into my room, so that they could shake on their deal by taking me together before you could come in! But you'd all forgotten about my allergy to gold, hadn't you? And so the brand was poisoning me as they conspired to rape me! I almost died as they tore at my gown, but apparently neither Constance or I are that easy to subdue, because we both fought back! Kohén tried to protest that he'd been deceiving Kohl and was just waiting for the moment to kill him, but she released a plague of wasps upon them-'

'What?' Amelia-Rose ripped the mask of her head. 'How?!'

'No! Not Constance-'

'Yes! It was always her and her plagues, Elijah! You ate away at her soul a little every day, so she did the same to your kingdom! Then, she attempted to destroy your evil sons when she overheard what they were planning to do with me, but Kohl drew a knife and stabbed her in the back and now they are *all* dying! And you- *you* should be in there dying with them!' I shook my head, disgusted as he began to cry. 'But I will not kill you and make Karol a king. I will not kill you and let you out of the guilt that must consume you this night!' I knelt before him. 'Give me that pardon for my friends now, Elijah and let me pass, or know that I will scream what has happened in here and to Martya-'

'I've already given it to them!' Elijah was sobbing as he tried to sit up on his haunches. He ripped his hat off his head and then stuffed his hands into his pockets, pulling out the lining so that I could see that they were empty except for a handkerchief and Karol's folded letter to me as his gaze shifted from my face to my wings and back again apprehensively. I knew that he understood that they were not fake, because unlike Amelia-Rose, he had seen the golden costume ones before and unlike Amelia-Rose, *he* had learned not to underestimate my potential a long time ago, so I smirked at him as I swiped Karol's letter and shoved it into my corset. I was gladdened to see that fear in his eyes again, but hesitant to believe that he had finally done one thing right by me so I stared hard back at him to see if he would crumble further. 'It's true!' he insisted, sniffling, and it pleased me to finally see him loose tears and break a cardinal rule. 'I saw them waiting out here, the guard can attest to that-'

'What are you two talking about?' Amelia-Rose demanded. 'What pardon? What *friends*? Your highness, don't tell me that you've struck some kind of bargain with this sinner? You are *supposed* to be a man of God!'

'You are supposed to be cowering in the throne room with the rest of the useless, greedy, social-climbing young ladies here, not riding me child!' Elijah barked at her in a vitriolic voice, and she recoiled. 'Every time I turn around, there you are trying to tell me how to run my kingdom and I have been tolerant as I can be because I respect your father, but I have lost respect for him over these past few days after seeing the wretched pain in the ass that he's raised and will abide your nagging not a moment longer!'

'As opposed to *your* perfect sons?' Amelia-Rose demanded, looking stunned. 'What are they good for, except for sniffing after this whore? Kohl's the only one with a backbone, and it sounds like even that had been splintered due to his lust over this trash now!'

'*Trash*?' I sprung at Amelia-Rose quickly, shoving her hard backwards so that she fell onto her backside. She tried to get up but I lifted my hand and sent a fireball bursting into the ground between her open knees. She screamed and retracted quickly, fumbling for her sword but I advanced further and she held up her hands. Beside her on the ground, Elijah's eyes bugged at the sight of the fireball, then swept to me and widened further. 'I'd like to see that tongue of yours blistered, Amelia-Rose, so if you part your lips on the subject of my character or appearance again, I will stuff it with fire you jealous cow!'

'Stop!' Amelia sobbed, shaking her head and holding up her hands. 'I won't fight a demon, I won't lower myself to that!' She bowed her head in another prayer. 'Oh Lord, please save me from-'

'Oh Christ- if you do that again I will set you on fire, you religious fiend!' I turned back to Elijah, heart pounding while she spluttered in offence. 'You swear to God that you gave them that pardon?'

'I swear to God, they have it on them!' he swallowed hard. 'The Trevasse's were obviously disconcerted to wonder why they were suddenly in need of one, but they took it gratefully, embraced me and then they went to wait for you with your other friends, all believing that you were about to join them! I went looking for Karol so that I could rush him back to help you heal, but Ora told me that he'd gone off somewhere to wait for Kohén to retrieve him, and then I heard the people outside and-' he hiccupped, looking towards the open harem door. Flames taller than me were leaping about in there now. 'Constance! I have to get to her!'

I held him down. 'You cannot! If Kohl has not perished then I fear what he will do to you, Elijah- and you should fear it too! Let T'are salvage her if he can, then take Saint Choir here out to the ballroom and protect your people from those invading the castle! It is the only good you can do, and all that I will allow you to do!'

'I will not fight you, I swear it! And for the millionth time: I did not hurt Martya! I have never taken a human life and until tonight, my sons have never hurt a fly either, so it wasn't them!'

'That you know of!' I sneered. 'But I've seen them kill another whore, Elijah and when you bury the bodies of your loved ones in the near future I urge you to bury Kohén and Kohl right beside Kelia! For the three of them belong together!'

Elijah clutched at his heart as his face constricted. 'They *killed* her? *My* boys?'

'To keep their secrets!' I shook my head, relieved to have my last secret out at last. Now, I could die unburdened by lies! 'So forgive me, or don't- but I'll not believe you innocent of Martya's murder until I cross into the afterlife and hear what happened from her with my own ears!' I sobbed, and my blackened wings shivered. 'Or would, if my life here hadn't damned me so!'

'You'll get into Heaven, Larkin! You have years to purify yourself left ahead of you, I swear it!' Elijah handed me the handkerchief despite the fact that he was the one weeping brokenly. 'Dry your eyes child, then tell me everything you want me to do to make amends for all of this and I swear to God that I will make you my daughter to honour my sweet- *arggghhh!*' His eyes bugged then and he let rip a scream of agony. I'd been kneeling down to stare him in the face, but now I looked up as I heard Amelia-Rose cry out in triumph as she ran the King through with her sword, which was apparently no more a mere accessory than my wings were.

'Weak piece of FILTH!' the pious young warrior hissed, eyes gleaming with malice as she withdrew the sword- and then plunged it in again. 'The lord would be ashamed of you for cowering before a demon so!'

Elijah's eyes locked on mine, and despite how much I had hated him for so long, seeing the brightness in those eyes flicker and fade away crushed me. I screamed and sank to my knees, catching his head before his face could hit the ground.

'C-Constance...' he spluttered, as his eyes rolled to the back of his head. 'My sweet...Constance...'and then blood dribbled out of the corner of his moth, and his head bowed to me.

Bowed, and stayed lowered. The king of Arcadia was dead! And damn him and the humanity that Constance's scream had evoked within me again, but I felt his loss like a punch to the heart. Snarling in outrage, I jerked up my head to glower at Amelia-Rose, and then stiffened when I felt the fire blare from me again, hitting her in the hand and hip and causing her to drop her sword and scream like Satan was after her.

'Help!' she shrieked, kicking the sword towards me so that it clattered into the wall by my right hand, spraying blood everywhere- including over my right arm, while I panted and tried to wet my mouth with saliva again. 'Help!' Amelia-Rose turned on her heel and run out into the ballroom. 'King Elijah has been slain by that whore! She knocked me down, took my sword and stabbed him! *Help!*'

I blinked, rising like a lion about to pounce, floored that she would tell such a lie- and so quickly! This was Calliel's saint? No wonder we were all fucked!

'Help! The whore has attacked the entire royal family!' Amelia Rose's boots squeaked against the floor as she barrelled out of the corridor, leaving me alone with the slain king. 'She may have killed them all!'

Amelia-Rose continued to scream as she vanished from sight, but she'd only been gone for a heartbeat before other screams joined her in chorus, and my heart fluttered as I realised that soon *I* would be hunted again!

She's killed the only witness here! I realised, my panic mounting as I looked from the bloody sword, to the fallen king. *And if Constance is dead too, then there won't be a soul in*

Acadia that will be able to vouch that anything I've done was in self-defence except for T'are, and he didn't actually see anything! Oh god! I have to get out of here!

'She is dark Nephilim!' Amelia-Rose went on, doing a convincing job of acting hysterical. 'She threw fire at me- the same fire she's used to burn the harem and all within it, someone *help me*! She must be stopped! Where is the crowned prince? He is our king now!'

Those words shocked me into action. I'd gotten out from beneath the king so now I bent down and gently kissed him on the top of his sweaty head, sobbing. My feelings for him were complex at best and loathsome at worst... but some of the good in him had encouraged the growth of some of the good in me, as it had with Kohén, and I would farewell him the way that I had not farewelled his son.

What are our enemies anyway, if not those who push us harder to be better than anyone that loves us ever could?

I sniffled again as I knelt awkwardly in my soggy skirts and took his hand in mine, squeezing it gently once before grasping his ring with shivering, heated fingertips and beginning to work it over his pronounced knuckle. Once it was loose enough I pulled it free, grimacing when his limp arm fell back to the ground with a lifeless *plop* after. Taking his ring was going to make me look even more guilty of his murder if I was caught, but I was already too far beyond help anyway and had no intention of getting caught much less trialled for anything by a shepherd, so I took it, telling myself that if he'd loved Constance as he'd claimed to with his final breath, then he would want me to have it.

'Goodbye, your highness,' I whispered to the king as I stood and then stepped over him and onto the stairs, headed up towards the monarch's wing where my contract was supposed to be. 'Thank you for the garden, if nothing else.'

And then I began to race up the stairs, no battering ram required.

29.

Every step I took up that flight of stairs squelched as the water ran out of my skirts, into my shoes and down the staircase behind me, but I held the railing with a heated hand and the ring in the other as I hurried up them, knowing that I only had seconds to vanish behind the door before people, drawn by Amelia-Rose's cries, would come flying around the corner and spot me making what would look like a hasty, guilty retreat.

I will be free soon, free! If only in name, and if only of this world! Just a few steps more, just one goal left to attain...

I reached the topmost landing, fiddled with the key until the prongs of the wings lined up with the odd little gashes in the steel lock (how did Kohén and Elijah do this so quickly?) and finally heard the lock click and twist. I pushed the door open as gently as I could, closed it behind me and immediately found myself staring into Kohén's open bedroom doorway. It had been tidy the last time I'd seen it but there were clothes scattered everywhere now, and though I knew I shouldn't, I hurried in there, scooped them up and walked them over to the laundry chute, bending my head briefly to inhale them, letting his scent tickle my nostrils and fill my being with a bit of light. It was a strange thing to do and I was aware of that, but for better or worse, Kohén had loved me in the best way that he could and I had killed him for it, and I had done so in such a way that I'd deprived myself of any closure on the matter too. But I needed that closure, and desperately. How could I farewell the world without fare-welling my home?

And yes, the only home I'd ever had, had been in Kohén's arms.

It didn't have to be like this! I thought, pausing briefly to look out the window, down to the roof of the harem burning below me. *If he'd seen me as an equal, we would have made memories in here one day, instead of in that harem! Oh Kohén.... if only you'd fought as hard to free me as you had to love me! We could have made Heaven on earth together, instead of raising Hell this night!!*

Suddenly overcome with regret- not for what I had done but for what all of the Barachiel's had done to bring us to this point- I pressed my face against the warming glass of the window and wept gently. I recalled Kohén's delight when he'd read my PCE scores, Kohén chasing me into the snow that day and swearing to me that he would never cross the line that would lead to me being trapped, Kohén's face when he saw me ready for his ball... Kohén's heart pounding when he slid himself into me the first time...Kohén's face when he'd begged me in Pacifica to do nothing but return his affections. Kohén Kohén, Kohén... my life was naught but a stream of recollections of him reacting to me, just as his life had ended up being a collection of moments framed on his bedroom wall.

'But I love you so much Larkin- I need to know that we are together on this! I cannot focus on rewriting laws over my conviction alone!'

Oh, how right he'd been that night on Caldera island, but too late! Even *then,* it had been too late because I'd already started to fall for the twin that I'd assumed to be his better and *why*? Because Kohl had never had the chance to prove what kind of royal he would be, and Kohén never the chance to prove how he'd fare with *less*! Their faces had been so alike so it had been easy to transfer such affection... but I knew now that even though Kohl had always said the right things, Kohén's eyes had always been brighter with love, darker with lust... and never as hard or soulless as Kohl's had become that night. And the eyes truly were the windows to the soul.

I could have stayed there all night crying and raging at them in my mind, but I knew that the time I was wasting could be the difference between the sweet relief of death- and another epoch of imprisonment and torture for me, so with a shuddering sigh, I walked back out into the hall and paused by the mirror there. I raised my eyes to meet my reflection and gasped, taking Elijah's handkerchief out of my bodice and immediately dabbing at my tears. I looked a fright! My make-up was still on but it had become streaked with pink beneath my eyes, so I wiped it gently away, and then firmly smudged the defining line at the bottom of the painted mask right across my face, leaving the upper half of it intact until it looked like it had been made to blend into my cheeks, not scrubbed off to hide the blood. My lips were still stained with colour but the gloss had been licked off my face thanks to Kohl (and the fire-breathing trick probably had not helped), so I wet them to give them a supple appearance again, and then scrubbed at the streaks of blood that had run down the rest of my face until I looked, well, less like a murderer and more like a swan again. A black swan, thanks to the wings, but I didn't know how to make them go away and wasn't sure that I wanted to so I shook them off and prayed that they would help me escape, not impede my chances of escaping. When that had been done, I started wiping Elijah's blood splatters off my arm.

I'll get the contracts if they're in there, tear them all in half, leave half of mine behind so they'll understand, smash a window and fly out of this place! I vowed. *I don't know how to fly, mind you, and if I'm too wet and heavy to, but if I fall well, that will just be a short cut, won't it?*

Once that was done I stood up taller, sniffled (thank goodness the blood didn't run out of my nose too!) and adjusted my corset, glad that it was still wet because it made the stains left by a few stray tears easier to rub into the gauzy, dark gold fabric. My ringlets had been tugged on and sweated beneath so much that they had dropped considerably, but the top of my hair still looked almost as perfectly coiffed as it had before so I ran my fingers through the lengths until they resembled natural waves. Then finally, I lifted my skirts, wringing them out firmly a few times until they stopped dripping so but had left a considerable puddle on the ground. I didn't look as polished and ethereal as I had in the spa earlier once I'd finished primping, but someone would have to look awfully hard at me under bright lights to realise that I'd been through a branding, an electrical storm, a flash flood AND a flash fire as well as half-stripped and molested while people were stabbed to death around me, and that was all I asked for- the ability to participate in a masquerade should I come upon a crowd on my way out of Eden.

Certain that I was as presentable as humanly possible under the circumstances (weren't all the frantic ladies downstairs going to look sweaty, flushed and wild-eyed anyway due to the Banished threat as well?) I closed my eyes, held onto the end table in front of the mirror and took in a deep, full breath before exhaling it slowly, counting to ten as I did. Not only did that give me the chance to slow my breathing and rapidly pounding heart, but it chased a bit of the heat away from my face, staved off my tears and gave me enough time to listen to the rooms around me, ascertaining that I truly was alone up there, and noting that it didn't sound like anyone was racing up the stairs after me.

And why would they? What fugitive in their right mind would run upstairs into the devil's lair, when the exit from the palace had been only five metres away from where I'd stabbed the king? Besides, even if they did come after me they'd need a key to get in, and the only other keys that accessed these rooms were on the hands of the corpses inside the harem, or the cleaning staff who left the castle at two in the afternoon.

You can do this! I told myself, breathing in deeply again as I reached back and tested that the lock on the front door had slid shut behind me. *You're not here, you're an insignificant silhouette on the wall. Creep in, creep out, and don't make a sound!*

Nodding, I opened my eyes, pulled up taller, and gasped when, after a rustle and a surge of warmth, I felt the pressure in my back dissipate. I looked at the mirror again, and was astonished to see just a regular girl standing there again. My wings- they'd vanished! Fearing the worst I twisted and surveyed the floor beneath me, worried that they'd disintegrated the way Satan's had in the Six Books Of Creation, but to my relief only one stray feather had fallen into the floor. I reached behind me, touched my back and smiled when I felt my skin smooth and even, and now free of that heavy ache. They'd not vanished, they'd withdrawn and now I would be that much less conspicuous for it. I wish I knew how I'd managed it, but I supposed that most of it had been an act of will- flight or fight reflex, perhaps, and I made a mental note to breathe deep and imagine them unfurling or vanishing the next time that I had cause to use them as I walked down the hall, to Karol's room with a growing sense of intimidation.

Oh god the last time I sought his room out, it ruined my life! I thought as I tiptoed down the hall, wincing every time one of my high heels squelched with the water that had soaked into the soles. *I must be crazy to be going back in there again!*

But I wasn't crazy, not anymore. I'd bypassed crazy in that harem when Kohl had branded me, and had moved onto something else entirely. How clear my thoughts were now! How deep and even my breathing, and how composed my nervous system! There were the usual ticks of course: trembling hands and an accelerated heart rate, but releasing that original fiery breath had cleansed me somehow and now everything seemed more vibrant to my suddenly alert mind. I could smell the scent of three separate colognes as I passed the bedrooms: Constance's, Elijah's and Karol's. They'd all sprayed themselves with the doors open and now their scents mingled in the hallway, leading my nose to the right room and confirming what my feet already knew.

The corridor was long and dark, and passing the living quarters on the way through almost set me off on another crying jag (how lonely this suite would feel tomorrow!) but soon enough I was at Karol's door and breathing harder. It was slightly ajar, but it was dark and silent beyond that so I exhaled low and slowly again and inched in, thanking Satan for the well-maintained hinges, which did not creak or squeak despite the fact that I knew that this wing of the castle had been built three hundred years before when the castle had gone from being one long, rectangular structure, to a cross. Ironically, the harem had been built before the monarchy had upgraded their own quarters, which gave one pause for thought- and a disgusted shake of the head.

And now it's burning! I thought, and my contemptuous expression morphed into a grin as I quietly closed the door behind me. I still didn't know how I felt about all of the karma that had just backwashed the Barachiel family, but I felt damned good about reducing that harem to coal! Never again would a

Companion have to endure a tour of the premises on her thirteenth birthday, and told that by moving in there, she was becoming part of Eden's long, rich and beautiful history!

It took my eyes a moment to adjust to the darkness in the room, but I'd remembered that Karol's desk was directly across from the door and so I crossed the room stealthily, my heart rate picking up again as I surveyed the blurred stacks of books and papers on the desk and tried to recall what the contracts had looked like! I knew that mine had been rolled up in a scroll after I'd signed it, but would it still be in that form now? Or would Karol have already un-rolled them in order to speed the process of releasing fourteen people up so he'd plenty of time to screw me, rinse off, and then go downstairs to get engaged? My fingers touched and brushed against paper that felt too new or too flimsy or too small until I touched the thick kind of parchment that Cadence Verity's book had been originally printed on. That was more like it! Paper that had been built to last for at least twenty-one years, if not considerably longer! Paper that five year-old Larkin had been told was precious and difficult to destroy.

Bingo! I thought, echoing the word that Satan had put into my mind just a few days before. *Now, where's a light? I need to know if Karol was stupid enough to leave mine out with the others, or if I'll have to hunt to find the ones that are intended to be kept locked away for years yet?*

I heard a door click open then and whirled around in fright, but the door I'd come in through was still closed and so for a beat I just stood there, a smile creeping across my face despite the fact that my heart was pounding, thinking that I'd left it open behind me, and that a wind had simply blown it shut.

'*Jesus*,' I whispered, turning back to the desk and reaching for what looked like the outline of a lamp that was similar to mine. 'Talk about-'

'It's Prince Karol, actually,' a deep voice said from my right and I squeaked, flinching from toe to eyebrow when a large shadow loomed up beside me. 'But as far as trespassers are concerned I am judge, jury and executioner so-' the light clicked on and Karol stopped talking like he'd flipped the switch to his brain. For one awful second we just gaped at each other in mutual astonishment, before we both moved- me pulling back while he tightened his grip on my wrist and yanking me towards him as he cried: 'Larkin? Oh my-' he broke off to whistle, eyes dropping to the tip of my shoes so that they could slide back up at a leisurely pace. 'Where's the rest of your gown?' He lifted his eyes to mine, and moved to touch my face. 'It's hard enough to think straight around you as it let alone-'

'Let me go!' I shrieked, cutting him off by sending a closed-fist strike into his lower jaw so hard that it hurt my hands and literally knocked the odd hat that he was wearing off of his head.

'*What* the...!' He released my hand as he moved to touch his bright-red cheek and I dove for the pile of parchments on the desk, scrambling to gather them all up into my arms before he could regain his composure. 'Larkin, wait, I'm sorry I should have known better than to say such a-' he tried to push off his desk to straighten but palmed a stack of books instead and sent them skittering under his weight as he cursed under his breath. 'Dammit!' he regained his balance and touched his face gingerly as he glowered at me. 'How did you get in here?' he winced, rubbing the pad of his thumb under the corner of his lip and inspecting it for blood. 'And more importantly, how many times are you going to clock me before I remember to keep a guard up around you?'

'As many as required!' I spat out as I surveyed the room for a window that I could exit through. There was just one large one behind his desk, and getting to it would be difficult. 'Grab me again, and you'll be in need of a fleet of healers to cure what ails *you*, your highness!' I glanced to the door that he'd entered through and saw by the tiled wall and basin within that it led to a more personal kind of throne room- an en-suite, and most likely dead-end. Realising that I was cornered, I began to back up the way I'd come, cursing when I felt the stack of heavy papers in my arms tilt and then began to spill across the floor.

'Larkin-'

'I mean it!' I cried, ducking quickly as I attempted to grab the papers that had fallen. It would be just my luck to leave my own on the floor behind me! 'Not if you value your bone structure at all, and I know that you do, you vain bastard!'

'You speak as though *I* am the violent one-'

'You are!' I got the final paper and began to scramble back with it. 'I've seen the dungeon room- I've seen your whips and crops and manacles and-'

'Have you seen *this*?' Karol asked, and I looked up at him, frowning when I saw that he had crouched across from me, and was now tapping a scroll in his hand that he'd pulled from a trunk on the floor near his feet. 'I mean, I assume that this is what you've come for, yes? Your freedom?' he wriggled his eyebrows, then used the scroll to motion to the papers in my hands. 'Unless of course, you're desperate to know how to make an authentic Asianic red curry?'

Something cold slithered around inside my abdomen again, and I looked from the scroll in his hand, to the papers in mine. I dropped my eyes and read the words: '*Lobster bisque,*' and felt my heart sink. 'What...?'

'Those are a collection of recipes that Shep Choir has amassed during his travels,' Karol said, standing up casually and adjusting the foreign-looking suit jacket that he was wearing, drawing my attention to two things at once: I was fucked, *again*, and he looked incredible.

Wearing a tightly-fitted, dark blue suit embellished with gold buttons, trim and a red sash around his lean waist he was a tall, dark and handsome drink of water. And that cunning 'I have you now!' smile was as disarming as it always had been, despite the fact that a good part of his face was hidden behind a dark blue velvet masquerade mask. I didn't know what or who he was supposed to be, but he wore it well, and the sword slung through a sheath at his side was keeping me in check. A sword wasn't a match for my fire, but I wouldn't be playing that hand until I knew that I had no other choice. I looked from him to the sealed scroll and felt my knees weaken for two good reasons.

'*No,*' I whispered, feeling the tears welling behind my eyes again. That was my contract he had in his hand, I knew it! If I'd had just twenty seconds more-

'Yes.' Karol casually picked up his hat and popped it back on top of his head again, tilting it at a jaunty angle while smoothing his sash. Was it my imagination, or was he watching me watch him with expectation in his sparkling green eyes? Was I supposed to compliment his outfit? Ask who the designer was? He was mad to think that I'd care about such things at a time like this, and when I just stared hatefully at him, he sighed and went on, posture dropping a little. 'Mother had one of them cooked up at his insistence last night and now considers him to be a man of great taste. She asked for all of the recipes that he has on him, and I was copying them into a book for her from his originals before he departs in the morning,' he pointed to the desk and I turned to see a notebook open to a hand-written recipe for chowder that he must have painstakingly transcribed already. 'But I've been a busy little bee today- making grand preparations, saving lives... you know... all standard responsibilities for a man like me...' he paused to wink while I rolled my eyes, 'so I haven't finished the bisque one yet.' He cleared his throat and chanced a step forward. 'Now I can see that you're very angry with me for some reason right now, and I'm sure I'll understand why once you expand upon it- but Shep Choir will be quite upset if I lose his copies, so if you don't mind...' he raised his eyebrows, then inclined his head to his desk again.

I sighed, stepped forward and replaced the pile of papers onto his desk, praying that Constance would survive and get to enjoy that bisque someday. 'Of course,' I said softly, wondering what the hell to do from here. Fight? Flirt? Flee? He obviously didn't have an inkling about the calamities taking place downstairs and although that was throwing me off, it also gave me more control over the whole situation, allowing me to set the tone- I just didn't know which to pick!

'Thank you.' I heard her Karol sigh and then step forward, and I instinctively stepped back, hugging myself. 'Larkin, can you please stop glaring at me like I'm a common criminal because I rudely interrupted your ransacking of my private chamber and just tell me: what on earth are you doing in here?'

383

'Stealing my contract back,' I said flatly, deciding that treating him as I always had would suffice for now. 'I thought that was obvious?'

He snorted, but his eyes hardened immediately after as he shook his head. '*Why?* You don't have to steal anything from me. I told you I'd tear up your contract tonight if you came to me and I *meant* it.' He wet his lips and then ventured. 'I assume that's why you're here, isn't it? Because you got my letter?' he stepped closer. 'How did you manage to shake off Kohén?'

I couldn't bring myself to think about the answers for those questions, so I rewound the conversation to a better starting place. 'Has it escaped your notice that my contract is out of your hands now, Prince Karol? Kohén has had me, and no longer needs that contract to keep me here.'

Karol winced. 'You make it sound as romantic as I assumed it had been.' He stepped closer, studying my expression while his remained unreadable due to that mask. '*Is* that what he did, Larkin? Did he have you... or did he *take* you?'

I swallowed hard. 'You suspect that I was raped, too?'

'I wouldn't use the word *raped...*' he said, looking distinctly uncomfortable. 'But I've spent every spare second this week plotting his demise for laying a finger on you and-'

'Of course you wouldn't use *that* word!' I hissed. 'Coerced, right? *That's* the word you're searching for? Or perhaps you believe I was black-mailed, yes? Guilt tripped even? All things that sweet, lovesick little Kohén could easily be suspected of doing! But not *raped*- that word is too ugly, your souls too pristine, and my free will a moot point, so rape couldn't possibly apply in this situation, could it?' I could feel that furnace inside me heating up again, flooding my blood with heat and rage. 'Well rest your shrivelled-up conscience, your highness, because *no* Kohén did not rape me on Tuesday night! The word that articulates what happened is *tricked,* okay? I was *tricked* into giving my virginity away-'

'Then why didn't you-'

'Because I had to! Because of the contract! Because Kohl's feelings for me and my empathy for him put his life on the line, just like the freedom of the people whose contracts you are standing in front of now is dependent on me keeping a clear head! I couldn't run, I couldn't scream- all I could do was sit there and try to convince myself that I deserved to end up exactly where I was, and I did such a grand job of convincing Kohén and my stupid, drunken, heartsick self that I was coming to terms with all of it, that Kohén didn't even *have* to rape me to get what he needed from me!' I cackled. 'Well, not until half an hour ago when he and Kohl decided to brand me and claim me in the name of Barachiel... *twice!*'

Karol tore the mask away from his eyes, and all at once I saw that they were awash with confusion and horror. '*What?* They did *what* to you?' he looked at my brand, pressed his hand to his chest and then balled it, turning around to smash the lamp off the desk. 'No! I'll kill them!' The lamp went flying across the room with a muted clunk that was softened by the thick carpet, and I winced, wondering how many people are arguing was going to draw up here. The bulb didn't go out, but it rolled a few times, casting odd shadows about that danced along to the beat of Karol's supposed outrage. 'No wonder he kept me away from you as he did!' he raged on. 'Blissfully happy, I was told you were. Afraid to come near me, for fear that *I* would berate you for turning down my offer, *ha*! Lying, sneaking little shit! Cherry told me that you swore that you were-'

'Bullshit!' I cried as Karol took off towards the door, switched on the overhead light and then stomped over to a timber armoire in the corner. There was stuff everywhere: suitcases, open books, discarded clothes and a disassembled gun, but the rifle that he pulled out of the cupboard after punching his key into the lock looked functional enough to make me step back a few paces more. 'They didn't do anything that you wouldn't have done yourself, if not given the opportunity to bypass consent and get straight on with it!' I pointed out. 'Why do you think I passed along messages with your biggest fans for you to you to leave me be? I'd already been used once, I wasn't about to let you near me to claim me too!

He had the gall to look wounded as he turned around and pumped the weapon once. 'You still believe that I'd rape you?'

he charged towards me, saw the way that I shrank back from the weapon and quickly rested it against the desk before coming at me with only the scroll in hand. 'Larkin-'

'If you did not believe you already had your consent to have me- or take me- or whatever the fuck else you expect to do to claim me *yes*, I do!' I wanted to open the door and flee as he closed in on me, but he still had the scroll in his hand, so if I was ever going to get the chance to snatch it, then it was approaching me now and I couldn't allow my fear of this man to override my determination to be free of his kingdom in every sense of the word. 'And if you want me to believe otherwise you can tear up that-' my rant came to a screeching halt as Karol hastily tore open the wax seal on the scroll, held it up so that I could see my name printed in calligraphy and then signed under in juvenile, sloppy attempt at a signature- and then ripped in in two.

'Wish granted!' he whispered, slamming his hands to the wall on either side of me, catching me off-guard and caging me in while I'd been gaping down at my contract. 'Now, it's *your* turn to make my dreams come true.'

30.

I sucked in a breath when I felt my back hit the cool wall, not knowing what to think or say. Karol had done as he'd promised- he'd voided my contract before making me return the favour! I should have been elated- I was free! And yet, I was in his arms, and he seemed pretty certain of the fact that I was going to stay there... *why?*

Because he wanted you to come to him when you were free, remember? This was never about cornering you, this was about earning your desire and gratitude! He thinks he has done so and now expects that you will respond with lust! And when he realises that you will not...

My eyes strayed to the gun and my abdomen clenched tightly. I'd read so many books about guns- books that other citizen had never even seen- but had never seen one used before. How fitting that I was now likely to be killed by one!

'Karol...' I wet my lips and looked towards the door, wondering how long I had left before someone charged through it. 'There's something you should know-'

'No, there's something that *you* should know,' Karol moaned and leaned in kissing my upper lip gently as he pressed more heavily into me and the wall. I was a statue- afraid to move or breathe- and terrified that at any moment I'd crack straight down the middle, like Miguel Barachiel's marble head. 'I can't get you out of my head! I've tried Larkin, so help me God I've tried...all week I've tried to convince myself that I'd lost my chance with you...' he bent his face and slowly pressed his parted lips against my lower one now, making me hold my breath. He hummed at the whisper-soft contact, and when my heart skipped a beat I told myself it was fear even though I suspected that there was a lot of anticipation in there as well. If it had been Kohén, he would have been kissing me madly already, trying to force the connection to suit his own urgency and if it had been Kohl, well, I couldn't bear to reflect on *that*... and yet Karol kept the kiss tentative despite the fact that his shallow breathing demonstrated that he wanted me a lot more than he'd ever actually let on.

Controlled, but shaking as he struggled to stay that way, Karol slowly lifted his mouth and caressed my top lip with both of his again, before parting his lips further to make the barely-there contact a little more balanced. I whimpered when I heard him draw in a ragged breath and slowly slide his hands down the wall, straightening a little as he did, leaning more into me before gently suckling on my lower lip and the pulling back to stare into my eyes with his brilliant green ones. 'But I cannot even *conceive* of staying away from you, let alone seeing it through. I know you don't want me…' he gently touched my upper lip with his again, and my fingertips curled into the wall as I felt my temperature spike. 'I know you don't need me…' the bottom lip was caressed again, oh God I was *panting!* I turned my face up to the ceiling and trembled when he tilted his head so that he gently kissed the outer corner of my lip, and though I'd been confused when Kohén had tried to delicately explain what made the girls come out of the dungeon room with Karol with smiles on their faces, I got it now! Lord, if he could draw out a *kiss* for this long, what would he do to the core of a woman if he taunted her sex with his barely there touches so? Goosebumps exploded across my skin- the first I'd felt in a while, and as though he sensed them, Karol went in for the kill:

'But I know that I need you. I'm in love with you, Larkin,' he finished huskily, finally sliding his arms around me as he straightened to tower over me. 'And I will do whatever it takes to make you love me in return.'

No! My brain cried in shock. *No, no, NO! Anything but that!*

'You-' but he kissed me before I could come up with a fitting string of nasty adjectives, and my gasp of surprise made it an easy victory for him. It wasn't really surprise that had me sucking in air so violently- more like un-adulterated horror- but Karol did not understand that (or wasn't going to try to) and so he slanted his mouth over mine as he enfolded me in his arms and crushed me against him, infusing me with his healing energy and making my muscles melt in relief while my brain screamed in horror.

No! I thought again, grabbing at him as I tried to wrestle myself free. No I could handle his sarcasm and contempt and lewd flirtations, but not his love! *He promised me he'd never throw his heart at me- he swore it! He swore he was too cold hearted to love anybody! And yet...*

The crowned prince was strong, I'd always known that, but I'd underestimated just how strong his power was and found myself melded to him before I could cry out. His kiss was smooth and controlled and overwhelming that my mouth moved back against his in reflex, and when his tongue tangled around mine, my indignant flush became an evanescent heat that made my knees buckle.

He's manipulating you! My mind screamed at me. *He's a healer- he's lulled you into compliance! You must break his hold!*

But I couldn't lift a hand against him. Karol moaned against my mouth and clutched a fistful of my hair, drawing me nearer but there was no way that we could get closer than we already were, so he lifted my knee around his waist and ground me into the wall while he began to kiss me more deeply, cupping my jaw and head now, holding me still for the lusty assault.

I could have done this... I realised, shocked by it. *If I'd had to go to bed with this firstborn prince to get free, it wouldn't have been so bad... better than getting licked all over the face by the second-born anyway...*

'Yes!' he whispered huskily against my mouth as he paused to pant and then slipped his tongue into my mouth again before gently touching his lips to mine once more. He panted, staring at me through those emerald eyes and thick black lashes that were lowered in lust. 'I knew it... I knew it...' he traced my brow with a fingertip, his expression conflicted. 'Larkin, forgive me for denying what I always knew!' And then he caught my lips with his once more and I wilted.

I can only plead shock for the fact that that kiss lasted five seconds instead of half of one before my hate for him overwhelmed my stupefaction, and cannot expect anyone to understand why I did not bite off his tongue any better than I can explain it to myself now, all of these years later. All I *can* say is that natural healing powers aside- that kiss may have just been the most physically perfect moment that I'd experienced in my life, up until then. As powerful even as my first kiss with Kohén had been despite the fact there was no sentimentality or attraction arousing me prior to it. Kohl had proven to be a clumsy lover, Kohén and I had come together as easily as breathing- but Karol had the passion and the experience to kiss me stupid and yet somehow make me feel as though I were the overwhelming *him*. Like a ballerina might light up from within after she executes a perfect pirouette, or an artist might finish a painting with a single brushstroke that brings all of those that had come before it to life- that kiss was the epitome of lust, chemistry and desire- a chemically perfect manifestation of all things regarding attraction- and I could not have stopped it from happening any more than I could have slowed an incoming tide.

But, like a meteor crashing to earth, a memory of the last time we'd been in here- and the last words we'd exchanged- smacked into me hard and ignited my hate and fear all over again just as I felt Karol harden against me and press me more purposefully against the wall- taking my hand in his and clenching it tightly before pinning it above my shoulder. That wasn't just a move- it was a declaration of possessiveness, and my blood boiled as my claustrophobia was triggered all over again.

'What are you going to do if I fall in love with you and try to prevent you from leaving?' Karol had asked, and I'd smiled sweetly.

'Probably kill you like I would Kohén.'

He'd laughed. 'I thought so. Good thing that I'm cold-hearted, huh?'

'You'd be cold either way,' I'd teased.

I could do this- it was physically doable. But he wouldn't let me leave after it was done now that he thought himself besotted, and that was crossing the only line I had left.

'Stop!' I panted, shoving him back with all of the force I had and watching him trip and slip over my contract. A Barachiel's love and sense of possession was not something to be seduced by- but fled from! 'No! The answer is NO Karol, I will not repay my debt, and I do not have to anymore! Your father has given

Lindy and Coaxley a pardon, so you cannot punish them for my refusal now!'

Karol looked dazed. 'What? Father…'

'He knows!' I cried, and his eyebrows shot up. 'Everybody knows what I promised you, and what I traded for it! Kohl, Kohén, your parents- they all know!'

'*No!*'

I nodded hard. 'Yes! And Karol this isn't just about me not wanting to do something that I've promised to, or how much I've always disliked you… I just can't bear to be touched or looked at by another man, don't you get it? I would have gone through with this, if that was what it took for you to keep your word. But not after tonight!' I felt my tears falling and touched them, terrified, but when I looked at my fingertips they were clear. Without his arms around me and his healing energy streaming through me, all of my shadows were coming back and so I wrapped them around me like a cloak. 'Not after tonight!'

'But if they knew, they would have been screaming this entire-'

'They did! That's why I was branded, don't you see? Your awful letter arrived while I was dressing and they all read it! Kohén refused to allow me to go to the ball and calm everyone down, so I was branded to keep you in line and to guarantee my attendance there!'

'*My* awful letter?' Karol pulled off his hat, paling as his eyes darkened. '*What* awful letter?'

'The one you sent me, along with the gown, and the Trevasse family!' I pulled it out of my corset. 'This one! Is that not in your hand?'

Karol frowned at it, then lifted his eyes to mine. 'Yes, I wrote it, but how was it awful?'

'You threatening to kill my friends and ruin the ball and the harem in one was supposed to be…. what?' I demanded, waving it. '*Sweet*?'

Karol's eyes bugged. 'That's not what I wrote! Let me see that!' he snatched the paper out of my hand and read it, his frown deepening. For an awful moment I held my breath, waiting for him to declare that the letter had been a forgery meant to incite chaos, which would probably mean that Satan had switched notes, but he looked up at me when he was finished with a helpless expression. 'God Larkin... what have we done to you here?' He held the paper up. 'This is a letter declaring that I love you more than any man has ever loved a woman, not a threat against you or your loved ones!' He stepped closer to me. 'My family... they translated this as *you* did too?' His face was falling as he saw the anger in my eyes when I nodded. 'Oh god.... I've been trying to win your trust and respect for five years... but you think me vile still, don't you? Worse than that! You think me...' He dropped his face into his hands and shook his head. 'Oh God... all of this trouble... and she still despises me!'

I stared at him, feeling scrambled and speechless. Was he honestly expecting me to believe that he'd penned those words with good intentions? That it was feasible to believe that a thirty-year old prince could fall in love with a seventeen year-old whore? Or was he just trying to plead insanity as his brothers had- by crying love where there was only unhealthy obsession?

I was fairly certain it was the latter, but I was stupefied enough by his convincing portrayal of a despairing saint that I was not prepared for him to leap forward suddenly, taking my shoulders and shaking me with flashing green eyes.

'Larkin Whittaker, what does it take to earn your trust?! Tell me, and I will do it! Even if it's only your companionship that I earn at first-'

'Let me go!' I squealed, jerking out of his hands and feeling my insides overheat again. 'Let me go, Karol! *That's* what it takes! I'm leaving Eden tonight, I will never be your Companion, and if you want me to believe that there is any good inside you, then stand out of my way and do not attempt to accost me again!' I moved forward but he was in my face in an instant, shaking his head while wide-eyed.

'No! No anything but that! Ask me for the stars, Larkin Whittaker and I will give them to you, but do not ask me to stand aside while you walk out of my life!'

'Go fetch me the stars then!' I snapped, face flushing, fingertips tingling. 'Off you go- I want thirty, at least. Whatever it takes to get you to turn your back on me for long enough--'

'No!' He tried to close his arms around me again, and my panic made my nerve endings shiver with a radiant heat. 'No I love you and I must-'

I struck him again but this time he deflected it and pushed me back up against the wall, trying to lean in for another kiss. 'Please!' he cried. 'Just hear me out! One moment to clarify-'

'I will not be your whore! And I have already been kissed by two different men tonight so pressing your lips to mine is doing nothing but participating in my debasement!' I bemoaned, turning my face from side to side so that he could not find my mouth for long enough to snare it. 'I came here for my freedom and I will be leaving here with it and if you try to stand in my way, I will knock you down! Don't think I can't! You cannot comprehend what I have already been through this night! And if you did...' I sobbed, wiping at my mouth feeling dirty and used. 'You wouldn't want me anyway. I'm filthy, your highness, inside and out!'

'Larkin no-'

'Get off me!' I screamed, shoving him back hard and sending a breath of fire after him. He staggered back, face waxen, eyes glassy, and when I advanced on him, I heard the rustle that caused his eyes to drift to my shoulders and then widen in absolute horror. 'I would sooner die this night then bend to your will! You asked me to come to you with a happy heart Karol but I know only misery and loss and soon, so will you! So let me by! You are the king of Arcadia now- *act* like it!'

'WHAT?' Karol steadied himself on the floor, eyes filling with tears- face hardening in anger and fear as his hand went to the handle of his sword. 'Larkin WHAT did you just say?' He looked at my wings again. 'How-'

'You are the king!' I sobbed. 'So stop wasting your time on your brother's whore, go downstairs, salvage what you can of your kingdom and never think of me again! I am not the one that has slain every member of your family, but their blood is on my hands all the same so do not reach for it again- it is beneath you, your highness! And I always have been!'

'You're lying!' he cried, getting up onto one knee. 'I'd never thought you capable of such ugly fabrications but now that I see that you are dark Nephilim, I guess that you must be!

'Believe what you will, just let me be!' I tried to dart past him but he grabbed my skirt and pulled me back. I heard the fabric he'd snared stretch enough to make a tearing sound. 'Karol stop! You're fighting for the wrong thing!'

'I cannot live without you, even if you are being awful right now! You're not a whore Larkin, you're a princess with the potential to be so much more!' he cried, hefting me back and making me scream. He caught me in his arms so that my backside rested on my knee and then he reached for his sword again. 'And if I have to do something drastic in order to prove what I'll do to keep you here-'

I screamed and burst into flames, and Karol let out an almighty bellow and jumped to his feet, knocking me to the floor and dropping a small box from his hand instead of the handle of the sword I'd thought he'd been going for. The flames did not hurt me or incinerate my dress as they ought to have, but they were all over me, making the very fabric of my world wobble before my eyes and setting the gentle woollen fabric of his suit alight in a heartbeat. I saw Karol smash into his desk and then into the opposite wall as he tried to beat at the flames that had flared up on his clothes, but his hair was on fire too and when he brushed up against the curtains, they went up as old fabric always does. Immediately the fire began to generate its own heat and wind, and I was so hypnotised by the horrid sight of him battling it, that I did not realise that my own flames had already gone out until Karol looked up at me with the most anguished expression I'd ever seen.

'Demon!' he cried, looking more wrecked than a man had ever looked before. 'I knew you'd stolen my heart- but I never believed that you would steal my soul! My father is dead?' he saw the confirmation in my frightened eyes, and his face transformed into a mask of anguish. 'And you scream it at me? And to think I was supposed to be the cold-blooded one...'

And those were the last words he said before a fresh crop of flames leapt up from the carpet beneath him. He jumped back, mouth open in an 'O' of horror- and then there was a smash as prince charming crashed through the tower window- and fell three floors below.

No! I spasmed and sobbed when I heard his bones hit the ground on the other side and then fell to my knees, shaking my head in horror and grief when I heard fresh screaming erupt from below. 'Karol!' I croaked, overcome with guilt to think that I might have just caused the death of Miguel Barachiel's final descendant. I should have been cheering, but I felt wretched. 'Oh God *no...*!'

'It's the prince!' someone screamed then.

'He's snapped his neck!'

'He's burning alive! The Choir girl is right, Larkin of Eden is a dark Nephilim, and she is coming for us all!'

'Upstairs, now! Grab weapons, we must destroy her before the kingdom burns to the ground!'

I cupped my head and shook it as I wept, not wanting to believe such awful things about me, but knowing they were true. I hadn't wanted to kill Karol- I hadn't wanted to hurt anyone! And yet *they'd* been the suicidal ones- they'd been the ones determined to have me or perish trying, and they'd made me a murderess for it! I remembered Satan telling me- *complimenting* me- on the fact that the last time someone had raised such hell on earth it had been her doing, and I bowed to the carpet and sobbed to understand that she was right, and that if I didn't end myself soon, there was a chance that the entire world would go up in smoke.

The door flew open behind me and as though I'd summoned her, I turned around as Ora burst in looking asphyxiated. 'Larkin!' she yelped my name, recoiling in horror. 'Oh! You dressed as a fallen angel? Oh, Larkin... well I can sympathise, of course, but we can't have you looking like that! Word has it that you've set fire to the harem and though I know it's a lie, nothing about that ensemble screams innocent now, does it?'

'Wh-where did you come from?' I stammered as she engulfed me in an embrace.

'The secret passage- I've been in and out of it all week, through Kohl's chamber. Easy enough seeing as how he's never in there anymore.' She knelt beside me in a figure-hugging black sheath that sparkled and made her look taller and more slender than ever before. She hadn't taken my styling suggestions, but she looked absolutely stunning, and a sequinned black mask on a stick was dropped into my lap as she took my hands. 'Come, you have to get up and get changed now, you reek of smoke! We'll go to Constance's room and raid her closet! I should be able to get in there without a key, yes? Well come on, hurry we need to find Karol so that he can hide you until this disaster is sorted out, then arrange for you to walk out there looking as ethereal and innocent as-'

'Stop!' I tugged my hand from her grip, feeling a headache coming on from the way she was talking at me without pausing for breath. I'd liked that about her the last time we'd met, but this new Larkin needed to be spoken to softly and slowly or not at all! 'I'm not going anywhere, least of all to a ball! Have you no compunction of what has happened this evening? Yes, I set fire to the harem, but only because the twins tried to rape me within it! Now I come in seeking to tear my contract and flee this place but-' I turned to the window but Ora's hand jerked my face back to face hers.

'The twins tried to rape you? What- *together*?' I nodded grimly, eyes spilling over and hers did the same. 'Oh, sweet Larkin! Who could blame you for setting a fire then? Screw the outfit- let them all see what was done to you!'

Arson was the least of what I feared being blamed for and I didn't give a hoot about making a statement with my risqué attire, but she obviously didn't know that Elijah and Karol were both dead either and that I was going to be held responsible for their murders, so I couldn't fault her for trying to micro-manage what she saw to be minor hiccups.

'*Every*one will blame me!' I was shaking like crazy now but when I tried to stand up, I almost twisted my ankle when I half-stood on the small timber box that had been in Karol's pocket. I winced and bent to pick it up, pausing to rub the pain out of my lower leg. 'This place is a nightmare and I want to leave! If you care about me at all, please- show me to the passage you used so that I might sneak-'

'No!' she tried to hold me again but I was trying to get the box open to see what was within and that made it difficult for her to manipulate my limbs. 'No, Larkin no! So many people want to believe the best in you, and they will once you've had the chance to clear your name! I don't know where Karol is- he was supposed to wait here for Kohén to come for him, but I was sure he would have heard about the fire and-'

I gasped when I opened the box and saw the beautiful solitaire shimmering within. All at once I realised what Karol had been about to tell me to motivate me to stay- that he had decided to marry Ora *despite* his supposed feelings for me- and my heart twisted painfully. 'Oh God... *oh*...!' I snapped the box closed and forced it into her hands as I turned away. 'I'm sorry! I shouldn't have...'

'What is...?' she opened the box and chuckled softly. 'Oh... good lord, he left the engagement ring on the floor? What a goose! Oh Larkin don't look so upset! It's not your fault!'

'Yes it is, I've ruined everything!' I lamented, voice tight. 'You were supposed to become our future queen this night but now I've gone and-'

'What? No! This isn't *my* ring, Larkin!' Ora stepped forward and tried to return the box. 'It is to be yours, you silly girl!'

I was sure I'd misheard her. I whipped around, dumbstruck. 'What?!'

'You heard me.' Ora was grinning and now she rolled her eyes. 'Why do you think it's imperative to get you to Karol and disaster-adjacent? *You* are the one that is to become the future queen this night, Larkin Whittaker, not *me!*'

The rug had been pulled out from under me many times in my years in Eden- but this was the first time that I had not seen it coming, and so I fell sharper and harder than I had ever fell before.

31.

'What are you talking about?' I demanded when I caught my breath again, looking from the ring to her. 'Are you drunk? Karol would never-'

'But he did, and if you do not believe me, then look closely at it and see the proof engraved within. There's an inscription there for you- and I know this because I helped Karol choose what he wanted most to say to you through a long process of elimination earlier today.' She smiled tenderly, taking the ring out of the box and showing it to me. 'You can't imagine how long it took for him to find the exact right stone- one that reflected blues and lavender and glare, as your eyes do, apparently.' She rolled her eyes and stepped forward and placed it into the palm of my hand. 'It should be him giving this to you, not I, but I will do whatever it takes to soothe your ruffled feathers right now, so you must know: you *will* be untouchable after midnight, because Karol already has the votes he needs to change your status from captive by contract, to captured by love!' She smiled, and her eyes shone with tears. 'If you'll accept, of course… and you must! Not only is he a wonderful man, but this is your ticket to freedom Lark! Possibly the only one you have left now, so take it, and let the love he has for you infect you as it has me!'

Proposal at twelve-fifteen. Proposal at twelve-fifteen…Yes there was to be a proposal made at twelve-fifteen, Kohén and I knew that! But to WHO? That is the question!

I gazed down at the ring, staggered, and through misty eyes, read the words within, twisting it gently so every letter appeared and vanished behind the gleaming platinum band:

'What is a Prince Charming, without a swan princess?'

My legs went cold as my blood began to chill. I looked up at Ora, mystified. 'Wh-what… no! He is confused- bewitched! *Look* at me, Ora! Who would want-'

'Karol wants you, that's who, and he's hardly the only one!' she smiled, tucking my hair behind my ear. 'And do not apologise to me for winning his heart before I could. I suspected that he felt something for you when we first met remember? I asked you if the feelings were mutual-'

'They're not!' I cried. 'I hate him and he knows it!'

Her eyebrows shot up. 'That's what you both believe but it's not the truth and anyone standing on the outside of the chemistry between you can see plain as day that you're more drawn to one another than magnets are!'

'No we're not! He's drawn to this... stuff,' I motioned to myself, 'but he's drawn to *every* woman's stuff, and I'm not attracted to him at all!'

She arched an eyebrow. 'I'm sorry... you expect me to believe that you don't find *Karol Barachiel* attractive... at *all*? Is that what you're truly trying to sell me on?' She waved her hands in front of my eyes. 'Are these plugged in?'

I turned away from her, feeling my heat working itself up into a frenzy again as I stared down at the beautiful diamond. It was shocking to think that Karol would consider marrying me at all...but making me a princess for LIFE despite the fact that we'd barely been friends? Talk about a risk! I didn't know if it was the most romantic thing I'd ever heard- or the most insane. 'There's more to attraction than physical appearance! You cannot love someone that you hate!'

'But you do not hate him as passionately as you believe you do, take my word for it.' Ora sighed sadly, as though I were the rain on her lovely, romantic parade. 'You two were unaware of me at that dinner the other night, but I was very aware of the two of you! In fact, there wasn't a person in attendance that was not riveted by your escapades together! What an attractive couple you made- teasing one another one moment, squabbling like an old married couple over his speech- and then forming an alliance so that you could side against Kohén together! No wonder he turned green with jealousy and stormed off! You and Karol were having a private party for two and the rest of us were just there as voyeurs!'

'You're crazy,' I wheezed, pressing my spare hand against my abdomen and feeling a sharp pain within as I continued to stare at the diamond. It was so beautiful! 'I barely know him, and I'm thirteen years his junior!'

Ora laughed. 'I am *twelve* years his junior, and yet you encouraged *me* to wed him! Surely it has not escaped your notice that a Barachiel man has never taken a spouse that wasn't at least ten years younger than they were? They almost always choose to join with someone that have only just turned twenty-one!' She rolled her eyes. 'A lot of things have changed since the dawn of time- but men seeking the youngest woman possible to wed is sadly not one of them.'

'But I won't be twenty-one for four more years!' I protested. 'And we're not talking about joining but... but so much more!'

'You weren't going to be free for four more years either. If he found a way to change that, don't you think he would have found a way to marry you as soon as that ring was on your hand?' She blushed. 'Especially if it meant getting to the consummation part? Karol's a dear heart, don't get me wrong- but I don't think he would have made it until midnight tomorrow before finding a way to marry you.'

'No!' I exploded as I whirled around, and she drew back in shock. 'No he wouldn't have! I'm not fertile- that would be a strike against us. I am a used whore- THAT would be another! I was his brother's plaything- that's the third! Shall I keep going?' I slapped the ring back into her hand and pointed to my brand. 'Or does this not shout the obvious for me?'

'All factors he was very aware of Larkin, except the brand of course, ' Ora came after me, looking dismayed and clenching the ring tightly. I suppose in her head we should have been in silk pyjamas while discussing this- gazing up at the stars while giggling about boys. It was a sweet notion, but only the kind of daydream that a noble girl could expect to come to pass. 'But he worried that it might become a factor, and that's exactly why he's spent the last day asking the other rulers for their support in changing the rules for you! He had two younger brothers to bear heirs- so what would it matter if he opted out of trying to do the same, if the bride he chose had the ambition, intelligence and charm required to change the world for the better on her own, instead of expecting offspring to do it for her like all of the others do?'

'I had the ambition to do WHAT?' I squeaked. 'I wanted to grow cotton, not wear a crown!'

'And yet you are more than capable of doing both- and more! I've seen it in you, Larkin! It doesn't matter if you believe in his love or in yourself- it doesn't even matter that it will take time for you to come to care for him as he has for you- just say *yes* when he asks, and you will begin to change the world with that lovely word!' She clasped her hands together, begging me to do what she did not know was impossible- accept a proposal from a dead man. 'He will win your heart eventually, I just know it!'

'Stop!' I pressed my hands to my ears and sobbed as I felt my flames returning again. 'You don't know what you're asking of me, but I assure you that it is all quite impossible!'

'To love a man that you believe is evil?' she asked, prying my hands off my ears and staring into my eyes. 'Yes, Larkin I do know- about the deal that you two made, that is.'

I tented my fingers around my nose and stared at her over them. 'What?' She knew I'd already sold myself to the man I'd encouraged her to marry? I was mortified!

'He confessed it all, all right? Told me that originally, he'd just wanted to bed you one day, but after you struck that deal, he'd contemplated convincing you to stay on as his Companion instead, should Kohén lead you down *that* dead-end road...' she wrinkled her tiny little nose. 'But on Tuesday he said that he'd realised that he'd wanted more than a tryst with you some time ago- following a fight you'd had or something along those lines when he stole a kiss? And that he'd freed you with the intention of pursuing you romantically- a secret he kept close to his heart, for fear that Kohén would catch wind of it and lock you in prematurely.' She made another face. 'As he did...'

I slid my hands down to clutch at my throat. 'What? But all he said was that I had to come to him at midnight tonight as pre-arranged-'

'He couldn't just blurt out the fact that he'd fallen for you, Larkin, he was certain that you'd rebuke him without him first setting a precedent for such a claim! *And* because he knew there was a good chance that you'd laugh in his face- an honour he's earned with his womanising ways- *and* because he knew that his parents would lose their fool minds if they discovered that he wanted to pursue an infertile woman...' she shrugged her tiny shoulders. 'But he desperately wanted the chance to try to start something with you despite those odds- so *that* was why he made that birthday wish Larkin. Not to wish you beneath him, as he now thinks you suspect- but to make you eligible for a *future* with him! And after recent developments, he was inspired to go one better and ask every monarch in the world to stand behind him against his father in order to make you a princess! Support that they have all agreed to demonstrate- even Yael, who was the toughest sell!'

My mouth popped open. All of this had come about after the fight we'd had in the courtyard? Was *that* why he had stopped sleeping with his Companions? I'd thought it was because I'd accused him of rape earlier that morning, not because he'd fallen for *me*! 'I don't understand!' I cried. 'When did you learn this? And when did *you* go from being the one he was courting, to his confidante?'

Ora blew out her bangs. 'Tuesday night, after all of that hoopla with Kohl and you vanishing into that God forsaken harem with Kohén...' She made a face. 'I found Karol in Miguel Barachiel's cottage; sobbing as though his heart were broken! I asked him what was going on and he apologised and confessed that despite his best efforts to pursue me or keep his options open, he had just learned that you had caved into your love for his brother, and that he was too torn apart by it to show his face! All of the sordid details poured out of him after that.' She stepped closer again, giving me a bittersweet smile. 'I will admit that I was a little crushed to hear it all, sweetie, but not surprised. The moment I saw him look at you- well! Who *could* hold a candle to Liberty and her blazing torch?' Her tentative smile morphed back into a concerned frown, and she rubbed my shoulder briskly. 'None of us wanted to believe that you'd willingly given up your freedom, but none of us wanted to believe that you'd been *un*willing to concede to Kohén more, so we both tried to get into that harem to speak with you after you vanished in there with Kohén, but were thwarted at every turn! Adeline could not even seek entrance to collect a book that she'd left behind and-'

'Adeline was in on this too?' I demanded.

Ora smiled. 'Apparently Adeline was the first one to bring her master's feelings for you to his fool attention, when she claims that his pillow talk became him talking about *you* on her pillow about a year ago.' She shrugged. 'She says that she knew what was coming on Tuesday long before the rest of us did, and had already packed her things before the dinner on Monday evening, and had warned Karol's other Companions to do the same.'

'Oh no!' I cried, remembering how solemn Karol's Companions had looked when we'd gathered on the lawn to hear Karol's speech. 'She must detest me!'

'Wrong again, Larkin. She adores you- as do I! Most of the people out there do, which is why you need to stop saying that you're not worthy of being a queen, and just *be* one already!'

'That's not possible,' my eyes flooded again. 'Too much has happened, and you can't possibly understand that right now but soon you will so-'

'I know that you have been through hell and I am sorry for it, but you can't let Kohén's prior hold on you determine your future! Oh Lark... I'm sorry that we didn't get to you sooner, I can see how it's rattled you! We tried! Karol would have started smashing windows to get to you and the truth behind your supposed submission that very night, but then Kohl ran off and made a scene and Elijah put us all on lockdown- we had to take focus away from your predicament not draw *more* attention to it, so we were forced to tread carefully... in case something awful happened to you...' I heard her sniffle and tentatively touch the elbow of my left arm. 'Something like *this*. How did this come to pass, sweetie? Was it Kohén's doing, or Elijah's?'

It was neither, and my heart burned like a coal to think of the boy that had been named for that very thing. 'I don't want to talk about it...' I slid my hands back up to hide my face. 'Please... can we stop talking about this? I can't bear to hear another word!'

'But you must hear it all!' Ora's fingers combed through my hair soothingly. 'Please believe me... I didn't think it could be as bad for you in there as some feared, because I didn't get an ominous vibe from Kohén at all... and after Karol received several messages from Chérrine, well, from *you* through her insisting that you were fine and that you wanted him to butt out of your private affairs, we both began to believe that maybe you were happy after all, you know? I can see *now* that you weren't, but all of the opposition forced Karol into a retreat. He even wanted to give up once he'd been convinced that a life with Kohén was all that you truly wanted, but I would not allow it!'

'You should have!' I croaked, glancing at the smouldering curtains again, but she did not follow my gaze for she was too busy trying to hold it.

'I could not! Karol was dissolving over you, sweetheart, barely coherent most of the time, and to keep people from suspecting why he was so withdrawn, we pretended to be courting. That allowed us to sneak away together often and conspire over you, and it also kept girls like Amelia-Rose from pouncing him.' She sighed. 'I'm sorry that we did not free you from that awful place, Larkin but you have to understand that getting to you was impossible with that gargoyle on the harem door and the smaller, royal gargoyle behind *yours*!' She feigned tearing out her hair. 'We might have done something drastic, but we kept thinking: 'Any day now! Any *hour* now she'll waltz out and we'll get to the bottom of it all...' But bloody Kohén kept coming up with one excuse after the other to keep you locked away and make it look like it was what you wanted and needed, so when we learned that you'd had the chance to bolt but had fought for Eden instead, we were gobsmacked. That might have been the end of it all- even for me- but when Karol heard that you'd almost died on Friday night, he lost his mind! He'd already suspected that he would live a miserable life without you, but finding out that he'd almost lost you without first getting to tell you how he felt? No, he was more determined than I to get you out of there after that, and that was when he decided to make the grandest gesture of all- to the fairest of them all. He spent the early hours of this morning in a secret meeting with all of the monarchs, explaining that the outcry over you was all the proof anyone needed to launch you out of that harem and onto a throne, where you belonged.'

I desperately didn't want to believe what I was being told but I was starting to, and it sickened me to my very core. I looked down to see that I'd already shed a few black feathers for what I'd done to Karol and I cried softly, understanding that like trust and love- feathers were not something that could be replaced once lost.

Oblivious to the fact that I was fading away, Ora went on. '... We went to storm the harem with all of your friends to liberate you the moment that we'd heard that you'd come to, but when we were told that you were coming to the ball, Karol decided to play his hand close to his chest again for fear of triggering his possessive little brother. He'd already ordered your gown months ago, and then had paid for your friends to deliver it so they would be here to see you released once he'd decided upon doing *that*- but he took me to select your ring the moment Kohén said that you'd be at the ball, and made arrangements to propose to you after the fireworks.' She wriggled her eyebrows. 'Oh Larkin, if I could show you the smile he'd had on his face this afternoon, it would be all of the proof of his love that you'd need! His mood changed so swiftly- in a heartbeat he'd gone from being sad and surly, to bright and bubbly once more! And *romantic...*' she shook her head, dimpling prettily. 'Wait until you see him in the special suit he had sewn for himself just this afternoon, to strike your interest!' she fanned herself. 'He looks absolutely delicious in it!'

'Wh-what?' I swallowed hard. '*What* special suit?'

She pressed her hands to her heart. 'I cannot say, that will ruin the-'

'I can't take another surprise!' I whimpered, knots twisting up my intestines. 'Please just tell me... what was that costume supposed to be?'

A line appeared between Ora's brows. 'You've seen it?' She glanced behind her, but still she did not see the way that the charred curtains were flapping frantically through the shattered window. 'Where is he? If he's around, why am *I* the one explaining all of this?'

'What was it?!' I demanded shrilly, taking her hands now and shaking her when her eyes landed on the rifle and widened. 'I have to know! What costume did he believe would appeal to me so, after years of me making my hate evident?'

'Ow! Shit!' Ora snatched her hands from mine and when I looked down and saw scarlet imprints around her wrists, my stomach flipped. 'What's wrong with your hands?' She pressed her soft palm to my sweaty forehead. 'Are you still ill?'

'Tell me NOW!'

Ora stepped back, looking cross and a little fearful now. 'He's dressed as a soldier, all right?!' she yelled the answer at me, but it only confused me more. What want did *I* have for a soldier? 'A confederate officer to be precise- like your hero, Rhett Butler-'

My abdomen buckled, and I felt Karol's letter to me beneath my corset crackle. *'No!'*

'Yes! He wanted to swoop out of the pages of one of the closest things to a love story that you've ever deigned to relate to- so he combed through history books all morning trying to find out how such a man would have dressed-'

'No!' I cried again, backing away from her more rapidly now, heartsick in the terminal sense. That's why he had been looking at me the way he had been- he'd been waiting for me to recognise his costume out of one of my favourite books! But how could I have? The only pictures I'd ever seen of the old south had been ones of cotton fields, negro slaves and the occasional plantation home! Never an officer of the Confederate army! *'No!* Oh Karol you stupid, impulsive...' I pressed my furnace-hot hands to my face and screamed. 'When will this torture end?'

I couldn't believe it. I'd finally brought an end to the Barachiel monopoly over the third-borns of the world, but in doing so, I'd also killed the only man in the world that might have actually loved me in the way I needed to be loved- freely. My heart turned to ashes and my soul with it. I wasn't a duckling or a swan now- I was fallen, and there was no coming back from that.

Ora cupped my shoulders, staring at me aghast as I sobbed. 'Get a hold of yourself! I know you're upset right now but if anyone has the ability to see you rise above this awful business it is...' her eyes darted to the right then, her slanted eyebrows furrowing together when she finally seemed to notice the smouldering curtains flapping about in the breeze that was now rushing through the broken window. 'Oh my gosh, what happened to the window?' her delicate features were awash with confusion as she turned back to frown at me, as though finally seeing me clearly- the feathers, the blood that had started running down my face again, distorting my vision- the anguish that had to be written all over my face. 'Larkin...why is there a gun out?' she swallowed hard and then narrowed her eyes at me. 'Larkin: *Where's Karol?*'

'I'm sorry...' my throat was so tight that the words ached more than my brand did. I pried her hands off me and placed the ring in her hand, squeezing it closed around it. 'Like I said... it should have been you!'

'But-' her face contorted again as she stared at me. 'Are your tears... is that...?'

'He gr-grabbed me, just like the others!' I mewled. 'I thought his letter a th-threat... and I.. I...' Footsteps filled the hallway, joined swiftly by furious, frantic voices, cutting me off from making my confession- that I'd killed the only man that may have actually loved me in a way that counted. A shiver raced through me as her suddenly cold, desolate grey eyes read the truth in mine, and she stumbled back, looking more scared of me than I was sure I had of Satan.

'No...' Ora shook her head, hugged herself as her face collapsed. 'Oh no, Larkin...' she looked to the gun, and then back at me. 'You didn't hurt him, did you?!'

'She must be up here!' a man cried.

'Prince Karol was pushed from his own window, there's no other explanation!' that was Amelia-Rose, and that was enough to send me staggering back towards the window now. I bumped into a box, looked into it and saw fourteen more scrolls, remembered what I had come here to do and pointed my finger at them, incinerating the contents of the entire trunk in one go. It should have felt amazing, and yet I couldn't feel my fire or my triumph.

'I am what they made me,' I whispered, 'I cannot change that- but I am sorry for it.'

And then I turned and dove out the open window and started falling as Ora began to scream. The ground rushed up to meet me and when I saw the way that Karol's body was sprawled out on the blood splattered pavement- twisted and motionless on the dark ground and practically covered in shattered glass and the people crowding around him, I screamed in anguish. Like startled insects the people looked up at me and then scattered, their mouths open in O's of horror, their eyes white and wide behind their masquerade masks, and it made me feel heinous. But my fear of crashing into them and hurting yet another innocent gave me a surge of energy that swept through me, tensing muscles I'd never used before along my spine.

One moment I'd been about to smash flat a horrified-looking little boy, and the next I was sweeping up into the dark sky and away from them, too fast and erratically for me to hope to have any control over my other limbs, which were freezing quickly due to the icy air outside. When I realised that I was about to perform a loop that would surely send me crashing into the ground again- only upside down this time- I crunched at the waist to prevent myself from flipping feet over head, and then dove forward sharply, hearing the crowd below collectively gasp or sob every time I changed direction, reacting to my clumsy flying the way one would watch a first-time rider mount a steed and then fumble at the reigns.

Yes that was how I was handling my wings- like a tiny clown from the old world being bucked off an angry bull in a rodeo, and embarrassment made my cheeks flush despite how frigid the air was. Was it not bad enough that I was doing this in my lingerie and a skirt, or that I had just killed the only Barachiel that I should have let live... now I had to be humiliated too? I probably looked like a rag doll caught up in a whirly wind!

I was plummeting towards the ground fast now, but I gritted my teeth and called on those unfamiliar muscles along my spine again, setting my eyes on Lady Liberty across the expansive lawn to give myself direction before I tried again. My wings flapped once, hard after I willed them to and I levitated up once more and finally began to coast forward in a straight line off inertia alone, exhaling a rush of misty breath. Realising that the air was as pressurised as water against my wings, and that flying seemed to require the same sort of effort that swimming did, I pressed my ankles together so the rest of my limbs would stop jerking about straightened my arms before me, which smoothed my passage through the air for a few seconds and actually elicited a relieved sigh off someone below me. Somewhat bemused to realise that at least one person on that lawn didn't want to see me crash land on Eden's manicured lawn, I glanced slightly to my left, and almost dropped my face when I saw the crowd of people thrashing against the fence in the distance.

'She's FREE!' someone hooted, throwing a hat into the air and causing me to suck in a gasp of icy air that my lungs needed but protested against. It was like I'd breathed in a blizzard, extinguishing all of my heat and power. Was this my weakness... the cold? Funny, I'd never felt it while I'd kept my fire inside me, but now my teeth chattered hard enough to snap.

'Liber-*ty*! Liber-*ty*!' others were chanting, and now that I was closer to the rear fence than I was to the palace, I realised that there were a lot more than a few people on my side- but what looked like hundreds! Not just pressed against the exterior perimeter fence in the wildwoods (how had they managed to clear such a broad area amongst those trees?!) but on the walkway that snaked a path between Eden's fence and the Banished one- actual Arcadian citizens rejoicing my exit, not just outlaws! There were guards positioned all along the interior fence with rifles aimed out at the crowd, but all of them were watching me too- and one or two seemed to be smiling!

Oh my God! What's come over them? Can't they see that my wings are black? Don't they know that I am damned?

I wanted to go to them so badly- to find out what it was that they wanted from me, but I dipped sharply to the right then, and surprise made my body flinch. I'd known that flying would be wonderful (and it was, in a way) and difficult, but I hadn't expected it to feel this unstable, and when I glanced back beside me and saw my wings were shivering- and coming loose like a cloud of ash behind me, I realised that my fall was more than fated- it was imminent. Just like Satan I'd sinned beyond the point of redemption and now I would be a flightless bird until I died. I'd made it this far, but if I wanted to make it to the tidal fall, then I was going to have to think and act quickly before my wings disintegrated completely, trapping me on this side of the fence.

Sobbing and trying desperately to control my chattering teeth, but slightly more in control of myself now and prepared for any matter of things to go wrong, I fisted my hands and shot them behind me, undulating my body as I aimed my nose at Liberty's torch, rather than at her head now that I saw that I was more likely to end up impaled on one of her spikes than I was to land on the sharply angled back of her head. I lifted like I was riding a wave and saw all at once that if I was going to land on such a small area then I was going to have to stop my forward momentum now, so I straightened and then thrust back my arms at my sides, spanning out my fingers and sobbing in relief when with a whoosh and a hiss, my trembling wings opened up like a sail that closed in around my shoulders, resisting the wind. The cage around her torch rattled and bowed when I crashed into it, and although I was shocked and disorientated, I found the strength to wrap my fingers around the guardrail as my slippery, completely ridiculous high heels kicked out, searching for a foothold. I managed to locate one as the air battered me and the cries from below rose in a crescendo of surprise, but it was so slippery that for a moment, I was certain that I was about to fall to my death in front of them all. It was just too slick and the breeze was so strong- I was aching all over and trying to spit my hair out of my mouth as the wind whipped it into a frenzy... but before I could just give up and let go, I felt a warm hand wrap

411

around my wrist and yank me over the side and onto the copper platform behind the intricate railing with an unceremonious thud.

Winded I looked up into the face of my saviour, and actually coughed out a laugh when I saw the beautiful woman kneel before me and open her arms.

'You're such a fighter!' Satan whispered, wrapping me in an embrace that was destined to be an eternal one. 'How can you imagine that you have what it takes to end your life, Larkin? You were born to start a revolution, not cower in the shadows!'

In response- I punched her in the face.

32.

Satan threw back her head after I'd struck her and for a moment I perked up, believing that she was as easy to overpower as any other mortal woman... but then I realised that she was laughing, not groaning or crying, and my triumphant smirk became a scowl.

'Oh don't look at me like that! I call you a fighter, and you strike me- despite the fact that I'm thousands of years old and almost as strong as God. It's funny!'

'Almost as strong as God,' I hissed, shaking out my now-aching fist. punching her had been like punching iron. 'Not so strong that you don't still come running to teenage girls for help, though!'

Satan sighed. 'That mouth of yours... I'm surprised you've lived this long. But you have, and if we want to keep it that way, we need to fly out of this place now! So for the millionth time, child, please take my hand-'

'No!' I turned my face away and tried to fight my way out from underneath her wings. 'Stop offering me your hand when we both know you're asking for so much more! I won't be responsible for ruining the world and bringing you back to life!'

'I have been brought back to life already, and it was not just your doing, little dove- but *theirs*, look!' Satan lifted her wing and pointed towards the fence, steering me that way by grasping my branded bicep which ceased to hurt the moment her touch flashed ice-cold against it.

'The people?' I sniffled, shivering as her raised wing had allowed the freezing night air to rush over me again. 'But they love God! I am in this mess because they've allowed his word to be translated into twisted, but apparently well-meaning laws again!'

'Not the people, look at the *harem*!' she turned me further and when I saw the violent blaze licking along the northern wing, I cried out in fear. It wasn't just on fire now, it was an actual inferno! And *I* had done that!

Oh God what if T'are and Constance didn't get out?

'… I needed people to call to me- to pledge themselves to me to empower me with the strength I needed to force my way back into this world in this form, and when you appealed to me so you brought me close, but not enough to tip the scales.' She twirled, making a big shop of inhaling the night air deeply and beaming at me after, fluttering her own wings. 'But when you shattered the hearts and the minds of the Barachiels tonight, *I* am the one that they called to in their hour of need, to gift them what God had not! Not just Kohén when that chandelier fell upon him, and not just Kohl when he caught alight- but all of them! Well, except Karol and Elijah, I suppose, but three Nephilim pleas for my assistance in addition to yours and those of the Banished at the fence? That sufficed, and now look at me, walking the earth again, with my sweet protégé at my side!'

'I am not at your side, and I hate you for not telling me what would happen!' I cried, forcing her hands off me. 'I should have been told that I was Nephilim! I should have been told about the flames! I should have been told that Kohl would turn on me so and I *definitely* should have been warned about Karol!'

'I did not know about anything except for your potential, I could not see into their hearts and minds before it was too late for me!' Satan protested, looking wounded. 'A potential that I knew would get you bound and gagged in a cold, wet place if it was discovered before the door was unlocked! But so long as you interpreted your power as your pain, you did what you could to swallow it down and keep it concealed and that has prolonged your life- not *shortened* it.'

'But you said that it was too late for Kohl and that I would kill myself!' I reminded her, giving her an odd look when she reached forward and tenderly stroked my hair. 'So you must have known a lot more than you let on!'

'Only what might happen to you! Every time you were hurt, I'd have a glimpse of your future and every time I saw it, you were on the edge of that tidal fall, silently cursing Kohén, then Karol- and then finally Kohl, which shocked even *me*.' She released my hair and stroked a finger beneath my chin next and I shivered at the glee in her eyes and the feel of her very mortal touch. 'Every time you leapt onto those rocks it was because another one of them had hurt you somehow, only I did not know why or how! The clearest vision I got was of Kohén and Kohl leading you into that dungeon room, and before I could see anything else, you blocked me out! If you'd just taken me into you, I would have been able to control your power and manipulate the situation to your advantage, but you refused to meet me halfway!'

'Because I don't want to be responsible for your continued existence!' I sobbed, backing away from her and treading on my own shedding feathers, which were flying about in the wind now. Satan bent and picked one up, pressing it to her face and inhaling it deeply- and it was then that I realised that she was probably touching things on Earth with her own fingertips for the first time in over six-hundred years- and enjoying it immensely. 'Even though I am hurt, even though I am desolate and filled with hate- I do not want to be responsible for instigating hell on earth for all of these innocent people! And Karol...' I looked back to the crowd of people that were weeping around him as they lifted his shattered body off the ground. 'He did not deserve that end, Satan!'

'Neither did Hell!' Satan snarled, advancing on me again. 'But no one was there to protect *him* from his feelings for Heaven!'

'Just like no one was there to protect Heaven from the way everyone treated her, just because she was that little bit more special, than God's own descendants,' my voice broke. 'The tragedy is not that they are dead, Satan- it is that *your* hate has kept them separated for an eternity, when they could have spent it together if you'd just taken God's hand instead of questing for mine! Forgive him, already!' I pleaded. 'Forgive him and be done with this!'

Satan's eyes flashed. 'Fine, I'll forgive God,' she wet her dark lips and smiled a pointy smile, like a serpent, 'just show me how, by marching back in there and forgiving Kohl and Kohén for how they have treated *you.*'

I shrank back, feeling that coal heat up in my chest again. 'Never!'

'That's what I thought.' Satan rested against the railing, staring out at the dark ocean behind us, her eyes undulating in shades of black and grey as the waves did. 'As cold and scary as the darkness can be... it always manages to feel safer than the light, doesn't it? Light is fleeting, and warmth is an awful thing to be deprived of once you've become accustomed to basking in it... Why opt to strive for that fleeting light offered by love, when hate is so much more constant and dependable?' She slid her gaze back to me and smiled sadly. 'That's why you want to die, isn't it? Not because you hate life, but because you fear losing it so. As a third-born slave, the only thing that has ever been in your control has been your own welfare, yes? This week that control was taken from you, and so it is the only time that you have ever truly felt the harsh bite of misery in that perfect, hopeful, forbearing heart of yours, isn't it? The first time that you ever truly believed that your own destiny was out of your hands?' She saw the agreement in my eyes and straightened. 'Well, I'm here to tell you that it's not, Larkin. Your heart is so much stronger and lighter than you believe it is- and because of that, you still have the potential to make everything you've ever dreamed of come true! That brand hasn't trapped you- it's unlocked the *true* you! And all you have to do to see who that is, is fly freely with me now, and listen to me for once!'

'With withered wings?' I asked her. 'Those you cannot repair, I know that- and you cannot reverse the damage done to my heart. There is too much hate in it for me to go on.'

'That's not true!' she cried. 'I told you, I could make you happy! You will forgive me, and the Barachiel's eventually and every other person that has ever wronged you because you will rise above them all-'

'But I'll never forgive myself,' I whispered softly, my hand tightening around the rail. 'For all the things I've done tonight- for all of the pain and death I've caused... I cannot live with that. It is *I* that I despise, Satan- not you, and not the world.'

Her features contorted. 'But you can't leave those feelings behind either, Larkin! If you die now before having done enough good to make up for all you have done wrong, you will be held accountable for them, and it will be torturous! You can trust me on that, for I am the one that will have to oversee your torture! I cannot change that any more than I can heal your wings, even if I desperately want to!'

'Then I will see you on the other side,' I whispered, and then flung myself over the side of the railing to the tune of her screaming.

As though they knew that this was all I'd ever ask of them, my decaying wings did as I willed and sent me soaring off the tip of the torch and to the right-hand side of Eden's grounds. I flitted above faces, some familiar but most strange, and heard them crying out my name. Knowing that I could not pause for fear of crashing into them all, I glanced back to blow a kiss to Cherry and Adeline (Adeline was on the walkway and not in the Wildwoods, thank God!) and then at the Golden man as he twisted to watch me pass, and saw tears streaming down his face.

'Larkin no!' he cried, bolting after me, shoving people out of his way. 'Daughter, child of mine! *Stop!*'

But I would not. My curiosity beseeched me too- tugging on my wings in an attempt to physically wrestle me down, but my curiosity had gotten me to this point and I would not allow it to drop me again. I turned my face back into the wind, swooped over a crowd of filthy-looking, excited people that had not shaved or washed themselves for years, and did not stop until I saw the river that led over the tidal fall emerge from the mist.

That river was technically set into the Wildwoods, beyond the borders of our country and had been used as a natural break between Arcadia and the desolate Northern lands of ice and impassable forest for centuries because its waters streamed from the north and were always perilous and freezing cold, especially here on the coast, where it forked off to border half the castle as a perilous moat that whooshed down from a nearby precipice in the foothills of our region, and then swerved back to the left before it crashed over the cliff face and down to rocks and sand, one hundred and twenty feet below. Not even in the hottest Arcadian summers would one consider a dip into the Pinnacle River because you could be swept from the access to it behind the villages on the other side of town and over the tidal fall in three and a half minutes. I knew- Finch and I had once seen a dead horse go in near our house and then get spat out the other side in under four. And it hadn't looked much like a horse once it landed! Thank goodness it had been high tide at the time or it would have been a ghastly sight indeed.

No one ever crossed the Pinnacle River intentionally either- not even the Banished. Usually the only way to get to Arcadia without crossing it was to slip in around a bend some five kilometres east of our city (up near Rachiel) and then either break tree branches away from the fence with an axe to clear yourself a path- a task that would kill you before it paid off- or find a way to dam the river where it was narrow or possibly build a bridge over it. I didn't know how this many Banished had gotten to the thin strip of Wildwoods that bordered this side of the river, but they'd either taken the 'secret path' I'd once heard mentioned as a child, or had accomplished one of the other feats together, which spoke volumes about their determination to terrorise our country's residents this week.

But they wouldn't get close enough to terrorise me, not if I acted quickly. The only time the Pinnacle River opened up enough to touch Arcadian land was by the natural moat that my father had helped dam off before building the bridge over it, and where I was going- the frothy precipice of the Tidal Falls themselves. The raging current had been eating away at the rocky embankment and the forest lining it on both sides for centuries, so it had taken a chunk out of the Wildwoods in the furthest corner of the Banished lands, near to us, and now the water poured over the very edge of our kingdom at a sharp angle. In one hundred years, it would probably eat away at the walkway too, and though that might cause the Barachiels a bit of grief in the future, for now, it made for a pretty view.

From the corner of Eden's slightly lower grounds, you could stare ever-so-slightly up at the crest of the falls, (the rocks around them had been fenced off on our side to prevent anyone getting too close) access the public look-outs that had also been fenced off at a few points down along the cliff, and even walk up close to it on the beach at low tide, near where my parents had been married. You couldn't cross the boundary line via the beach either though, because the Wildwoods were bordered by sharp, jutting and ever-slippery cliffs on the other side that turned a sharp corner north of the falls and then stretched on for hundreds of kilometres after without a beach to be seen. They were sheer drops that were almost always frosted with ice, and the current in the ocean that edged them was so fierce that Arcadian ships could not sail north of our harbour, which was a good half a kilometre south of the falls, just beyond the most southern point of Eden's farming lands, where I had toiled for so long with Martya.

There were three fences standing between Eden and the top of the falls- Eden's, the Banished fence across the public walkway, and a small barrier fence that had been built to prevent suicidal people- like me- from getting too close to the ultimate temptation. The girl I'd been half an hour beforehand would have had to scale Eden's fence and then rush down to the look out, climb over it and negotiate slippery boulders to get within an arm's reach of the falls, but the Nephilim I was now swooped over all three fences and then gently lowered herself down to the highest rock, on the very edge of the raging river where the Banished fence to my right cornered-off with the safety one that was behind me. I folded in my wings as I was covered with the spray coming off the thunderous falls and landed in a crouch, almost slipping off the glassy rock's surface beneath me, but latched my fingers around the ice-cold fence behind me until I'd regained my balance, grateful that the corner of the Wildwoods to my right was just overgrown enough to conceal me from sight of anyone on the footpath behind it.

There! I thought, smiling grimly as I pulled Karol's letter out of my corset again, grimacing as the fierce winds almost immediately tore it out of my hands. *This is close to where I came to read my sister's letter, which changed how I saw the Barachiel family forever- so it's fitting that I should read this here too, one final time- to see if it can't change it all back!*

I lowered myself staring back up the river, momentarily awed by the beauty and power of it, and then over the edge of the falls to the bottom where I'd once dreamed of being wed. The drop was hundreds of feet high, but the tide was on my side and so I saw the sharp rocks that would surely rip me to shreds glinting in the darkness below, beckoning me to them the same way Satan did. I didn't know how many people had ever stood where I had- had felt the wind pummelling them and had been lucky enough to feel God's glory as intensely as I did right then- but I knew it could not have been many, and so I felt privileged to stand on the wrong side of it now.

Just as I would soon feel privileged to fall. My death would not be pretty- but it would be my choice, as Satan had said, and that was a miracle to the likes of me. Now all I needed to see it through, was the conviction that had gotten me this far- to be reminded of the fact that I was a jaded, joyless, untrusting and wicked girl that deserved to die- not the would-be hero that the people back by the footpath were crying out to. And they *were* still crying out! I didn't need to turn around to know that they'd run to the corner of the fence and were now straining for a glimpse of me through the trees! Luckily, however, the wind and the water streaming past me was strong enough to mute their roars, and so with shaking fingers and absolute focus, I dropped my eyes to read the letter again.

Dear Larkin.

I'd rather hoped that we'd be meeting at midnight tonight to tear up your contract along with all of the others before enjoying a private celebration for two, and though circumstances have changed, my desire for you has not. It may appear that way, but you would be foolish to believe that anything would prevent me from taking you in my arms at long last. I have fallen silent and I have kept away- but only physically for the sake of keeping up appearances, Larkin. Inside my body I am screaming for you and reducing that harem and anyone who tries to stop me from getting to you to rubble. Were it not for my desire to maintain some dignity as far as my family name is concerned, I would have done so already!

But dignity can be restored in the Barachiel name in many ways, and we cannot be watched every second, despite what they all believe, so you will come to me before midnight, or I will come to you. That is not a threat, sweet angel- but a heartfelt promise. And Barachiel men take promises awfully seriously, so I beg you to keep the one you made to me- and your gratitude for all I have done to you- at the forefront of your mind when you ask yourself what I mean to you and what I still could, because birthday wishes can only be granted after the candle has been blown out- and the candle I hold burning for you could withstand an electrical storm and a monsoon, my love- so it can mostly certainly weather those that would oppose it!

So fight for me the way I am fighting for you. Slip your beautiful being into this beautiful gown and then come celebrate my birthday with me, your dear friends, and the Blue-Collar family have travelled across the country to tell you how much your sacrifice meant to them, and know that I will be counting the seconds until you arrive-

...and that I will remain the most eligible bachelor in Calliel until I have first had the opportunity to capture you the way you have captured me.

Sincerely,

Prince Charming.

Tears were running down my face by the time I finished, and my heart felt exactly like balled paper as I closed my fist around it and sobbed. When I'd first read this, I'd translated it to suit the monster that I'd presumed him to be, but now that I read it from the perspective of a man in love, everything changed and after, I knew that *I* was the monstrous one. He'd said that it hadn't been a threat but a promise... but like with Satan, I hadn't understood that there had been NO double-meaning until it was too late. Weeping bitterly, I cursed my wicked self and threw the paper over my shoulder.

I'm so sorry, Karol! I thought, leaning over the edge and breathing in deeply through my nose. Then I opened my eyes and whispered out loud, believing it as I never had before: *'I deserve this!'*

'Larkin, don't do it!' a soft voice cried, and I lifted my eyes to see a figure appear on the boulder across from me- on the other side of the river. I should have been shocked to see her again, but I was not- I understood that she was just a figment of my imagination. 'You have too much to live for!'

'So much less, since you left me dear friend,' I whispered to Martya, my tears falling like rain now to see her pale clothes glowing in the milky moonlight. 'But you know what? I swore that I would avenge your death, and tonight I did. Not as I expected to, but I don't think this kingdom will ever allow another Given Girl to be murdered again, okay? I don't know if it was Elijah or Karol or even bloody Kohl, but whoever did it-'

'I was not murdered Larkin!' Martya cried, and my heart skipped a beat, first at the admission, then again when I saw the smile on her pretty face. 'And I will never leave you again.'

33.

'No!' I cried, fingernails snapping off as they dug into the rock beneath me in outrage. 'Don't tell me you've been alive this whole time Martya don't even DREAM of it!' I cried, beside myself as I remembered reading her letter- and then slipping a bread knife into my toga before I spoke to Karol about it. 'When you died, something inside me died, and I've never been able to get it back!'

'I know. That was the whole point! I'm sorry, Lark, so sorry...' My friend had the grace to look nervous and ashamed as she whipped off her glasses and stepped forward so that I could see her more clearly. 'But I had to get out of there to carve a path for us, so I escaped, all right? I escaped and I made it look like a murder so-'

'What?!' I gasped, falling to my knees and tearing at my hair. Was she a ghost, a figment of my imagination or a complete traitor?! 'You're lying!' I pointed my finger at her. 'You're Satan again, aren't you? You're just showing me what I want to see! Trying to convince me to take another hand when really it's hers!' I looked around. 'She'd be here otherwise, trying to stop me herself!'

'Satan sent me to try and stop you, and I can explain why if you just calm down, okay? We're on the same side, Lark. She and I- we almost always have been!'

'No!' I breathed, my chin wobbling. 'No, that can't be true! You had so much going for you! You had your freedom! Why would you throw that away to align yourself with the dark?'

'Because I AM the dark, Larkin. In the definition of the word anyway, but I'm not *evil*!' If this was truly Martya, then I was astounded by how she'd grown in the short time since I'd seen her last. She'd shot up at least a foot and had developed muscles under her clothes, which looked worn, threadbare and filthy. She was gaunt too, clearly underfed, and there were dark circles under her eyes and scratches and bruises all over her. 'The roots of my family tree have been tangled with the Barachiel one since the beginning of this new time, Larkin!' Martya cried, raising her voice to be heard over the fall. 'It started with one of my ancestors, who loved Elijah the first, but was forbidden from being with him because of the circumstances of her birth, but it *will* end with me! I let you believe they had killed me, because I knew it would give you the healthy dose of distrust in them that you needed to free yourself from this place! That's what it's always been about, all right? Getting you out of here while garnering my own freedom!' She held up her hands. 'What started as such an easy task turned out to be a nightmare because no matter how much you should have hated your master, you could only love Kohén, just like my fool cousin, Adeline, could only love *hers*!'

My chin dropped forward as shock rippled through me. 'But Adeline is a part of your family too, isn't she? How could you end up on opposing sides of such a fence?'

'Because Adeline was the descendant of Rosa, Gabrielle's daughter, whereas I am a descendant of her half-sister, Julieta!' Martya screamed, and I cupped my face, horrified as I remembered the book that Satan had given me, and the name that had been crossed out: Julieta.

'Julieta? How?' I asked, shivering as the water misted me. 'You told us that her mother was your mother's little sister!'

Martya shook her head. 'That was what I believed but my mother told me many misleading things as a child to keep certain secrets from me- including the fact that I have more relatives than I believe- out here on this side of the fence! We would have been out here too, Larkin, but my mother had an important job and… and I was it.' She sniffled. 'There was dark Nephilim on my side, all right? And I know Satan has tried to tell you about it! Rosa and Julieta's bastard father was a rapist, and after Miguel followed Gabriella's pleas to find and salvage her daughter's half-sister, he discovered that he was a dark Nephilim too, as was she! He was terrified of having her in the family even though she was sweet and beautiful and flawed only by her haunted eyes, for he knew that her soul may have been corrupted for having been raised by such a bastard! He brought her back to Eden to be kind, but he did not let the two girls know that they were related- raised one with his family, and set the other up in an orphanage with other children that had survived the apocalypse!' she paused, and both of our breaths misted as we panted for air. 'She might have grown up to be happy for she was treated well, but one day, she and Elijah met while he'd been out on a ride, and fell madly in love at the age of eighteen! Miguel could have let them be together for the sake of all that was good and light, but he was too scared of what their child might be- a powerful Nephilim infected by her father's shadows- so he moved her away and found consorts to keep his son entertained with instead!'

'Oh my god!'

Martya grimaced and nodded. 'But Rosa had already started to get to know Julieta, and she'd seen how alike they were, and when she'd asked Miguel what he knew about her, he'd denied any inside knowledge. But she was curious, Rosa, like you, and when she continued to pump Elijah and Miguel for information over the disappeared girl, Miguel offered her husband a considerable estate in Miner as a bribe, and so Jasper moved her thousands of kilometres away in the opposite direction! Don't you see, Larkin? The very first companions weren't just saved by the royal family, but *manipulated* to break up a love affair!' My head was spinning from the influx of information but Martya had probably forgotten that she'd always been smarter than me, so she rushed on without pause. 'Julieta didn't believe that Elijah would forget her so easily, but he was because of his lust, and so she was forced to go live in a remote property in Rachiel while pregnant with the first TRUE Arcadian heir, all alone, on Miguel's command! But she was too heartbroken to function, so the infant- a daughter- was born prematurely and without breath! Miguel offered her riches in compensation- more land, a larger house...he did everything he could to make it up to her, and although Julieta took all he offered and broke the soil on the farm that my family still owns today, and although she eventually went on to marry and have normal children with another, kinder but completely powerless man, she had already been thrust into the darkness by Miguel's scheming, and had cursed his entire family from that day forth- had vowed that no Barachiel man would ever know the love of a daughter, until they had learned to love the mother more than they loved themselves AND their bloody God!'

'What? I gasped, reeling to learn that Elijah had been telling the truth- he had wanted a daughter, just prohibited from doing so, and utterly clueless as to why! I'd accused him of so much, and I'd been wrong at every turn, and now he was dead and it was too late for me to make amends for it. It was, quite frankly, the worse news I'd ever received, and I could not believe that it was something that Satan had... *what? Wanted* rectified? Was that why she had thrust that book at me? *Why?* Didn't she want them miserable and turning to her? 'How?'

'She hadn't done it intentionally!' Martya cried. 'She'd simply had more power than she had been aware of, and too much grief in her heart and head to think clearly, and so a woman's heartbroken pleas with the universe became the wish that Satan granted- a wish that Satan does not have the power to undo now, despite the fact that the consequences of that wish have been crippling to us all on both sides of this moral fence! Michael Barachiel's infant twin sister was born dead years later after Elijah the first finally procreated in a loveless union, and when Julieta found out she felt awful, but there was nothing she could do to take it back so she ended her own life for causing the man she'd loved so, so much pain- damning herself *again* and bringing shame upon her new family name! Miguel confessed that they were related to Rosa after her funeral, because he felt guilty over her now motherless children, and Rosa and Jasper moved to Rachiel to help Julieta's widower raise her niece and nephew until they were full grown, and so our families have been closer since...but Adeline's side was not stained by the sordid happenstances as ours were: they are as loyal to the crown as distant relatives of it can be, because Rosa believed that her step father was KIND to only move Julieta away, because the last time a light and dark Nephilim had had children together, God had ordered them to be destroyed!' Martya sighed. 'Whereas my side of the family is still affected by it all to this day. At first my ancestors felt guilt-stricken, but now that this many centuries have passed without a Barachiel marrying the mother of their children and breaking the curse on their end- we have reverted to being angry! Which is why I hated Elijah The Second so, especially when I saw the way he tried to repeat history by trying to turn Kohén's love for you against *you*!' Martya snapped off a gnarled branch off a tree in the Wildwoods and hurled it into the water. 'That's why we are where we are! Hundreds of years have lapsed but due to the Barachiel's misguided belief that they cannot risk marrying a woman in God's name for fear that they might hurt her, balanced with their need to have a woman in their arms at all times, the curse is still an entity within Eden's walls- one that *I* fell prey to when I was born third!' She smiled grimly. 'But my birth was not an accident, Larkin, and neither was yours! It was *all* pre- ordained!'

'What?!' I squeaked, grasping at the rock so that I wouldn't tip over prematurely. 'How?'

'Satan put you in here on purpose!' Martya declared, and my jaw dropped, filling with river-spray. 'On the night that we learned of our Companion fate, I was furious! I looked in the mirror and saw that my pain and fear had manifested Satan! She told me that she'd asked my mother to break a rule by having me- to give my family a shot at making things right! She said we could all be free of this place and break the curse and that would steer humanity back on course, but only if I helped you either win Kohén's heart, or got you out of here before you could be sucked into the system, like you're determined to become sucked into this waterfall!' She gripped the rocks, kneeling to look me in the eyes. '*You* were to be the woman that a Barachiel could love, Larkin! You were planted here for that purpose alone, and I planted near to you, to cultivate it! *You* were to be the one that broke the curse and changed it all, but that would not happen if you were made infertile, so when I saw that Karol was beginning to leer at you, and Kohén beginning to gaze at you with lust, I did all that I did in the hopes that it would force you to run from this place! Hoping that you would leave before you turned sixteen and went through that dreadful induction...' she shuddered, and when she opened her eyes again, she looked desolate. 'But not even my death could shake any sense into your well-meaning mind! That cure was your ticket out of here and you used it to make someone else's world a better place instead of your own!'

'I couldn't help it!' I wept, head swimming as my eyes were. 'No one told me anything! I was raised to aspire to be good and kind and strong- not to manipulate myself into the position of becoming a queen!'

'You would have been all of that and more if you'd had one selfish bone in your body!' Martya cried. 'Your goodness and light was supposed to be what earned you a Barachiel soul mate, while your awkward looks were intended to help conceal your appeal, but you bloomed too soon, so all it did was play you right into their greedy, grasping hands! *Now* look at you- considering ending your life over those smarmy bastards, who deserve all that Julieta cursed them with and more! Well I won't stand for it! I did not give up my hopes and dreams and freedom to see my best friend plunge to her death, Larkin!' She stood up again. 'So fly over here now, okay? Fly over here, embrace me, and let me show you all that is waiting for you on the other side of this fence! Your father! Your friends! Anyone you wish to follow you *will* follow you, but you must take that leap first into my arms!'

I stared at her, aghast. 'You're asking for me to trust you?' I demanded, incredulous. 'You admit that you're a dark Nephilim driven into my life by a curse, and then ask me to trust you? How do I know that you're not really Satan right now, playing tricks with my mind?'

'You can't know that, only trust in your heart that I am telling the truth!' Martya extended a hand to me. 'There are no light or dark Nephilim, Larkin, only different coloured feathers, remember? I could be as light as you- as good and kind and selfless and sacrificing, *everyone* in the world could be! But only if you use what is left of your feathers to bridge the last gap between us and join The Sequestered! We will rise with you as our queen, and we will make the world a truly equal place at last! Satan has *seen* it!'

The Sequestered again? Is that who Constance was telling me to run to? What have they got to do with my life?!

I looked from Martya, to the woods behind her, then down at the white water and over to the rocks below. The river was narrow here, but even then, it was still at least ten metres wide. Did I have what it took to bridge that gap? I looked down at my feathers, and knew that I did not. 'Satan has seen it?' I asked quietly. 'Me... as a queen?'

Martya nodded eagerly. 'Why do you think so many people have amassed here tonight, Larkin? Why do you think they've been screaming for your release? Because we all know what you could do for humanity- she has been spreading the word, congregating us here to witness this glorious moment so that we will know to follow you as surely as the first residents of this place knew to follow Miguel! She has manipulated every moment of your existence to get you to this point, and over that infernal fence, so that you can lead the ones that slipped through the cracks, *together*! It could have come to pass by getting you on the Barachiel throne too, but they fucked it up and I am glad for it! The world has been making a saint of Miguel Barachiel for too long, to its detriment- well *no more*! It's time to see what would happen if a woman were left in charge, and that woman is you, so jump for your life and let those who share your dreams catch you!'

My heart cramped up inside my chest, beating its last. 'If Satan wanted me to have the strength to lead people, or to get over that fence... then she should have given me a darker heart, an uglier facade or stronger feathers- because as desperately as I want to live, Martya... for all of you...' I sniffled and wiped at my last tears while I tried to shake off my ellipism, 'I want to die more. Witness *that*, why don't you? Witness me leap to you- and fall short of everyone's expectations! Perhaps then, they will turn to *you*- a woman with an actual backbone- to lead the way!'

'Larkin!' I heard someone behind me call, and twisted around just in time to see a perfectly-healed Barachiel in a white toga stagger after me, grasping the fence and shaking it as he howled. Kohl. He had survived and had been healed, and if I'd

429

needed further proof that I was done with this world, then the sight of him up and about while poor Karol remained dead somewhere clinched it for me. Thunder cracked above us and the skies opened so that ice-cold rain could pelt down on us- and at all of the people reaching for him. 'Get back here, Larkin Whittaker, and answer for your crimes!'

Martya screamed as he did, but I moved quickly, only making it a few feet over the river's edge before I flapped my wings- and felt the air rush through them. One moment I'd been bounding off the ground with all of the strength I had right towards Martya as she'd asked, and the next I was free-falling into the water below, which grasped me and sent me tumbling over the side, forcing rocks into my hips- snapping my bones immediately. My dear friend's scream followed me for as far as it could before that violent white water swallowed me, sucking me into itself, and it was like being pounded by a thousand fists as I was hit with rocks, sticks and chunks of ice. Ice-cold water filled my ears, eyes, and mouth until I was choking on my own scream, and the world around me fuzzed and bubbled angrily as it thumped me downwards.

It's ending! I thought, closing my eyes and letting the freezing water put the coals in my heart out for good. *It's finally ending! I'm sorry Martya, but I cannot live in this world and love without trust!*

But suddenly I was spat out into more of a free-fall, which was as thrilling as it was terrifying, but just as I opened my eyes, gasped around the rush of adrenaline making my extremities tingle, said a silent prayer to God to forgive me for all I had done- especially to poor Karol- and mostly for being too weak to go on living, I saw the last thing I'd expected to see-

'*No!*' I spluttered, as I plummeted not into rocks, but the swiftest incoming tide in history. Not into Satan's eternal hellfire, but into the ocean, which was as good as falling directly into Kohl's own, hateful hands again as he manipulated it to work his will- and break mine anew. The rain had stopped, but only because Kohl had switched tactics, and had decided to cushion my fall by filling the cove beneath me with the tide.

Son of a-

I hit the water hard like a stone being dropped into a stream, but though I let my breath rush out of me in order to sink down quickly, begging the rocks below to rise from the earth so that they'd still shatter me, all my flailing arms and legs touched was water. Ferocious, heavy, mind-numbingly cold water that began to swirl as I reached the bottom, sucked me backwards- and then spat me back through the surface like flotsam, making me gasp. The sky was as dark as the water was, and I could not tell if I was still rising up, or falling back down until bubbles burst into my nose as a wave crashed over me, pounding me down hard again.

'No!' I cried, but my mouth was already filling with water and I was vanishing under the surface, completely disorientated and terrified. I'd wanted to die, but not like this! Not as a result of Kohl's control over anything, least of all my fate! I was spat out onto the surface again, and then I heard a roar and looked up in time to see a huge wave bearing down over me. I sobbed in fear and tried to duck dive beneath it so that I could avoid being caught up by the powerful surface movement and hurtled back to the shore, but it was a mystical wave forged with murderous intent and so I was not equipped to fight it, especially not with waterlogged wings and dread-filled limbs that were not cooperating.

Oh God, Kohl- how are you doing this? Large bodies of water are supposed to intimidate you, not accommodate you!

My feet were frantically pedalling but my heels were stabbing into my frothy, sodden skirts, getting caught until they tore free, and my hair was wrapping around my face and neck like angry serpents, keeping me blinded and therefore panicked. The wave caught me and flipped me and started to drive me towards the shore, and just as I caught the lighter hint of land and sand rushing forward to meet me, I felt a warm, familiar hand catch my leg and drag me back with twice the strength of the wave. I balled up and twisted, saw Satan glowering at me from behind and beneath like an anchor, and sobbed anew, churning out a cluster of bubbles from my nose. The wave passed over us and then she let go of my foot, took my wrist and then began to kick her legs, towing me behind her until we both surfaced simultaneously.

'Is *this* what you wanted?' Satan screamed over the groan and crashing of the wave that had just hit the shore while I used one hand to tug the band of my skirt over my hips so that it would slide away. 'So many millions of people have opted for suicide over the years, wanting to add romance and drama to their death- wanting to set things up for themselves to be as easy and poetic as plausible! But you cannot plot an idyllic death, Larkin, it is always ugly! It is the one thing that *is* an equaliser!'

'You know this isn't what I wanted!' I spluttered as she hefted me over a large log that had been about to crash into us. It only just supported my weight, but I appreciated it all the same. 'I wanted it over fast! I wanted it to happen somewhere beautiful, just so beauty on earth would be the last thing I saw!' I scowled at her. 'And I know this is your doing! The only healer powerful enough to have restored Kohl so swiftly is Karol, and he's dead, so you must have master-minded his recovery, just as you apparently master-minded my entire life!' I knew it was pointless but I scooped up an armful of water and sloshed it at her. 'I hate you-'

Another wave smashed into us and I was picked up as easily as the log beneath me and shoved down through the surf again. I was in shallower waters this time so I hit the bottom hard, but all that crashed into me was cold, grainy sand. I rolled for I don't know how long and tried to suck the water in- tried to drown myself- but it was too hard to do and before I knew it, someone had clutched me and dragged me back upwards again. I wanted to fight, but I was already exhausted.

'Yes I did it!' Satan screamed as I surfaced in the frigid night air again. 'What can I say? It's not every day that a descendant of Miguel's cries out for my help, so I was moved to answer his prayers!'

'What did he ask for?' I choked on the words and salty water. 'Me? More power?'

'The chance to emerge from the harem with his reputation and his physical being unscathed!' Satan retorted, and I gaped at her, thunderstruck. 'So I healed him, on one condition!'

'You got to keep his soul?' I growled, despising her for granting him the ability to get away with all that he had done to hurt me.

'No, that's actually not the first thing I ask for Larkin, but the last,' Satan's eyes flashed with amusement. 'I told him that he'd make it out of the harem alive, but only he saved his baby brother first!' She shook her sodden hair. 'He actually considered not doing it, can you believe it?' Satan tittered as we rose and fell on a gentler wave. 'But in the end vanity won out- it always does- so he put out the fire and pulled Kohén to safety, getting him to a healer in the nick of time.'

I felt like I'd been slapped. 'But they must have been burning for twenty minutes by-'

'Oh don't be daft- this was done by the time you'd made it through the door, child. What do you think...I sat there listening to your re-cap of the evening's events with that bloody bouncer when there were pristine hearts to capture just metres away?'

'You're so twisted!' I cried, hating myself for being surprised to learn that Satan had double-crossed me. 'You act like you want to help me, but you help the very people that have led me to this moment!'

'I cleared two deaths off your conscience, and have now motivated you to stay alive- all things that prove that I am looking out for you!' she argued. 'And that is exactly what I'm doing. I'm offering you HELP. I am offering you the WORLD! But all you're going to know from now is pain if you don't take me up on those offers, Larkin! Perhaps you haven't been caught alone on a dark beach while in a fragile state by a bunch of ravenous men, but *I* have, remember?' She pointed to the shore, and my heart sank to see dozens of flaming torches working their way down the paths that had been cut into the hillside and to the scrawny, dark beach alone. 'And that's the fate that waits for you now, sweet Larkin! This tide will work to sweep you directly back into his clutches so that he can make a spectacle out of remanding you! He will have you bound, gagged, humiliated and dragged to that dungeon where he'll be able to do unspeakable things to you and call it justice... is THAT WHAT YOU WANT?!'

'No!' I cried. 'Of course it's not!'

'Then trust me, and swear yourself to me so I can get you out of this! I need that blessing Larkin I need your free will to love you as best as I am able, just like Karol did!'

'But I can't trust you now any more than I could have trusted Karol ten minutes ago!' I wept, feeling broken into pieces on the inside. 'Didn't you once say that exact same thing to God? In the book of creation he asked for your love, but thanks to the way he had ruined you- you could not give it!' I choked on salty water and spat it out, coughing. 'That is how I am with trust! I want to be able to give it, but I have none left!'

'Find some, Larkin!' Satan was crying now, her tears bloody and dark in the dim, smoky night. 'Learn from my mistakes if nothing else and trust *me*!' She twisted my weary body in the water and showed me the silvery wave looming up over us in the near distance. 'Or see your distrust knock you hard into the arms of the man that has created it!'

I looked at the wave, then back to the beach, then back to Satan. 'Wh-what's the price?' I asked weakly, sinking again because I had no strength left to paddle anymore. She caught me and jerked me up.

'I want you to swear to do three things for me- you must do them all without hesitation or argument, and if you don't...' she glanced back at the beach, then back to me. 'Then this is where you will end up again- right here, this moment, this night- *that* end.'

My teeth were chattering. 'Th-that's not fair,' I whispered. 'If you get three, I want three too!'

Her eyebrows shot up. 'I am not a fucking genie I am Satan- and you are rubbing me the wrong way.'

I shrugged, kicking away from her. 'Fine. Then rape it is-'

'Fine! What are they?' the 'R' word seemed to push a panic button in her eyes, and I found it unsettling to think that she was still traumatised by what had been done to her thousands of years ago. 'Spit them out now, or there's no deal!'

I looked back over at the wave and to the beach. There were dozens and dozens of people on the grey smudge of sand now, their torches blazing brightly as they waited for me to wash up onto the shore. They'd find me too- these waves were smashing only into that part of the world, and the current was strong and seemingly tireless. I didn't know how long Kohl could keep this up for, but I knew his reserves of energy were greater than mine. As were his reserves of darkness. If the ocean were towing me out, that I could tolerate…. but washing me up in his arms? No, absolutely not.

'I want Karol to be revived,' I whispered quietly, and Satan sucked in a breath. 'Completely, one hundred percent restored to how he was before I burned him tonight, no matter what it takes!'

'Oh, Lark, *no*! Do you think he'll wake up like the princess in a fairy-tale and come bounding after you to propose a second time?' Satan demanded, incredulous. 'He'll detest you! He thinks you're demonic!'

'Perhaps, but I know that *he* is not, and that's what counts!' I glanced back at the wave, heart racing more swiftly to see it cresting with silvery white water. 'Elijah's gone, which leaves his throne up for grabs and I will NOT see Kohl's backside upon it! Karol must live- as he was, you hear me? No tricks! No undead corpse staggering about- as he *was*!'

'Fine! Done!' Satan shook my arms. 'Hurry with the others! Now! Like I said, I'm not a genie- there is only so much control that I have over you until your free will is given! Finish wishing quickly, or never will I get the chance to start granting them!'

'Then I want Kohén to fall out of love with me!' I exclaimed, beginning to brace myself for the wave to hit us. 'If he's going to live, then I can't bear to think of him mourning what we had and how we hurt one another forever! I hate who he has become, but I will always carry a torch for the boy he was, so I want his perfect heart restored to how it was at the age of five, before I came into the picture so I can see with my own eyes, who he would have become if the harem hadn't messed with his head so! He must see all that I have done, and move past his obsession- and fall as hard for the next wonderful girl he meets with an unblemished heart!' I saw Satan open her mouth to protest again so I rushed on: 'And finally, I wish for equality on earth!'

Satan's eyes bugged. 'That I cannot grant! Do you think we'd be in this position if I could? God decided how man would be made differently from one another, and as you so kindly pointed out earlier, I am not even equal to God!'

'Surely there's-'

'No, I've tried! Choose a different third wish Larkin, because if it's not within my capacity, it will be wasted!'

I gulped when I saw the wave but really, I already knew what I wanted- what I'd been prepared to live and die for. There were other things I wanted- for Kohl's wish to be rendered null and void so that he'd be tarred and feathered by his people, not loved, and for the Given caste to be eliminated, but they were too limiting- they would only fix part of a problem, not the whole problem, and if I was who I'd been told I was, then it was very possible that maybe I'd be able to fix those problems, and more, with a bit of hard work and focus. 'I wish to be free forever!' I whispered quickly, looking back at the people wading into the shallows, searching for my body. 'Never again will I be owned by ANYBODY, locked up or forced to act against my will!'

'All that you have asked for will be done!' Satan crowed, and then, I felt an ungodly pain began to stab at my lower legs. 'But first, you must fulfil my first request- by going to *HELL!*'

I tried to scream, but the air was sucked out of my lungs and replaced with water as a liquid tornado swirled in the water around me and spiralled me down into the inky depths of it.

34.

I don't know how long I spiralled through the black water for, but eventually I was blasted out against the hard ocean floor that was just light enough to see in so fast that it knocked the water out of my lungs- and caused me to open my mouth in a scream that immediately saw them inflated again.

Oh God! She went through all of this just to kill me anyway? That must have been her on the cliff, not Martya! She was appealing to my vanity- trying to make me want to live so that she could snatch that from me again! Demon! She's trying to make me hate life until I hate God! Well too late!

I grunted as my lungs were filled to the point of bursting while pain ripped through my lower body again. I tried to kick my legs, to thrash the agony out, but when I looked down I was astounded to see that they'd become one! Not just one appendage but a distinct one- a scaly tail!

I'm a mermaid now? One that's drowning? That's her idea of Hell?

'For a claustrophobic like yourself that is weakened by water? Yes! You're not supposed to cry in grief, remember little one? That was one of the first rules you learned- and the first you broke and have consistently broken since! You hurt God with your tears- you weakened him and now, the weight of them will weaken you while you are held accountable for your other crimes against God and your fellow man!' Satan snapped inside my mind, and when I tried to move, I realised that she was right- the ocean filling my mouth tasted exactly like my tears, and having my legs seared together like that was making me feel even more panicky than the pressure in my lungs was so this probably the most fitting punishment for me. 'That's what Hell is all about, remember? Being punished for what we did wrong in life! You wanted death and equality more than anything else, Larkin, so don't curse me for your current terror- I'm giving you only what you asked for! The death you deserve, and the punishment that every other human would receive in hell in your place!'

Why? I tried to bring in my legs- to shoot up towards the surface again using the tail to propel me, but suddenly things were wrapping themselves around my fluke and wrists and I was being pulled back down! My eyes bugged and my heart began to grow faster and weaker- I would explode! I would explode soon, but at least I would be done, right? I wanted to be calmed by the knowledge that I had wanted this- but I had not. *Why beg for me to live if you only wanted me to die anyway?*

'God's not the only one that works in mysterious ways! And why would I answer your questions now, curious little kitty, when I know that unanswered questions will enhance your torment so?' Satan jeered, as seaweed continued to sprout out of the sand and weave around me, anchoring me to the ocean floor. 'Welcome to accountability, Larkin Whittaker! Welcome to the *other* side of life! You have asked for so much love and yet, you have caused so much heartbreak! So as your introduction to hell... I ask you to now feel what Kohén, Kohl and Karol suffered over you returned to you now, little swan, and if you survive that, we will move on!' she chuckled. 'Just be warned, I do like to compound the damage done in life by ten in the afterlife, just to make sure that a lesson is learned- so there is a good chance that you won't survive long enough to be repaid for your next sin- *lust!*'

I tried to scream when I felt the oxygen sucked out of my lungs, but it was too late for that so all I could do was choke and smack my useless tail against the bottom of the ocean floor as my lungs contracted like a stampede of horses were being driven over me.

My heart! I thought wildly as I thrashed about. *Oh God, it hurts! It hurts it hurts it HURTS!*

'It smarts doesn't it?' Satan hissed inside my mind. 'The breathlessness, the racing heart, the fear, the hurt- the PAIN! You have made the men that cared for you feel this time and time again with your indecision, and you think yourself the only one wronged when you are on the receiving end of it? You call *me* wicked? When my feathers were white, all Miguel *knew* was my *devotion*, whereas all Kohén has known from you was

Miguel's indecision! I think it's funny, of course and well deserved, but that doesn't let you off the hook with me or God!'

It was so painful that I immediately began wishing for death to return to me, but she kept me conscious enough to feel every heart contraction, so I grasped at fistfuls of sand as what felt like every inch of pressure in the ocean pressed down upon me. I wanted to be astonished to think that I'd caused any one person this much grief at one point (even divided by ten!) and cry about how unfair it was for me to be subjected to punishment for an ailment that *I'd* also suffered, but I hadn't the self-possession to even do that so I gasped and choked and sobbed and ripped at the sand. I could not breathe and could not think- all I could do was sob out bubbles and writhe while an icy fist clamped down around my heart and as visions of the Barachiel men's tormented expressions flitted before my eyes- still images from memories that I'd always avoided reflecting upon. Kohén after he kissed me for the first time and I mocked him- Kohén when he saw me wrapped around Kohl before his birthday, Kohl when he saw me giggle and flirt with Kohén in Pacifica, Kohén when Kelia had shown him the letters from me! I'd not even been present for that one but I saw it now- felt his terror and the harsh kick of my betrayal, square to his- and my- heart. Karol when I'd called him a rapist and finally, Karol when I'd set him on fire.

Their pain had always hurt me, but now I felt every ounce of suffering they'd experienced over me even when I hadn't been around to witness it, and so their torment became *my* torment- hundreds of little moments poured into one funnel and shoved down my throat. So many images of my haughty, retreating figure shown through Karol's stinging eyes while he pressed a healing hand to his own wounded heart through his chest- and countless nights that Kohén had spent sobbing into his pillow! Even the moments I'd faked- mostly moments from the past week when I'd reached for Kohén to make a point of it to Kohl to save him assailed me until eventually, I started trying to scream again and eventually succeeded, the sound tearing out of me in a cascade of bile-flavoured bubbles.

I'm sorry! I raged at everyone and no one. *I'm so sorry! But you hurt me too!*

'That they did, and to be fair- you gave the boys their fair share of thrills too... thrills I myself have always been happy to dole out...' Satan drawled as the ocean began to slowly morph from blue, to purple, 'kisses that were stolen, heavy breathing that fogged windows... the incredible sensation of being touched, and taunted and teased...' the colour lightened from amaranthine to deep pink and my heart began to throb so loudly that it was almost all I could hear. I was now so desperate for breath that it felt like I was going to be able to float free of my binds- but then they began to writhe more fluidly around me, touching places on me that stiffened and ached and throbbed in response. 'Lust...such a beautiful thing when sated- but such a hideous ache when one is left wanting!' I opened my eyes wide and looked down at myself and cringed when I saw that the seaweed had become vines that were now exploring me as intimately as Kohén's hands had. They slid under my corset, popping it free, and then began to caress my breasts slimily, feeling more like Kohl's clumsy ones in a matter of moments. I watched my undergarment float away, panic rising when I felt those vines begin to slither around my neck and nibble at the place where my scales met my lower abdomen, seeking entrance but finding none. 'And you left them wanting, Larkin! Time and time again! You wielded your beauty like a weapon and cried foul when they tried to disarm you! Scarlett O'Hara of Eden, you were, but cornered little bird you claimed to be... were they solely responsible for what happened tonight? Fiddle-de-dee!'

Stop! Stop, STOP! I cried silently as that thing began to strum against me rhythmically, making my sex hum despite my desperation to drop dead.

"Fuck me Kohén- now! Fuck me twice before you must leave me!" Satan mocked me and when I moaned, she laughed. 'Don't misunderstand me Larkin- lust is my favourite sin and certainly the one that comes most naturally- but God's not a fan of it, and it's one of the many things about himself that he cast off into Hell, I'm afraid, so you must be punished for giving in to yours!' Something forced its way into my open, silently

screaming mouth then and I felt my entire body shudder as the vine that had wound around my neck suddenly slammed between my teeth and down my throat. At the same moment, the others all tightened around me, constricting like thread around a bobbin. 'I know it's not fair to be punished for something you were born with when you were made in God's image, but even I must admit that you would have avoided tragedy if you *had* had a tail keeping those shapely legs shut over this past year!'

'*Fuck you!*' I raged at her silently. '*Fuck all of you twice! I was trained to do that and I am NOT-*' I hacked and gagged and felt my eyes roll violently back into my head- but then suddenly the vine jabbed into my lungs, popping something in there until the water rushed out of me like a geyser. I sat up, vomiting water for what felt like forever on a cold, hard floor, my body heaving with it but contorting freely because the vines had vanished.

Kill me! Kill me now! I begged her, spitting out sand and broken fragments of shells. *Because if I survive this for another minute longer I'm going to find a way to kill YOU!*

'Oh, that temper!' Satan chortled as the suddenly cold, cavernous space around us transitioned from pink to red. The water was only spluttering out of me now, allowing me to breathe again, but I was exhausted and aching, still stuck in the tail, soaking wet and feeling like I *had* been raped. I tried to calm myself, but every snatch of breath that I sucked up was a sharp rasp in my ears and when I tried to roll over onto all fours, I cried out in pain and collapsed, realising only then that the bone in my left wrist had snapped, as had the bone in my right arm- injuries that had probably been sustained when I'd plummeted off the tidal fall, but hadn't noticed until now due to shock and exposure. I'd not even felt them before but they burned now, making the muscles around them throb painfully. And my wings- when I twisted to regard them I sobbed, for they resembled charred Spiderwebs wrapped around broken sticks now.

'I've run out of tears to return to you, but we're not even close to being done yet, so let's move onto your anger!' Satan clucked her tongue. 'So many things you've screamed at people, Larkin- so many feelings hurt and wise-cracks pelted like stones! Oh yes by human, third-born standards you were well within your rights to let off a little steam, but God's perfect beings are not supposed to express hate and you have done so on a daily basis your whole life, so listen to a replay of your rage, endure the physical manifestation of your own anger, and *learn* from it! Sticks and stones may break bones, but hateful words chop up souls like bullets!'

The sound started like a whistling wind that was travelling towards me through a crack in a wall some distance way, and before I could prop myself up again, that whistle became a howl and then a scream and then suddenly my ears felt like they were being stabbed at with knives. I shrieked and bowed, trying to curl up into a ball and shield my ears, but my broken limbs wouldn't cooperate right and suddenly, I felt myself being hit by hard, sharp objects. I peeked up- just in time to see a rock the side of my fist fall down on me, striking me hard in the cheekbone. I wailed and turned my face but another hit me, just another smacked into the centre of what was now my naked back, and a fourth where my calf muscle would have been under the tail. The screaming sound continued as hard objects rained down on me, and I felt my brain and bones begin to turn to thick dust as I was crushed by the wrath that I'd lashed out at others with, tenfold. My bones broke and popped through my skin as Kelia's had, my teeth disintegrated into chalky fragments and my face was slapped again and again from both sides, to make up for the times that I'd struck Kohén and Karol. I heard voices emerge from the screaming calling me names, but they weren't other peoples' voices- they were my own and every word landed like another hurled rock, and ripped a fresh tear through the atmosphere as loud as a whip cracking.

'Liar! Thief! Bastard! Asshole! Rapist! Bitch! Shrew! Weak! Coward! Double-crosser! Spoiled pig! Predator! Son-of-a-bitch!' the insults rained down upon me until I began to fall apart like my feathers had, and I felt death's inky tentacles curl around me, tugging me into the descending darkness which

suddenly erupted in flames as I was subjected to being burned alive.

'Manslaughter is a funny word, isn't it?' Satan asked, her words hissing like steam from a valve, blistering my skin, and suddenly I was gasping for the pain of seeing Karol catch alight and fall back out of that window. Things exploded around me, glass shattered and the atmosphere became a conflagration as the chandelier that I'd dropped on Kohén fell around me, but no matter how much I screamed, Satan's voice remained steady and cool. 'How is slaughtering a man different from killing one? Does it hurt less? No. Did you want Karol to survive grabbing you? No, no you didn't...so I guess you murdered him Larkin, and that's the worst sin there is, isn't it? I know better- but God sure thinks so.... so here we go!'

But I couldn't respond to her- all I could do was burn.

I don't know how much time passed for me in that state, but the punishments continued to change before I'd had the chance to recover from the last. I crawled out of the flames that I'd hurtled at Kohén, Kohl, Karol and Amelia-Rose, and headfirst into a drunken state where all I could do was writhe on the floor, turn and vomit before rolling into it and being sick again. I grew dizzy from the alcohol flooding my mind and nauseous off the stink of bile and sickness- finding relief only from that when I slithered into a crowded room full of masked people and was laughed at for the state I was in- humiliated for all of the times that I had joked at someone else's expense, or made someone feel foolish. I'd only just deduced that I was being repaid for my sin of pride when the roof above us crashed down, trapping me under a mound of rubble. I was almost too weak to lift even a flaky bit of paint off of me, and yet I had to find a way to emerge from it- to toss shattered bricks and plaster aside while I fought to catch a breath and broke into a prickly sweat, and it didn't take long for Satan to inform me that I was being held accountable for the times when my depression had led to me having idle hands and a lazy brain- most of which had occurred that past week.

I'd read about the seven deadly sins before, and though it was evident that I was being punished for most of them as a matter of course, it was clearer that she'd tailored my hellish experience to make amends for everything that I'd ever done wrong so that no stone- or sin- was left unturned or went un-punished. I crawled and flinched and bucked and sobbed my way out of what felt like a gauntlet of nightmares, and by the time I emerged in quicksand, I knew that my character wasn't strong enough to endure it, and that I was probably going to suffer like that forever. I wept and closed my eyes as the pungent-smelling stuff filled my mouth and ears, not even having the strength to wonder what I'd done to deserve being smothered alive, just exhaling slowly through my nose and letting it all go, including my rampant curiosity. I'd wanted to die, hadn't I? That had been my fondest wish and now, it was being granted so how could I be anything but grateful *for* that?

And then I fell out the other side of the mud and into a pool of ice-cold water. I hit the sandy ground hard on two flat feet and immediately felt tiny waves rising behind me and breaking over me, knocking me to my hands and knees and dissolving against my skin in a burst of foam.

'Oh hell... *oh*...fuck!' Gasping in greedy mouthfuls of icy air and shivering violently, I crawled and spluttered my way out of the water and directly into the mouth of a cave, going up a steep, muddy hill and wondering what fresh hell waited for me within- but I was surprised to see Satan step out of the darkness beside me, barring my path as she helped me to my feet on hard packed sand. I looked behind me, wondering if I should just swim for it, but though I saw nothing but a sheer rock wall behind me, I could hear the tidal falls pounding into the ocean on the other side of it. Talk about claustrophobia-inducing! I was now stuck in an underground cave, and the only way out of there would be to swim out and pray that the pressure of the falls would drown me once I got out the other side.

'Congratulations, Larkin Whittaker...' Satan lifted my chin so that I was staring into her inky black eyes. 'You survived passing through the mouth of Hell. How does it feel?'

Say what? Huh? Where am I then? I stared at her, astonished, and could do nothing else for a few beats until she lifted her eyebrows inquisitively.

'Sweetheart- that was an actual *question.*' She took my hands, inspected them and then squeezed them before lifting one to her lips and kissing it tenderly. 'Are you all right? I've only ever seen one other human being enter Hell alive and come out alive so-'

'What?!' I demanded, thawing out a little at her words. 'I'm out? It's over? But.... how am I not *dead*? You just drowned me, and set me on fire, crushed me-' fury overwhelmed me- fury to see her looking at me with concern after what she'd just put me through. I opened my mouth to give her the sharpest, ugliest piece of my mind I had- but she wriggled her fingers and I saw a misty breath escape me and curl up in the palm of her hand. She'd taken my voice again!

'Sorry- it's really hard to get a word in edgewise with you sometimes, so just breathe while I explain myself, all right?' Satan smiled while I slitted my eyes at her. 'I held you accountable for your sins while you were still alive, but nothing happened to your physical being Larkin- it thrashed in the shallows behind you as you were punished inside your mind.' Satan smiled while I turned to look behind me at the water that was breaking against the sand bank that I was standing on, blinking to see the Tidal fall from the wrong side. Had I truly been there all along? 'Yes. And before you go off accusing me of deception again, or attempted murder, you must understand that I knew you would survive it, and that I wouldn't have subjected you to that if I'd thought otherwise.' She touched her fingers to my lips, drawing my face back. 'Okay, now *you* go.'

'What are you talking about?' I demanded, looking down at myself and blinking when I saw that I was wearing a corset identical to the one I'd fallen into the sea in, but one that was black and dry and... *fine.* As was the rest of me! My skirt was gone and had been replaced with form-fitting, black suede pants, and my lower legs were encased in sturdy black leather boots that were sinking into the wet sand but keeping them dry. My hair was still sopping wet, but when I reached around me to wring it out, I felt a familiar rustle, both against my hand and in my ear, and twisted to see that my wings had flared out behind me again, and that they were as lush and full as they had been when they'd first sprouted! They were still black, which hurt something deep inside me, but when I pressed my hand to my chest, I realised that it was the only thing that hurt now; a gentle twinge of regret, and nothing more. Tears filled my eyes- happy ones, and when I looked at Satan, I was stunned to see that her eyes were spilling over too.

'I know,' she whispered, touching one of the feathers over my shoulder gently and reverently, 'they're beautiful, aren't they? It killed me to put you through all of that, but to see your wings restored….' she swallowed hard and nodded, cupping my chin. 'It was worth it. And I hope you feel the same.'

I couldn't get a handle on the emotions coursing through me now- excited, happy, content emotions! 'How?' was all I could ask, and she smiled, wiping away one of my tears and examining it almost lovingly.

'I told you that you didn't understand Hell, but you didn't understand that either and hopefully, this experience has enlightened you a little more.' She took my hands and squeezed them. 'It is common knowledge that God accepts everyone into Heaven so long as they love him, and that those that do not come to me by default and are punished for their sins, but what no one alive knows- except a handful of people that I trust- is that atonement is only the *first stage* of Hell. Souls come to me- battered or merely bruised, guilty, evil, warped- and I cleanse them by putting them through what you just went through, and then I take the power filtered through their wrong-doings back into myself, and that regenerates me without compounding my already blackened soul.'

I stared at her. 'You… you filter evil out of power before you take it into you?'

'Yes.' She smiled. 'Surprised, hey? You're not the first and you won't be the last.' She took my hands and looked into my eyes. 'It is said that I grow from hate as he grows from love and technically that's the truth… but I was still made in his image and when he cast me out, he didn't change that, so I am not that much different from the Satan that first walked this earth because I still crave the things that God did before he split himself in two: comfort, happiness, pleasure, creation and success.' She paused. 'Even love. Actually no- especially love. I crave that more than I crave anything else... I just don't have the ability to hope or dream or believe in it anymore.'

I was beyond confused. 'Are you telling me that you are not evil?'

'Not in the way you have been taught to believe.' She wrinkled her nose. 'I admit, I get a rush out punishing bad people, and acting lustfully and eating and drinking and cursing and... well, basically everything you got up to this past week.' She smirked, squeezing my hands to let me know that she was teasing me. 'But causing bad things to happen to people is not fulfilling at all, so I strive for other things. They're selfish goals, I'll admit that, and if I was ever made to go through hell again I probably wouldn't survive the 'pride' part but no, I am not evil- I am merely as afflicted by humanity as all of you are, can only grow from that hate that I am offered and incapable of loving anyone.'

I digested that. 'What about liking people?' Silently I was asking: *Do you like me?*

'If they make me laugh or impress me or out-wit me or another human I grow fond of watching them and come to like them very much, and if something bad were to happen to them and take their energy from the earth I would be crushed. I just won't ever be able to put another human before myself or my ambition, and that's what love is, isn't it?' she asked, and I nodded thinking that didn't seem so evil at all- just limited. She nodded politely and went on: 'Most people that enter Hell go through a lot worse than what you just did Larkin and it takes them much, much longer to pass through to the afterlife that I built out of his negative energy as I atoned for my own sins... and some lived lives so corrupt that they never make it through before they dissolve- like vapour.' She smiled sadly. 'But when they have made it through, what awaits them is... considerably more attractive a prospect than it is made out to be, and not as dissimilar from Heaven as God believes.' She sighed. 'Crossing over is an awful thing to experience though, and believe me when I say I know because for what I did to Heaven and Miguel, I writhed in agony as you just did for what felt like centuries and was, in actuality- decades.' She smiled sadly as I winced in sympathy. 'But your sins paled in comparison to mine, and I knew you'd be out in minutes, so I sent you there to free you.' She swallowed hard. 'I also apologise for how I spoke to you when you were in there, but I cannot help that- punishing people is my responsibility and mine alone, and when it must be done, it takes me over.'

I wrapped my feathers around myself and hugged them tightly. 'So... so Hell *isn't* a bad place? It's just *getting* there that hurts?'

Satan held a finger to her lips, as she had before, and smiled with sparkling onyx eyes. 'Let's not share that around, right? I'm as fond of the earth as I am of Hell, unlike God, and do not desire to see people act wicked upon it in their eagerness to join me after because my ultimate goal is to gain control of the world and if it gets wrecked then God will try and intervene again and then we'll all have nothing. All you need to know is that you have atoned for your sins, Larkin. That is why you feel so light now, and why your feathers have returned. Most people have to die in order to be cleansed by Hellfire the way you just have, but I made an exception for you, and sent you in with a pulse.'

I was so confused. 'Why?'

'Because I wasn't going to save your life, just to have you find some other way to end it,' Satan said simply. 'If I'd saved you from Kohl, you would have found a way to feel guilty about accepting my help or any of the other million things that were weighing on your conscience, and you probably would have swallowed poison or jumped off a cliff or Lord knows what else in your haste to be free of all of that hurt and shame and pain that you carry around with you the moment my back was turned- I saw many things occur to you, even while you were making your wishes.' She shrugged. 'But now... it's gone, isn't it?' She studied me carefully. 'When you think of all of the things you have done... you know that you have already been punished for them, and no longer feel like you ought to be...don't you?'

I lowered my eyes, not knowing what to think, but to test myself, I thought of Karol and felt.... nothing. I remembered laughing at his jokes, melting under his kisses and screaming as he'd gone out that window- but my heart didn't clench up as it had before, and so I tentatively thought of Kohén- and felt only a rush of warmth followed by another twinge of... no, not regret... loss maybe? I missed him. I missed the *old* him a lot- but the desire to throw myself at his feet and apologise for all the ways I'd wronged him was gone, as was the desire to ever see him again. Besides, they were all going to recover anyway, weren't they? So what did I have to feel guilty for?

They couldn't be allowed to escape their guilt so easily though- that I realised when I recalled the ways that they had wronged me! In fact, the memory of the way that Kohén had slipped his fingers inside me while Kohl had held me down made my blood boil and feathers shiver with silent age as I realised the absolute truth:

I didn't deserve it, and they will pay for what they did to me! All of them! My wings, they were so white! So lovely! And they stained them! Maybe that was never their intention so they cannot be considered evil, but it was the outcome of their family's rules, and that is the evil that must be changed! I want equality, and fairness.... and I want my white feathers back!

'I can't fix that any more than I can reverse the staining of my own,' Satan said, and I looked up and blushed when I realised that she was reading my mind again. 'The condition of your feathers is a reflection of how you feel about God, and that's why killing Karol- even unintentionally- ravaged yours so. Going to Hell washed your sins away, but the colour of your wings... that determines whether you will get into Heaven or not-'

'I don't want to go to Heaven, I want to live!' I snapped, heart pounding with enthusiasm for life again- and revenge- and Satan snorted lightly, looking somewhat pleased. 'God wasn't there to help me in my hour of need- *you* were.' I wrung out my hair. 'Where is he, anyway? God, I mean?'

'He's everywhere,' Satan said simply. 'He's in everything good and light in the world as I am in everything dark. But physically...' she shrugged. 'He's not here- thank *God*,' she smirked, 'and he won't return unless we give him cause to. Which is precisely why I have intervened - not only because I am desperate to see you live and make a change, but because if you'd died- I know that God would have felt your loss and returned.'

'My- my *loss*?' I repeated, confounded. 'Why would a God that has never answered my prayers feel my loss?'

'He's answered more of your prayers than you think, Larkin- just not as many as I have. And he certainly would have felt your loss- being that you're an angel.'

'A Nephilim,' I corrected her, thinking of what Martya had told me about Julieta. She had died, and the earth had rolled on without God's interference, and that had only happened thirty-odd years after he'd turned his back! 'One that doesn't love him, remember?'

'A Nephilim refers to a being that is created via breeding with an angel, or another Nephilim- and a human,' Satan said, taking my hair and wringing it out for me. 'You're... *more* than that.'

I frowned at her. 'But Sapphire Whittaker wasn't a Nephilim- even though I know that my father was-'

'Sapphire Whittaker wasn't your mother, Larkin,' Satan said sadly, and I felt my heart sink. 'I lied about that... somewhat. I had to, for risk of provoking your flames while you were still their ward. Don't get me wrong, Sapphire was a formidable woman, but your true mother was a lot more powerful than she was-'

'*Some*what?' I hissed, jerking her hands out of my hair and stepping back, hanging onto it for dear life and whimpering when I felt that it was dry. 'How can you *somewhat* lie about such a thing? She either gave birth to me, or she didn't!'

'She gave birth to you, that part I was honest about!' Satan said, wringing her own hands together now and looking...

nervous. And that worried me- how could it not? If something made the devil nervous then how on earth was I going to deal with it? 'But she was just a womb, the purest one I could find at the time, the most beautiful...' she bit her lip. 'And the most likely to do as the law commanded- and hand you over to the crown like I needed you to be, before you could return to your real mother- the Nephilim that Bastien impregnated.'

'The most likely to not care about me, you mean?' I asked roughly.

'The most likely to love God more than she loved her own child,' Satan admitted, and my heart twisted. 'I felt bad for using her like that, and subjecting you to such a cold home... but it had to be that way, Larkin. I couldn't risk that anyone- your mother, your father, your master would notice how special you were, which is why I cloaked your beauty for as long as I did too.'

I frowned. 'Cloaked my beauty? Is that what you called it?'

She smiled, touching my hair again but I recoiled and she sighed. 'You would have been the most dazzling little thing on the planet if I hadn't taken pains to hide your genetics, so I enchanted you to stay as plain, scrawny and unappealing as possible to protect you. Not just from men's eyes, but from vanity and arrogance and everything Kelia developed that *you* escaped.'

I leaned back and held up my hands. 'Whoa! Was Kelia a dark Nephilim too?'

'No, she was a fucking twat and the world is better off without her,' Satan said, making a face, and my corrupted soul loosed a giggle. 'Anyway, I know that giving you such a plain face to wear was difficult for you and potentially detrimental to your self-esteem, but after what happened with Heaven Barachiel back in the beginning...' she sighed. 'A woman has no business being beautiful if she is not also clever, cunning and kind. Not that it did *you* much good. Your first kiss was to be won with your inner beauty and break the enchantment once you were shielded from a boy's lust by love, but that happened much earlier than I'd hoped because you agreed to do Kohén that favour and give him his first kiss so…' she gestured to me. 'Here you are! Five foot-six inches of Barachiel bait.'

I put my hands on my hips and glowered at her. 'So I wasn't supposed to be bait all along? Martya sure inferred otherwise! And who was my mother if it wasn't Sapphire? Siria? Lindy? If Lindy had the means to save her own ass all along then I'm going to-'

'No! she cried. 'It wasn't Lindy and you were never supposed to risk yourself like that! That was your father's influence on your soul, not mine. I… Your father and I… we…' she glanced behind her and sighed, stepping aside so that I could see a tall, golden silhouette unfurl from beside the fire. 'Shep… *you're* the articulate one.' She swallowed hard, looking back at me and beckoning the golden man forward while I stumbled back. 'Do you think you could come explain all of this and who her mother is to your daughter before she hurls a fireball at me?'

I'll hurl fireballs at everyone if I don't get answers soon! If I'm half angel, half Nephilim, then who was I conceived with? Siria? Gabby? CHERRY?

'I wouldn't blame her if she did, and don't call me Shep- you know I hate it,' the man said, approaching me as tentatively as one would a Salt and Pepper bear. 'But I'll gladly take over- hello Larkin,' he said, smiling softly, 'I'd say its lovely to finally meet you… but I don't know if that's going to be the case yet, do I? Not until it is the past tense and not just wishful thinking on my part?'

'You're a Shep?!' I squeaked, glancing at Satan. 'My father is a Shep *and* a Nephilim?'

'The purest soul I've ever known,' Satan said. 'His wings have stayed white for a millennia.'

It was like being beaten over the back of a head. 'A millennia?!' I gasped, gaping at Shep. 'You're…?'

'One of the originals, like me, and Miguel,' Constance said softly and I covered my mouth with my hand, astonished. 'A soul-mate. And yes, sweet girl- that makes *you* the first angel to survive past infancy on earth in over two-hundred thousand years.'

35.

'**H**_ow?!_' I cried, looking at the golden man in alarm as the words '_two-hundred thousand years_' echoed over and over in my head.

Satan cocked her head. 'Well, others have been born but because they were mixed God had them destroyed-'

'Not how am I the only surviving...' I couldn't even say the word 'Angel' without my fever spiking and mouth going dry! 'I mean how is he _here_?' I turned back to my father. 'All of you were only allowed to stay and help until your feathers had been repaired by your good deeds, but then you were all supposed to leave and never return! God made that a _rule_! He said he was surrendering his eyes and ears to safeguard your souls-'

'He gave us all the free will to return that he denied Miguel,' the golden man said softly, 'and the others did all return to Heaven, eventually. But I _couldn't_. I was enamoured with the human world as Satan and Miguel were and had spent most of my life in Heaven at God's side before Armageddon, so living here was more of a novelty to me than it was to the others, so I stayed longer and God allowed it because my feathers had always been the purest and were never compromised.' He glanced at Satan. 'Plus, I was terrified that she'd return once God's back was turned, and knew that once Miguel's mortal life came to an end, the world might end up in the clutches of her dark Nephilim, so I lingered to hunt them out while helping the humans, knowing that the gates to Heaven would remain open to me so long as my feathers remained white.'

'Translation- he was as nice as the most boring pie there ever was,' Satan said, and the golden man gave her a _look_ that was probably supposed to be threatening but translated only to being a blander smile. 'He never sinned, was never ambitious or proud or vain- he was perfect, just like you were before the Barachiel's got to you.' She nudged him with her elbow. 'Inside and out, right baby?'

'_Baby?_' I repeated, horrified, but my father laughed. 'You're an item?!'

'She's teasing me, Larkin. Satan has never gotten over Miguel, and so she and I have no romantic feelings towards one another whatsoever.'

'I don't even like him much,' Satan joked, 'but he is rather handsome, isn't he?' and when the golden man blushed and smiled, I smiled too to see that he was taking her sharp humour with an abundance of good humour. It reminded me of how Kohén had always taken my gentle ribbing with a smile.

'She was never very aware of the rest of us soul mates when she was still counted as one of us, not with Miguel around to catch and hold her eye as he did,' the angel teased back, 'and she didn't even know I was still alive until after I had begun to die.'

'Oh I was aware of you,' Satan huffed, 'I just didn't care.'

'You... you died?' I asked, wondering if that meant that he truly was a ghost. 'What happened?'

'A lot of things...' The man pulled me down, perching on one rock while indicating that I should sit on the other by the fire, and I sank willingly, fascinated by his story and the dynamic between them, which was confounding. 'I'd lived dozens of human lives by that point, Larkin, always in a new place, with a new name, and I was fully invested in every one, trying to find a new way to make Miguel's sacrifice count while living life to the fullest while I could. I'd always accomplished what I'd set out to do, righting some wrong or preventing some disaster, and I think I got addicted to being pious, and that became vanity and...' he sighed. 'Eventually I got in over my head, my feathers began to lose their integrity and like the opportunist she is, Satan felt me at my weakest and pounced-'

'You called to *me*-'

'While out of my head with fear!' the angel smiled reassuringly at me. 'She promised me to save my life when it was first threatened. I tried to resist her, just like you did, but I was put through more distress and my feathers began to malt so rapidly...' he looked down at my hand in his and smiled tenderly before looking back up at me, and it was only then that I realised that not only was I holding onto him, but I was *hypnotised* by him! For so long I'd dreaded this moment and yet here I was... awestruck. He was as beautiful as I'd remembered-tanned skin, golden hair with bright eyes that shifted colours, just like mine, and he spoke with a clipped accent that made music out of his words. 'I got trapped in a human conundrum, you may say, caused by a heartless Nephilim-'

'That *I* had no connection with!' Satan pointed out quickly, looking at me. 'Yes they are all descendants from my old soul-mates, but as soon as they lost their wings, I lost the ability to keep an eye on them, as God did with the light, all right?'

'She's telling the truth,' my father conceded. 'But I still had my wings, and dark Nephilim are attracted and intrigued by energy like mine when they feel it- as they are inclined to destroy it. So this girl knew what I really was, and wanted to make an example of me to spite all that is holy, which she reviled.' He sighed. 'It quickly became apparent that I'd been softened by my experiences on earth- shielded from how dangerous some beings could be because the humans I'd all known had been relatively harmless and as devoted to God as I- so I was not equipped to face off with her.'

'What did she do?' I asked, hurting for him when I saw the anguish in his eyes.

'Told them that I was dark Nephilim... or alluded to it, at least, and then set a series of traps for me to prove it true that I naively walked right into. They believed the lies that she told about me after that, so they punished me for things I had not done... they whipped me, accused me of unspeakable acts, branded me, poisoned me with gold-'

'You're allergic to it too?!' I demanded, and he nodded grimly.

'Yes, and she knew it. So when I reacted to it, that was proof to them, see?'

'To *whom*?'

'The Barachiel family, who I sadly despise now, which saddens me because once, I'd thought the world of Miguel Barachiel too, and had only wanted to help his ancestors, not harm them as she led them to believe!' the man shook his head and I squeezed his hand, letting him know silently that he was not the only one to have suffered that fate. He smiled weakly and went on: 'And of course, they didn't want anyone finding out that there were still dark Nephilim about, so they hid that fact and threw me over that fence, where I lay for days dying a slow, torturous death- the kind of death that they believed only a dark Nephilim deserved, to send a message to any others that might be loitering nearby.' His golden brows pulled in together. 'It was awful, but I didn't care about my life- I didn't even care about getting into Heaven by that point, so hurt and jaded was I... but then I remembered that if I died while my feathers were skeletal, God would feel my loss and be drawn down to avenge it- and *that* would mean the end of the world, most likely, not because the humans deserved it, but because a Nephilim had interfered as *I'd* always feared. So...'

'So he called out to me and I showed up and made him an offer that he couldn't refuse,' Satan said, winking at me as she quoted one of my favourite books. 'Well, he refused it *and* eight others but finally we agreed on an arrangement that was to his liking-'

'She'd save and then prolong my life until I'd gotten my feathers back,' he said, squeezing my hand again, 'buying the human race time to evolve beyond needing so much divine intervention, and giving me the chance to finish what I'd started while maintaining the right to one day, return to Heaven. She wouldn't get my soul because I refused to hate God for what a Nephilim had done, but God wouldn't find out that another archangel had fallen and draw him back either, so she generously lowered the price for me when she saw that it would benefit her too, and I have been paying it since.'

I glanced at Satan. 'What price?'

She met my eyes without flinching. 'He'd be my slave, of course. I let him keep his pesky soul to give to God one day, and haven't made him do anything untoward that would blacken his remaining feathers... but until he finishes what he started- he belongs to *me.*'

As I do until I've done the three things she's asked of me, right? I thought, and shivered when Satan winked and nodded.

'And we made that deal some years ago,' my father admitted, casting a weary look Satan's way. 'I thought I'd be able to accomplish all I'd dreamed of by now, but *someone's* kept me in purgatory by keeping me busy with a never-ending to-do list-'

'Which suits your purposes as much as it does mine,' Satan pointed out, looking irked and telling me that this wasn't the first time they'd bickered over this point.

'So you say…' but he was still smiling and I was amazed to think that I'd ever considered that smile to be off-putting. It wasn't his darkness that had made me feel so uneasy, but his light! Who could trust such kind words, in a world where kind words were usually spoken to cover an insult? Who could stare so directly into such an unfaltering smile and steady gaze? It was like staring into the sun! And I'd inherited half of his genetics? It was astonishing to me!

'Anyway Larkin…' he said, and I looked from his smile back to his eyes, which I were amazed to see had turned lavender. 'Creating you with her at her behest was the scariest thing I've ever done. I feared the repercussions for us all, and have hated being trapped on the other side of that fence since you were born- forced to watch and wait and pray for you… but when I look at you now, and think of all you've endured and accomplished…' he smiled, regarding me with wonder as his eyes scanned my face. 'I feel like perhaps conceiving you was my true purpose all along, and that I wasted my last life trying to do something that you were always meant to accomplish anyway.' His hand squeezed mine. 'It makes me wish that I had procreated earlier and saved the world by giving them you when you were first needed.'

My heart thunked in my chest, as I tore my eyes off him and flitted them to Satan, and back again. Gone was her teasing smile- and the apprehension in her eyes had returned. 'You conceived me…. with *her*?' I felt the blood rush to the surface of my skin again. That pain in my stomach twanged again, becoming hot all of sudden, and I gasped to realise what it was. 'I am *Satan's* child?!'

'An angel!' Satan repeated, looking indignant. 'Half-light, half dark and the only one in existence! And I've already been more of a mother to you than Sapphire was so please, dial down the revulsion a notch, okay? You're hurting my feelings.'

'Why don't *you* dial down the flippancy?' my father demanded of her. 'Acting so aloof at such a moment when you know that I know how much you've anticipated this! And how desperately this child needs to feel loved and protected!'

'I can't help it, Bastien!' she snapped, and I almost fell off the rock she'd sat me on. 'God made me the way I am, so it is not my fault that I don't have the ability to communicate my affection for her as eloquently as you do, is it?' she pointed her finger at me. 'I wept! Just minutes ago! I was so gladdened to see her emerge from Hell that I *wept*! Can't that be enough to satisfy you for now, or must I bake cookies and braid her hair to prove how exalted I am to be a mother again while you explain immaculate conception to her?'

'Bastien?!' Flames flared out of my fingertips as I scurried back against the sand and into the water, inadvertently dousing them and causing them to hiss and steam. 'Shepherd Bastien *Birch*?'

Shep looked at me, eyebrows raised. 'You've heard of me?' and then alarm flickered across his face as he rose. 'Oh Larkin, nothing you've heard is true, I swear it! That girl made it all up- I was trying to save her from Eden, but she wanted to destroy it and anyone that got in her way! I would have seen it coming if I'd used my wings but I've never allowed any human to see them for fear of what they'd do to me!'

'His real name is Raphael, if that helps,' Satan said, coming over to help me out of the sand. 'He didn't get a personal mention in the Six Books Of Creation so it's okay if you haven't heard of him. It was different in the old world, but he's been rather inconsequential to this new one, nellipot that he's become…'

Raphael, the angel that tried to guide people with wisdom and healing! I thought, casting my mind back to my theology studies, and then to what I recalled of the bible. *That's why he's spent so much time helping people privately instead of forming a new country with his ancestors as the old ones did! His calling has not changed since the dawn of time!*

'Huh... you *are* well read...' my mother said, taking the thoughts from my mind and I ground my teeth together in anger, tugged my arm out of Satan's grip and then collapsed back against the cave wall, glowering at her. 'Or, thoroughly read, at least.' She smiled at my father. 'She knows you,' and he looked pleased. 'Big fan.'

'Shut up!' I snapped at her. 'Yes I've heard of him, but your reputation is the opposite of inconsequential and that's what's throwing me here! If all that is good in me is due to him, then all that is bad in me is due to *you*, right? I am literally the spawn of Satan!' Tears filled my eyes as I pressed my hand to my aching stomach. 'I read banned books because of *you*! If my blood had been tested, I would have been killed- and yet you put me in that place on *PURPOSE?!*'

'Yes,' Satan said quietly, taking my wrists and pulling them down while my head spun in dizzying circles all over again. She winced at the sight of my tears. 'But I had a good reason for doing it Larkin and if you'll remember... I tried very hard to get you out of there when I realised that you were in real peril- but you didn't listen to me, did you? A point I hope you're going to rectify from now on!'

But I could barely hear a word she was saying now that it all hit me. Martya was alive, and so were all of the Barachiel sons, if Satan had done as I'd asked. I was an angel, my father was Bastien Birch and the Archangel Raphael, my mother was the devil and I was supposed to champion all their causes now or something with*out* pissing off God and causing him to intervene? It was all too much! In fact, I think it was more than anyone else in the world had EVER been expected to do, and it was terrifying! And the way I'd come into the world... it was mind-boggling, and sort of gross. My biological parents didn't even like each other, and if Sapphire had lain with a woman then she must have lain with Satan but...

'She was a vessel,' Satan said softly, watching me carefully with her eyes while picking through my thoughts with her mind. 'She took me into her arms, and I took over her. Then I beckoned Bastien in and... I had no other options, Larkin. I couldn't create people out of my energy the way God could while ninety-eight percent of the existing population were devout to him, and without a mortal, fertile body of my own I was limited-'

'Weren't you castrated?' I demanded of Bastien Birch, already doubting all I'd believed to be good about him. 'Chemically?'

'The gold did the job, but Satan reversed that too,' Bastien said.

'But you seem like a ghost!' I cried. 'I've seen you flicker and fade, and you can't seem to breech that fence so how could you touch me now- or touch mother dearest here at all?'

'The flickering and fading is part of my own powers,' Bastien said softly. 'I can vanish, if need be- on a molecular level, which is why I encouraged you to take my hand because it would transfer to you, and keep you safe. And I could not breech that fence because your mother - *this* one- forbade me doing so to keep me from liberating you early, which I was desperate to do the moment I saw you with my own eyes...' he smiled sadly. 'But I'm not *dead* Larkin. Often I don't feel alive and I always feel as though I am haunting this world... but I cannot physically die until I have earned my feathers back by fulfilling my purpose- to eliminate the Given caste once and for all with your help.'

'But Constance was intuitive and she sensed darkness in you!' I cried.

'She sensed my hate for her because she had hurt you!' Bastien snapped, showing a flare of temper for the first time. 'There isn't a Barachiel on this earth that wouldn't feel my hatred for them all with one look at my face! In fact, it is probably my hatred for them that keeps my feathers in disrepair!'

I racked my brain, fanning myself as my temperature steadily rose. 'But what about the other baby?' I demanded, thinking of that awful trial I'd witnessed. 'There have been others, haven't there? So do I have little angel siblings getting around that you-'

460

'I have NEVER had another child!' Raphael protested, lilac eyes darkening as mine did. 'Not since I was first created, and that I swear to you, my darling- I may not have been a father to you, but you are the only daughter I have ever known.'

'They were lying, Larkin,' Satan said quickly, when my mouth popped open. 'Those women got babies on their backs the old fashioned way and cried rape or coercion to hide it. When they tried to throw the babies over the fence however, your father was always there to catch them, and so they used him as a scapegoat. The babies that they'd claimed had been immaculately conceived were taken away, had their blood tested, and then were spat back into the third-born system once it was determined that they were all completely human- and often matched the DNA of the mother's male neighbour when it didn't match her actual spouse's.'

'That's awful!' I cried.

'That's humanity,' Bastien said sadly, stepping up beside her. 'And it's always been repellent to you because you have less of it than any of them and a divine soul.'

I stared at him, digesting that while feeling an awful headache coming on. 'So what happened to the babies that you were passed that didn't get discovered?'

He smiled at me warmly. 'They are waiting for you to join them, just like all of the others.'

'What *others*?'

'The Sequestered,' Satan said. 'That part Martya has already explained to you, yes?'

Oh Martya had explained it, partially at least, but it still didn't make any sense to me, and my curiosity was so overwhelmed by questions that I was feeling light-headed. There were babies waiting to meet me? I was going to help father wipe out the Given Caste? This had to be a warped dream, or another, impassable level of Hell!

Having wings is hard enough to come to terms with! I thought, feeling panicky and claustrophobic again. *But... saving the world from God's wrath? Immaculate conception? Jesus Christ!*

'Close,' my mother said, reading my mind again and smiling, 'but you're a lot prettier- and twice as powerful as Gabriel's first child was.' She leaned in and wrapped her arms around me in a tight embrace, lifting my face to hers and smiling wickedly. 'And soon enough, *every*one will know it!'

I stared into her eyes and felt not fear- but a growing sense of anticipation now. 'What is it I have to do?'

Satan sighed, looking apprehensive. 'You have to break that curse or find your way onto a powerful throne. That would have been accomplished more easily if you'd let them all die, but you have asked me to save them and I can only do what is asked of me or what I want for myself so long as it doesn't interfere with free will. It is good for your feathers that you have saved them, and good for mankind because I think God would return if he felt the loss of Miguel's entire legacy... but despite your powers, you were born from a mortal woman and not hand-crafted by God, so you can still be killed my dear- rather easily- and soon, they will try to do exactly that, and I will not be able to linger much longer to shield you as I have tonight.'

My eyes widened at that. 'Why?'

'Like God, I must retreat from the mortal coil to recover, and I have exhausted myself this night- I will have to be gone by morning before my body begins to fade and will be unable to return until your actions have won me more hearts, or the Barachiel's evil actions have won me more hate.' She motioned to Bastien. 'He will stay with you to guide you to a safe space and fill you in on a lot of important details along the way, but his power isn't an offensive one like yours, merely defensive, so you will have to find a way to protect yourself from the Barachiel crown's reach however you can, until it is time for you to be the one that attacks from an equal if not greater position of power.' She met my eyes steadily. 'Can you do that, sweet girl? Can you make your life a priority over all else if it means saving others? It might mean doing things that are unpleasant... but ultimately for the greater good.'

I thought it over while my heart pounded in my ears. 'I think I can,' I eventually admitted, feeling power stirring inside me. 'But first... do you have a knife?'

Satan looked confused for a moment, but then she read my thoughts and winced.

Don't tell him! I warned her. *It must be done! And he will try and stop me if he sees it coming!*

Yes, he will. Oh dear... this will take the last of my energy, you know. And I'm afraid it will pain me to watch it happen.

And watching me deep throat a vine didn't set off your maternal red flags? Please- you should have thought of it before you checked me into the whore hotel.

I told you, I can't separate that part of myself from this part of myself! And before you sass me with one of your snappy little comebacks... ask yourself who you inherited your quick wit and forked tongue off, hmm? You think it was bashful Bastien? Pfft. Some of my supposed 'negative' traits have been a crutch for you, little bird- one of these days, I hope you find a way to see me in your reflection, and be grateful for what we have in common! Starting with that superb chest of yours.

Oh yes my breasts have been so helpful! They're like an evil-male magnet!

One you needed!

'What?' Bastien asked, seeing the way we were glowering at one another. 'What's the knife for?'

I shook my head. *I have to do this quick before I lose my nerve, so get out of my head, all right? And please... just heal me after? I swear that's the last thing that I will ask of you.*

Like I'd leave you to bleed to death! Just... be careful, and slice only where you feel it! Here... I nodded when I felt her trickle a warm line across the inside of my lower abdomen and Satan opened her hand, producing a beautiful, silver knife. Bastien had been watching us with confusion, but now alarm lit his lavender eyes.

'What's going on?' he demanded, stepping forward as I grasped the handle in my hand. 'What is-'

I twisted the knife and jabbed it into my stomach, screaming as I did and buckling at the waist as actual, physical agony ripped through me. My father bellowed but my mother held him back and they both watched horrified as I pressed my fingers into my womb, felt around- and then tore out the tiny vial that had been inserted on my sixteenth birthday. It was blood and gore covered, but it was glowing a faint golden colour in a way that it hadn't before, and I tossed it onto the sand before I fell to my knees.

'It's time to follow a real leader boys,' I croaked, cupping my hand to my stomach as Satan rushed forward and pushed it away so that she could heal the gaping hole. 'But do it without your beacon or my trail of feathers to make the path easier for you!' I collapsed onto all fours, panting and sobbing as my mother's warmth radiated through my womb, restoring it at last while the tide lapped beneath my hands, catching the tracking device, rinsing it free- and then dragging it out to sea.

And then I gave into the blackness again for what I hoped to be the last time, letting it consume me without panic this time, knowing that when I awoke, Satan would be gone and I would finally be free.

Loss of consciousness is indeed, a funny thing. Sometimes it's your body's way of telling you that it cannot cope with your life as it is. But sometimes, it is your body's way of ensuring that you get the chance to recover from all you have endured, and wake up again with eyes that are finally wide open.

EPILOGUE

KOHÉN BARACHIEL

I watched my brother's twisted body twitch as the healers ran their hands over him, feeling like I was having an out of body experience. My mirror image was standing in the doorway of our private suite, arguing with Ora about damage control and she was arguing back about how she didn't know what was damage control and what was concealment of crimes, my uncle was sobbing in the corner over the bodies of my parents that had been stretched out on a large day bed, my former Companions and a few others were huddled on the other side of the felled king, crying like their hearts had been collectively broken, John of Arc was insisting that they should leave this wing of the castle at once so that the family could grieve in private and I... I felt *nothing*.

I knew I'd lost the girl I'd thought was the love of my life forever, and yet I felt nothing. Nothing at all, not internally anyway. Not anger, not empathy, not grief, not desperation or anguish... just everybody's palpable dislike of me, which I knew I'd earned. I was the prince that had been healed and then commanded to go sit in the corner like a naughty dog while they focused on healing the one that actually mattered, and *that* wasn't even bothering me the way it should. The healers has written off my dry eyes and vacant stare as being symptoms of shock or possible concussion, but I wasn't so sure if that was the case, or if I was just an awful person. Could a *good* person sit in a room with his dead parents and feel such indifference to the bodies? It didn't seem likely. We'd quarrelled yes but...shouldn't I be crying? Or at least acting out like my twin was? He seemed more upset about Lark's disappearance into the ocean than I did, and yet she'd been mine! So where was my despair for the girl I'd been obsessed with since the age of five?

'If you want to handle it that way, then you go out there and do it while I stay with him for I can only report, in good conscience, what I know to be true!' Ora cried, throwing up her hands and storming past Kohl, who watched her go to the long couch that my elder brother had been stretched across while wearing an anguished expression. T'are's corpse was on the floor in the middle of the room too, covered with a sheet, but no one seemed to pay him much mind as they stalked past, and that actually struck me as being sad, because I knew he'd died trying to get my mother out of the burning building after spending days serving me and decades serving my father. How important he'd been once to castle life, but how quickly he'd been disregarded, and how insignificant and lonely he seemed now! I wiped at a tear, and wondered if my shock was wearing off and if I was about to be slammed with a wall of grief forged by everything else that I'd lost this night. I hoped not- I was rather enjoying the numbness, and actually kind of wished that someone would tell me to just go to bed or something, because the dominant feeling in my body at that moment was definitely exhaustion.

'And I don't know if I believe that a word you've said *is* true, Kohl! I've heard so many sides of this story tonight that I'm starting to wonder if any of this is happening at all or if I'm having a horrible nightmare!'

'Did you not see her wings?' Kohl wheeled on her, following her across the room, and I watched him, wondering if I walked and looked exactly as he did when I was angry. 'Can you not see the state we are all in, especially your darling Karol? This wasn't done with fire or electricity- *she* did this, Ora! You've told me that she admitted as much!' he sobbed. 'I don't want to believe that any of it has happened either, but it has and the kingdom has to be warned about how dangerous she is! Especially if she went around saying awful things about us first to turn people against us before she flew out of the bloody building!' he stomped his foot, clutching at his chest. 'I loved her more than anyone else did! I would never have hurt her! She simply lost her mind when that brand came out, and I tried to talk them all out of it but...' he dropped his head into his hands and moaned, leaning against the edge of the grand dining table between us. 'This *is* a nightmare, but it's not yours alone!'

'If you are speaking the truth, then eventually, I will believe it, Kohl...' Ora said, slipping in to grip my elder brother's hand and not looking back at my twin. 'But I will speak to Karol about what happened in his room and what Lark said to him before I believe another word anyone else says, understood?' she sniffled. 'That's if he ever comes to! Bloody hell Karol...' she sighed, cupping his hand with both of hers as though praying, and I thought how lucky my eldest brother was to have someone fussing over him so. 'It's not yet midnight, so you can't leave us! Think of all of the birthday kisses you will miss out on if you do?'

'God...' Joan Of Arc got up from beside my father's body, smudged her own sheen tears away with her fingers and moved to embrace Kohl, blocking my view of all that was happening on the other side and thankfully, of T'are's corpse. 'I saw Lark kill your father Kohl,' she whispered to my twin, touching his face tenderly. 'I believe that she is all that is awful and more, and I will help your people understand that too, all right?' she turned to me and the shadows around me, smiling sweetly, and it was the first time that she'd struck me as being incredibly pretty. 'You too, Kohén. I know how much you loved her, and how she took advantage of that fact.' She stretched across to grip my hand and squeezed it in her soft one, comforting us both at the same time. 'No companion has ever been as well treated as she, and I will not let people twist your vulnerability to her into something ugly.'

I didn't know if she was being honest or not- but I smiled crookedly and mouthed a thank you, then took my hand back as Kohl pressed his face into the Shepherd's daughter's shoulder and sighed.

'Thank you, Amelia-Rose,' he said hoarsely, and I moved to cover a yawn- certain that Ora would stab me herself if she heard me do something that insensitive while my brother was fighting for his life. 'It's nice to know that at least one person in this room has faith in me.'

How long has it been now since I awoke under the hands of that strange, black-haired healer? Ten? Twenty? How much longer am I going to have to stand being inundated by everyone's feelings, without having any of my own?!

'Oh Lark...' one of my Companions moaned from beside my father's body. I couldn't tell which though- they all looked so alike in their white togas from across the room- and I really didn't care. 'How could you?'

'You don't know that she-'

'We know that she killed Elijah, if nothing else,' the weeping girl whispered. 'And if she did that then it's likely that she's responsible for the others too, isn't it?'

'Kohl's not a liar,' another admitted softly. 'I'd think it was a story if it came from Karol or Kohén, but not *Kohl.*'

I raised an eyebrow at that and looked back at my twin, wondering how he'd managed to garner so much faith from *my* companions. Hadn't I treated them well?

Not well enough, apparently... the thought came to mind unbidden. *At least one was miserable enough under your watch to be inspired to go on a murderous rampage!* I swallowed hard, my palms sweating and then crackling with energy. I needed to get out of there but where could I go? Apparently the castle was overflowing with people that wanted to throttle me now! People that wanted to ask me questions that I didn't have answers to!

My room! I thought then, glancing around. *I'll say I'm going to wash my face and change my clothes, and that will buy me some time alone, won't it? Maybe once I'm alone, it will all hit me and I'll feel... something...*

'Oh! Karol!' someone suddenly cried: Ora.

'Oh! His eyes are open- he's regained consciousness!' another voice, one that made me stand up and look over with renewed interest. Was he truly going to live? That would mean something, I knew! If he'd died, my father's crown would be passed to my uncle Ewan because I was the second in line but nowhere close to being thirty and old enough to assume a throne yet, but if he lived, I would step up and become the crowned prince- something that I knew would matter to me once the shock wore off.

'How?' Kohl cried, bursting from Amelia-Rose's grip and storming to our brother's side. 'Wasn't his neck-' there was a collective gasp and then I saw my older brother sit up looking... fine! He'd been a blistered, charred body minutes before, one twisted like wreckage, but now he leapt off the bed, knocking his saviours out of the way and causing everyone else to shrink back. His eyes were green fire as he searched the room and finally, saw me. Those eyes slitted and then his head jerked to study Kohl's face- and by the time they'd seen our parents' bodies, they'd darkened from being the colour of emeralds, to algae. My heart rate began to accelerate as his muscles bunched, and for a moment I was sure that he was going to bound across the room and flatten me, but then he looked at Ora, then Amelia-Rose and then finally, lifted a hand and thrusted it towards the door.

'Everyone out NOW!' he roared, and though Ora tried to protest and step forward, he pushed her out of the way. 'All of you! Leave us! I thank you for saving my life, but we are facing a disaster and an emergency at once and I MUST speak to my brothers about the witch that brought it upon us in confidence before I speak to anyone else! So *go*!'

It wasn't the fastest recovery in history I was sure, and possibly the ugliest one. Couldn't he at least hug Ora? Kiss one of his healers on the cheek or something?

'Witch? Oh god, so it *is* true?' Ora tried to reach for him again but he turned away from her, and she was quickly collected by my startled companions as they swarmed around her and began to hurry her out the door. 'She really *did* try to kill you? Karol.... talk to me! Surely you and I have become closer this week than you have been with your brothers?'

But: 'Out!' was my brother's only response, and mine was to flinch on the heartbroken girl's behalf.

Well if I am a monster, there's a good chance it's hereditary...

There had been at least eighteen people in there with us before, but it emptied quickly. Amelia-Rose had been the last out and had turned, asking if she could stay and offer spiritual guidance, but had received a hostile look in response that had provoked her to close the door behind her. Once she'd skittered out, that left only me, my brothers and the three dead bodies on this side of it.

Oh man... I shifted in my seat uneasily as Karol prowled towards me. *This doesn't look good...*

'Fuck Karol, you almost *died*!' Kohl said, sounding both nervous and agitated. 'Why don't you sit down for a minute and collect yourself so I-'

'Kohén Barachiel!' my brother's eyes were startling and bright again, seemingly glowing from within as he cut Kohl off dead and then loomed over me, smacking his palms so hard into the table that the entire thing shook. 'What the *hell* happened here tonight? Larkin says you branded her? That Kohl killed mother? That you *both* tried to rape her-'

'All lies!' Kohl declared, stepping forward and ripping Karol back by taking his shoulder, making me wilt in relief. 'Father tried to have mother brand her, and mother refused and branded Kohén instead the second father left to go looking for you! She screamed that the entire family was evil, except for me, and tried to attack Kohén again! I knocked her out of the way to shield him, and she hit her head on the spring, falling unconscious!' I watched Kohl with eyes that had been stretched to the point of watering, as horrified by the grisly tale as Karol was. 'Lark became a psychotic in a heartbeat, and accused me of killing mother! We tried to restrain her and assure her that mother was still breathing, but she started screaming rape and all sorts of things, and declared that she was running away from us so Kohén branded her so she wouldn't get far- and she burst into *flames*! *Nephilim* flames!'

'They were siding together?' Karol asked, looking dazed. 'But mother hated Lark for so long-'

'Well apparently they've been two peas in a Nephilim pod since Pacifica, because neither seemed surprised to see the *other* unleash their powers on us,' Kohl snarled, and Karol's eyes bugged and I saw how red and veiny they were now, telling me that he hadn't been getting much sleep either.

'Mother's *what*?'

'Her powers, because yes, she is Nephilim too- or *was*.' Kohl threw up his hands while I shot my dead mother's corpse an uneasy look. 'She unleashed a plague of fucking wasps after Kohén, which also threatened *my* life even though she'd been begging *me* to get Lark out of here to begin with!'

'That can't be true!' Karol cried. 'She-'

'It is! Amelia-Rose was in the hall with father when Lark attacked him, and confessed that mother had been the one that had been plaguing us with locusts all along, trying to get back at him for not marrying her!'

Karol gripped at his hair. 'No! She wouldn't have hidden that from me!'

'But she did, and she used it to try and kill us.' Kohl gestured to me. 'They probably would have succeeded, but Lark had already set fire to Kohén and I both *and* the chandelier out of the ceiling- just like she MUST have done at Kohén's ball last year- and when it fell, it set fire to mother's dress and trapped Kohén. I put those flames out by drawing a wave from the spring and went to save them both, but the security guard kicked down the door to see what all of the chaos was, and Lark escaped! And then when he picked up mother to carry her out of here, a beam fell from the roof and hit them *both* while I was trying to get Kohén out from under that bloody chandelier!' Kohl gulped down oxygen while Karol's eyes began to overflow. 'I raced out right after her, carrying Kohén to a healer, and that's when I-' his voice cracked and I felt a lump form in my own throat, 'when I found father dead on the floor...' Tears were streaming down his face now, and Karol's too. 'It was *all* Larkin, Larkin and mother! Karol I loved that girl but after she got that letter from *you* she lost her damned mind and became something else entirely, all right? So wipe that accusatory look off your face right now- the question isn't just what did we do to her, but what did *you* do to her after, huh?' He stepped forward, his stance menacing. 'Obviously, if you think we did something ugly to her to deserve being incinerated, then what did *you* try with her to warrant getting thrown out a three-storey window?'

'Not what you think!' Karol snapped. 'And not what she thought either! Something I would have explained before she'd set me on fire if I'd understood how un-glued she'd become!' He turned back to me. 'Is everything he just said true? Did she truly lose her mind? It seemed that way but...' his features became pinched and he pounded the table in front of me. 'But it was you that set her off! How could you contemplate branding her? You're lucky this place is full of witnesses, or I'd kill you myself for the pain and disgrace you've brought upon this family this week!'

I shrank back, mouth falling open but nothing came out. My skin hummed though and my hands sparked and when Karol saw that, he lifted his eyebrow in a challenge as his green eyes deepened to become the colour of algae again. 'Oh is *that* how it's going to be? You'd take me on before you explained-'

'He can't explain himself because he doesn't know anything!' Kohl said quickly, waving his hand at me. 'He can't remember a fucking thing. Guess that's what happens when the girl you love drops a timber chandelier on your head, hmm?'

'Oh get out of here!' Karol frowned at me, stepping closer and looking sceptical. 'You're seriously telling me that you can't remember a thing that happened after that light fell? How convenient!'

I swallowed and shook my head before I ventured: 'Actually... Prince Karol...' he blinked rapidly while I held out my hands. 'I can't remember a single thing that happened *before* it fell, either.' I frowned. 'Least of all... this girl that I apparently just attacked... and loved?' I looked to Kohl. 'It was Larkin, right? That was her full name? I've heard *Lark* a lot too...'

'Yes,' Kohl said, and then looked at my brother, who was now gaping at me. 'But you called her duckling or swan, depending on your mood at the time...'

I made a face. 'I'm starting to get why she dropped a chandelier on my head...' I wet my lips. 'It sounds like I treated her appallingly.'

'Oh my God...' Karol leaned in, peering at me closely. 'You have got to be pulling a fast one on me, right?'

'That's what I thought at first, and I think everyone suspects the same thing because they're giving him the silent treatment for his strange behaviour... but I think he's on the level, Karol,' Kohl said softly, studying me. 'He didn't know anything- not my name, this castle's name- and his face hasn't flashed with recognition once since he was healed, not even when his old Companions came in. I filled him in on a lot of stuff so he knows names and stuff *now* and that this is his house and who he is and what he is.... but I only had like, two minutes to bring him up to speed about most of it before I had to go outside...' Kohl looked at me, shaking his head. 'The healers say it's amnesia brought on by concussion, and that they have no way of knowing how long he'll be like that for. It should be short term because he was healed by two of them, but it could last months if not years...' He sighed. 'Or he could just be in shock. He knows what Nephilim are and about God and Miguel and even Calliel- he just cannot relate to any of it in a personal way, and doesn't seem to have any emotions- at *all.*'

'From what I've heard- he never did!' Karol said, but not as angrily as before.

'I have them now,' I whispered quietly, wetting my lips as I looked over at T'are. 'I feel sorry for the man I was told was my bodyguard this past week and I am terrified of our older brother right now and felt bad for the girl that he dismissed rather rudely... and I feel *really* bad about all of the things that I was told about myself... I just don't feel grief any private grief over any of it. Like you are all strangers, and that I am a stranger to myself.'

'Unbelievable...'

Kohl nodded. 'You should have seen the look on his face when a healer showed him a mirror to prove how his third-degree burns had been healed from his face, neck and hands- and he looked at me and asked if we were twins 'or something...'. It was the creepiest shit I've ever seen.'

'I've seen a lot worse...' Karol said, still studying me thoughtfully. 'Are you being honest, little brother? There are ways of finding out the truth, you know. And if you're lying-'

Finally my eyes filled with tears. 'I think so. But I don't know anything for sure and I...' I looked over at the bodies in the corner. 'This is going to hurt me, isn't it? When my memory comes back? I loved this girl... and she accused me of rape and then killed my parents?' I pressed my hand to my forehead, tearing up at the idea of it even though I had no idea what this girl looked like except that she'd had wings. 'Who could survive that?'

Karol looked dazed. 'Holy sh-'

'Don't,' Kohl said roughly. 'I already know that Satan's in this place with us, Karol- and I'd very much like to encourage her to haunt another family, if you don't mind knocking off the blaspheme shit.'

Karol shot him a look. 'You take the lord's name in vain more than any of us.'

'I did,' Kohl looked down at his bloody toga and sighed, shaking his head. 'But I never will again after tonight, and neither should *you*.'

'That's usually good advice, but I'm starting to think that Amelia-Rose is a budding evangelist, so I caution you about how often you use the words 'the lord' little brother, or I'll start to believe that she's influencing you in an illegal sort of way and start searching your possessions for crucifixes and Bibles...' Kohl rolled his eyes while I frowned, puzzled, and sighing, Karol straightened, and looked from me to my twin again. 'Well... where is she now?' His lips twisted in a cruel smirk. 'The black swan, I mean?'

'No one knows,' Kohl said, looking haunted himself. 'She flew off, crashed into the statue of liberty and then flew off again and landed by the falls, right near the top. I ran after her as soon as I had Kohén with a healer, found you and then made it rain when people pointed to her standing up on the rocks. She jumped, but she didn't fly, Karol, I think she was starting to fall to her death like she once told me she planned to...' Kohl gestured out the windows, looking distressed. 'But I drew in the tide to stop her from being obliterated on the rocks. Partially because I couldn't stand to see her ended like that, but mostly because I wanted to make her pay for the destruction she caused on her way out of here.'

Karol had gone grey at the mention of her jumping, but now his lips drew tight and he nodded. 'And then?'

Kohl shrugged. 'I manipulated the waves, trying to get her to wash up on the shore, but after ten minutes nothing happened, and then people started screaming that you still had a heartbeat so naturally- I joined everyone inside again, waiting to see if you could be revived.' He stood taller. 'The guards are still on the beach, waiting for her and I plan on keeping them there all night and well into tomorrow, but we can't send out boats to comb the waters until daylight-'

'We won't need to,' Karol said, pushing off the desk and motioning to the small television screen across from the dining table that I'd been sat at. 'I'll activate her tracker now- that will help us narrow the search to a one-hundred metre radius of wherever she ends up.'

'Tracker?' Kohl leaned back, looking startled. 'So she really does have one? I thought Kohén was making that up!'

'In her womb...' Karol looked back at him and made a face. 'Sorry, I keep forgetting how much of this stuff you couldn't know.'

I made a choked sound and they both turned to stare at me. 'Good grief...' I said, rubbing at my eyes, 'sorry but that just all sounded so...a tracking device in her *womb*?!' I exhaled slowly, looking from one face to the other. 'I've been told that I was obsessed with this girl by your girlfriend Ora, Karol, and yet I allowed her to pleasure me for jewels, denied her freedom even after it was granted, permitted someone to stick a tracking device into her womb, branded her as a whore and continued to sleep with other girls the whole time?' The guys looked at one another, then me, then nodded. Feeling something sharp stab inside my gut I stood and pulled on my hair. 'And everyone's what... *surprised* that she went on a rampage? I don't blame her! What the fuck was the matter with me?'

'That was a popular question an hour ago Kohén, but right now, I'm not so sure if you were the problem- or if she was working her hellish thrall over us for all of these years and making us act like heathens while believing...' Karol sighed heavily, scratching at his hair in an agitated manner. 'I hope to find out, though. Dead or alive, this tracking device will lead us to her. And I *really* hope she's alive...'

'Still want to make good on all of the things you promised her in that letter once you find her?' Kohl asked, and it sounded like he was mocking him. 'Good luck with that.'

'No. So I can take them all back, actually.' Karol wiped at his face, and I got the feeling that he was crying. 'And then, once it's clear that I am never, EVER going to long for her again... I'm going to *kill* her.'

'You're not going near her!' Kohl cried. 'If anyone in this family can take her down, it's *me*! Fire... water... you see where I'm going with this, yeah?'

'The only place you're going is back to Pacifica- and as far out of from Larkin's reach as possible. She's too dangerous for you to risk confronting again Kohl!' Karol said brusquely. 'If your powers were a match for hers, how the hell did that fiery nymph get out of this room to start with, let alone past your tide?'

'What would *you* have done in my place, oh powerful healer?' Kohl demanded. 'Soothed her fevered brow? Kissed her brand better?'

'Someone fucking should have before she boiled over but no, that's not how I plan on handling the bitch now!'

'You're not gonna handle her at all! You're the one she got dead, remember? It's *you* that's not match for her, not I!'

'You're the one she wasn't afraid of enough to *try* to kill!' Karol pointed out. 'And I am your king so you will do as I say- you're not going anywhere near Larkin Whittaker without a fucking army, got it?'

'Maybe I'll raise an army then, hmm?'

'Maybe you should TRY!'

Acid bubbled in my stomach. 'Can either of you do that? Kill someone, I mean? I thought we were descendants from angels!'

The king looked back at me and smiled grimly, eyes dark as night. 'Yes we are descendants of angels,' he said, and his face was glistening with his tear tracks. 'Which is why I'll never allow the devil masquerading as a swan into our hearts- or lives- *again*.' He stood taller and began to move towards the door, motioning to the screen. 'That will take a few minutes to start tracking her... watch it until I return please? I need to speak with Ora quickly, but we cannot afford to waste a second locating Larkin Of Eden, so come and find me if something shows up before I come back, all right?'

'Off to make that marriage proposal now that the one you wanted on the side is officially off the menu?' Kohl demanded snarkily

'If I ever use the word 'marriage' again, feel free to bludgeon me to death with something, all right?' Karol grumbled. 'No I just need to make sure that certain things that I have confessed in Ora of late will remain between us now that my temporary insanity has cleared up.'

Kohl sighed. 'You're going to let a lot of people down, Karol.'

'Frankly, my brother- I don't give a damn.' And then the door slammed shut behind him. I flinched and saw Kohl look to me.

'You really don't remember her?'

I shook my head.

'Huh...' Kohl turned back to the screen. 'I don't know if you're the luckiest man alive, or if I pity you. But I suppose time will tell, won't it?'

I felt a searing pain in my chest then and averted my eyes, trying to feel around in my brain to see if it was linked to some memory, but it wasn't. And then I looked down at my filthy, blood-smeared chest and saw the cause of the pain- in a large, lumpy wound that resembled a boil that I hadn't noticed before because I had an outlandish feather necklace covering most of my chest. I looked closer and saw that it was a brand to match the ones on my Companions and realised what it was- my mother's parting gift to me. I frowned down at it, confused. My healer, a strange, dark-skinned man with beautiful, haunting eyes had examined me so thoroughly after I'd come to... how had he missed it?

'I don't know why we seek to cover scars...' the healer had said as he'd brushed his fingers over my shoulders and torso, but not my chest. *'I think they're important- a map that tells us where we've been, and where we ought to go.'*

'What can you tell from my skin?' I'd asked him, and he hadn't looked at me as he'd answered:

'You don't have any scars,' he'd said, rising to go back to Karol. *'Where you have been and where you need to go has been recorded on the flesh of others and now that they've scattered, I'm not sure that you'll ever find your way...'*

And then he'd left me.

As Larkin had left me.

As my parents had left me.

I didn't need my memories back to suspect that somewhere along the line, God had left me too.

But as I looked down at the only scar I had- the only thing about me that I could see that made me different from my twin, I cupped my hand over it protectively and vowed to keep it as my compass point of finding my way back to God.

And for her sake, I prayed that Larkin of Eden remained lost to all of us. Though if the look in my brothers' eyes was anything to go by- she didn't have a shot in hell of escaping us now. Not unless she raised an army of her own.

That was when a gasp sounded across the room, and before I could even look that way, I was hit hard in the face with a spray of water that knocked me off the chair- but did not block the sight of my mother's 'corpse' sitting up, or the sound of her screaming as my twin raced across the room- and punched her square in the face.

-End-

LARKIN'S ADVENTURE CONTINUES, BOOK #4 THE WILDEST WOODS

ABOUT THE AUTHOR

S.K Munt is a happily married mother of 4 from Queensland, Australia. When she's not reading, writing or wrangling her kids, she enjoys the dabbling in the local performing arts, surfing, working out and going on long road trips. The Given Garden is just one of her 29 published titles, and in addition to those novels, she has written and/or produced five stage shows, with a sixth in the works as of 2021.